Paperback

ISBN: 978-1-918039-13-9

Published by: *Good Reach Publishing*

Content Advisory

The *Warborn* series delves into dark and mature themes, including violence, war, and combat-related injuries; torture, captivity, and biotechnological experimentation; death, grief, and trauma such as PTSD; and government betrayal and corruption. It also features explicit language, smoking, alcohol use, and consensual on-page intimacy between adults, along with depictions of prisoners of war—including children and detailed descriptions of war zones and civilian casualties.

Blending military realism with elements of biotechnological horror, the story is anchored by an emotionally intense romance at its core. This series is intended for mature readers; please read with care and take breaks if needed, as your wellbeing always comes first.

Dedication

For every survivor who walked through fire and chose to rise again. This story is yours.

You'll never walk alone.

.

Acknowledgment

This book could never have come into the world without the kindness, patience, and belief of others.

To Stephen Brown at *Good Reach Publishing* – thank you for your steady kindness and patience, for guiding me through this journey with encouragement at every turn.

To Bushra (my editor) – thank you for taking care of my dyslexia with such care and respect.

To my daughter, Sophia – my heart, my reason, my fiercest teacher.

To Hugh – my anchor, my steady ground in every storm.

To my mum – my fire, the flame that shows me how to stand strong when the world tries to push me down.

To my dad and Helen – my calm, my zen, the safe space I can always return to.

To the railway boys – you taught me what true brotherhood feels like, and I carry it always.

To Meg and Bekki – my ride-or-die queens, who remind me of my worth and give me the confidence to walk tall.

To Rebecca Munro – who showed me what it means to be a strong woman in a man's world.

And finally, to every reader holding this book: thank you for believing in Evelyn, James, and Obsidian. This story belongs to you now.

Table of Contents

Chapter 1

It wasn't pretty, love.

It wasn't the kind that blooms gently, soft-edged and slow-burning like a romance novel.

Their love was born in foxholes and stitched together in desert med tents, with bloody hands and fractured bones.

It was forged in gunfire and grown through whispered nightmares, clinging to each other when sleep was no longer safe.

It was the kind of love that didn't ask permission. The kind that knew, really knew, that tomorrow wasn't guaranteed.

It was ugly.

It was relentless.

And it was the most honest thing either of them had ever known.

It was ten years of walking through war zones on every continent.

Ten years of dragging each other through the dark, of pulling shrapnel from muscle, of cleaning blood and ash off skin that still trembled.

Ten years of watching each other's six, of knowing the other's pulse better than their own, of holding on, because letting go would've killed them both.

And in the times when war tore them apart, when oceans and orders and different conflicts split their paths, they still found each other.

Not by chance.

But by gravity.

As if the world itself bent around their bond.

As if even chaos knew they belonged on the same battlefield.

Chapter 2

Virginia Beach – Obsidian Operations HQ

The war room never truly slept. It thrummed with a low, electric hum, as though the walls themselves were wired into every battlefield Obsidian had ever bled on. Screens lined the far wall, cycling through satellite feeds, encrypted Intel drops, and helmet-cam footage grainy with dust and blood. At the center of the room a table dominated the space. A huge slab of matte-black steel, its surface alive with shifting maps like arteries, with red and blue light crawling across continents like veins under skin.

The air smelt of cold coffee and gun oil. Familiar. Ritual. Along the edges of the room lay racks of tactical gear stood in soldierly silence: Kevlar vests, radios, and trauma packs tagged and ready. Above them, the flags hung like ghosts with colours muted and fabric scorched at the edges, memorials to every place Obsidian had walked where governments swore they hadn't.

James Reaves stood at the head of the table. He didn't have to command the space; he was the space. Broad-shouldered, muscle stacked over decades of violence and survival, his fitted black t-shirt clung to forearms corded with strength, faint scars catching in the overhead glow. His jaw was square, shadowed by a day's stubble. His eyes were near-black, steady and unflinching. They were eyes that had seen too much and still kept showing up. When he did speak, the Detroit in him still lingered, low and rough with steel threaded through it, softened only when he forgot to guard it.

He was studying the mission rotation on the main board when the door swung open.

3

Evelyn Blackthorn didn't enter rooms. She claimed them.

She leaned against the frame, a silhouette of poise and defiance. She adorned black tactical pants that fitted like armor. The boots she wore told a story worn by sand, rain, and mud from three continents. A black T-shirt bore her callsign, Valkyrie that she wore with pride. Her arms equally showed a life of grit and war, with Celtic ink curling down her arms like living knots, broken up with old scars from shrapnel wounds. Her dirty blonde hair was braided long, with her frost-blue eyes that could cut through a room, sharp as a blade.

Evelyn spoke with a spark equal parts challenge and greeting.

"You're the only commander I'd commit six months to," the Liverpool vowels were softened by years on the road but it still carried that music. Her smile curled slyly. "How the fuck are you?"

For the first time that morning, James looked away from the board.

Captain Evelyn Blackthorn had been there at the start, when Obsidian was just a rumour, a handful of operators taking jobs no one else would touch. Together they had survived deserts that ground sand into their teeth, jungles that soaked every wound with rot, and cities where sniper scopes lingered longer than breath. They had carried each other through monsoon rain and mortar fire, stitched flesh closed in the back of rattling trucks, bled for one another and dragged each other back across the line again and again.

"Hello, Red," James lifted his head, a smile pulling faint at the corner of his mouth. "Where the fuck have you been?"

4

She shrugged, casual as smoke. "About."

Her tone was light, but the way her gaze held him said she knew he didn't believe a word.

James tilted his head, a smirk tugging wider. "Is that the official report?"

"That's the one you're getting."

She stepped inside, closing the space between them, her braid sliding over her shoulder as she moved.

"Still can't follow orders to save your life," he said quietly.

"And you still look like you haven't slept in a week." Her eyes traced the stubble shadowing his jaw, the crease etched deep between his brows. "I'd call it rugged, but you've been milking that excuse for years."

His smirk widened. "Good to have you back."

"Good to be back," she answered softly. For a moment, the banter dropped away, leaving only something unspoken between them.

Her smile warmed, the edge softening. "Where's our team?"

He straightened, glancing toward the corridor. "Mack's lit the fire pit. They're waiting for you."

Mack's place sat off a quiet back road outside Virginia Beach, where city noise gave way to cicadas and the hiss of wind through pine trees. From the front, it was all warm wood and weathered charm, two stories and a wraparound porch like something off a postcard. The paint was sun-faded, the porch steps groaned underfoot, and a pair of muddy boots always stood by the door like an unspoken welcome.

Inside, it was the opposite of sterile base housing. The walls were alive with framed photographs, grainy team shots from nameless outposts, laughter frozen mid-beer in some dive bar, and mission patches pinned beside spent casings. The air carried its own signature: oak smoke and strong coffee, no matter the hour.

The kitchen was the heart, wide enough for everyone to crowd in at once, leaning on counters, stealing bites from pans while Mack cooked. The furniture was mismatched but sturdy, every chair worn into the familiar shape of exhausted bodies returning from hell.

But the backyard was where the soul lived.

A stone firepit stood at the centre, the circle Mack had painstakingly built himself brick by brick. The pit was blackened from years of nights burning hot enough to fend off winter. Around it, wooden benches bore scars from boots, knives, and drunken carvings. Here rank meant nothing. Here they weren't operatives or commanders; they were family. Debriefs turned into stories, bad missions were purged in smoke and laughter, new scars were shown off, and old wounds were quietly acknowledged. They celebrated here. They mourned here. They found the strength to go back when they swore they couldn't.

It was always where they returned. Always where they breathed.

And tonight, the fire was already burning.

The screen door creaked under James's hand. The smell of oak smoke and spilt beer from old nights wrapped around them before they even stepped ouside. Conversation drifted from the backyard, undercut by the steady crackle of the fire. James's boots thudded across the worn boards first, Evelyn following close behind.

Mack spotted her instantly.

He was impossible to miss – tall, broad, the kind of build you get from a lifetime of hard work and heavier lifting. His ash blond hair was salted with grey, his beard trimmed close, with a Metallica T-shirt stretched over biceps that looked like they could break axe handles. But his eyes softened the moment they found her.

"Ev!"

He didn't walk. He strode across the decking in a few thudding steps and swept her clean off her feet.

She laughed, with her boots dangling off the floor. "Put me down, Mack!"

"Not a chance," he rumbled, squeezing her tight enough to crack the ribs on anyone else before ceremoniously setting her down. "Good to have you home, you absolute legend!" The relief in his voice was thick, the type that only came from seeing someone return when too many never had.

Before she could steady herself, a blur of motion cut in.

"¡Mi reina!"

Bullet.

Chaos and charm wrapped into one, all grin and motion, and zero chill. He looked like the devil's favorite son, with his Cambodian blood adding to his boyish charm. He had sun-bleached streaks running through his wild hair that was catching the light, his signature kohl eyeliner was smudged around his wicked eyes. Tattoos curled along his skin, a bold claw mark running up his throat. He didn't slow; he never slowed. One second he was across the yard; the next he was spinning her in a circle, her laughter rising with his momentum.

"You gonna warn me next time, Coyote?" she managed between laughs.

"Not a chance," he shot back, accent thick in his Spanish, like it was just for her. "You disappear on me, you get the full welcome-home package."

He dropped her back on her boots but not before planting a dramatic kiss on the top of her head. "Damn, I missed you, Princesa."

Evelyn shook her head, still laughing, but her gaze was already searching beyond the chaos until it found him.

AJ.

He stood a little apart, calm in the storm, his dark hair cropped neat, his beard trimmed sharp. He wore black jeans, a fitted shirt, trainers a little too clean, and beads circling his wrist like a reminder of another life. His face still carried something of the boy James had dragged out of Syria, but he'd grown into it now, a man, dangerous when he had to be, steady when it mattered. And yet to her, he would always be the hollow-eyed kid she'd held until he learnt to breathe again.

"Hey, ḥabībī," she said softly.

His answering smile was small but real. She crossed to him without hesitation and folded him into her arms. He hugged her back hard, no hesitation, just like blood.

"You still making my playlists sound like a war crime?" she teased into his shoulder.

"Only the serotonin-inducing ones, In shā' Allāh. Gotta keep your head clear**."**

When she pulled back, his deep dark eyes lingered, scanning her the way family did after too long apart, before he finally let her go.

"I'm ok, I promise." Evelyn whispered into his ear, with her hand resting on his cheek.

She moved on. The intoxicating hum of a guitar floated through the night, stopping mid-note.

Frost.

Seated near the edge of the circle, with his guitar resting across his lap and the firelight catching the curve of its wood. His face was all calm lines, black skin and dark eyes that had seen too much but gave nothing away. He set the instrument down carefully, rose, and met her halfway. No theatrics. Just a steady clasp of her palm in his, the tug pulling her close enough to feel his weight and his silence. That was their language, quiet nights trading her bass for his guitar, neither perfect, but neither judging the other. That was their therapy. When the nights got too loud, they drowned it out with renditions of Fleetwood Mac songs, until they could breathe again.

Then Selena.

The Oracle. She held her call sign as she knew everything yet she never judged. Born in the high valleys of Himachal Pradesh, India, where mountain air sharpened her lungs and politics sharpened her mind. She carried that stillness with her, even here, in her black obsidian hoodie which she somehow made look elegant. Her jet-black hair was immaculately braided back, and her deep brown soulful eyes were sharp enough to cut through anyone's lies.

For Evelyn, though, all that composure melted in an instant. Selena's hands rose to her face, thumbs brushing her cheekbones, eyes closing as their foreheads touched. They held on, long and unbroken. They were sisters by soul, bound by wounds no one else ever needed explained.

When they finally pulled back, Selena's gaze lingered. "You look like hell," she murmured.

Evelyn smirked. "Good. Wouldn't want you thinking I'd gone soft."

And then, at the fire's edge, Irish.

Fifteen years of history lay between them; they had meet Afghanistan when Evelyn was just nineteen years old. He was tall, with a kind weathered face and undeniable rugged Celtic charm. He hadn't moved to greet her; instead, he just leaned against the bench, his red hair tied back and his piercing blue eyes fixed firmly on hers

"Fifteen years," he said evenly. "And in fifteen years, have I ever missed anything of yours?"

Her voice faltered. "Irish... I'm sorry."

"Married, Ev." His words cut but were not cruel. "Hand wrote the invite. Left you calls. Nothing. Not even a reply."

The team went still, listening but not intervening, Irish had always been the only one who could call her out on her bullshit.

10

"Where were you?" he asked, sharply. "And don't say 'classified."

She stepped closer, shoulders squaring. "I wasn't working. Gaza City. UN vest. UNICEF field support."

His eyes searched hers. "Shit... really?"

"On my life."

A beat passed between them, his face softened, and he let out a long exhale. "Fuck, Ev. You're forgiven."

The firepit circle hushed, drawn in by the weight of it. Evelyn told them where she'd been and about the water systems she was supposed to install; instead, she ended up with the medics. Pulling people out of the rubble when the bombs fell, and the sounds that followed her into sleep. By the time she finished, no one spoke. The fire snapped, the smoke curled upward, and even the night itself seemed to hold still under the weight of it.

The silence held for a few beats longer, the weight of her words settling deep into the cracks between them all. Then, somewhere off to her left, Bullet broke it.

"Well... shit," he chocked, tipping his beer toward her. "Leave it to Red to make even her humanitarian work sound like an action movie with PTSD."

AJ smirked. "You're just mad she didn't take you with her."

"I would've looked amazing in a blue UN helmet," Bullet shot back. "International heartbreaker."

Selena rolled her eyes "Humble as ever Bullet. Not everything is about looking beautiful. Trust you to take it there."

11

That cracked the tension. Frost huffed a quiet laugh and Mack leaned forward on his elbows.

"Truth is," Mack said, raising his own bottle, "we've all been a bit lost without you. The commander's been less broody since you walked in tonight, so…" He looked across the fire at James. "Thanks for proving my point, boss."

James didn't take the bait, instead he just sipped his beer, though the corner of his mouth twitched in the direction of a smile.

"Broody?" Evelyn arched an eyebrow. "That's what you lot have been calling him behind his back?"

Irish snorted. "Behind his back? We call him that to his face."

"Yeah," Bullet grinned, "cause it's either that or 'AF… Angry Fucker."

James finally shook his head. "You're all children."

"Your children," Selena said smoothly, lifting her mug.

Evelyn leaned back on the bench, the firelight catching the curl of her smile. "Feels like home."

"Damn right," Mack said, tipping his drink toward her. "Now shut up and pass me that whisky before Bullet drinks it all."

The fire popped again, sparks drifting up into the night, and the air filled with the familiar rhythm of their voices, the old stories, jabs, and laughter weaving back together like the silence had never been there.

The laughter had ebbed into the dark. One by one, the team drifted off, with Mack herding Bullet into the kitchen for more whisky, AJ disappearing with a nod, and Selena and Frost slipping quietly inside. Irish had kissed her cheek before heading upstairs. The firepit burnt low now, with its embers glowing red, as smoke curled in lazy ribbons into the night sky.

Only James and Evelyn remained, sitting benches opposite each other, with firelight flickering across their tired faces. The cicadas hummed in the background. But the night was still.

Evelyn sat hunched forward, with her elbows on her knees and a bottle dangling loose between her fingers. Her braid had half-unraveled, with strands falling around her face. She stared into the flames like they might burn the memories out of her if she stared hard enough.

James watched her. Silent, patient. He knew this posture, the weight pressing down until it had to spill somewhere.

When she finally spoke, her voice was quiet, raw.

"Gaza City."

The words alone carried ash. James leaned forward with his forearms braced on his thighs, already listening.

"I thought I was going there to help," she whispered. "Blue helmet, UNICEF badge, water filters, aid supplies. Thought I'd do something good for once. But it wasn't that. It was…" She shook her head, eyes bright in the firelight. "It was horror."

She drew a breath, voice breaking.

"The first night, bombs fell when we were handing out food. People had queued all day… families, kids… and the planes came in low. No fucking warning. The ground just shook, buildings shattered. Then screams… so many scream… and suddenly it was just bodies everywhere. I was pulling children out from under rubble, carrying them in my arms while the sky lit up red. One

13

was missing half her face. Another... another just kept screaming for his mother, and she was already gone. Buried under concrete. I carried him until my arms gave out."

Her hand tightened around the bottle, while her fingers picked at the label as she recalled hell.

"I held a boy while his father bled out next to him, intestines in my hands, and the man wouldn't let go of his daughter's corpse. Just held her like she was sleeping. He died still holding her. Do you understand that, James? He chose to bleed out just so he wouldn't have to let her go. And it happened again and again and again. Relentless. No reason and no mercy."

Her voice fractured, breaking on the edges.

"One night... I had a toddler die in my arms. Two years old. Big brown eyes. He looked at me like I could fix it, and then he just... went. I tried Jamie, I really tried. I have never seen so many die. They were innocent Jamie."

James's jaw locked with his throat working, but he didn't speak. His gaze was fixed on her, and his eyes were heavy with recognition. He remembered this feeling all too well. He has been in similar situations far many times to count. That gutting feeling. Helplessness.

"I've been in every war zone," she said, barely more than a whisper. "But Gaza..." She shook her head again, her hair falling into her face. "That was different. I thought I was strong enough, but it got into my bones. It got into my soul and ripped it apart. I can still hear it. Smell it. The dust, the blood, the smoke. Children crying for parents who weren't coming. Running through streets while bombs fell on people queueing for food. Not soldiers. Just... people."

14

The fire cracked, sending sparks into the dark. Evelyn's voice was almost gone when she added,

"I took a black ops job before. Something filthy, off the books, just to fund my way in there as a volunteer. I wanted to be useful. I was useful. But it was not enough... its never enough in places like that. It broke me, Jamie. It broke me worse than any op."

The silence was thick and suffocating.

James steadied himself and dragged in a slow breath. His voice was rough with recognition when it finally came.

"I remember."

Her eyes lifted to him, startled.

"When I went to Gaza with you and Irish," he said, voice low and steady. "Different year, different hell, but same smoke. Same children. Same screams. I've never been the same since, Ev. I still see their faces when I close my eyes. The dead don't let you forget them. Not ever."

His gaze didn't leave hers.

"And that's why we don't stop. Because the day we stop feeling it, the day we stop seeing them... that's when we're the monsters they think we are."

For a long moment, neither of them moved. The fire burnt low, throwing shadows that seemed older than the night itself. Evelyn blinked, a single tear sliding down her cheek before she could stop it. James didn't reach for her, not yet. He just sat with her in her darkness, carrying the silence so she didn't have to.

The ghosts hung heavy around them, but in the circle of firelight, neither of them was alone.

Chapter 3

The fire was dying out back when James finally asked, voice low, quiet enough to feel like a secret.

"Do you need me tonight?"

Evelyn didn't hesitate.

"Yeh, mate," she said, tired but honest. "I need you."

So he took her upstairs, into Mack's spare room. It was their ritual. A decade old. When the weight of the world pressed too heavy, they didn't drink themselves to sleep or crawl into separate corners. They curled around each other like armor, laughed when they shouldn't, and pressed stolen kisses into each other's hair and shoulders until the nightmares loosened their grip.

James pushed the door open and flicked the light.

"You can crash in here," he said, his voice low and fatigued.

Evelyn poked her head in first like a gremlin casing new territory.

"Very… beige," she muttered. "Even in Mack's house you live like a monk. A tall, emotionally constipated monk."

James huffed, tugging his old shorts on. Evelyn couldn't help but laugh.

"They're comfortable."

"They're a crime against humanity." She teased.

"Better than your ancient Fleetwood Mac shirt."

"Bite your tongue." She slipped inside, already smirking. "That shirt's got more history than you do."

Evelyn peeled her T-shirt off without ceremony, leaving her in just black knickers and a bra that had survived a hundred deployments and had definitely seen some shit. She stretched like it was the most natural thing in the world, scarred and bruised and utterly unbothered.

James turned away fast, like his life depended on it.

"Christ, Ev."

"What?" She shrugged, highly amused by his reaction. For such a hardened soldier, who never showed emotion to anyone else, making him blush almost felt like a petty victory to her.

"You've seen me naked a hundred times. You literally held my hair back while I had the shits behind a medic tent in Syria."

He pinched the bridge of his nose, making her grin wider.

"You're not in a Jane Austen novel, Jamie. You don't have to 'avert thy gaze' and pretend I'm some delicate flower... Wait, that's Shakespeare, isn't it? Whatever. You get the point."

James smirked, dropping his bag with a grunt. "You want a t-shirt or something?"

"A dirty one," she fired back instantly.

He tossed one at her. She caught it triumphantly with her left hand, exaggerated a deep sniff, then moaned dramatically.

"Mmmm. Paladin pits. New fragrance. Notes of gunpowder, stress, and repressed feelings."

James burst out laughing, real, helpless laughter that cracked out of him before he could stop it. She beamed, proud of herself, legs tucked under her like a gremlin in borrowed armour.

"You're enjoying this," he muttered.

"Deeply."

"You're a menace."

"You're obsessed with me."

He didn't answer, instead he just shook his head with a smile that could kill and crossed the room, lowering himself onto the bed beside her. Not touching, but close enough.

James dragged a knitted blanket over his lap and stayed on top of the covers like a man surviving a Category 5 Evelyn storm.

Evelyn squinted suspiciously at him.

"Really, Paladin? What is this? Some kind of chastity fort?"

"I'm being respectful," he muttered to the ceiling. "It's been a while."

"Respectful?" She burrowed under the covers like she was reclaiming territory. "James, you've dug shrapnel out of my arse with a rusty scalpel. Don't suddenly go modest on me. I'm not scary."

He finally looked at her. She was bruised, bandaged, with wild blonde hair spilling everywhere, drowning in his shirt and still a fever dream he couldn't look away from.

"Get under," she ordered, grinning wickedly. "Come on. I'll build a pillow fort if you're worried about accidental morning glory contact."

His whole body went rigid.

"Jesus Christ, Ev."

"It's a natural biological function," she said solemnly, stacking pillows like a toddler. "If it happens, we ignore it. Like adults. Or British people in awkward family conversations."

"You're the worst."

"You love me."

He sighed heavily and gave in, sliding under the covers at last.

They began with their backs to each other, the only sound the creak of the house around them. As always, the distance didn't last; slowly, they gravitated closer. James kept his eyes on the ceiling while Evelyn lay very still beside him with her long braid pulled forward. Careful, deliberate, she never let him glimpse her back, not even here, in their ritual refuge.

He noticed. He always noticed. But he didn't press.

Minutes later, she murmured into the dark, allowing her banter mask to slip, showing just a tiny ounce of vulnerability and truth.

"Thanks for letting me stay."

His voice matched hers, quiet, full of that unspoken ache.

"Always."

Mack's Place – Upstairs, 03:17 Hours

The house was silent. Somewhere downstairs the last of the firepit embers had gone cold, the cicadas had quieted, and only the faint hum of the fridge broke the stillness.

James stirred first, half-awake, his body heavy, head fogged with sleep. Beside him, Evelyn shifted, rolling just enough that their foreheads brushed in the dark. Her eyes blinked open, unfocused but soft. For a moment neither moved, the world was suspended between the dream and waking world. Then, without thought, their mouths found each other: a slow, tired kiss, lips warm and lazy as breath.

No urgency. No performance. Only instinct. Only home.

When they pulled apart, she let out a small hum, eyelids drooping again. James pressed another kiss to the corner of her mouth, feather-light, then tucked his chin against her hair.

She rolled into him without asking, her head on his chest, leg draped over his stomach and her braid spilling across his arm. His arms closed around her automatically, locking tight across her ribs and pulling her flush to him. He held her as he always did on nights like this, not as a lover, not as a soldier, but as a man bracing himself against the dark with the only person who knew his weight. Her hand found his forearm and squeezed once, wordless. He buried his face in her hair, breathing her in. And so, tangled together, armour wrapped around armour, they drifted back under.

The first light crept pale through the blinds, with streaks of grey-blue softening the edges of the room. The cicadas had stilled, replaced only by the distant lap of the tide and the occasional gull's cry.

James stirred, with his breath heavy and his arms still locked around her. Evelyn lay warm in his hold, with her arm and hand pressed to his chest and her body curled into his like they'd been carved that way. For once, she was still. No restless twitch, no half-sob caught in her throat. Just sleep.

He didn't move. Didn't dare. He just lay there with his face buried against her hair, breathing her in. Salt and smoke and something that was her.

For the first time in too long, he felt peace slip in. A quiet he didn't trust but couldn't push away.

But even in the peace, he noticed.

How she stayed curled forward, always front-on. How she'd kept her back away from him all night, even when they'd shifted, even now, half-asleep. The way her braid slid forward deliberately so it didn't press against her back, her shoulders tilted as if shielding something she didn't want him to see.

He didn't loosen his grip. If anything, he tightened it, pulling her closer, as if by holding her he could keep the ghosts at bay. His mouth brushed her shoulder, the kiss so light it barely stirred her.

"Always, Red," he whispered into her hair, his voice rasped and low, a promise only the dawn heard.

Her fingers twitched against his arm in her sleep with a small squeeze, like her body had heard him even if her mind hadn't.

James closed his eyes again, not ready to face the day yet and certainly not ready to let go of the one place he found peace.

For now, she was here. In his arms. Breathing.

James had dozed back off, but it didn't last. The smell of stale whisky and woodsmoke clung to the room, and Evelyn shifted in his arms with the gracelessness of a cat falling off a sofa.

"Ughhh," she groaned into the pillow, her voice wrecked with sleep. "My mouth tastes like I've been getting off with an ashtray."

James cracked one eye, still half-buried in her hair. "Mornin' to you too."

She twisted her head just enough to squint up at him, eyes bloodshot but already sparkling with mischief. "Christ, look at you. Staring at me like we're in some BBC drama. You making a brew or just brooding me to death?"

He smirked, voice low. "I was actually enjoying the silence."

"Silence?" She scoffed, propping herself up on one elbow and her hair sticking up like she'd been electrocuted. "Jamie, you've been clinging onto us all night like I'm your emotional support Scouser. Don't pretend you're zen now."

He rolled onto his back with a sigh. "You asked me to hold you."

Her grin widened. "Aye, and you did. Like a big, broody hot water bottle. Dead romantic."

James shook his head, but the corner of his mouth betrayed him. "You're impossible."

"Impossibly funny," she shot back without missing a beat, snatching his pillow and whacking him lightly with it. "Now shift. I need coffee before I start threatenin' murder."

James sat up, dragging a hand down his face. "You threaten murder even with coffee."

"Exactly." She dragged his oversized t-shirt further down her thighs like it was armour. "So you best get on it before I start practising on you."

He chuckled, pushing himself to his feet. "You're trouble."

She flopped back dramatically with her hair fanning out, grinning up at him. "And you love me for it."

He glanced back at her, shaking his head as he headed for the door. "God help me, I do."

James stood at the counter, methodically scooping coffee grounds like he was defusing a bomb. Evelyn sat on the counter itself with her bare legs swinging, drowning in his t-shirt and her hair a wild nest that gave her a feral sort of glamour.

"Serious face," she muttered, eyeing him. "You're making coffee like it's a military op. What's next, Paladin, an after-action report on the fucking kettle?"

He ignored her, poured the water, and kept his jaw tight.

She smirked. "You know what your problem is? You keep pretending this is unusual."

James glanced over with one brow raised. "What's unusual?"

"This." She waved a hand between them, grinning. "The 'oh no, I and Red had a little smooch; better act like it didn't happen' routine."

He frowned. "We didn't…"

"Oh give over." She cut him off, leaning forward with her eyes sparkling. "We've done the 'kissing mates' thing twenty-six times last year alone. Twenty. Six. I've been keeping tally."

James froze mid-stir, with the spoon clinking against the mug. "…You've been counting?"

"Course I have," she said proudly. "You think I'd forget Sarajevo? Or that night in Berlin when you were sulking in the rain, and I had to cheer you up with a snog outside a kebab shop?"

He pinched the bridge of his nose, muttering, "Jesus Christ."

"And don't even get me started on New Year's in Belfast," she added, grinning wickedly. "You started that one. Proper needy kiss, that. Like one of them tragic blokes in rom-coms."

James turned with his mug in hand and his face dark with embarrassment. "Ev…"

"What?" She beamed, all cheek. "Don't get broody about it. You're a great kisser. World-class, even. If there was an Olympic sport for repressing feelings until they explode into random snogs with your Scouse mate, gold medal, lad. Gold."

James shoved another mug into her hands just to shut her up. "Drink your coffee."

She took a victorious sip with her eyes never leaving his. "Mmm. Tastes like denial."

Chapter 4

Morning light hit the Obsidian compound in sharp, clean lines, the Atlantic wind carrying the tang of salt over the outer wall. The main building rose from the coastal scrub like a shadow made from glass, steel, and reinforced concrete tucked behind a nondescript security gate that looked civilian enough to make passing drivers ignore it.

From the outside, it was quiet. Inside, it was a hive.

The war room was the nerve centre, satellite feeds bleeding across the wall screens, comms chatter rolling in from every corner of the globe. Long tables ran the length of the space, cluttered with mission files, encrypted tablets, and coffee mugs that looked like they hadn't been washed in weeks. It smelt of coffee and cold steel, the scent of operators who spent more time here than in their own homes.

Evelyn stepped in behind James, her eyes sweeping over the space. The team called it HQ, but its full name, Obsidian Directive, wasn't something you said loud outside these walls.

The Directive had been built out of necessity. James and a handful of others had broken away from sanctioned black ops units, sick of watching red tape and politics get people killed. Obsidian operated in the margins, taking contracts no government would claim, carrying out missions that officially didn't exist. If the world needed something done that couldn't be done in daylight, Obsidian was the name whispered down the line.

They worked cleanly with no civilian casualties, no political games. But they worked hard, and they worked everywhere. The Arctic, Afghan mountains, West African ports, South American jungles, Syrian cities, if there was a war zone, they'd walked it. If there was a hostage, a rogue asset, or a target too dangerous for official channels, they'd go after it.

And the price of being off the books? No official backup. No cavalry. If they went in, they came out on their own terms or not at all.

James moved toward the mission rotation board, his eyes scanning the shifting lines of names, dates, and codenames.

"This feels familiar," Evelyn murmured, coming up beside him.

"You've been gone too long," he said without looking up.

"You missed me," she teased.

"Maybe I just missed someone who could keep up," he replied, though the flicker of a smirk gave him away.

She crossed her arms, leaning casually against the edge of the mission table. "So… fill me in. What've you been working on while I've been gone? What am I walking into?"

James didn't glance away from the rotation board. "What can you expect from the next six months?" He tapped a finger against the top section, scrolling through the Intel feeds. "High-yield munitions disappearing from storage sites in Eastern Europe. A new black-market route for VX-series gas moving through West Africa. Three confirmed cases of ex-military engineers being snatched in the Middle East. And…" He switched to a grainy overhead image. "…an arms lab in southern Ukraine we think is doubling as an R&D site for long-range missile guidance systems, that don't belong to the Ukrainians."

She whistled low. "Busy boys and girls."

He finally looked at her, his expression even. "Most of it leans on your skill set. Explosives disarmament, countermeasure extraction, live ordnance retrieval. There's no one on the roster who does it cleaner."

Evelyn shook her head with a faint grin. "Jesus… I can see why you needed me back."

"Needed?" The corner of his mouth lifted. "Try 'begged'."

She smirked, pushing off the table. "I'll remember that next time you try and give me orders."

"You never follow them anyway," he said, turning back to the board. "Let's get you up to speed before you start blowing up my op plan."

James keyed a sequence into the mission board, and the digital wall came alive with multiple windows opening at once. Satellite images, cargo manifests, black-and-white recon stills. The hum of processors and the faint buzz of comms filled the room.

The rest of the team drifted in, coffee cups in hand, taking their usual places around the long matte-black table. Mack stood near the end, arms folded, the picture of relaxed but watchful. Bullet perched on the edge of the table like he owned it, tapping his boot against the metal leg. AJ had a tablet open before James even started, Frost was leaning back in his chair like nothing could rush him, and Selena's eyes flicked between each feed before James said a word.

James didn't waste time.

"Alright," James said, voice steady. "We've got four active priorities for the next quarter. First—" He tapped the panel. A long, low building flickered onto the screen, its roof half-collapsed under tarpaulin. "Arms lab, southern Ukraine. Posing as a vehicle repair depot. Intel suggests they're developing long-range missile guidance systems with stolen NATO components."

His gaze cut toward Evelyn. "Guess who's the only one here who's disarmed one of these live before?"

She gave him a mock salute. "Happy to make your life easier, boss."

He ignored her smirk and moved on. "Second: VX-series gas. Someone's moving it through port facilities in West Africa. Low volume, high risk. Frost, AJ, you're primary on intercept. But Ev..." He nodded at her. "If it's live, we'll need you on containment."

"Copy," she said, leaning forward, eyes narrowing at the glowing pins on the map.

"Third..." James tapped again. A cluster of red markers lit Eastern Europe. "High-yield munitions disappearing from NATO stockpiles. Mack, you're lead. If we can trace it to a holding site, Ev goes in to assess and neutralise."

Bullet leaned back, hand shooting up like a kid in class. "What's number four? Something fun?"

"Fun for you, maybe," James replied dryly. His eyes swept the table, steady. "Extraction ops. Right now, we're the go-to for anything dirty. No support. No backup. We go in quiet."

Evelyn tilted her head. "Missiles, gas, stolen ordnance, hostage rescue…" She gave a slow whistle. "Jesus. You weren't kidding. This is my wheelhouse."

"Told you," He said, moving to the head of the table.

She leaned back, scanning the Intel feeds, then looked at the others. "Alright, boys and girls, let's go ruin somebody's day."

Mack grinned. "And here I was worried she'd gone soft."

Bullet smirked. "Don't worry. She'll have us in an international incident before the months out."

James rolled his eyes. "Briefing's over. Ev… stay a minute."

The others filed out with their voices fading toward the comms room and kitchen. Evelyn stayed perched on the edge of the table, watching James close down the rotation board.

He didn't turn right away.

"What'll it take to get you back in Obsidian full-time?"

Her brows lifted. "Straight to the point, lad. No flowers, no wining and dining?"

"I need you," he said, finally looking at her.

She grinned, leaning back on her hands. "You need me?" The Scouse lilt gave it bite, but her eyes searched his face.

His gaze didn't waver. "We need you. Half the ops in the next six months lean on your expertise. There's no one else who can walk into a live missile bay and walk out with the guidance core in her back pocket."

She tilted her head, mock-thoughtful. "Flattery'll get you somewhere. Just not permanent."

"I'm not asking you to stop being you," he said evenly. "I'm asking you to stop leaving holes only you can fill."

For a moment, the air between them hummed. Then she slid off the table and stepped close, chin tilted up.

"For now, I'm here. See how you handle that before you ask me to sign my soul back over."

Something flickered in his eyes, maybe a touch of relief or satisfaction, maybe both.

"Fair enough."

He reached for the last folder but didn't open it, glancing at her curiously instead.

"So… where you crashing this time?"

She smirked despite herself "Too old for sofas and washing me gear in hotel sinks."

His brows lifted. "You've actually got somewhere? A home?"

"I've got four walls rented. Flat."

"A flat? You?" His mouth curved. "Sounds permanent."

"Don't get ahead of yourself," she warned, though the spark in her eyes betrayed her. "But yes… I've got an address."

He leaned back against the table, folding his arms. "Bet it's still got half your kit piled by the front door."

"Front door, back door, kitchen table." She shrugged. "It's a system."

He shook his head, the corner of his mouth twitching. "Some things never change."

She slung her jacket over one shoulder, already moving for the door.

"Come by later. I'll cook."

That made him pause, Evelyn was not one for welcoming someone in her sanctuary, not even him. "You're inviting me over?"

"Don't look so shocked," she called back, a wild grin flashing. "It's just dinner, not a bloody marriage contract."

"Last time you 'settled'," he said, with a smirk tugging, "you had a mattress on the floor and a kettle you used as a weapon."

She winked cheekily over her shoulder. "This is different. You'll see."

Throughout the day Ev drifted through the rooms, catching up with the crew. First, she found Selena in the galley, pouring over a thermos of herbal tea. Ev slid in opposite her; her grin was full of questions and mischief.

"What have you been up to? And I don't mean work, are you still pretending you and Frost aren't a thing?" Ev teased.

Selena's mouth twitched. "You're one to talk. What about you and James?"

"There's nowt going on between us," Ev shot back, deadpan.

"Us neither!" Selena snapped, then like true sisters, both of them burst out laughing, the sound bright and a little wild against the dust and diesel.

Ev wiped her eyes with the back of her hand and threw her head back. "Anyway... fuck men. I need a night out with my fearless queen. And you know all the best places with the hottest waiters."

Selena raised an eyebrow, with her stunning half-smile forming. "Oh, we will make a night of it. You pick the dress. I'll pick the boys to ogle."

They clinked their coffee flasks like champagne glasses and for a beat the world shrank to two stubborn women, loud and alive.

She nearly collided with Bullet in the corridor, shoulder bumping his as she turned. He grinned up at her like a rogue who'd just robbed the sun. Stunning, beautiful and rebel to the core.

"You still breaking hearts, beautiful boy?" she teased, with her fingers snagging the collar of his jacket for emphasis.

"Hey... enough of the 'boy'!" he shot back, mock-offended, with his hand splayed over his chest. "I'm a man of many sins, not a child."

Ev rolled her eyes. "You, a man of sin? Please. You're a gourmet of disaster in a leather jacket."

Bullet leaned in, conspiratorial. "Gourmet, yeah. And tonight, I'm serving spoilers... front row for the hottest cage fight in town, exclusive access." He waggled his brows. "You coming or what?"

She laughed and shoved him playfully. "Nope. Can't do! our fearless leader is stalking me tonight."

"Ow really...." he said, grin widening. "I will fight on my own then. I'll try to keep it tasteful."

Lastly, Mack found her by the doorway, leaning like he'd been propped there by habit. He grinned when he saw her, like the sight of her was a small relief.

"You know what's been, what do you brits say..." doing my head in?" he said, dropping his voice like it was a scandal. "James has missed you… and he has been driving himself mad. I mean, I like bachelor life, no drama, no woman, beers, terrible films, right? But not him! This brooding thing? Heavy. He's taken to roaming the compound at two in the morning like he's waiting for a parade that never turns up."

Evelyn raised an eyebrow. "So, what, he paces. Men do that."

"He's polished his boots so many times they're filing reports. Last night he tried to rehearse poetry to an empty chair and cried at the bit where it talks about love." Mack shrugged, helpless and amused. "It's theatrical, Ev. And honestly? It's getting a bit much. Somebody needs to tell him being tragic looking doesn't help the mission."

Evelyn laughed, shaking her head. "Fuck off Mack!! He would destroy you if he knew you were taking the piss like that… But lucky for you our kid, he's coming to mine tonight, so you've got a night with no James and all the shit films you want."

Mack let out a dirty laugh slapping her hard on his back. "Well thank fuck for that!"

Chapter 5

Ghent, Norfolk – Evelyn's Flat

The street was lined with thrift stores, cafés strung with fairy lights, and murals bleeding colour across brick walls. Boho, a laid-back place where no one asked questions, and everyone minded their own.

James clocked the garage before anything else. The matte-black CBR900 sat gleaming like a predator at rest. Next to it, her Cherokee Jeep took up most of the space. Strange choice. Bikes usually got the prime spot. But she'd parked the Jeep in the garage and her motorbike ready like she expected to need it at a moment's notice, like she was preparing to outrun someone.

She led him up the narrow stairs, keys jingling.

The door swung open.

The first thing he noticed was the smell: warm, earthy, faintly spiced with sage, cedar, and something grounding. The second was the colour. Moss green in the living room, rich terracotta in the kitchen, layered rugs softening the creak of old floorboards. This was her in a room, grounded at first glance yet chaos if you looked too close.

And then he saw the crash helmet, the leathers, and a grab-and-go rucksack sitting on top. Always ready.

Plants were everywhere hanging, climbing, sprawling. Crystals and candles nestled beside framed photos: blurry bar nights, dusty compounds, and the team caught laughing mid-mission. A bass guitar leaned against the wall by the record player, with Rumors already on the stand.

It was lived in. It was hers.

James stepped inside slowly. "This… is an actual home."

"Told you."

"It's… you," he admitted, surprise softening his voice. "All of it."

She shrugged, tossing her keys into a crescent moon dish. "Told you not to get ahead of yourself. But yeah… maybe I put my heart in a building."

He moved through the room, catching on to details she'd never had in those transient bolt-holes before. A small shelf by the far wall held three sets of medals in worn cases. He stopped.

"These yours?"

"Yeh," she called from the kitchen, knife tapping on wood. "First ones are mine. The second set's my grandad's … Korea, UN. Taken prisoner, but he made it home. The last ones are my great-grandad's navy medals."

James nodded slowly; she saw a moment of sadness uncharacteristically etched in his eyes, with the gleam of old metal catching firelight. "Didn't know that. I don't know anything about my heritage, joys of being a care kid… No idea about my family…"

She glanced up at him. "Wherever you come from, I promise you, you have got stubborn blood in your veins and a big heart. The past doesn't matter; it's who you are now, and you should be proud."

James let himself relax a little as music drifted in; it was Niki & the Dove, Ode to the Dancefloor, and there she was in the kitchen, changed out of her obsidian gear, barefoot in worn denim shorts, a velvet kimono catching light as she moved. Stirring a pot of chilli with her hips swaying, and the spoon twirled like a mic.

She belted the words out, shameless, spinning before diving back into the song.

James leaned in the doorway, grinning despite himself.

She caught him watching. "What?"

"Just… Jesus, Ev."

She flicked the spoon at him. "Don't knock my cooking playlist. You're lucky it's not ABBA."

"That a threat?"

"Promise," she smirked, turning down the heat and dancing into the next verse.

For a moment, he felt it: ease. Real, impossible ease.

Later, he ducked into the bathroom. It was small but neat, with plants on the sill and dark towels folded on the rack. He was washing his hands when something caught his eye.

Tucked behind the sink, almost invisible, was a SIG Sauer P365. Matte black. Suppressor fitted.

His posture shifted instantly, that soldier's awareness snapping sharp.

Back in the hall, his eyes scanned. And now he saw it.

A pair of custom Glock 43s, discreet on a narrow shelf, half-hidden by a drape. Etched into each grip: a blackbird in mid-flight, wings sharp and deliberate. Beneath it: E.N.A.B.

Spare mags stacked by the record cabinet. A box of .380 rounds wedged between books. Clips in a drawer that looked like it should hold tea towels.

Everything discreet. Everything reachable in seconds.

This wasn't just a flat. It was a fortress.

He was still holding one of the Glocks when Evelyn appeared in the doorway, with a bowl steaming in her hand.

"Ah," she said, not even blinking. "You found them."

He turned the pistol in his palm. "These are nice. What's the A stand for? Evelyn Natasha Blackthorn... but the A?"

For just a heartbeat, her eyes dropped.

"They were a gift. A name I used to have." Then she nodded toward the kitchen. "Anyway. Chilli. Fuckton of cheese, just how you like it."

He took the bowl, but his gaze roamed the flat again with the warmth, the colour, and the music. The guns tucked into corners.

This wasn't just a home.

This was Fort Knox with fairy lights.

James set the Glock back exactly where he'd found it, not because he wanted to, but because leaving it told him more. The fact she could walk in here blind and still reach for a weapon within arm's length meant this wasn't just a home. It was a redoubt.

He followed her into the kitchen, bowl in hand, watching the way she moved. She was loose, unbothered, and completely at ease in her own skin. Like this was normal. Like she didn't notice the way his eyes kept tracing the room.

He dropped into a chair at the little wooden table. The steam from the chilli curled up, thick with spice and cheddar. Evelyn slid her own bowl down, snagged a beer from the counter, and twisted the cap off with one hand.

"You've changed," he said lightly, scooping a spoonful.

"In the last five minutes?" She deadpanned, a grin tugging at the corner of her mouth as she stirred her chilli.

He chewed slowly, deliberately. "You used to keep your gear in a lockbox. Now you've got more firepower stashed in here than most safehouses."

She shrugged, unbothered. "Different times, different habits."

"Mm." He let the sound sit heavy, watching her over the rim of his bottle. "And the A?"

For just a fraction of a second, her spoon faltered. Then she kept moving. "Why are you getting hung up on a letter?"

"That's the kind of thing you only say when there's something to worry about."

Her eyes lifted, sharp, meeting his with that spark of Scouse defiance. "You gonna eat seconds or interrogate me, Commander?"

He held her gaze, steady, unblinking. Then finally, he took another bite. "Both."

The silence after wasn't tense, not exactly. It was familiar. Comfortable on the surface. But James's eyes kept wandering the

39

room, cataloguing. A mag case on the bookshelf. A knife tucked behind the curtain tie. A flashlight clipped inside a plant pot. None of it careless. Every piece chosen is hidden and reachable in a heartbeat.

She'd built herself a home. But she'd built it to hold under siege.

When she caught him glancing again, her smile curved like she knew exactly what he was thinking. "Told you. Too old for sleeping on sofas."

James gave the smallest nod, pushing his bowl away, but the thought stayed razor-sharp in his head.

She's not settled.

She's ready.

Chapter 6

The sun lifted over the Atlantic, turning the HQ's glass front to liquid gold. Inside, printers hummed, keys clattered, and laughter drifted from the kitchen. The team were filtering in, pulled toward the war room for the final brief.

James stood at the coffee machine, scanning the rotation board with his mug in hand. Irish slid in beside him, hoodie half-zipped, a paper cup steaming.

"Hey," James said low, eyes still on the board. "Random question. In Britain... you guys have hidden middle names?"

Irish gave him a sideways look. "Only if you're Catholic. Communion name. Mine's Michael. We don't use it; it's just a church thing. Why?"

James's jaw flexed. "Just heard one I hadn't before. Wasn't sure if it was a thing."

Irish's snort was quiet. "If it's Ev you mean? Good luck. She's tighter than a bank vault when she wants to be."

James nodded once with his mug tapping the counter. "Yeah. I figured."

Across the room, Evelyn strode in, braid neat, sidearm holstered, and black Obsidian tee fitting like armour. Already at Mack's shoulder, gesturing at the sat feed, laughing at something he muttered. She looked like she'd never been gone.

James's eyes followed her for a beat longer than he should've. The letters burnt behind his gaze: E.N.A.B.

41

A name she hadn't wanted to explain.

He pushed off the counter, mug in hand, and joined the team at the matte-black table. The screens shifted through live feeds and schematics with Selena walking them through entry points.

Halfway in, James took over. His voice was clipped and steady, laying out roles and fallback positions. When he reached hers, his finger tapped the schematic, knuckle sharp on steel.

"Blackthorn, you're on point for disarmament. Secondary extraction if things go loud. Standard protocols... unless, of course..." His eyes flicked up, steady, unreadable. "...you'd prefer us to use one of your aliases over comms."

The table stilled.

Bullet's grin spread immediately, sharp and feral. "Oooooh. Red's got secrets?"

AJ leaned back, lips twitching. "Doesn't she always?"

Evelyn's head tilted slowly, her lips curving with that dangerous Scouse lilt. "Aliases?" she echoed.

James didn't blink. "Wouldn't want to call you the wrong thing in the middle of a firefight."

For half a breath, no one moved.

Then she smiled, slow and razor-bright. "Commander, you can call me whatever the hell you want. Just don't call me late for exfil."

Laughter rippled around the table. Bullet whooped. Mack shook his head with a smirk.

42

James moved on without missing a beat, but his eyes lingered a fraction too long before the screen pulled him back.

And Evelyn caught it. That look. That promise that he wasn't dropping this, not by a long shot.

Her smile didn't fade, but in her chest, she felt the weight of it:

Yeah. He's not letting that one go.

Nightfall – Blacksite Alpha-9, Southern Ukraine

The van rattled over the dirt track with the suspension groaning under the weight of eight bodies in full kit. The air inside was thick with gun oil, sweat, and the kind of pre-contact stillness that stole oxygen from lungs.

One by one, voices crackled through the comms as they ran their check.

"Paladin, online," James said, low and steady.

"Zero, online," Frost followed, calm as ice.

"Grim, Online," Mack, steady as always.

"Coyote, loud and clear," Bullet grinned around the words, tapping the mic.

"Rook, ready," AJ muttered, eyes already glued to his wrist display.

"Oracle, link established," Selena confirmed, voice sharp, clipped.

"Wrath, online," Irish finished, his tone a low growl.

Last was Evelyn. She clicked her mic, eyes forward, voice cool.

43

"Valkyrie, standing by."

The callsigns hung in the air like a litany. Obsidian Directive. Alive, together, rolling into another shadow.

The van jostled over a rut with the silence thickening again. Evelyn sat forward with her eyes locked on the map pinned above the driver. Less than two klicks out. Target: an unmarked warehouse. Paper said vehicle depot. Reality: a black-market arms lab.

The mission was simple in concept. Infiltrate. Neutralise. Extract. The devil, as always, lived in the details.

And under Evelyn's skin, something buzzed. Low, electric, thrumming through her muscle and bone.

The van rattled over the dirt track; the team inside were wired and ready. With pre-contact silence, it was that suffocating hush before violence, where the team's breath felt stolen and hearts beat too loud. Her skin buzzed. Low and electric, like a static charge that didn't belong to nerves. It threaded through her bones, settling under her nails, making the world sharpen too much.

She didn't look back.

"Three guards. Four-minute rotation. Blind spot. Eight seconds to cross."

James's eyes lingered. "You good?"

Her lips barely moved. "I'm fine."

Within the compound, the hatch gave with a groan, and they were inside: dark air reeking of rust and decay with machines humming like they were alive. The team flowed inwards in silence with efficiency; as they journeyed into the belly of the

44

beast, they were seamless and well-practiced. They moved in silence like liquid smoke until they approached the area that AJ had identified as the location of the targets.

Then Evelyn saw it.

Two benches were normal enough: optics, casings, and parts stripped down. But the third…

The third was wrong.

The alloy gleamed slick as wet stone, veins of light pulsing faintly beneath the surface. Symbols crawled across its casing like living script, shifting whenever her eyes locked onto them. Not etched. Growing.

The hum in her bones deepened until her teeth ached.

"I've seen this before," she said, too calm. "Extract the team. The third is volatile, but I can handle it."

James's head snapped. "Valkyrie…"

"Do it." Her voice carried no argument, just a flat certainty that made the hair rise on his neck.

The others withdrew, uneasy, with AJ last to go. James lingered until her eyes cut to his; there was something sharp, almost alien, in them, and he moved and withdrew too. She knew exactly what to do; this was her remit, and he trusted her judgement and with the life of his team beyond anything. If Valkyrie said extract, it was never without good reason.

Evelyn stood in the empty space, faced with imminent death to anyone but her. Her body stilled, a razor focus enveloped her and with one flick of her gloved hand, she cut the comms and every feed froze. Silence swallowed the team outside.

She was alone with it.

The weapon wasn't just alloy. It was tissue. Veins of light pulsed in rhythm with her chest. The air seemed to thicken, metallic and warm, like a breath against her skin. The symbols shifted faster, reacting to her stare.

Her pupils blew wide as the weapon beckoned her, taunted her, almost daring her to touch it. She should have stepped back. Instead, she moved forward with no fear and rested her hand on the casing. Heat surged up her arm like liquid wire. The casing rippled under her palm, not moving but responding, as if it knew her. The weapons' veins flared bright, syncing to the rhythm of her pulse; they were in a symbiotic state of trance, communicating without talking, feeling each other's rhythm.

It whispered without words as data slammed into her skull: blueprints, locks, the way it wanted to be armed, the way it wanted to kill. It wasn't showing her how to dismantle it. It was inviting her.

Her jaw clenched as she forced her body to obey. Disengage the core, break contact. Her hand trembled with her tendons screaming as she peeled away.

The hum dropped, but not all the way. Not inside her.

In twenty seconds, the bio-core was sealed in a pouch. The casing is inert.

Her comms flickered back to life, voice cool, clipped.

"Triple threat neutralised. You're clear."

To the others, it was seamless. To James, waiting by the hatch, it wasn't.

46

She emerged steady, with her pupils still blown wide. Her breath just slightly off. Her left hand flexed once before she stilled it. The pouch at her hip sat angled away from the others, like her body itself was shielding it.

Mack cracked a joke as normal. Bullet lit a cigarette. Selena filed reports. Nobody else saw.

James did.

In the van, she sat across from him, stripping her gloves with her gaze fixed on the rear doors.

He watched her for a long beat, then asked, quiet but cutting, "Anything I should know?"

Her eyes met his, they were pale and unreadable. "Nothing that matters."

The van jolted over a rut. Laughter and chatter masked the air, but James still heard it. The faint, unnatural hum. Not in the room. In her.

And he knew…

She was hiding something.

Chapter 7

Temporary Base – Polish/Ukraine Border

The big screen was frozen on the final frame from Evelyn's bodycam. Her silhouette stood over the third workbench, just as the alloy casing began to ripple. The image warped mid-pulse, her pupils blown wide, one hand reaching down, then static swallowed everything.

Selena stood with her arms folded, her sharp profile lit by the blue glow. "Comms went dead. Every camera feed cut at the exact same second."

Evelyn sat casually on the edge of the mission table, stripped down to her black Obsidian tee, a mug of coffee cupped like she had all the time in the world. She didn't even glance at the frozen screen.

"Technical fault," she said smoothly. "It happens."

Selena's brow arched, unblinking. "It's never happened to all systems at once. Not without an external surge. And our sensors didn't pick one up."

Across the table, Bullet smirked, trying to bleed the tension. "You're saying Red fried our tech for fun?"

"I'm saying," Selena countered, eyes still locked on Evelyn, "that it's a hell of a coincidence."

Evelyn took a slow sip, calm as still water. "If it was sabotage, I'd expect you to have proof by now."

The silence stretched across the team, as Selena eyes her suspiciously.

James stepped forward from the far wall, with his arms still tightly folded, his voice even cutting through the quiet.

"So, Red… anything I should know about what happened in there?"

Her gaze snapped to his, steady, indecipherable and guarded. "Triple threat neutralised. Core dismantled. Containment sealed. That's all that matters."

The words were crisp and almost rehearsed, like she knew the questions would come.

Selena didn't move, but James saw the flicker in her expression. She knew there was more. And she wasn't letting it go.

James let the silence hang a beat longer, then gave a single nod. "Fine. We move on."

Selena's jaw tightened as Evelyn just smiled faintly into her coffee, like she'd won something no one else realised they were playing for.

And James couldn't shake the thought as he studied her…

No one should look that calm after touching something alive and lethal.

Border Showers – Temporary Base

The showers were little more than tiled cubicles with cracked drains, steam curling into the cold air from battered pipework overhead. The hot water came in bursts, stinging and cooling too quickly. But after hours of dust, smoke, and diesel fumes, it felt like a luxury.

Evelyn stood under the spray with her head tipped back and streaks of dirt and filth-tinted sweat running down her arms. Across from her, James sluiced the grime from his hair, water tracking through scars old and familiar. Around them, the low hum of the other showers mixed with laughter and shouted jokes from the rest of the team.

Their banter cut easily through it all.

"Missed a spot," James said, nodding toward the mud streaking her shoulder.

"Then get it," she shot back, turning so her back faced him before she could stop herself.

He stepped closer, running the flat of his hand across her shoulder blade with his fingers quickly working the dirt away. It was automatic after ten years of patching each other up, checking cuts, bruises, and burns. Just as casual as breathing.

Until his fingers found something new.

His whole body stilled.

Beneath the spray of hot water and soap was a scar. Jagged, six inches long, curling dangerously close to her spine. The edges were too straight, too deliberate. Not torn skin. Not shrapnel. This was surgical.

And wrong.

As the water coursed over it, the scar didn't pale like normal tissue; instead, it darkened. Faint blue threads pulsed beneath the skin, just for a second, like veins of light tracking under her flesh. His fingertips twitched as it felt warm, not with blood but with a low hum, a vibration that seemed to travel into his hand.

50

James froze with his breath stalling in his throat. He knew her body as well as his own after a decade of battlefield patch-ups, and this had never been there. This wasn't hers. It didn't belong.

Evelyn felt it, the hesitation in him, the sharp shift in his breathing. And she knew exactly where his mind was going.

Without missing a beat, she glanced over her shoulder, smirking.

"You checking out my arse, Reaves?"

It cracked the tension enough that his mouth twitched, but his eyes stayed on that scar. The way the water slid over it and seemed to catch, pooling faintly as if the skin itself resisted.

"Ev…" His voice was low, careful. "These showers are for decompressing. DECON. No flirting. Last place we take care of each other before we come back from being war dogs."

She rolled her eyes, turning back into the spray. "Yeh, sorry. Now hurry up before Mack drains the last of the hot water."

He let it go. Out loud, but the scar burnt in his mind, seared there along with the faint hum that hadn't been water or pipes.

A question lodged sharp and deep with all the others she'd been giving him reason to ask lately.

Temporary Base – Kit Room

The low hum of the generator was the only sound, vibrating faintly through the concrete floor. James leaned against the edge of the table with his arms folded tight, watching Evelyn strip and repack her kit for the next day's move. Most of the team were

51

racked out or grabbing food, leaving the room to just the two of them.

He didn't ease into it.

"When did you have surgery?"

Her hands didn't pause, not even a flicker of hesitation, as she fed a strap through a buckle. "Hello to you too, Commander."

"Don't." His voice was low and iron-edged. "Ten years I've been patching you up. I know every scar you've got. That one on your back... six inches, clean cut, curling to your spine. It's new. You don't get something like that without telling me."

Slowly, she lifted her head, meeting his stare head on. Her mouth curved into something faint but unreadable. "Maybe I just didn't think it was worth mentioning."

"Not worth..." He broke off, jaw tightening. "Ev, it's surgery. What was it? You should have declared this."

She held his gaze for a beat too long. Then, with perfect calm, she states, "Elective." Her tone was even, but her pupils tightened, but there was a flicker of something sharp flashing in her eyes before it vanished. She cinched a strap with unnecessary force, the metal buckles clinking loud in the quiet. "You done playing medic?"

James didn't move. His arms folded tighter, his eyes narrowing. Her body was calm, precise... but he saw it. The way her knuckles whitened on the canvas. The way her breath sat shallow in her chest. And in her eyes there was no annoyance. Not dismissal. Fear.

"You're hiding something," he said, softer now, but heavier.

For the first time, her hands stilled. Just for a fraction. Then she stepped past him, brushing his arm as she moved for the door. Her smile was light and evidently fake, she was wearing a mask and he knew it.

"Or maybe I just like keeping a little mystery alive."

Her boots echoed sharply against the concrete as she vanished into the hall.

James stayed with his neck corded, tendons standing out, and the hum of the generator suddenly sounded louder in the silence she left behind.

All he could see beyond the mask she wore, was the trepidation in her eyes.

Chapter 8

James sat beside Selena at the comms desk, the dim light from the screen painting them both in a cold blue glow.

"Check her medical records for when she was in Gaza," James ordered, leaning in. "And any hospitals… elective surgery, field trauma, anything."

Selena's fingers flew over the keys, quickly pulling up encrypted logs. "Nothing. Not even a dust inhalation note."

"Before that?" he pressed. "She told me she was on a black ops contract before Gaza."

Selena narrowed the search, her brow furrowing. "Colombia…Venezuela border. She was with NATO… listed as a tactical de-conflict specialist, joint ops. Embedded as a sole operative in a NATO specialist unit. Officially she was doing a military audit… military/civilian protocols, narco-zone de-escalation for non-combat extractions."

James straightened. "That's the cover story?"

"Yeah. But…" Selena's mouth tightened. "All details of what she was actually doing, mission logs, operational reports, medical records… they're gone. I can see she was in La Guajira…but that's it."

"Wiped?"

Selena nodded. "And not by anybody military. This isn't the kind of deletion I've seen in NATO's internal purges. Someone took the files out at the source, scrubbed them clean, and didn't bother to reformat the gaps."

James leaned back in his chair, exhaling slowly. "La Guajira… that's fucking dangerous ground."

Selena glanced at him. "How dangerous?"

He rubbed a hand over his jaw. "Narco-trafficking corridors, paramilitary enclaves, cartel families older than most governments, and enough black-market arms running through that jungle to start a war every week. You don't go there unless you're heavily backed… or suicidal."

"And she went in solo," Selena said quietly.

James's gaze stayed on the empty search field, the wiped records like a black hole on the screen. "She's been in something deep, Sal. Something that didn't want to leave a footprint."

Selena tapped her pen against the desk, trying to decipher the missing Intel. "And she's not going to hand us the truth."

"No," James said, his voice low and certain. "But I'll get it anyway."

Selena's eyes narrowed at the code running across the screen. She'd pushed past the NATO firewall hours ago, but this… this was something else. The gaps weren't just deletions; they were surgical removals, each byte lifted out with precision that left no residual trace.

She leaned in closer, her fingers dancing over the keys to run a deep-source probe. A faint digital watermark ghosted in the corner of the encrypted void, so faint she almost missed it.

Her heart dropped.

"Shit…"

James looked up from the ops table. "What?"

"This wasn't military," she said quietly, her voice different now, measured, almost reluctant. "And it wasn't cartel or civilian scrub work. This was done by an outsider. Highly skilled. You don't even see the work unless you know exactly what to look for."

The laptop fan hummed, the only sound besides Selena's keys. James leaned on the table, mug in hand, watching the blue glow flicker over her face.

Selena's probe hit another wall. The deletion wasn't random; it was perfectly excised. Byte by byte, Evelyn's record had been carved out like a surgeon removing tissue. No shadows. No metadata. Nothing.

Selena leaned closer, her eyes narrowing as a faint digital watermark ghosted in the corner of the void. A recursive cypher, folding three times over itself, sigils shifting as though alive.

Her pulse jumped.

"Oh, fuck…"

James's head lifted. "What?"

"This isn't NATO. Not cartel. Not private contractors. This…" Her voice dropped. "This is Ghost. This is the deletion signature I have only ever seen when Ghost has a hand in it. It's the Ghost signature."

James frowned. "Who the hell is Ghost?"

Selena sat back, her pen tapping fast against the desk, eyes fixed on the empty file.

"Ghost isn't a soldier. They're not even in the field. They're worse. A phantom in the wires, a name whispered in backrooms for forty years. Hacker, infiltrator, archivist. The one person who can slip inside any system and pull the truth out like a thread. Governments fear them because Ghost doesn't fight wars... Ghost shifts the balance of them. Cartels, mafias, corporations... they've all tried to kill Ghost, but he always comes back because he doesn't exist anywhere except in the cracks."

James stayed silent, listening, but he had that foreboding feeling deep in his gut. His solder's instinct lurched into high alert.

Selena's gaze hardened. "Every time a government tried to bury its own corruption, Ghost made it bleed in public. Thatcher's Britain, 1980s. Ghost leaked her private files... her manipulation of the Falklands crisis, her backdoor pressure to keep Mandela locked, and her hand in choking Northern Ireland. Even the miners' strikes... Ghost dropped records proving how she gutted communities for profit. Half the country already hated her. Ghost lit the rest on fire."

James exhaled slowly, leaning back as the wave of anxiety hit him. "Yeah... I remember that." His voice carried a different weight now, almost personal. "Ev told me about it once. Said she grew up in a house that hated Thatcher with passion. She even made me watch Brassed Off just to hammer it home."

Selena's eyes flicked to him a sense of gravity.

James shook his head, muttering, "Christ. Don't tell me Ghost is tied up in this too."

Selena tapped the screen with frustration and at the black void where Evelyn's file should have been. "I'm telling you, whoever Ghost is, they didn't just wipe her clean. They shielded her. And that means she's more important than she's ever admitted."

James leaned forward, eyes hard with realisation. "Why the fuck would a political heavyweight hacktivist risk coming out of the shadows to delete someone's medical files? That makes no sense." His voice was edged with disbelief, almost anger. "That's not his remit. Ghost doesn't protect soldiers. He doesn't babysit operatives. He works in shadows for the greater good, and half the time what we do can be seen as morally grey at best."

Selena didn't flinch. "Exactly. Which is why this is bigger. They wouldn't do this for anyone. The risk of being caught is too high. If Ghost moved for Evelyn, it means she isn't just another operative. She's leverage, or legacy, or something they couldn't afford to lose."

James sat back, jaw flexing the way it always did when he was calculating risk. "Or someone they couldn't afford to let go."

The words hung between them, heavy, unspoken with questions filling the silence.

Temporary Base – Quiet Hours

The base had gone still for the night. No hum of generators, no chatter from the mess. Just the faint drip of a leaking tap somewhere down the corridor.

Evelyn sat on the edge of her bunk, the small weapons case opened in front of her. Inside, nestled in dark foam, were the twin Glock 43s. Lightweight. Discreet. The blackbirds etched into the grips seemed almost alive in the dim light, their wings caught mid-beat.

She reached out with her fingertips brushing the metal like they were an extension of her skin.

The moment she touched the carved lines, a faint shimmer of blue crawled outwards, blooming along her fingertips, threading down into her veins like light forcing itself beneath her flesh. The Glock pulsed in rhythm with her heart, too exact, too intimate.

Her breath caught as she felt the weapon sync and move through her body, it gave her a calming, grounding sensation, pulling her into a sense of security.

The blackbirds seemed to flex under her touch, the wings twitching as if they wanted to lift free of the grip. The etching was just cold metal, but the sensation through her hand was warm and wrong, like bone-deep static. She swore she could feel the gun breathing against her palm.

She turned her hand slowly, watching the glow flare then sink beneath her skin again, like it was hiding there, waiting. The hum in her chest rose with it, low, insistent with something that didn't feel like hers anymore.

Her pulse stuttered as sudden fear flickered across her eyes.

Then, abruptly and sharply, she snatched her hand back. Flexed her fingers hard, shaking them as though she could fling the shimmer off like water.

The light gently faded back into nothing.

The guns lay silent, innocent again, just weapons in a case.

Evelyn slammed the lid shut, locking it with a sharp click, and sat back on the bunk. Her face was unreadable, but her hands wouldn't stop trembling.

Chapter 9

Three Days Later – Outskirts of Kherson, Ukraine

The cold bit straight through the gear today, that damp, marrow-deep chill that clung even under body armour. Obsidian moved in staggered formation through an abandoned industrial block, boots crunching over frost-bitten gravel.

Objective: recover encrypted drives from a compromised NATO relay station before Russian-backed militias sweep in.

Simple on paper.

Never simple in reality.

Selena held the middle of the column, tablet angled in her hands, thermal feed scrolling across the screen. But her eyes weren't on the map. They kept drifting forward. To her.

Something was off about Evelyn.

Not her technique, as that was flawless. Every movement from her was sharp and efficient, it was a textbook sweep you could use in training films. No. It was the way she focused. The way her head tilted ever so slightly, like she was listening to a frequency only she could hear.

The relay station loomed ahead, a squat concrete bunker daubed with faded graffiti. Frost stacked on the entrance, Mack and Bullet fanned to the perimeter with their rifles steady. Evelyn slipped through the door first with her combat boots crunching on broken glass. She cleared the main room with clinical precision, rifle sweeping, before moving to the server racks at the far end of the compound.

And then Selena saw it.

Subtle. But real. Evelyn's posture shifted as she approached the racks, her spine loosening, her shoulders rolling back like a tension she hadn't known she was holding had suddenly released. Her gloved hand brushed the server housing, just a casual contact, and yet her pupils flared wide in the dim light.

James's voice crackled low in their comms.

"Valkyrie... status?"

"Clear," Evelyn said. Calm and cold

But her hand lingered on the steel casing for a second too long. Then...

Selena's tablet stuttered. Every feed on her HUD dropped to static with white noise tearing across the display. It was just for a heartbeat, no more. Then the picture reformed, like nothing had happened.

Selena's eyes cut up, sharp. Evelyn was crouched low now, tugging the first drive free, her face was impassive. James hadn't noticed as his sight stayed locked on the entryway, on point with his rifle locked.

Selena said nothing, but her pulse hadn't steadied by the time they regrouped outside.

As they moved toward exfil, Selena slid in beside Evelyn with her voice light and conversational.

"Something you want to share?" she asked, adjusting the strap across her shoulder.

Evelyn didn't even look at her. "Nope."

Selena's lips curved faintly, but her eyes stayed flint-hard.

"Thought so."

By the time the extraction vehicle rumbled into view, Selena already knew she wasn't just going to watch Evelyn.

She was going to pull every thread until the whole truth came apart in her hands.

That Night – Temporary Base, Kherson - Temporary Base – Comms Room

Most of the team had turned in.

Selena sat alone with her tablet jacked into her own network. The feed from Kherson looped again, frozen on the instant Evelyn's hand brushed the server rack. For a split second, every camera glitched simultaneously with a ripple of static like the world had blinked.

She dug into the anomaly; it was too clean, like the system had rewritten its own history. Cross-checking the signature, her stomach dropped; it was the same faint trace buried in the La Guajira scrub.

Then without warning, her screen froze. The cursor stilled.

Words appeared in white text, crisp and deliberate:

If you dig for the answers, you dig her grave.

— Ghost

The screen then blinked twice, then went black, leaving only her reflection in the glass.

James was flipping through a mission report in his quarters when the knock came with three sharp raps. Selena abruptly stepped in with her tablet clutched tightly to her chest.

"We have a problem."

"Evelyn?"

She nodded. "Same signature as La Guajira. And then... they made contact."

She turned the screen toward him: with a frozen screenshot of Ghost's warning.

James's jaw tightened. "You're sure?"

"They signed it," she said flatly. "They were inside my system before I even knew he was there."

James moved from his bed and began pacing. "So Ghost is not just covering her past. Ghost is watching her now. In real time."

Selena's arms were folded tight, but her voice was razor-steady. "What does that even mean?"

James stopped dead, eyes hard with tension, his brow creased with unease. "Then the question is... why does Ghost think Evelyn Blackthorn is worth dying for? They could be traced reaching out"

Night – Base Corridor

The hallway was dim, the generator's carried that familiar hum faintly through the walls. Evelyn knocked twice on James's door.

It opened a crack, then wider. James stood there in a plain black tee, hair still damp from the showers. He shifted into the frame deliberately, one arm braced against the door, blocking the entry.

"Can I bunk in with you tonight, Jamie?" Her voice was low, almost vigilant.

His brows knit. "Why do you need to bunk in with me, Ev?"

Her eyes flicked up pointed with irritation. "You never normally ask for a reason."

"You never normally give me reason to question…," he said, tone flat, indecipherable. "But here we are."

The pause between them stretched with the silence pressing heavy. Her chin lifted in defiance, armour sliding back into place with perfect precision.

"Forget it." She turned to go.

"Ev…" His voice dropped, not commander's orders, but something rawer. "What is going on with you?"

She stopped only long enough to glance back, frost-blue eyes hard in the dim light. "None of your concern, Commander."

Then she walked away with her boots echoing down the corridor, leaving him in the doorway, with a tight jaw and every question left blazing within his chest.

The following morning James found her hunched on a bench with her boots unlaced, nursing coffee like it was the only thing holding her together.

"Ev." His tone was low but hard as steel.

She didn't look up. "You here to lecture me about last night?"

"No." He came around to the other side of the table, leaning on his knuckles. "I'm here to ask what happened in Colombia."

Her head snapped up with her eyes narrowing in indignation. "I didn't tell you I've been there. You digging up shit on me? Jesus, you of all people should know the word "classified".

"I know you weren't on any NATO brief. I know you used a false name in Phnom Penh. And three days later, a warehouse full of biotech went up in flames. You telling me that's coincidence?"

Her blood went cold, not at the accusation, but at the fact that he knew everything. Those files were gone, wiped so deep even the people who paid her couldn't trace them.

She forced her face blank. "Don't turn this on me."

"I'm not," he said tightly. "I'm trying to keep you alive... or safe. Look, you're carrying something radioactive; the team deserves to know."

Her jaw ticked. "Fine. When we're back in Virginia, I'll go. Then you won't have to worry."

"That's not what I..."

"It's exactly what you're saying."

She slammed the mug down with coffee slopping over her fingers and then froze. For half a second, the liquid glimmered faintly blue across her skin, veins lighting like buried wires before it snuffed out.

James's eyes snapped to it, blindsided by what he had just seen. Her hand clenched, trying to hide the tremor as she wiped it on her sleeve like nothing had happened.

66

"You want control," she bit out, shoving past the slip. "You want every scrap of my past laid out so you can decide if I'm worth the risk."

"I want you alive!" His voice broke with raw fury. "And I can't do that if I don't know what the hell you're walking us into."

His jaw strained. "At least let Irish take a look at your back."

Her head whipped up, with her eyes blazing. "No!" The word tore out of her edged, almost a shout, too piercing for the empty mess.

The silence that followed was oppressive. James just glared at her, and for the first time in a decade of war and chaos, what he saw wasn't defiance or anger.

It was consternation.

She looked away fast, shoulders taut, like she could physically hold herself together if she just didn't meet his eyes.

James's voice dropped, rough. "Something's going on, Ev. You know I won't let anything happen to you. But for Christ's sake…" He leaned closer, his words a razor meant only for her. "…let me the fuck in."

Her silence stretched, louder than any argument. And that, more than anything she could have said, told him just how deep whatever this was really went.

Chapter 10

Night – Evelyn's Quarters

The barracks was deathly still, like it was bracing itself for a fallout. Evelyn's quarters were claustrophobic, with two bunks stacked against one wall. Irish was already out cold on the top, one arm dangling lazily over the edge, his steady snore was proof that the whisky earlier had done its job.

The door clicked open, and James filled the frame. He didn't speak right away, he just stood there in a plain black tee, hair still dampened from the showers, looking more unsettled than she'd seen him in a while.

"Can I bunk in with you tonight?" he asked finally, voice low.

Evelyn blinked, then a slow smile tugged at her mouth. "What's this then? Paladin finally admitting he gets lonely?" She slid off her bunk just enough to close the space and hug him, her head landing naturally against his chest. His arms came around her instantly, like he'd been waiting for it all day.

"You're warm," she teased, voice muffled against him. "Like a big human radiator. Might keep you around just for that."

But when she pulled back, his eyes stayed on hers, steady, protective, and too serious for her joke.

"And you're deflecting with your smart arse mouth…But I see it Red, I know you're scared," he said softly, so only she could hear it. "And I just want to help you, Ev. Not as your commander…" His jaw tightened, then eased. "…but as yours."

Something flickered in her face, a combination of fear, relief, and the temptation to actually believe him. Then she looked down while chewing the inside of her cheek like she always did when her armour threatened to crack.

From above, Irish's voice cut through the quiet, gruff and half-asleep.

"For fuck's sake," he muttered, rolling over, "will you two just get together already? Christ almighty, its painful listening to."

Evelyn snorted against James's chest, shaking her head. "Even in his sleep, the ginger bastard's got opinions."

James didn't laugh. He just kept holding her a little tighter, like if he let go, she might vanish into smoke again.

Morning Run – Outskirts of Kherson, Ukraine

The following morning, Evelyn woke James early; she hadn't slept much that night, with a world of chaos running through her head, making it impossible to rest. The remainder of the team were still sleeping off mission fatigue as Evelyn started putting on her trainers. She turned to James. "Run with me, and we will talk. I promise I will tell you what I can… Leave your phone… tell no one."

James only answered, "Okay."

The air was knife-cold, with their breath rising white into the pale dawn. The gravel path crunched beneath their trainers. Neither spoke for the first stretch, the rhythm of running acting as a silent pact.

They pushed past the 10k point before she stopped dead. Her hands braced on her thighs, head down, her breath was steady in that unnatural soldier's way.

"You were right," she said flatly. "Sort of."

James didn't break the silence.

"I was in Colombia. Sent under NATO cover as an auditor. Six months of non-combat... that's what they promised. A breather." She laughed without humor. "Instead, I was torching bio-weapons labs. That's why I recognised those warheads in Ukraine...Seen them before."

She looked at him then, her eyes glassy but hard. "But it wasn't the warheads that fucked me."

Her voice dropped. "I found a building. A door. Reinforced like nothing I'd ever seen. Not to keep people out... to keep something in. You could smell it before you touched the handle. The smell pulled me in. Rot. That thick, sweet stink you never forget after pulling POWs out of cages. Only worse. Concentrated."

James's gut twisted tight.

"Inside were... labs. Rows of cots with kids hooked to drips. Soldiers tied down, fed this shit called Revenant." She spat the word like it was venom in her mouth. "Nanotech, rotten, unstable. You could see it chewing them up alive. Skin blistering like it was boiling under the surface. Veins lit blue, pulsing like worms under the skin. They screamed until their throats tore. Some didn't even have voices left... just this wet, rattling noise..."

Her words faltered; she was speaking so rapidly, almost like she was afraid to speak longer than necessary. James's mind filled the gaps.

He'd read the classified reports. "Revenant casualties" are sanitised words for horrors no paper could hold. Men with black froth bubbling from their mouths, lungs liquefied. Women with eyes milked white, nanotechnology threading under the corneas like spiderwebs. Bodies rupturing from the inside, skin splitting to reveal circuitry where veins should be. He'd seen the photographs stamped RESTRICTED: NATO INTEL ONLY. Once seen, never forgotten.

And Evelyn had walked straight into it. Alone. His stomach bottomed out. A strategist's instinct told him this wasn't chance; he knew dam well that coincidence was a lie in their world. Someone wanted her there. Someone wanted her to see it.

She kept going, her voice hardening like brittle glass. "Then I found the pit. Mass grave. Flies so thick you could hardly breathe. People tangled, melted into each other. Some are still twitching. I put a round in one man's skull. Mercy."

James swallowed as bile creeped up his throat.

"I don't remember much after. Just reloading. Shooting. Twelve guards, maybe more. I killed every bastard. Got the survivors out. Took a round to the leg, ended up in a military hospital. They put me under, though I didn't need it. Woke up with this scar across my back and no clue what they'd done. Doctors are always watching me. Like I was the fucking experiment."

Her hands flexed as she tried to ground herself. "Four days later, a mafia courier smuggled me out the hospital and onto a container ship. Dumped me stateside. Was due to work in Gaza a month after, so I went early… Most dangerous place to work… but safest place to hide…. Then Gaza was a shitstorm…"

Finally she looked at him, eyes wrecked and hollow. "That's what happened."

The silence was suffocating. James couldn't breathe right. He saw it all... pits full of twitching half-corpses, kids with their veins glowing blue, the smell of bodies not even human anymore. And Evelyn, his Ev, buried in it.

"Jesus Christ..." The words rasped out of him.

She flinched like he'd struck her.

James paced forward with his voice low and fierce. "Why didn't you tell me?"

Her mouth twisted. "Because you'd look at me like you're looking now."

James caught her arm, steadying her. "I don't care what they did to you. I just want to protect you... Just trust me...let me in..." His throat closed, then he forced it out. "You and me... Like always..."

Her eyes flickered. Raw. Hesitant.

"And the worst part?" she whispered. "The courier gave me guns. Twin Glocks. On the grips, he'd carved ENAB. Evelyn Natasha Ada Blackthorn. Ada. My Holy Communion name. No one outside Our Lady's school ever knew it. Not even Obsidian. Just my mum."

James's body hardened.

Her voice shook. "And the grips had blackbirds carved into them. That was her name for me. My mum. She's dead, Jamie. I buried her myself. The night before, open the casket... I pinned a blackbird brooch to her dress. And now it's on my guns. Which means someone saw her body. In my house. While I was fifteen and grieving. Or it's a fucking big coincident."

The words ripped out of her, ragged and trembling. "Whoever got me out that hell hole has watching me since I was a kid. Inside my house. Inside my life. Or knows someone who did. And I don't know whether to be scared shitless or relived for being smuggled. But someone is watching me. And I don't know if they are an ally or an enemy. I feel paranoid. It's suffocating."

James felt nauseated. Whoever had eyes on her had been inside her bones for decades.

She was shaking now, fists balled. "I'm sorry I've clung to you since I got back. But after Colombia, Gaza, and that fucking scar, Jamie... My head is a mess. I don't know who the fuck to trust. And there is this thing crawling through me... I can feel things, Jamie... things I couldn't before... and I don't know what the fuck..."

He cupped her jaw, his thumb brushing the tremor in her cheek. His voice cracked with steel and devotion both. "Whoever's behind this... they don't get to have you. Not while I'm breathing. You're mine, Ev. Not theirs. Not anymore."

For once, she didn't argue. Didn't smirk. She just leaned into him, letting him hold the weight of it.

Temporary Base – Kherson, Ukraine – Late Evening

The base was full of the clatter of gear being packed down the hall. In the dim kitchen, James sat at a metal table, coffee cooling in his hands. Evelyn was opposite, with her legs tucked under her, eyes fixed on the steam rising from her mug.

Neither spoke for a long time. They didn't need to.

Finally, James said, low and steady, "I've got you, Red."

73

Her gaze lifted, frost blue and tired. "I never wanted to drag you into it. Thought I could keep it separate. But every time I try to outrun whatever this is, it finds me again. And the worst part?" Her voice thinned. "I don't even know who I'm running from anymore."

James leaned forward, hand open on the table. "Then stop running. Whatever it is, we face it together. I'm not going anywhere."

She hesitated, then brushed her fingers against his. The touch was brief, but it was enough.

"Thank you," she whispered.

His answer was quiet and ironclad. "Never."

The moment held until a voice shouted from the hall, 'The transport is ready.' Evelyn pulled back, her composure slipping back into place.

"Come on," she said, standing. "We've got a party to get to. And Irish's wife to meet."

James rose beside her, eyes still on her. No more words were needed between them, just the promise hanging unspoken between them.

Chapter 11

The garden glowed as the sun sank, fairy lights tangled through the hedge and AJ's solar lanterns flickering like stars. Fleetwood Mac bled into filthy garage remixes no one admitted to liking, but everyone danced too.

Mack planted himself by the firepit with the tongs like he was commanding a mission.

"Back off, all of you. I've got this."

Bullet leaned in, eyes glinting. "You said that last time, hermano, and we ended up with charcoal pretending to be chicken."

"Charcoal's good for the gut," Mack shot back, flipping a skewer with exaggerated precision.

Bullet snorted. "Maybe for a goat. Not for me. Hand it over before you poison us."

Selena folded her arms. "He's worse than my uncle at weddings. Thinks standing near smoke makes him a king."

Frost, dry as ever, added, "Just let him have it. Man needs one place in life where he feels in control."

AJ smirked into his grill. "My halal chicken looks beautiful; there is extra if anyone wants it."

"Deal," Bullet grinned. "Yours looks like actual food."

Mack flipped them all off "Fuck you all… I am in control. Mostly…" as a flame shot up.

The team sprawled around the firepit, Evelyn sat barefoot on a log, with her bass in her lap. Frost leaned over, guiding her fingers, their notes weaving through the laughter.

Irish appeared at the gate, hand in hand with a woman.

"Oi!" Mack bellowed. "Look what the dog dragged in…finally brought proof he's married!"

Rose's laugh was warm as Evelyn ran barefoot to hug her. Introductions rolled quickly. Selena with a drink, Bullet with too much charm, and AJ with a quip and within minutes Rose was folded in, her Belfast stories drawing the circle close. Evelyn leaned to Selena, whispering, "I love her."

Mack tipped his bottle toward her. "So tell us a bit about yourself, Rose. What's it like marrying this miserable sod?"

Rose grinned, eyes bright in the firelight. "Black ops medic. That's how I met Con, in Yemen. Field triage in the middle of hell, dust storms, gunfire, and men dropping faster than we could patch 'em. And this lunatic here…" she nudged Irish with her shoulder… "Refused to bleed out. Stitched himself shut while helping me save a kid. Thought he was indestructible. Still does."

Rose's voice softened. "He saved me as much as I saved him. After that… well, I wasn't going anywhere without him."

Bullet whistled low, shaking his head. "Romance, Obsidian style, nothing says true love like cauterising your own spleen."

Headlights and tired crunched on the gravel driveway. Evelyn jumped up far too excitedly. "Only one man sneaks off a debrief like that."

James stepped out the black Ford Raptor with his boots heavy and his eyes already scanning until they found Evelyn. She jogged over to him and handed him a cold beer before he even reached the firepit. "Good. We needed our brooding Paladin."

He froze at the sight of Rose. She stood to greet him and kissed his cheek like she'd known him forever. To everyone's shock, including his own, James didn't resist. Even Bullet muttered, "Fuck me. Paladin's thawing."

They all fell into stories with ease with the fire pulling all their confessions loose.

The fire spat and cracked, smoke curling into the night. Bullet tipped his beer toward Irish, a wicked grin playing at his mouth.

"Still can't believe Wrath's the only one of us married. What's that say about the rest of us? Walking disasters, the lot."

Mack barked a laugh. "Disasters is polite. My longest relationship ended when she tried to run me over with her sister's car."

"Should've married her," AJ quipped. "At least she cared enough to aim."

The laughter rolled, quick and sharp.

Selena shook her head, smirking. "I once went on two dates and came home to find the guy googling my property records. Decided celibacy was the safer option."

"Safer for him," Bullet muttered.

Even Frost cracked a small smile, low and dry. "My last serious one told me I was emotionally unavailable. She wasn't wrong. She left with the dog."

Irish spread his hands, smug as ever. "See? You're all proving the point. Took Rose to look at me bleeding out in a Yemeni dust storm and still decide I was worth keeping."

Evelyn raised her glass, eyes glinting in the firelight. "Or she just knew if shit goes down, she always has a medic to path her up... smart!."

The circle erupted again, laughter carrying into the night, warm and unashamed.

Rose's laugh quieted. "So James... How did you find this bunch of rogues and vagabonds?"

Bullet's eyes went wide with sheer excitement when Rose asked the question.

"You mean... You've never heard the origin stories?" His grin exploded. "Ohhh, princesa, you're in for it now."

He practically leapt to his feet, grabbing Evelyn by the wrist like a kid dragging a partner into mischief. "Come on, Red...we need supplies!"

They disappeared into the kitchen with their voices bouncing off the walls whilst clattering through cupboards. A minute later they came storming back out like pirates, Evelyn carrying a six-pack by the neck, Bullet balancing a bottle of whisky in one hand and clinking glasses in the other. Evelyn dropped a cold Coke into AJ's lap with a wink.

"Serotonin, qalbī," she teased.

Bullet spread his arms wide as though presenting an altar. "Behold! Fuel for legends."

James groaned, rubbing a hand over his face. "Are we really doing this?"

"Absolutely," AJ said, cracking open his Coke. His grin was wicked, but his eyes shone. "This is how legends are made."

James muttered something under his breath but reached for the whisky anyway. He poured himself three fingers, the liquid catching the firelight, and let the silence stretch just long enough for everyone to lean in.

The circle stilled, the fire popping, the night drawing tight around them.

James shifted, eyes catching the firelight before flicking toward AJ.

"Permission to tell it, brother?"

AJ hesitated, then gave a small nod. James draped an arm around his shoulders, pulling him in close before he spoke.

"Amir Jafari. Aleppo-born. When I found him, he was sixteen. Half-bombed server farm, dust still settling, and this kid was sitting barefoot on the racks, clutching the drives like treasure. Starving. Shaking. But grinning at me like he'd already won."

The firelight caught on AJ's profile, his smile faint but tight.

"I had a Glock on him," James went on, voice low. "And he doesn't flinch. Just waves the drives at me like a dare and says, 'One chocolate bar.' That's the price."

"It was Galaxy!" AJ tried to grin, though his voice cracked with anguish at the memory. "Best bribe I ever got."

The circle laughed softly, but gentler this time.

James's arm tightened on AJ's shoulders protectively. "He had no family left. No one. Just wreckage. And instead of breaking, he chose us. Then he came back with us; Ev and I put him through education, and he trained with the best, though he was better than all of them. Then we recruited him when he was willing and ready. I didn't recruit him…he chose to stay."

AJ's voice broke in, quiet but clear. "The first few months were hard…" His eyes flicked to Evelyn. "She held me while I broke."

The fire fell silent, every crackle echoing the weight of it.

Evelyn's hand found his across James's chest, squeezing tight. "Mā shā' Allāh, And I've never let go since Habibi…"

James's voice was rough. "Chaos wrapped in genius. So fucking clever, fights like a street brawler, hacks like a ghost. The little brother none of us asked for… but the one we'd burn the world to protect."

The toast rose heavy, reverent.

"To AJ."

James tipped his bottle toward the fire.

"Now this little Bastard, Diego Zavala. We call him Bullet. He goes off like one. We found him in a Guatemalan fight pit, covered in blood, boots two sizes too big, that he won in a bet, laughing like a lunatic after dropping three mercs bare-knuckled. He thought I was police… or worse."

Bullet's grin was pure chaos. "Figured he was gonna traffic me. Or make me his sex slave. And honestly…he's hot, but not that hot."

The team erupted. Mack groaned, "You can't open with that."

"I can and I did," Bullet shot back, swigging his beer. "Point is… he didn't cuff me. He threw me a towel and said: You done showing off, or should I place a bet?"

James shook his head, but there was nothing but fondness in his eyes.

"Fastest hands I've ever seen. Best shot I had ever seen as well. Impossible angles, reckless as hell, and still alive by nothing but instinct. He's chaos, yeah, but he's ours. And I'd never bet against him."

Evelyn's smile softened. "He's the laughter that reminds us we're still alive."

Bullet blinked once, then covered it with a crooked grin. "Don't get sappy on me, boss. And I am fucking sexy!"

The toast rose easy and warm.

"To Bullet."

James leaned back with his eyes flicking toward Selena.

"Selena Varma. Our Oracle. And the only person who ever truly outplayed me."

Selena arched a brow, sipping her drink. "Only once?"

He smirked faintly. "We were building the Task Force… vetting comms, securing Intel nets. And then… she slipped straight through. No alerts. No trace. Just a voice in my headset, asking if I wanted a lesson in how not to be so predictable."

AJ choked on his drink. "You hacked James?"

"Destroyed us," James corrected, though there was utter admiration in his tone. "And then she made me tea. Sat me down in a teahouse in the mountains and explained exactly how she'd dismantled us."

Selena's lips curved. "'You're lucky I'm friendly.'"

The circle groaned in unison.

"She doesn't just break systems," James said, voice lower now. "She sees patterns none of us do. Speaks half the world's languages. Keeps us sharper, calmer, and smarter than we'd ever be without her. Voice of our missions. Mind behind the rest."

Evelyn lifted her glass. "And a personal therapist when we're emotionally constipated. Our zen queen, who can fix everything with knowledge and tea."

Laughter rippled, but the toast that followed was steady.

"To Selena. Our Oracle."

James's gaze settled on the man reclining with pure ease in his chair with a beer balanced precariously on his knee.

"Mack. Mackenzie Larson. Grim. Known this stubborn bastard for years. San Francisco born, with a soldier's blood in his veins. By the time I met him, he'd done more tours than most generals and never bragged about a single one."

Mack shrugged as he was never the sort to accept praise. "Still can't grow a proper beard either."

The group chuckled.

"When Obsidian was just an idea," James went on, "I didn't even finish the pitch. I said, 'We're building something that matters.' He nodded once and asked, what time?"

Irish lifted his glass. "Aye, that's Grim. Don't shout. Doesn't flinch. Just moves."

"He leads like a wall of stone," James said. "And fights like it too. While the rest of us are screaming, he's just reloading."

Bullet snorted, with beer cascading down his chin. "And eating. Don't forget to eat."

Frost smirked. "Remind me what you said when that RPG missed our Humvee in Ukraine?"

Mack leaned back, with a sharp grin. "Said, 'Close shave. Anyone bring snacks?'"

The firepit roared with laughter as Evelyn lifted her bottle.

"To Grim. The big brother we'd follow into hell."

Glasses clinked in unison, sloshing liquor up and over the sides.

James's eyes found the quietest man in the circle.

"Now you, you smooth bastard, are my favourite origin story... Mr Malik Deveraux. Frost, named after his uncanny ability to stay chill and evaporate into thin air. Born in Atlanta to his French mother and creole father. And the most accurate shot records for distance that I have ever seen. I had to have him. Took me eight months to track him down. Every contact had said the same thing: ghost. Not a footprint, not a whisper. Three times he walked right past me without even trying."

The corner of Frost's mouth twitched.

"And when I finally caught him?" James shook his head. "He was in a jazz club in Paris. Guitar in hand. Spotlight on him. And the bastard looks me dead in the eye… and starts playing Smooth Criminal".

The firepit erupted, AJ nearly spilling his drink.

"Coolest thing anyone's ever done to me," James admitted. "Whole room vibing, and I'm stood there thinking… this is the guy I've been chasing?"

Frost finally spoke, voice low, velvet. "Finished the set. Bought you a whisky. Said one word."

James nodded. "'Talk.'"

The team groaned as one.

"Before Obsidian, he was the kind of operative you only read about in files that didn't exist," James said. "Diplomatic compounds, black sites, embassies… he could map them in his head and walk out without a trace. But I didn't bring him in just for that. I brought him in because when the rest of us fall apart, he's the calm in the storm… and he is one hell of a sniper"

Evelyn lifted her glass. "And the silence we trust."

The toast rose, steady.

"To Frost."

James then lifted his glass toward the man sitting solid and quiet by the fire.

"Conall McBride. Rose your husband you don't really need his story, but here it is, we call him Irish. Nickname speaks for itself. One of the originals, before Obsidian even had a name. I found him in Iraq, passed out on a dirt floor, half-covered in blood that wasn't his. Seventeen hours of surgery with nothing but makeshift tools and a will stronger than steel."

Irish didn't flinch, just took a slow drink.

"Belfast born," James continued. "Grew up in the last stretch of the Troubles. Saw more before fifteen than most men see in war. His mother was a nurse, his father a bricklayer. He learnt to fix things and fight things in the same breath. By the time Black Ops found him, he was already a ghost."

Selena spoke quietly. "He stitched my shoulder and reset my elbow under fire in Prague."

AJ grinned. "He set my rib with a crowbar."

"Explains a lot," Frost muttered.

Irish only shrugged. "Didn't have the right tools. Had to make do."

Evelyn leaned forward, voice softer. "My first tour, I was nineteen, bleeding out in the back of a moving truck. He patched me with duct tape, morphine, and his own belt." Her eyes met his, warm. "He's been my best mate ever since."

James nodded. "When I started Obsidian, he was the first man I called. Because if I was going to build something that lasted, it had to be with the man who never breaks."

Evelyn raised her glass. "Not just a medic. Our constant. When the world burns down, he's still standing."

The toast rang heavier this time, recognising the man who at one point or another had saved them all.

"To Irish."

Rose looked absolutely smitten at her husband and landed him a kiss, and the fire pit erupted in cheers. Rose then tilted her head, curious. "And what about Evelyn?"

The team fell silent, like rose had asked to know a national secrete.

"Nooo," AJ protested. "We don't go there."

"She pays us not to," Bullet smirked.

"She'll throw someone in the lake," Mack warned.

Evelyn laughed, curled into her seat beside James. "Oh, get fucked, I'm not that bad."

"You are exactly that bad," Irish grinned. "But... fair's fair."

She sighed, rolling her glass between her palms. "Fine. But only if someone else starts it."

James's voice cut through the firelight, low and steady.

"Evelyn Blackthorn. Liverpool girl with a sharp tongue and a sharper blade. Lost her parents too young. Grew up angry, broke, and fast, too good at the wrong things. By the time I met her, she was already running rings around NATO brass."

Selena smirked. "Still does."

"Afghanistan," James went on. "She pulled seven hostages out of a black site with nothing but a knife and a stolen comms line. She reads a battlefield like some people read palms. Leads from the front. Doesn't wait for permission. Scares the hell out of half the brass. Saves more lives than they'll ever admit."

"She bit a man once," Mack added.

"He grabbed my arse, dirty fucker..." Evelyn shot back.

Laughter rippled across the firepit, but James's tone stayed reverent.

"She's chaos. A gypsy soul. Swears like sailor. And the spark that lit this fire."

The firepit quieted. For a heartbeat, the only sound was the crackle of flames.

Selena lifted her glass. "To Evelyn."

"To Red," AJ echoed.

"The spark that lit the fire," James finished softly.

Evelyn hesitated, then raised her glass with a crooked grin.

"Alright then. I'll drink to that."

The fire burnt lower, wood collapsing into glowing embers. Smoke curled up into the night like ghosts, and for a while the only sounds were the crackle of flames and the clink of bottles.

They'd laughed themselves hoarse with banter and toasts and half-spilt stories until the night softened around them. AJ was slouched against Evelyn's side, Bullet sprawled with his boots too close to the fire, Selena graceful even in her quiet, Irish steady as stone, Mack grinning in the half-light, and Frost unreadable but present.

Rose sat back, eyes moving over the circle, and then her gaze landed on James. "And you, James?" she asked gently. "Where did you come from?"

The air shifted. The laughter stilled.

Evelyn's brow arched wickedly, and before he could protest, she hooked him into a headlock, running her knuckles over his head. "Speak now or lose your follicles!" she crowed as the others roared with laughter. James twisted free, smoothing his hair with mock severity, but his smirk faded almost at once.

The quiet that followed was different. Expectant. Heavy.

James stared into the embers, with his thumb rubbing slowly against the neck of his bottle. When he finally spoke, his voice was rough but steady.

"…Detroit. Father in prison for life. Mother drank herself into the grave. By sixteen, I was stealing cars to keep my sister fed. The recruiter gave me two choices: enlist… or jail."

No one moved. Even the fire seemed to still.

"I didn't put on the uniform out of patriotism. I put it on so Ruby, my sister, could eat. Every op since, every scar, every war… it wasn't noble. It was survival. Just the next step forward."

His eyes lifted, finding each of them in turn. The firelight made them burn with something harder than grief.

"And when they told me to build a new task force, I didn't ask for the best. I asked for the survivors. The ones who knew how to crawl, bleed, and still stand the next morning. That's how Obsidian was born."

The silence was reverent. Even Rose, new to their circle, felt the weight settle over her.

Mack lifted his bottle first. "To Paladin…the man who built a family from the kind of pain that should've eaten him alive."

AJ's voice was soft. "To the brother who gave me a second chance."

Selena's eyes shone. "To the man who fed his sister… and fed all of us."

Evelyn's gaze burnt into him, steady and unflinching. "To the boy in the cell… who chose the hard road and dragged us with him."

Glasses clinked. Sparks spiraled into the night like stars torn free.

James only nodded, that faint, tired smile tugging at his mouth. "Still. You're a violent little shit."

Evelyn smirked. "And you still love it."

The firepit erupted again with laughter rolling over them like a tide. But beneath it, Rose understood. This wasn't just a team. This was blood, chosen and forged in fire.

And for one rare night, under the stars, Obsidian was whole.

Scarred. Unshakably real.

Family

Chapter 12

Mack's kitchen, which was normally sacred ground, defended with spatulas and threats, was now utter chaos central.

Evelyn had hijacked the sound system, four whiskies in and waging war on everyone's ears. She stood on a chair, arms thrown wide, hair wild, eyes alight.

"Right, you beautiful bastards! Tonight… it's full Britpop! Pulp, Oasis, Kasabian, James…"

Her gaze cut through the crowd until it landed on their commander. She pointed, cheeky and unashamed.

"Oi, Jamie. You're so cool they named a band after you."

James shook his head, but the grin gave him away. God, she undid him with nothing but a glance.

Bullet whooped obnoxiously "Drunk-Ev is my favorite Ev!"

"I'm not drunk," she slurred, wobbling on the chair. "I'm cultured."

Rose was crying into Irish's chest with laughter. "This is what I signed up for!"

"Welcome to the circus," Irish laughed, kissing her head.

Then Oasis, Live Forever, blasted and Evelyn screamed like she was summoning the dead. She leapt down, grabbed Bullet, and dragged him into the center.

What followed wasn't dancing, it was utter bedlam with flailing limbs, head-banging, air-guitar solos. Bullet dipped her like a romcom lead and she howled the whole way down.

From the far side, James didn't move. Didn't dance. Didn't sing. But his eyes never left her. Every spin, every ridiculous stunt like she was a storm and he was helpless against it.

Rose leaned into Irish. "Does he always look at her like that?"

Irish didn't glance away. "You're noticed. Yeah. Always. Like she's his sunlight."

Girls & Boys by Blur hit next. AJ launched in like a man possessed, Selena followed with her wine glass raised high, elegant as ever. Evelyn slid across the floor in a knee-drop worthy of Glastonbury, somehow keeping her beer upright. She sprang up, bottle aloft.

"Nailed it!"

The room erupted. And James, James laughed. Not the polite chuckle they were used to. A real laugh, head back, chest open, so rare it pulled the whole room with it. They laughed harder just because their commander finally had.

Common People by Pulp slammed through. Evelyn flung her arms wide and shouted with no grace whatsoever, "I need a piss!"

"Thanks, Ev," James said dryly. "Good to know."

"Hydration is tactical!" she shot back, dancing towards the stairs.

She clipped the top step with a thunderous bang. Silence. Then her head popped back up, hair in her mouth.

"I'm OK!"

AJ doubled over. "That was so loud! How the hell is she in overt ops."

Two minutes later, Song 2 by Blur dropped.

"WOOHOOO!" Evelyn shrieked, sprinting down the stairs. She launched herself off the last two steps, drastically misjudges it slamming her straight into the coat rack with an explosion of boots and jackets.

Dead silence followed. Then from the heap: "Not dead yet!"

James pinched the bridge of his nose. "Coat rack: zero. Evelyn: undefeated."

She grinned up at him through scarves. "I meant to do that."

"Of course you did," he muttered, tugging fabric off her head.

She jabbed a finger into his chest. " I'm your favorite hazard."

His mouth twitched, as he desperately tried to hide his amusement "Yeah. Unfortunately."

The team howled. Bullet intoned, "The Obsidian Princess, carried off by her Paladin…"

"Fuck off…" James growled, but he bent anyway, lifting her like she weighed nothing.

He set her down on the couch, gentle, careful, hands brushing over ribs, ankles, wrists searching for any injuries.

"She's fine," he told the others with his voice firmer than he felt.

"Mate," Irish said flatly. "You've got heart-eyes."

Then Laid by James hit. Evelyn abruptly bolted upright, grabbed James's hand, and spun under his arm, screaming every lyric.

"You're not dancing!" she accused.

"I am," he said quietly. "I'm just letting you orbit."

And she did, wild, relentless like a storm circling its mountain.

"Jesus, Red…" James laughed as she spun around him, dizzy, magnetic.

Rose, still giggling, leaned in. "Why do you call her Red?"

The music almost skipped.

"Oh Christ…" Mack groaned.

"Oh fuck, now you've done it," Bullet whispered.

Evelyn stopped dead, then hauled a chair into the centre of the kitchen, and mounted it like a throne.

"Liverpool," she declared, deadly serious, voice carrying over the music. "Is not just a city. It's a heart. It's history, pride, sarcasm sharp enough to shave the King himself. We fight for the underdog. And we never buy The Sun! And as for Liverpool Football Club…" she raised a hand high, "it's not just a team. It's a fucking religion. Anfield is our holy ground. We will never forget our ninety-six lives lost at Hillsborough. And when we sing our anthem from the Kop…"

She broke off, darted to her rucksack, and came up triumphantly with her LFC scarf. Laughter rolled through the room as she vaulted back onto the chair, scarf held high like a banner.

James shook his head, grinning despite himself. God help him, he was smitten. She could've been standing on a battlefield or a bar stool, and she'd command it the same way.

Then she belted it out, lungs and heart in one wild roar:

"YOU'LL NEVER WALK… ALONEEEE!"

The kitchen exploded with Bullet on his knees like she was preaching, AJ swaying with a lighter in the air, Mack trying and failing to keep a straight face, Frost smirking like someone had just finally given in to the chaos.

Rose blinked through her laughter. "Great. Glad I cleared that up…"

Evelyn threw her arms wide and bowed. "Boss night. Fucking epic. Banging. Mint!!"

James was already moving when the chair wobbled. He caught her waist before she toppled, steadying her down onto the couch. She collapsed with a dramatic sigh, scarf pulled over her face and her head dropping squarely into his lap.

James looked down at her and at the damp patch spreading where she'd drooled on his jeans. "She's dribbling on me."

"Closest thing you're getting to head, boss," Bullet crowed.

The room detonated with laughter, but James barely heard them.

He brushed her hair back anyway, fingers gentle, lingering against her temple.

"She's out cold," Irish said, matter-of-fact.

"Still looks like she won the war," Selena added.

James's throat worked as he gazed down at her, with her eyeliner smudged, scarf crooked, chaos even in sleep. And still, she was radiant. His beautiful disaster. His ferocious wildfire. His Red.

"She always wins," he murmured, but the words carried more than fondness. They carried surrender.

And when the music dimmed, boots kicked off, laughter fading into tired warmth, one truth rooted deep in James's chest:

Whatever came tomorrow, whatever war waited at the door—tonight, with her asleep in his lap, was worth surviving for.

Morning – Mack's House

Morning crept into Mack's kitchen through half-drawn blinds, the light far too sharp for James's skull. His head pounded with every heartbeat, whisky still coiled in his gut like bad ammo. He sat hunched at the table, elbows braced on the wood, bloodshot eyes buried in his hands.

Across the room, Evelyn was already moving. Barefoot, hair tied in a messy knot, T-shirt hanging loose over her hips, she worked the stove like she'd slept eight hours instead of three. Bacon sizzled, AJ's separate pan was sizzling with love, coffee steamed, and she hummed low under her breath steady, bright and untouchable.

It wasn't fair. He felt like death warmed over. She looked like sunlight.

She slid past him to grab a plate, her shoulder brushing his as she reached up into the cupboard. That was when he saw it.

Her fingers pressed absently to the side of her neck, rubbing into the muscle like something had seized. For a split second, a thin blue thread flickered beneath her skin, racing up toward her jaw. She rolled her shoulders and exhaled, and just like that, whatever it was, it was gone. The tension in her face eased, her movements loosening as if some invisible weight had slipped off.

James blinked, sitting up straighter despite the pounding in his skull.

She noticed him watching, with a smirk tugging at her mouth. "What?" she teased, sliding eggs onto a plate. "Can't handle your drink, Paladin?"

He shook his head, more to clear it than to answer. He was hungover to an apocalyptic level, but he knew exactly what he saw.

And as the smell of coffee drifted over, one truth sank low and heavy in his chest: Evelyn wasn't just tougher than the rest of them, she was becoming something else entirely. Something he couldn't yet name.

Evelyn leaned against the counter, making the most of the quiet while the rest of the team nursed hangovers. Beside her, AJ sat cross-legged on the kitchen island, fiddling with his phone before shoving it away. The cheeky grin he usually wore was missing.

She tilted her head, studying him. "So… you seeing anyone special?"

AJ blinked, startled. Then laughed, too quick and too thin. "That obvious?"

"Only to someone who knows you." She nudged his arm with her boot. "So? Spill."

He hesitated for a moment, chewing on his thumb nail, then finally let the words out like they'd been locked up too long.

"Yeah. There's someone."

Evelyn's lips curved. "Good for you. Who's the lucky…"

"Ev…" His voice cracked tight. "It's a guy."

The words hung there, fragile, heavy but Evelyn didn't flinch. Didn't blink. Her smile only softened.

"Good," she said simply. "He must be bloody brilliant if he's got your attention."

AJ let out a breath he didn't know he'd been holding. His shoulders sagged, but something deeper still flickered in his eyes.

"I haven't told anyone. Not Bullet, not even said Ryan's name. Because…" He swallowed, gaze darting away. "I'm Syrian. I'm Muslim. It goes against everything I was brought up with. Everything my family believes. If they knew…" He shook his head.

Evelyn stepped forward, crouching until her eyes met his, her hand resting on his shoulder.

"If they knew you were happy, they would be happy. You don't have to explain, habibi. And you don't owe anyone your truth until you're ready. But hear me, I am so so happy for you. You deserve love. You deserve joy. No matter where it comes from."

His throat worked as he swallowed, his eyes turned glassy with love.

"You're the first person I've ever told," he whispered.

Her hand tightened on his shoulder, steady as stone. "Then I'll guard it with you, until the day you're ready to shout it from the rooftops."

The weight lifted from him just a little. AJ smiled, it was small, shy, but real.

"Show us a picture then…"

He hesitated with his thumb hovering over his phone before he sighed and unlocked it. Scrolled. Then he slowley turned the screen around.

Evelyn's eyes widened. The photo showed AJ grinning wider than she'd ever seen, shoulder-to-shoulder with a sun-kissed blond man at a beach bar. Both glowing with the kind of joy you can't fake.

"Oh my goddess, AJ…he is hot!" Evelyn slapped a hand over her mouth, then pointed at the grin on his face. "And look at you, all smiley. That's not your usual 'I've just hacked the Pentagon' smirk….that's the 'my soul's on holiday' smile."

AJ tried to stifle it, but the grin broke free anyway.

"So that was three weeks in Ibiza, then?" she teased.

He chuckled, shaking his head. "Yeah. We made the most of it."

They both burst out laughing.

Evelyn leaned closer, still staring at the photo. "So what does this Adonis do?"

AJ's grin turned sly. "Hacker. Goes by SyntaxError. A fucking good one. He caught my eye when he hijacked an arms conference James had sent me on. Every screen flashing: Stop bombing Syria. That was the first time I noticed him. And… the rest is history."

Evelyn's chest warmed. She reached out, squeezing his hand. "I love this for you, Habibi."

AJ ducked his head, but pride flickered in his eyes. Evelyn was still grinning when he gently tugged the phone back, slipping it into his pocket like something sacred.

"Ev… don't tell anyone," he said softly. "I'm not ready for that yet."

She frowned. "Not ready to come out?"

He shook his head. "No…that's not it. I don't care who knows I'm gay, not anymore. It's just… if James finds out, he'll try to recruit him. And I don't want him anywhere near what we do. He's a lover, not a killer. And…" His voice dropped, fragile but certain. "I do love him."

Her chest ached with pride. She touched his cheek lightly, grounding him. "Then it stays between us. Swear on it."

Her grin returned, wicked. "But you realise Bullet's gonna lose his mind when he meets him. Someone more beautiful than him? He'll never recover."

AJ barked a laugh, nearly doubling over. "Oh god, you're right. He'll combust on the spot."

"Good," Evelyn smirked, leaning back against the counter. "About bloody time someone knocked that heartbreaker crown off his head."

For the first time that morning AJ's smile was easy. Unguarded. Real.

The front door creaked open with the slow hesitation of someone who'd survived the night but wasn't ready for the morning. Selena slipped inside, sunglasses immaculate, a bag of pastries tucked under one arm like contraband. She looked flawless, of course she did, even though her hangover had to be screaming.

She didn't hesitate. Made a beeline for the deck, where James sat hunched over, cigarette burning down to the nub, body sagging like every bone had been hollowed out. The man looked wrecked.

She slid the door shut behind her, sealing them in a pocket of quiet.

"You okay, boss?" she asked, voice steady, though the concern was there if you knew where to listen.

James didn't answer straight away. His eyes stayed fixed on the ember at the end of his cigarette.

"Nope," he muttered finally. He took a drag, exhaled slowly. "Got the hangover from hell... and a head full of trouble."

Selena leaned against the railing, waiting. She knew when to press and when to give space.

"Ev?" she asked softly.

That got him. He turned, face tight, eyes rimmed with exhaustion. One sharp nod.

"She told me everything, Sel. Where she's been. What's happened to her." His voice was low, hoarse. "It's dark. Darker than I knew. She liberated a Revenant camp, kids, prisoners, a mass grave. She was shot. Cut open. Doesn't even know why.

100

Then smuggled out on a fucking ship. Then dose a tour in Gaza to top it off"

His hand trembled as he ground the cigarette out against the railing. For a second he just stared at the ash smeared on his fingers, like the weight of it was carved into his skin. Selena clocked the tremor. She clocked the grey fatigue in his eyes, the sleepless lines etched deep. He wouldn't admit it, but he was running on fumes.

"There's more," he said, voice rough. "But I can't tell you. Not yet."

Selena stayed silent, but her eyes softened. Then, quieter:

"So last night's madness?" She tilted her head, sharp edge creeping into her tone. "The dancing. The karaoke. That was all a mask, wasn't it?"

James's jaw tightened. "Yeah. All of it. You know Ev, She hides herself behind chaos and humor, like if she is loud enough… fun enough… no one will see beneath it all. She is close to breaking point, Sel…. She went to Gaza to hide as much as to help. Thought it was the only place she wouldn't be followed."

Selena stepped closer, folding her arms. "Ow my goodness James. Poor girl. So who's she running from?"

James finally looked up at her. The exhaustion in his eyes had hardened into something colder, resolve.

"I don't know," he said. "But I'm going to find out."

The air between them went heavy, taut with the storm that hadn't broken yet. Selena studied him for a long beat, then nodded once. No fuss. No theatrics. Just the truth.

"I have got your back," she said quietly. "Always."

James breathed deep, ash still smudged across his fingertips. His gaze drifted to the horizon, with his shoulders squaring like a man bracing for war.

"Thanks, Sel," he murmured. "I'm gonna need it."

Selena didn't answer. But in that moment, watching the faint shake in his hands, she silently made the decision to start guarding him, whether he asked for it or not.

The world outside stayed deceptively quiet, but both of them knew the silence wouldn't last.

Chapter 13

Three days later – The Fire Pit

Three nights later, the fire pit roared, flames licking skyward as the team gathered close. Bottles clinked, laughter tangled under fairy lights strung across the courtyard. Mack had the grill smoking, meat spitting and sizzling, the smell mingling with spilled beer and woodsmoke. For once, it felt like life was allowed to be simple.

Evelyn leaned back in her chair, feet propped on the edge of the stone pit, cheeks flushed from the second drink warming her blood. Bullet had just cracked a filthy joke, and she was doubled over laughing, her voice raw with the kind of release that only came after weeks of tension. Her eyes shone brighter than James had seen in a long time.

James sat beside her, his body loose for once, the firelight softening the hollows of exhaustion etched into his face. AJ downed Red Bull like it was intravenous, grinning wide as Selena gave him shit for it. The night was easy. The night was good.

Then James's phone buzzed.

He didn't reach for it right away. His gaze flicked across the fire to Mack. The subtle change in his posture sent a ripple through the group. Even the flames seemed to quieten, the warmth collapsing into something colder, sharper.

Mack lifted a hand. A silent command.

"Phones down," he commanded, low but iron. "Stop drinking."

The chatter died on impact.

James had already pulled his phone, scanning the message. His body shifted suddenly alert. He stood, tossing the device onto the bench with enough force to rattle wood.

"The Americans just called." His voice carried like steel in the night. "Emergency op. Libya. Black-site Revenant lab."

The words detonated in the silence.

Evelyn's fingers tightened around her beer bottle until the glass squeaked. Blood drained from her face. She didn't blink, didn't breathe, the ghosts flooding back: cold corridors, screaming children, pits of bodies. The lab.

"Fuck," she muttered, too loud in the quiet.

James's eyes caught hers, soft for just a second. He knew. He'd seen her flinch.

"I know," he said, quieter. "But we move now. No hesitation."

"What's the target?" Frost was already on his feet, calm but razor-sharp.

"They're calling it a 'clean-up.' Neutralize whatever's left. But we're not the only ones hunting. Clock's already ticking." James's gaze swept across each face, the fire reflected in his eyes like something alive. "You've got fifteen minutes. Gear up. HQ. Go."

No one argued. No one moved slow. The firepit still crackled, but the night was dead.

Without hesitation, chairs scraped back. Boots hit the ground. The firepit glow seemed too warm, too alive for what had just landed in their laps. The truth clung to the air: this wasn't just another op. It was personal. It was dangerous. It had teeth.

Evelyn felt it in her bones before her mind caught up. The weight of it pressed down, dragging old ghosts back from where she'd buried them. Screams in concrete corridors. The stench of rot, of death piled high. Gaza, different war, same nightmare. Children gasping in her arms, hands shaking as she tried to pull them back from the brink. Both memories crashed together, a tide she couldn't stop.

She stood, shaking her head like she could physically rattle the panic loose. But it clung. It always clung.

James saw it instantly. He stepped closer with his voice pitched low so it carried only to her.

"Ev... we've got this. Whatever you need... say it now... we don't need any hesitation on this... You need to sit this out?"

She nodded, too tight, too practiced. The familiar weight locked back into her chest. Responsibility. It never left.

"I'll be fine," she mouthed. It was a lie that they both heard. "Besides I have most experience with Revenant labs"

Mack's voice cut through, sharp but steady.

"You don't need to be fine, Red. You just need to be ready."

That was all it took.

The team moved. The laughter and smoke of the night evaporated in an instant. The shift from downtime to combat was muscle memory now, silent and seamless. No speeches. No hesitation. Just soldiers falling into the rhythm of survival, bound by blood and by the scars they carried.

Obsidian HQ pulsed with motion.

The order had landed like a hammer, sharp and absolute. The air was thick with tension with heavy boots pounding against the concrete, voices echoed the building, clipped and urgent. The plane was inbound in thirty. No time for hesitation.

James moved fast, scanning the Intel feed flashing across his tablet, his eyes cold, his shoulders squared. He was already in commander mode.

Mack was the first to rise, downing the last of his coffee in one gulp before slamming the cup down.

"Thirty minutes," he broadcasted, already striding toward the gear room.

James stepped forward with a voice low, carrying that iron weight that made everyone in the room focus.

"Alright. Wheels up in thirty. High-stakes recovery, hostile territory, and the clock's against us. We hit fast, we hit hard. No fuck-ups. Non-negotiable."

He turned on his heel.

"Frost secure high ground, not so much as a whisper getting past you."

Frost gave a sharp nod, already moving with calm precision in every step.

"Ev you're lead on extraction. Biohazard protocols are live. You're on the ground first. Get the Intel, get it out."

Evelyn's hands were steady as she racked her weapon, checking the chamber. "You don't need to tell me twice, boss."

"Bullet."

"Yeah, yeah," Bullet grinned, strapping on his harness. "I'll make sure when the shit hits the fan, it splatters the other guys."

"AJ."

Helmet in hand, AJ's grin matched his fire. "We've got this. Same as always."

James pivoted to Selena, who hadn't looked up from her tablet once, with her fingers flying.

"Selena, Intel hub stays with you. Keep our comms clean. Feed me anything the second you see it."

"Already on it," she confirmed, her eyes narrowing at the screen.

James scanned the team one last time, his voice dropping low, hard as steel.

"We've got one shot. One. Don't fail me."

That was it. No pep talk. No speeches. Just the click of magazines locking home, the rip of velcro straps, the hiss of tactical packs being sealed. Silence fell, heavy but sharp with soldiers bracing themselves for another plunge into the abyss.

Evelyn checked her gear again, pausing just long enough for her eyes to find James's. No words were needed. Just the silent agreement they always carried into hell: together, or not at all.

Outside, the rotors of the waiting black ops helicopter already chewed the night, ready to take them to the airfield. James stood at the doorway, with his gaze sweeping the room, and then he moved.

"Obsidian—let's roll."

And once again, they stepped into the chaos they were born to control.

The plane's hum was deafening, a low metallic growl that rattled through the fuselage. In the back, there was nothing but quiet focus. Every man and woman on Obsidian was locked into ritual, checking mags, adjusting straps, fingers brushing over steel like prayer beads.

James sat shoulder to shoulder with Irish with his eyes fixed on the tablet in his hands. The mission feed scrolled in cold green lines across the screen, but he wasn't reading anymore as he already knew every word.

"Irish." His voice cut low through the roar of the engines, steady but sharp. "Brief them. Revenant. Everything."

Irish set down his coffee, the plastic cup rattling in its holder. His face was carved deep in shadow, the kind that comes from seeing too much. For a moment he didn't speak, he just exhaled slowly through his nose. Then he tapped his own tablet to life, flicking up a briefing feed.

"Alright. Listen in." His voice wasn't loud, but it carried the weight of the situation. One by one, heads turned. Even Bullet, normally all restless energy, leaned forward, with his eyes narrowing.

"You've all heard the word. Revenant. Nanites. Biotech. Enhanced combatants. Here's the truth." He looked each of them in the eye before continuing.

"These aren't soldiers. They're victims. Prisoners of war. Civilians. Kids. Refugees. They're injected with swarms of self-replicating machines designed to make them stronger, faster, harder to kill. But the cost?" He shook his head. "The nanites, nanotechnology, don't stay in balance. They adapt. They mutate. They eat their host from the inside out."

A ripple of unease passed through the cabin.

Irish's tone dropped lower, weight settling on every syllable. "I've seen men split their own bones just trying to stand upright. Skin tearing like wet paper while their muscles doubled in size underneath. Nerves burning out like wires sparking in an electrical fire. Sometimes they don't even die…they just… keep moving, half-rotten, half-machine. Unpredictable. Unstoppable until you put them down."

No one moved. Even the sound of the engines seemed farther away.

Irish glanced at James, then back to the team. "These camps… we're about to walk into one. They've been running them for years. Human test beds. Hell on earth. They'll use anything…children, refuges, prisoners, soldiers who won't be missed. And when the experiments fail…" He let the silence speak for him.

The weight of it pressed down heavy.

Finally Bullet broke it, his voice quieter than usual. "Anyone here ever been inside one of those?"

Silence settled.

Then Evelyn raised her head. Her eyes were shadowed, face strained as she gritted her back teeth and her knuckles white where her fingers wrapped her rifle.

"I have," she said. Just two words. Gravel-rough, but steady.

The cabin stilled. Even the air seemed to hold its breath.

Her gaze didn't waver. "We're not walking into a mission." A pause. "We're walking into hell itself."

Irish's throat bobbed as he swallowed, his gaze softening in grim recognition. "She's right. It won't be easy."

James's fingers found the edge of his dog tags as he ran his thumb down the edge of them to ground himself, his eyes fixed dead ahead. He didn't soften, didn't blink. His voice was iron.

"Then we stay focused. We go in fast, get the targets, and get out. Nobody gets left behind. We're not just fighting to win... we're fighting to survive."

The hum of the plane filled the silence again. But now it wasn't background noise. It sounded like a dirge, carrying them all straight into the dark.

The team had been absorbing Irish's briefing, the weight of it pressing heavy on their shoulders, but now the silence seemed too thick, too loaded. Evelyn, who had been silent since the start, shifted in her seat. Her shoulders were coiled tight; her eyes fixed on the cold horizon beyond the glass.

James caught the change immediately. He knew that look, with memories clawing their way to the surface.

"Valkyrie?" His voice cut through the hum, quieter than he intended. "You want to add something?"

She didn't answer right away. Her fingers flexed against her gear, knuckles pale. Finally, she drew in a sharp breath.

"The full Revenant has never been perfected," she said, her voice low but steady. "But every experiment gets them closer.

Closer to something horrific." Her eyes flicked briefly toward the others. "What no one tells you is this… Revenant only bonds under pain. They believe the nanites fuse stronger if the body is breaking. So they make you break."

A beat of silence. The air seemed thinner, harder to breathe.

"Most die before it takes. Some overdose. Some bleed out when the nanites eat through their organs. But most?" Her throat bobbed as she swallowed. "Most die because of the torture. Because the body just… gives up."

Her words hit like lead.

AJ cleared his throat, his voice too young for this kind of war. "But… if they survive?"

Evelyn's gaze snapped to him, her tone flat, merciless. "They don't. Not really. They're walking corpses. Skin stretched too thin, bones warped, eyes gone black from nanite burn. You can smell them before you see them. Death, wrapped in a body that won't stop moving."

The aircraft seemed to shrink.

Her voice dipped, a tremor threading through it. "In the beginning, they used soldiers. Prisoners. Volunteers. People who thought they were serving something bigger. But it wasn't the science that destroyed them. It was the agony. The years of being broken. And now…" she faltered for the briefest second, "…now they've started taking women."

Her eyes burnt, but her words carried ice.

"I've seen it. I've seen kids strapped down while the machines tore them apart from the inside. Screaming until there

111

was nothing left to scream with. And when it was over… there was no one left to save. Just husks."

Her voice cracked, and she bit down on it, hard. "And I couldn't…" Her hand tightened into a fist, shaking. "I couldn't save them."

James moved before the silence could devour her. "That's enough, Valkyrie." His voice cut like steel. Firm, commanding, but gentled at the edges. "I won't have you carrying that in with you."

She snapped her gaze to him, breath sharp. "I can. I'm in. No hesitation."

He held her eyes, steady as a rock in a storm. "We deal with it as a team. You faulter… you feel yourself doing down… you find me…"

For a moment, it was just the two of them, that unspoken vow hanging in the air. Evelyn exhaled, shoulders loosening by inches.

"Alright," she muttered. "We do this. And we do it right."

Around them, the team exchanged grim glances. The silence wasn't just heavy now; it was sacred.

The plane kept humming, but the sound had changed. It wasn't a hum anymore. It was a dirge, carrying them straight into hell.

Chapter 14

The plane shuddered as the green light blinked overhead. The briefing was done, silence clawing at every corner of the cabin. Evelyn's words still hung in the air, heavy and raw, impossible to shake.

The ramp whined as it began to lower. The roar of the outside world rushed in with the air thick, humid, choked with something that wasn't just heat.

It was the smell.

Not the clean burn of fuel or the dry earth of the desert. No. This was rot. Sweet and rancid, like meat left too long in the sun, layered with the metallic tang of blood and chemicals. It punched them all in the chest.

Bullet gagged, pulling his sleeve over his nose. "Jesus Christ... huele a muerte"

No one answered.

The hatch thudded fully open, slamming against the ground like a coffin lid. The team filed out, boots hitting dirt. The world around them was dim, the night pressing in like a living thing. The compound loomed in the distance with floodlights casting harsh white scars across barbed wire fences.

And then came the sound.

Not the usual chaos of a military site. No orders shouted. No engines. Just... crying. Thin, broken wails carried on the wind. Human, but not quite. Children, maybe. Or something that used to be children.

Irish froze mid-step, the blood draining from his face.

Mack muttered, low and furious, "Christ above…"

James kept moving, his rifle steady, eyes narrowed and focused. But even he felt the way the ground seemed wrong beneath their boots. Soft, almost spongy, as if soaked through with things that should never have been spilled.

Evelyn paused at the threshold. The floodlights caught her face, pale against the dark. She stared out at the compound, cheek muscle twitching with each unspoken word, she had seen this before. Every shadow, every sound, every stench, it was déjà vu wrapped in a nightmare.

Her throat worked as she whispered, too low for most to hear. "It's the domain of the undead."

James heard. He shifted closer, his shoulder brushing hers, his voice a steady growl.

"Stay with me."

She blinked, snapping back into the now, nodding once.

The team moved forward, into the compound's shadow. The cries grew louder. Shapes shifted in the dark, figures pressed against wire fences, faces pale and raw, eyes reflecting the floodlights like animals in the wild. Their mouths opened and closed, some soundless, some shrieking, some muttering in voices too broken to form words.

AJ's whisper cracked. "Are they…"

"Don't look," James cut him off, voice sharp.

But it was too late.

One figure staggered into the light, flesh warped, veins glowing faintly like embers under the skin. Nanite burn. Its body twitched, jerking like a puppet pulled on broken strings. It pressed a hand against the fence, skin peeling as metal fused into it.

And it smiled.

They were not human. Not sane. Just teeth and blood and a low, gurgling laugh.

Bullet swore under his breath, gun halfway raised.

Evelyn didn't move. Her eyes locked on the thing, every muscle taut, breath shaking in her chest. She whispered, voice like gravel, "That's what I meant."

James's command was low and final.

"Eyes forward. We move."

The team tore themselves away, stepping deeper into the compound. The hatch behind them sealed shut, cutting off the outside world.

They were in.

And the nightmare had only just begun.

Evelyn's breath caught as the team swept through the sterile corridors. Every step echoed too harshly, every door they opened revealing a new atrocity.

The cages came first. Too small. Too close. The stench of piss and rot burnt their noses. Children crouched inside, no older than five or six, their thin arms wrapped around their knees, eyes huge and vacant. Their skin clung to their bones like wet paper. They didn't cry. They didn't even whimper. They just watched, like beaten animals who had long since learnt that noise earned pain.

Then came the older ones. Their bodies told the story before their eyes did with limbs that twisted into grotesque shapes, bones bowed under the strain of injections and restraints. Some had patches of flesh like wax, melted and refrozen. Others twitched in unnatural rhythm, nerves firing wrong. They weren't children anymore. They were test subjects.

Evelyn's breath shallowed, clipped at the edges, like her lungs had shrunk. Her movements became sharp, as she forced herself to scan each room with military precision. But James saw it, her fingers uncharacteristically trembled when she gripped her weapon, her breath caught too often, and her eyes refused to linger on any one face too long.

And then it happened.

A flicker. Blue lightning, faint but unmistakable, danced beneath her skin like a serpent coiled under glass. It flared along her wrist and vanished before anyone else could notice.

James's stomach dropped. He moved instinctively, angling his comms away.

"Valkyrie…" His voice was low, dangerous. "What the fuck was that?"

She didn't answer. Just pushed forward, eyes dead ahead, like momentum was the only thing holding her together.

"I'm fine." The words scraped out of her throat, too quiet, too quick. "Keep moving."

James refocused his attention and didn't press. Not now. Not with this around them.

116

The deeper they went, the worse it became. The air grew thick, copper and chemicals stinging the back of their throats. The cries came next. Weak. Wet. Breathing machines hissing over ragged whimpers.

They reached a chamber. Metal walls sweated with condensation. Strange equipment clung to the ceiling like mechanical spiders, their arms bristling with needles and clamps.

And the gurneys.

Rows of them. Children strapped down, their bodies jerking in silent convulsions, skin riddled with tubes and metal prongs. Veins glowed faintly blue, nanites crawling like fireflies beneath paper-thin flesh. Some didn't move at all, their mouths frozen in eternal screams.

One stirred as the team entered. A boy, eight, maybe nine, his chest rattling with each shallow breath. His eyes fluttered open, pupils blown wide, glowing faintly with something not human. They locked onto Evelyn with terrifying clarity, like he knew her. Like he recognised her.

His lips cracked open. A whisper escaped, broken Arabic.

"Help… please… stop them…"

The words were barely audible, but they struck like gunfire. Evelyn staggered, a sound tearing from her throat before she crushed it down.

James froze, every instinct screaming. He didn't move until he saw Evelyn fall to her knees beside the boy, hands shaking as she reached for him. Professional. Efficient. But her face… James had seen that face before. It was the face of someone fighting their own ghosts.

117

And then the pulsing flair came again. Stronger. Her whole arm flared with that electric blue glow, veins burning like lightning branches under her skin.

James's heart thundered. He was right there, close enough to see the light crawl toward her neck, then vanish just as fast.

"Valkery…"

"Paladin," she cut him off, her voice trembling but commanding. "I need you here. Med kit. Now."

He snapped back into motion, shoving the fear down, pulling the kit open with quick, practised movements. He passed her what she needed, his eyes never leaving her.

Together they worked, stabilising the boy, giving him a chance, however small. But James knew. He knew as sure as the smell of blood in the air. Something was changing in her. The lab wasn't just a graveyard. It was a mirror. And it was pulling her into it, one shimmer at a time.

The boy's whisper still hung in the air when it happened.

From the far end of the chamber, one of the strapped-down children convulsed. At first it was just a twitch, an arm jerking against leather restraints, a guttural gasp leaking through clenched teeth. Then the machines around him began to shriek. Alarms screamed, nanite monitors spiked red, and liquid hissed through clear tubes into his veins.

The child arched violently, back bending at an impossible angle, bones popping loud enough to echo off the steel walls. Skin stretched tight, veins flaring a sickly blue that pulsed like something alive was trying to crawl its way out. His mouth tore open in a silent scream as his teeth began to lengthen, his jaw distorting until it cracked.

"Fuck…!" Mack had his rifle up instantly, but Evelyn threw her arm out, stopping him cold.

"Wait." Her voice was raw, shaking.

The boy's body split with seams of light, nanites boiling just under his flesh. Muscles bulged, tearing through skin that couldn't contain them. His eyes snapped open, white drowned in burning blue, and locked onto Evelyn.

And then Evelyn ignited too.

The eerie blue pulse ripped across her skin like lightning in a storm. Not subtle this time. Not a flicker. Her entire arm blazed electric blue, veins burning so bright it lit the chamber in pulses. The boy screamed, thrashing against the restraints, and every movement of his body mirrored a surge in Evelyn.

It was like they were linked.

James swore under his breath, moving closer, hand tightening on her shoulder. "Valkyrie... You need to shut it down. Right now."

"I can't," she choked, her body convulsing violently. Her eyes were locked on the boy's, pupils dilated to nothing but black, sweat dripping down her temples. "He's pulling me…"

The gurney snapped. Metal restraints tore like foil as the child's mutated arms lashed free, fingers now claws. He sat bolt upright, shrieking, nanite glow erupting from every pore.

The team scattered for firing positions, their weapons raised, but Evelyn screamed, not at them.

"No! Don't shoot him!" Her voice cracked, raw with desperation. "He's just a kid!"

The boy lunged with machines ripping free in showers of sparks, and James barely managed to tackle Evelyn aside before the claws shredded the floor where she had been kneeling. The Revenant-child's body convulsed mid-movement, snapping from human to monster and back again, a grotesque half-shift that made his bones grind audibly.

Bullet gagged at the sound as bile surged up his throat, the smell overwhelming him. Irish whispered, "Dear god help him…" under his breath.

Evelyn desperatley tried to crawl toward the boy again, her skin still glowing, as if his agony was bleeding into her body. James pinned her down hard, with his full weight pushing into her.

"Ev, look at me!" His voice cut through the chaos, steady and commanding. "You can't save him. Not like this. He's gone."

But the boy's gaze stayed locked on Evelyn, glowing and wild, until he spasmed again, blood spraying the floor as his body ruptured under its own transformation. The scream that left him was not a child's anymore.

The chamber reeked of ozone and copper. The sound of rending flesh and steel filled the air.

And Evelyn's glow didn't stop.

It burned.

The child convulsed one last time his small body snapping forward and mouth wide open in a shriek that rattled the chamber lights. And then silence. His head lolled back, eyes wide and unseeing, blue glow draining to nothing.

For a heartbeat, no one moved.

Evelyn's scream was inhuman ripping the stillness apart.

She lunged forward, hands shaking violently, trying to shake life back into the boy's ruined body. "No! No no no no! He was right there…"

James grabbed her wrists, pulling her back. "Ev, stop… He's gone. He's gone!"

Her eyes were empty, hollow, like the light had been ripped out of her chest. She stopped struggling, just… folded in on herself. Her body shook with shallow breaths. Catatonic. Staring straight through James like he wasn't there.

Then her gaze dropped. Straight to the rifle on the floor.

Her hand snapped out, fast as a striking snake. She gripped it and chambered a round with a metallic crack that echoed like thunder.

"Valkyrie. Stand down." James's voice was iron. "That's an order."

Her head turned toward him, slowly, eyes blazing with something feral. "Fuck your orders."

She rose to her feet, her body trembling but unbreakable, dripping with rage and vengeance. She made a beeline towards the exit, straight into the dark and dank compound corridors.

James swore, grabbing his comms. "Grim, Coyote… Cover her. Now."

Mack's voice: "Copy. On her six."

Bullet: "On her flank."

The three of them moved like wolves unleashed.

The first corridor lit up with gunfire. Shadows moved: guards, lab techs, and security drones. Evelyn's rifle barked three sharp bursts. One guard dropped, head blooming crimson against the steel wall. Another stumbled back, gasping as half his torso disintegrated under her rounds.

"Two, right. Elevated platform," Bullet called out over comms.

"Cover me," Evelyn snapped, vaulting over an overturned gurney. She slid low with her rifle angled up. Her rounds punched through the grated catwalk, blood raining down as the guards above screamed and collapsed, their legs folding in ways they shouldn't.

Mack advanced hard left, shotgun booming, blowing a man into the wall with such force his bones shattered against the tiles. He kicked the body aside without slowing.

Bullet took the high angle, moving like liquid chaos. "Three bogeys, surgical bay. Heavy armour." His rifle chattered in controlled bursts, each shot tearing through helmets and visors. One man fell, his hands clawing at the exposed Revenant graft on his jaw as it split wide open, with its teeth pushing through skin in a grotesque half-shift before he died gurgling.

Evelyn stormed through it all, silent but for her ragged breaths.

"Door left," Mack called.

"Stack." Evelyn's voice was stone.

She pressed flat to the wall, Mack opposite, Bullet on the breach. Hand signals: one… two…

The door blew inward under Mack's boot.

Inside, there were three lab coats frozen mid-step, one holding a tray of syringes. They didn't even have time to scream before Evelyn's rifle tore through them. Blood sprayed the sterile walls. One staggered back with the syringe still in hand, before Mack's knife silenced him with a crunch of vertebrae.

Bullet snarled darkly over comms. "Clear. Fuckers never stood a chance."

The deeper they pushed, the worse it became. There were half-men strapped into frames with tubes running into their throats, eyes rolling with terror. Some broke free when alarms wailed, their bodies twisting, limbs mutating in spasms of nanite surge.

One lunged, its jaw splitting vertically into two, shrieking. Evelyn's rifle snapped up with a double tap to the skull. The creature fell twitching, its nanite glow sputtering out like a dying star.

Another charged from the shadows with its stomach swollen grotesquely, veins crawling like worms under the skin. Mack didn't hesitate; one shotgun blast, and the thing ruptured in a flood of black sludge and blood that coated the walls.

Through it all, Evelyn never stopped. Every pull of the trigger was a purge. Every kill was for the boy she couldn't save.

James's voice crackled through comms, taut with fury and fear. "Valkyrie! Fall back. That's an order!"

She didn't answer.

She just reloaded, racked the rifle, and pressed forward into the fire.

Chapter 15

The sounds of chaos still echoed down the corridors with gunfire, shouting, and bodies hitting the floor, but James didn't hear any of it. All he could hear was Evelyn's ragged breathing as he caught her by the back of the neck and wrenched her off the kill path.

"WITH ME. NOW!" His voice was steel, raw and loud enough to slice through her frenzy.

Her wild, glowing eyes locked on him for half a heartbeat, unfocused, twitching like she didn't even recognise him. Then she stumbled forward, following his drag as if pulled by instinct.

He shouldered them into a disused lab, slammed the door, and killed the feeds with one vicious jab of his fist. Silence. For the first time since it began—silence.

"LOOK AT ME!" James snapped, grabbing her arms hard. His hands burnt where they touched her and her skin was burning hot, lightning racing under it in jagged veins of neon blue. Sparks crackled over her pulse points.

"Shit…" He muttered it under his breath, almost to himself. He didn't understand what he was seeing, but he knew one thing: if she spiralled further, they'd lose her.

He ripped his kit off – vest, comms, shirt – tossing them into a pile. Then he was on her gear, yanking straps, pulling buckles open with brutal efficiency until her plates hit the ground. His own shirt went over her head, drowning the glow in fabric, grounding her in something human, something his.

"Ev. Ev, look at me." His voice softened, but the tremor in it betrayed him. "Breathe. Just breathe with me."

She was shaking, her chest heaving and eyes wild and lethal. But slowly, painfully, her gaze started to clear, like he was pulling her out of a drowning current by sheer force of will.

And then her voice cracked out of her, raw and broken.

"What the fuck am I, Jamie?"

The question shattered him. Her tone wasn't anger; instead, it was terror. The kind that cut deeper than any wound.

James pulled her in, crushing her against his chest, arms wrapped so tight she couldn't slip away even if she tried. "You're mine," he whispered fiercely into her hair. "You're Evelyn. My Evelyn. I don't give a fuck what just happened …you hear me? You're mine."

She trembled in his arms from adrenaline, the glow fading and the sparks dying like embers.

He pressed his forehead to hers, forcing her eyes to meet his. "Breathe. Stay with me. I've got you. I'll always have you."

Her legs buckled once, almost dropping her, and James caught the full weight without flinching. He keyed his comm with one hand, his voice was clipped but laced with something his team had never heard from him before: Terror.

"Valkyrie's down. PTSD hit her hard. I'm extracting her myself."

There was static and questions, but he killed the feed before they could answer. This moment wasn't for them.

He looked back down. Evelyn's face was pale with sweat beading on her brow, but the madness in her eyes had receded. The storm was still there, caged now, burning in silence.

"Come on, Red," James said hoarsely, guiding her up, his arm steady under her shoulders. "We finish this together. Same as always."

She nodded once, weak and shaken but certain.

No more words were said, as they didn't need them.

The medevac bird screamed through the night, with rotors hammering the air. Inside, it was chaos. Survivors were being loaded onto stretchers, medics weaving between them, hands slick with blood. The team were helping, lifting bodies, securing IV lines, and holding down kids who thrashed in fevered confusion.

Evelyn didn't move. She was strapped in against the hull, her eyes locked on one woman across from her. Pregnant. Barely conscious, her lips were cracked, hand resting on the swell of her belly as if she could shield the child inside. Evelyn's gaze didn't flicker once, like she was staring at a reflection of a nightmare she already knew.

Irish moved through the bird with practised speed, checking pulses, barking to the medics in his clipped Belfast growl. When he reached Evelyn, he crouched low with his hand already reaching for her wrist.

James was faster. His palm shot out, blocking Irish's hand before it landed, with his body locked and eyes like knives.

"She's fine," James said flatly. "Screaming was PTSD. She threw up on herself. I checked her over myself; that's why she's in my top."

Irish didn't move; he didn't blink. His gaze slid to Evelyn's pale face, then to the faint blue shimmer still fading from her veins. He'd seen enough back in the facility.

"Roger that, boss," Irish said, his voice steady, but his eyes lingered.

Across the bird, Bullet and Mack weren't as subtle. They'd both seen her light up in the corridors. Their stares lingered just a moment too long.

James leaned between them, low enough that no one else could hear, voice like gravel:

"Not. A. Fucking. Word. Either of you."

Neither man spoke. Neither man nodded. But both understood.

For a long moment, the only sound was the rotors, the screams, and the medics working. Then Evelyn's voice cut through it all.

"Anyone else feel like this wasn't a rescue extraction?"

Her tone was flat and hollow. Her eyes didn't leave the pregnant woman.

The team froze. AJ's hand stilled on a bandage. Mack's body went ridged with the accusation. Even Irish looked up.

Evelyn blinked once, slowly. Then she said the thing none of them wanted to admit.

"Feels like we didn't save survivors… feels like we just retrieved assets."

There was a deathly silence that fell on all of Obsidian. No one moved. No one breathed. The word hung there, heavy and poisonous, cutting deeper than any wound they'd pulled from that hell.

Chapter 16

The evac bird dumped them into a makeshift operations base somewhere outside Tripoli. The walls were raw concrete, the air heavy with dust and diesel fumes. The hum of generators vibrated underfoot, radios chattering with clipped Arabic and NATO code. Medics moved the rescued into cordoned-off bays, triage tags swinging from their wrists. Children whimpered in their sleep with mothers clutching them like fragile glass. The pregnant woman was wheeled past on a stretcher, Evelyn's eyes followed her until she vanished behind a screen.

The team stripped out of gear in silence. No jokes, no banter. Just the slow, haunted motions of soldiers who'd seen too much. James kept moving, quiet and methodical, checking on everyone's mental status: a hand on Bullet's shoulder, grounding him before the kid spiraled; a nod to AJ, whose hands still shook as he cleaned his rifle; a squeeze on Mack's arm, forcing eye contact until he nodded back; a glance to Selena, who didn't flinch but hadn't blinked in minutes. Irish... no words, just the kind of look two men shared when both knew the truth but neither could say it.

He didn't forget Evelyn. He never could. She sat on the edge of a steel table, still wearing his top, staring at nothing. Her hair was damp with sweat, her hands resting limp in her lap. But her words hung over them all. This wasn't a rescue. This was retrieval.

Every time James moved past one of his people, he saw it in their eyes: the silent question, the terror etched in their minds of what they had just witnessed. If Evelyn was right, if this wasn't liberation but inventory, then what the fuck had they just walked into?

He kept his mask on. Stoic. Paladin. His voice was steady as he asked each of them if they were "green". But inside, his chest was burning. Because Evelyn wasn't wrong and, worse, he had no answer for her.

The war table in the Libyan base was dimly lit, screens glowing faint blue across their faces. No one spoke at first. The air felt heavier than the desert heat outside. Selena's fingers flew across the console, replay commands snapping into the system. Nothing came up. Again. Nothing. Her brows knitted, her jaw tightening as she dug deeper for back channels, cached feeds, anything. Still nothing. She hit the comms archive. Dead. She opened the body cam logs. Erased. Not corrupted, but cleaned.

"...No," she whispered, the sound barely audible over the hum of equipment. Her throat felt torrid. "No, no, no…"

"What is it?" Mack asked, already leaning forward.

Selena's face paled as she turned to the team. "It's gone. All of it. Every second of feed, every comm log, every camera." Her voice cracked against the silence. "It's like we were never there."

The words sank like lead. Evelyn's head snapped up, eyes dark and distant. Retrieval, not rescue. Irish swore under his breath, pacing away, dragging a hand down his face. Bullet muttered something in Spanish, his voice tight, but no one laughed. AJ sat forward, his laptop still open, typing furiously.

"She's right. I just pulled trace signals from the uplink. Data didn't vanish. It was intercepted and rerouted before it hit the servers. Someone scrubbed us live."

James's knuckles whitened against the edge of the table, his face unreadable, but the muscle in his jaw ticked. He scanned each of them, voice quiet but carrying weight.

"Then somebody wanted this mission buried."

Silence fell again. He could feel Evelyn's eyes on him; they were wild, hollow, and still trembling with the aftershock of her power. He couldn't look at her yet. Not with the others watching.

Selena broke it with the words they all dreaded but knew were true:

"We weren't just rescuing survivors. We were retrieving... military assets."

The hum of the ops room was deafening in its silence. Monitors blinked, untouched. The air was suffocating with the weight of what Selena had said.

Irish was the first to break. He slammed a med kit down on the table so hard that the contents rattled.

"Jesus Christ, we're supposed to be the ones who stop this. Not clean up after it. Not bury it."

Mack's voice came in low, sharp, and dangerous. "Don't you dare say it, Irish. Don't you fucking dare...."

"...What? That we've been used? That we just did their dirty work?" Irish shot back, stepping forward, his voice rising.

Bullet stood, pacing, flicking a lighter open and shut. "Madre de Dios... we dragged out kids like cargo. That's what they wanted. We handed them right over." His voice cracked, his fury boiling. "We weren't rescuing anyone. We were... we were collecting stock."

AJ's laptop snapped shut with a sharp crack, he started drumming fingertips against his thigh. "The feed was scrubbed before it even hit NATO's net. You know what that means? Someone high up knew. This wasn't oversight. This was… orchestrated."

The room threatened to tip into chaos. Voices overlapping, anger and betrayal bouncing off the metal walls like ricochets. Then Evelyn spoke.

Her voice wasn't loud, but it cut through everything like a blade. Steady. Cold. Terrifying.

"Fuck…" She swallowed, her eyes hollow, her thoughts locked on the pregnant woman fighting for her and her child's life "Fuck, Obsidian is on the wrong side of history."

The words landed like a gunshot.

The team froze. No one breathed.

James's started to grind his molars with the vein at his temple ticking. He wanted to deny it, desperate to shut her down. But he couldn't. Not with Selena's dead screens flickering in his periphery. Not with the screams of children still echoing in their skulls.

Irish rubbed his face, staring at the floor like it might open up and swallow him. Mack muttered something guttural and unfinished. Bullet sat hard on the edge of the table, shaking his head like he could physically dislodge the truth.

And Selena? She just stared at the empty monitors, whispering the words like a confession.

"She's right."

The silence stretched until it became unbearable. The weight of Evelyn's words pressed down on them like a boot on the throat.

James finally moved.

He stepped forward, slow and deliberate, until he was standing dead centre, cutting through their fractured circle. His eyes swept each of them in turn – Irish, Frost, Mack, Bullet, AJ, and Selena – all holding them there like iron clamps.

"Listen to me," his voice was low and steady. Not loud. Not a bark. But commanding. The kind of tone that cut deeper than shouting.

"We don't get to break here. Not in front of them." He jerked his chin toward the survivors and the medics still working triage in the building opposite. "They see us crack; they don't make it through the night. That's not an option."

Irish clenched his jaw, looking like he wanted to spit nails. "And what about us, James? What about what we just saw?"

James took a step closer, eyes locking on his. "We survive. We process later. Not here. Not now."

He turned, pinning Bullet and AJ. "Not a word. Not a fucking syllable leaves this room. Not until I say so. Understood?"

Bullet opened his mouth to argue, but one look at James's face snapped it shut. He nodded once, sharply. AJ followed with his lips pressed into a thin line.

James's gaze shifted to Selena. "You get me proof. Quietly. No chatter, no leaks. You dig until your fingers bleed if you have to. But you don't breathe a whisper until we've got something solid. I will contact my sister, she works on human rights violations, she can get the feelers out on what the fuck is going on."

Selena gave the smallest nod, her expression unreadable, but her hands twitched like she wanted to tear the whole system down with her bare nails.

Finally, James looked at Evelyn. She hadn't moved. Her mind still locked on the thought of the pregnant woman, her eyes were haunted and hollow.

He softened, just a fraction, enough for her to see him through the commander's mask.

"Ev… Valkyrie. You stay with me. One foot in front of the other. That's all I'm asking. You give me that, and I'll handle the rest."

Her lips parted, like she wanted to say something, but no words came. Just a faint, broken nod.

James straightened again, pulling the full weight of command back onto his shoulders.

"Until I say otherwise, this was a successful rescue. That's the story. That's what you tell yourselves; that's what you tell anyone who asks. You lock down, you stay sharp, and you don't fucking blink. Because the second you do, they win. And I'll be damned before I let that happen."

The team looked at him, torn between fury, despair, and obedience. But one by one, they nodded.

James didn't let them see it, but inside, the truth Evelyn had spoken was burning him alive.

The post-op shower was less about dirt and more about betrayal. Both of them wore it like a second skin.

The team had already scattered to their quarters, chasing silence or sleep, anything to blunt the edge of what they'd just lived through. But James had noticed the way Evelyn lingered, silent, her energy drained like a battery gone dead.

He stepped to the entrance, hesitation flickering for only a beat.

"You okay if I'm your shower buddy?" His voice was low, softer than his usual command, carrying a tenderness he rarely let anyone hear.

Evelyn looked over her shoulder, her eyes were rimmed red and her shoulders hung heavy. "Just you?"

"Just me," he said, steady. "Let me take care of you."

Inside the steam curled off the tiles. He drew the curtain closed; a small thing, but the team would notice. James never closed the curtain. Except now. For her.

She stood still with her head bowed, waiting. He stepped closer, peeling her shirt over her head with practised hands that lingered just enough to scan her skin. His gaze combed her for that shimmer and the nanite light that haunted him.

She whispered, raw, "Are they gone?"

He turned her gently, checking every inch with the precision of a man who had lost too much to chance. His palms were steady and deliberate, cataloguing each line of her.

"You're fine," he murmured at last. "You're okay."

That was all it took.

She broke, and her body collapsed into his chest, sobs tearing loose, hot water beating down around them. James didn't move. Didn't flinch. He wrapped her in arms meant for war and turned them into shelter.

"It's okay. It's okay," he whispered, his voice fraying at the edges.

Her fists curled in his skin like a lifeline. His hand threaded through her soaked hair, grounding her with every touch. When she lifted her face, streaked and trembling, he cupped her jaw, forcing her to see him.

"Look at me." His voice was soft but unyielding.

She met his gaze, her eyes wide and broken, but alive. He nodded once. "Breathe. That's all. I've got you, Ev."

The world outside vanished. Just heat, water, and his heartbeat against hers. Just the two of them.

She lifted her face and kissed him, tentative at first, then desperate, pouring fear and relief and trust into it. He answered with the same raw honesty, holding her like he might never let go.

When they broke apart their foreheads pressed together, she whispered, "We're gonna be okay. I need you."

James's thumb brushed away her tears. In all the years, he had never seen her properly cry, and he knew her well enough to know she needed comfort. This was their ritual after hard missions, but tonight was different. His voice was rough, pulled straight from the marrow.

"You're hurting. I won't cross that line. Tonight, we get dry, get food, and get some sleep. Tomorrow... tomorrow we go home. Just us."

"Home," she echoed, like it was a language she hadn't spoken in years. She nodded, eyes closing against his chest. "Okay."

Selenas and frosts bunkroom was claustrophobic, just a metal shell with two cots, but that didn't matter, not to them.

Frost climbed into the top bunk, with his boots hanging off the edge, the light catching the hollow under his eyes. Selena leaned her back against the metal wall; for a few heartbeats they let the small noises of the base be their world.

"I'm glad I'm bunking with you tonight," Selena said, the sentence almost swallowed as it left her. It was small, almost too brittle to hold truth, and yet it held.

Frost didn't answer at first. He reached his hand over the lip of the mattress and let it hover, as if testing whether being reached for would pull him apart or keep him whole. Then, slow and careful, he dropped his fingers down until they brushed the edge of Selena's hand and found it.

Her palm was warm. He closed his fingers around it like a tether.

"You okay?" she asked, quieter than before.

"No." His laugh came out thin. "I keep seeing them. Crates, incubators. Little faces that…" He stopped because words failed there, because there was no way to put that sound down on paper without it ripping.

Selena squeezed his hand, thumb rubbing the back of his knuckles in a motion she'd learned when there wasn't time for speeches. "Ow Malik, nothing I say will make this ok. I am sorry we were a part of that."

He let out a breath that might have been a sob. "They were kids, Sel. Babies strapped down. Eyes that didn't know mercy. I kept checking the crates 'cause I wanted there to be something that moved."

"I whispered names to them," Selena said. "Mira. Unit 004. I burned a copy of the manifest and memorised what I could. It's the only thing I could give at the time... words so they aren't numbers."

Frost closed his eyes and let the name settle in him like a bruise. "What do we do?" he asked after a while. The question was small and huge at once.

Selena looked up at the low ceiling, at the single bulb that made everything too honest. "James is on it. I can't tell you what he has done, but it won't be buried."

He hummed, a sound of tired assent. Sheltered in that metal room, with the desert wind trying to pry the world apart outside, they didn't make grand plans. They made the first, ugly, honest steps: names tucked into a pocket, a promise held in a squeeze of fingers. Frost let his hand rest over hers, not a rescue, not a cure. Just a small, human thing to hold while the dark worked through them.

Bullet entered his and AJ's room to find his best friend pacing like the floor could answer him, words tumbling loose and sharp.

"I'm a child of war," he said, voice raw. "That could have been me. That may have happened to my people, taken from their homes, treated like they were less than human... for what? For what...?" His hands trembled; he scrubbed them over his face as if he could wash the image away.

139

Bullet sat on the edge of the lower bunk with his elbows on his knees. He watched AJ for a moment, the room swallowing the rest of the world. When he finally spoke, it was flat and furious. "Money, hamito. Rich men prosper from war." He spat the words like they tasted of bile. "People are money to them. Weapons. Metrics. Contracts signed in glass towers while kids get turned into experiments."

AJ's laugh was a raw, small thing. "I keep seeing the tiny hands. The way they didn't cry because they'd been taught not to. I kept thinking… what if I'd been there as a kid? What if my cousin…" He broke off, the name stuck in his throat.

Bullet leaned forward, eyes dark. "Then don't let them keep doing it. You ain't the only one who knows how to burn a file, dog. You know how to make noise. You know how to snip a feed and pull a packet and leave a breadcrumb trail so the bastards choke on whatever lies they hide behind."

AJ's shoulders rose and fell. "I'm not a revolutionary. I'm a thief with a laptop."

"You're more than that," Bullet said. He flicked a toothpick in his teeth, a little, violent motion. "You're the kind that makes suits sweat. They listen when you whisper into a hole in their system. You think they'll notice a missing crate? They notice when every ledger thinks a crate never existed."

AJ sank onto the other bunk, with his fingers threading under his knee. "But what if nothing changes? What if we leak and they bury it deeper? What if our names get pulled and we're the ones who end up in boxes next?"

Bullet's laugh this time was short and bitter. "Obsidian means we will die to protect… that's what we do. We make sure the world knows what that box contains. We hand the names to people who don't sleep at meetings. We put photos where mothers can see them. We make the problem too loud to ignore." He reached out, palms open, not pretending this would fix anything. "You don't have to do it alone. Rebels together."

AJ looked at him, the fight and fear flickering in his face like a cheap neon. "You'd help? What about Paladin, he would kill me for leaking anything."

"Wouldn't leave you to choke on it," Bullet said simply. He pushed himself up and wrapped AJ in a quick, rough hug with no words, just the pressure of a brother who'd been dragged out of his own holes before. "We do what we can. We don't let those kids be numbers on a manifest. Paladin wouldn't kill you; he is already working on something… No way he would let this rest. Not him. But if anything happens to him and Ev… we become the rebels with a cause."

The mess hall was too bright, too clean, and too normal after what they'd seen. Evelyn sat hunched over her tray, letting the heat from the food spread through her like an anchor. Around her, the team worked hard at pretending.

Mack was ripping AJ about his coffee skills, calling it "chemical warfare". Bullet leaned back, pretending he was bored, but the twitch at his mouth betrayed the fact he was clinging to the noise. Selena picked at Irish's jacket, teasing him about being "vintage military issue".

It was chaos. Forced, desperate chaos, trying to push out the memories of what they had just been through. But it was theirs.

Irish slid an arm around Evelyn's shoulders. No words at first, just the weight and warmth of her best friend's hug, and she leaned in before she realised.

"You alright, Scouse?" he asked, voice low and teasing, but she heard the raw thread under it.

Her smile was faint and weary. That nickname still felt like home. "Yeah," she whispered. "Just need some time."

He gave one sharp squeeze, then let go, but his eyes didn't leave her.

Silence bled into the room. One by one, voices trailed off until all that remained was the scrape of cutlery.

Bullet cleared his throat, forcing brightness back into the air. "Alright then… who's doing the first toast?"

Laughter came, brittle at the edges. Evelyn found herself chuckling too, though it hurt in her chest. She lifted her cup slowly, her voice quieter than the scrape of boots on the floor.

"To the ones who never got to leave. To the ones still trapped. And to us… for clawing our way out of that hellhole."

Her words froze the table. Nobody moved. Nobody breathed.

James was the first. He raised his cup, eyes locked on hers, voice steady but rough. "To us."

Paper cups clashed, soft and hollow. The sound echoed like gunfire in the silence that followed. For a heartbeat, it felt like the ghosts in the room raised their cups too.

And then nothing. Just the quiet, heavy, unshakeable weight of the ones they hadn't saved pressing down on every single one of them.

The mess hall carried the weight of silence long after the cups clashed. Evelyn's toast still hung in the air like smoke, and for a moment, none of them could move, and none of them could breathe.

It was Mack who broke first. He slapped his palm against the table, muttering, "Christ, that was depressing. AJ, next time you're in charge of toasts. At least then it'll be about Wi-Fi signals and your love life with your laptop."

AJ groaned, "I don't have a love life with my laptop..."

"...yet," Bullet cut in, smirking as he leaned back in his chair. "Give it another deployment. Man and machine, forbidden romance. I can see it now."

Laughter cracked the tension like a bullet through glass. Evelyn's smile came without her permission; it was small but real.

Mack wasn't done. "Actually, no. Let Bullet do the toast next time. He can raise his cup to all the ex-girlfriends he's left crying in different countries. Might take a while though... we'll need refills."

The table erupted. Bullet pointed at him with mock outrage. "Bold words from a man whose last date was a chicken kebab at three a.m. Don't make me pull up the CCTV footage."

Selena groaned, but she was smiling, and Irish shook his head, muttering, "Eejits," and even James let the corner of his mouth twitch.

The weight hadn't gone. The ghosts were still there. But for a few minutes, the mess hall was loud again. Familiar again. The way it always had been.

And Evelyn, pressed between Irish's warmth and James's steady gaze, let herself breathe in the noise. It wasn't healing. But it was the noise of survival.

The barracks slept.

Muted breaths and the creak of bunks carried through the silence, the kind that weighed heavy after blood and fire. Only the ops room still lived, with a cold blue glow spilling across the bare walls, casting shadows long and unnatural.

James sat rigid in the corner with his laptop open on the steel desk. His face was carved in hard lines, eyes raw with sleeplessness. Every few seconds his fingers twitched over the keys, restless, like if he stopped moving, the ghosts in his head would catch him.

Selena sat opposite, with her mug untouched and steam long gone. Her eyes never left him. She didn't press. She didn't need to.

Then the screen glitched.

Just once

The cursor froze mid-blink. The glow flickered, too fast to be a power surge, too sharp to be chance.

A message bled across the screen, letters pulsing faint white before fixing into black:

Paladin, you walked our Blackbird to her death.

Be your namesake. Protect her.

Or I won't protect you.

– Ghost.

The hum of the laptop cut out. The room fell silent.

James's lungs seized, and his pulse slammed in his throat. It wasn't just words; it was a presence. The ops room felt crowded, like someone else was standing between them, invisible but watching.

"Boss…" Selena's voice was barely more than a whisper, sharp with alarm. "That's not just a message."

The cursor blinked again. Once. Twice. Then the speakers hissed, a soft static that slid like breath across the room.

James's hands hovered above the keys, but the screen shifted before he could touch them. His own reflection warped in the black, the faint outline of his face overlaid with another, eyes that weren't his staring back.

Selena's knuckles whitened around her cup. "They're in the room…"

James swallowed hard, the words rasping out of him like broken glass. "No one should know. Every camera feed… every comm log… scrubbed."

"Unless they're the one scrubbing." Her voice was steel over a tremor. "Ghost doesn't warn. Ghost condemns. If they're here…" She glanced at the screen, at the warping reflection. "….it means the blade's already above us."

James leaned back, dragging a hand through his hair. The air felt wrong, too heavy, like breathing through wet cloth. "I swore I'd keep her safe. And I'm lying to her. I'm failing her."

The lights flickered. The cursor blinked in rhythm with his pulse.

Selena leaned forward, her voice low and insistent. "You're not failing her. But you are killing yourself keeping her blind. Tell her, James. Or Ghost will."

The door creaked, and footsteps approached.

Irish stepped inside, stopping dead when he saw the looks on their faces. His voice was careful, like he'd walked into a funeral. "You alright, boss?"

James snapped the laptop shut. The glow vanished, plunging them into shadow. The air eased, just a fraction, but the weight lingered like smoke.

"I'll be fine," James muttered, though it sounded more like a prayer than the truth. "But I've got a problem."

Selena rose, her gaze steady, her voice low as she passed Irish.

"No. We all do. And it's already here."

Chapter 17

The moment they stepped inside the oceanfront Virginia Beach house, the air hit different. James's place smelt of coffee and polish, leather and salt, grounding and maddeningly domestic. Evelyn lingered in the doorway like she didn't belong, like if she breathed too deep, the whole place might vanish.

"Christ," she muttered, eyeing the bookshelves, the family photos, and the half-folded laundry. "You've gone full middle-aged man. All you're missing is a Labrador and a fucking barbecue set."

James smirked behind her, unfazed. "Make yourself at home, Ev. Everything here's yours too."

She shot him a look sharp enough to cut. "Don't start with the Hallmark lines, Paladin. I'll puke on your rug, and then where will we be?"

He saw it instantly: her humour wasn't banter: it was armour. But when his hand brushed the small of her back, she didn't move away. She walked straight into the kitchen, like if she stopped, her knees might give.

James followed with maddening calm, already pulling out pans. "Hungry?"

"Not really." She dropped onto a stool, tucking her knees to her chest, trying to look casual when every nerve in her body buzzed. "But sure, knock yourself out, Gordon Ramsay."

He cooked in silence, letting the rhythm of it fill the space she usually stuffed with words. When he set a steaming bowl in front of her, she just stared at it like it might be the thing that broke her.

"Eat," he said simply. "You'll feel better."

She gave a sharp, humourless laugh, twirling the spoon once before jabbing at the food. "You always think feeding me solves everything. Like I'm one meltdown away from being a gremlin. Midnight snack, and I'll stop setting shit on fire."

His mouth twitched, but he didn't take the bait. He just held her gaze until she caved and took a bite.

The first forkful landed heavy in her chest. She chewed slowly, staring at the counter. "Fuck," she muttered, softer now. "It's good."

James said nothing, just watched her shoulders drop with her armour loosening, piece by piece.

"When you're ready, we'll talk," he said finally. "But not tonight. Tonight I take care of you."

Her throat tightened. She wanted to snap back, to laugh it off, but the words stuck. Instead, she shoved herself off the stool and walked straight into his chest. His arms came around her instantly, steady, immovable.

"Fuck me, Jamie... What did we just walk into? That's the second time I've seen it. I can't... I can't process it... I need to scream or cry... but I can't..."

"Yes, you can," he murmured, his hand steady on her back. "Not out there. Here."

Her fists knotted in his shirt, face pressed against him, the storm spilling over.

"What do you need? Water? Wine?"

She shook her head hard, words breaking loose. "What the fuck am I, James? I lit up! You saw it!" Panic cracked through every syllable. "I don't understand what's happening to me."

"I know what I saw," he said, steady as stone.

"It's not normal!" Her hands flew up, frustration sharp. "I'm not normal. There's something in me, and it just…" She snapped her fingers, desperate. "…it just took over. And I don't know if I can stop it. I was like… like a Christmas tree had a baby with an ambulance!"

Her laugh came too high, too sharp, collapsing under itself. "Not being funny, but covert ops while glowing blue? May as well hang a strobe light out my arse. And it's blue, Jamie. Not even Liverpool red! Imagine the derby; I light up and…" Her voice cracked, the joke breaking into a choke. "…and I look like an Everton fan."

The humor shredded, leaving her raw and shaking.

James moved closer, his hands firm on her knees, anchoring her. "We'll adapt. Armor. Cover. Ski mask, balaclava. Fuck it, we'll paint you red if we have to."

Her eyes blurred, tears threatening. "Why aren't you scared of me?" she whispered.

"Because I've been beside you in worse hell than this. And none of it… none of it… has ever scared me as much as losing you." His voice softened, devotion cutting through. "You've never been the danger to me."

Her chest heaved. "The first time it happened… I was pulling kids out of a Revenant camp. Felt it in my bones, my skin, like

149

something was using me. Then again with biotech weapons. And tonight…" She forced herself to meet his gaze, eyes glassy. "…tonight, you saw it."

"What if I'm one of them?" she snapped, panic surging again. "What if I'm not even human? What if it's this scar on my back? What if they put something in me? I've changed, James. Something's woken up, and I can't put it back."

Her voice broke sharp. "I don't want to die like them. I've seen it. I've seen the way it ends."

James caught her hands before she could curl them into fists, his grip steady and commanding. "Ev. Look at me."

She dragged her eyes up, braced for the worst.

"You are not one of them," he said, slow and deliberate, like he was hammering truth into her bones. "You're Evelyn Blackthorn. You've fought through more hell than anyone I've ever known. Whatever this is? We'll figure it out. But you are not dying in some lab. And you will never be alone."

Her chin trembled. His hold didn't.

"I don't care if you light up like a fucking star in front of me, Valkyrie." His voice went raw, breaking through his own walls. "You're mine to protect. And I'll burn the world to ash before I let anyone take you."

It broke her, and she sagged against him, panic bleeding into exhaustion.

He eased her to the sofa, crouching in front of her. "Stay here."

She heard the tap run and the clink of glass. Then he was back, pressing cool water into her hands. "Slow sips."

She drank, her breaths steadying, his hands light on her knees.

"Alright," James said. "We take this apart piece by piece. Ghost. Tell me everything. Doesn't matter how small."

Her laugh was humorless. "Feels like homework."

"Feels like staying alive."

So she told him: Yemen, Venezuela, Kyiv. The anonymous Intel. The blue flicker at her fingertips every time contact came. The warnings sent saved lives, even from IDF airstrikes. Ghost was always one step too close.

James listened with his thumbs steady against her knees, anchoring her.

"Then he's been closer than either of us realised," he said quietly. "Ev... tell me about your dad."

Evelyn hesitated with the question throwing her. This was a topic she always made sure was off limits at all times.

She took a deep breath, gathered herself while making sure her mask was on, and relayed her well-rehearsed answer. "Left when I was six. Died when I was eight. Military. KIA. That's all."

"You never told me that."

"I don't like talking about dad, I miss him, it's hard."

His voice dropped. "I know, I'm sorry Ev. But what if Ghost knew him? Think about it, he could have served with him. If it were me, I'd know their kid's name. I would have known their mother, I would have been at baptisms, funerals, and your mums' funerals, and I would have explained the blackbirds if the guns were off him and why he would have known your communion name. I would know everything about an Obsidian child. If their parents fell. I'd watch the kids back always."

Her answer was almost submissive, like she needed to close the conversation down quickly. "Yeh maybe, you could be right."

James nodded once. "And if he served with your father, then he may know exactly what's waking up in you now. Maybe your dad was the same."

Her chest tightened. "Surly if that was the case they would have approached me?"

"If it were me?" James's gaze locked on hers. "I'd wait until you were ready to hear it."

The panic fog still clung, but her voice dropped. "You think I have a protector."

Her lips curved, and her brain calculated. James watched her face almost switch, perhaps changing the subject too fast. "James, you're so fucking clever. I love that brain of yours. I mean…" her voice cracked, truth spilling raw, "…I love you. In general."

The words hit like a shot. James froze with his mask slipping, his eyes wide.

She tilted her head, smile crooked. "What? Don't look so shocked. It's not the first time I have said it."

His jaw flexed, eyes burning into hers. His voice came low and rough. "You normally say it when you're taking the piss. Say it again."

Her voice trembled. "I love you."

The breath left him slowly, like she'd knocked the air clean out of him. For once, the soldier's mask broke. A small, true smile curved his mouth.

"You have no idea what that does to me, Valkyrie."

Her laugh came out shaky but lighter. "Good. Feed me pudding, and I'll say it a few more times."

His smirk tugged back. "You drive a hard bargain."

"Damn right I do. Pudding first. Love declarations second."

Chapter 18

Evelyn jabbed her fork through the cheesecake like she was threatening it.

"So… Are we gonna talk about me going all soft and telling you I've got the feels, or you just gonna leave me hanging?' Cause that kiss in the shower in Libya…don't even. That wasn't our usual chaos. That was… different."

James leaned back, a smirk tugging at his mouth. "You really want the truth?"

"I'm thirty-four, Jamie. I think I've earned it."

He dropped his fork and leaned forward on his elbows. "It was adrenaline. Exhaustion. And…" His eyes softened. "…me realising if I didn't kiss you right then, I'd regret it for the rest of my life."

Her chest skipped, but she rolled her eyes. "Christ above. So, it was something more."

"Yeah," he said, blunt as ever.

She chewed another bite, watching him over the fork. "So what are we doing about it then?"

His brow twitched. "About what?"

She leaned forward, voice low. "About you being stark bollock naked, kissing me when my heart was breaking, kissing me like you meant it. 'Cause newsflash….that's the safest I've felt in years."

He didn't answer straight away, just stared like he was weighing it all.

Then: "That's not exactly the kind of bomb you drop mid-pudding, Valkyrie."

"Why not?" she shot back. "We have just come back from a mission from hell. Just seen the worst in humanity. I'm knackered. We get these moments where we go full-on feral for each other, then pretend it's just two mates grabbing a quick serotonin hit. Like necking a pill in Concert Square and hitting a club. It's bollocks, Jamie."

James leaned in, forearms braced. "Fine. Then we stop pretending. But if we go there…." His eyes flicked to her mouth, then back. "…I'm not doing half measures. Not with you."

Her fork clattered onto the plate. "Good. Neither am I."

She dragged a hand through her hair, shaking her head. "We've been orbiting each other for a decade. I've had decent fellas… proper ones. Never stuck with any of them. Do you wanna know why?"

He just held her gaze, silent.

"Because I was waiting for you to pull your finger out of your arse and say it straight, that's why. Ten years of us sleeping in each other's arms, stealing kisses half-asleep, and more at times… pulling each other out of the gutter… You're it, James. Always fuckin' have been."

Her grip tightened on the table. "But I can't keep playing chicken with it. I need to know what you want. If it's not me, then that's sound. I'll deal with it. But don't keep me dangling."

James's jaw flexed. His voice came out rough. "You think I've been holding back 'cause I don't want you?"

"Looks that way," she muttered, though her throat was tight.

His palms pressed flat to the wood, eyes fierce. "Ev… you've been it since day one. First op. First time you walked into a room and the whole place shifted. You're not someone I can fuck once and forget. You're the only one I can't get out of my head. And if you're sat here telling me you're ready for something real… I'm done holding back."

The silence that dropped was heavy, years of the unsaid finally pressing in.

Evelyn's breath came shallow, then she shoved her chair back with a scrape. She rounded the table slowly, eyes locked on him, and slid onto his lap, straddling him like she'd been doing it all her life.

Her hands cupped his jaw, steady despite the tremor in her chest. "Ten years, Jamie. That's long enough. I am ready for something real" Then she smirked, Scouse through and through. "Now shut up and kiss me before this cheesecake goes warm, Jamie baby."

They didn't fall into it gently.

Their mouths crashed together, years of restraint shattering in the rush of the moment. Evelyn's hands tangled in his shirt, tugging it over his head and swearing with frustration when the fabric clung. James laughed into her lips, low and rough, before ripping it off himself and pressing her back against the bedroom door.

They devoured each other like they'd been starving, kisses desperate and impatient. His hands slid beneath her top, his fingers splaying across her skin, and she arched into him with a sound that made him groan.

Their clothes lay scattered in their wake, urgency spilling from every touch. But just when it felt like they might burn too hot, Evelyn pulled back. She pressed her palms flat against his chest, pushing him gently back just enough to look at him.

Then she lowered her mouth to his skin.

"I don't want to rush this."

His eyes locked on hers as he bowed his head slightly to honour her words. She needed his trust, and he was more than willing to give it.

Evelyn slowly kissed the scar across his collarbone, followed by the one at his ribs, then the jagged line at his hip. Each one was reverent and deliberate, like she was memorising his battles with her lips. James's breath stuttered, the heat in his eyes softening into something far deeper.

"Ev…" His voice broke on her name.

She looked up at him, her lips brushing his stomach, and whispered,

"You're still here. Every scar, every fight… you're still here… we've survived."

Something in him shifted as his frenzy stilled. He caught her face in his hands, lifting her until their eyes locked. Slowly, carefully, he laid her back against the bed, his body lowering over hers like a vow.

No rush now. No battlefield hunger. Just time.

His hands mapped her body, learning every curve and every single sensitive spot. He read her like terrain, watching for her reactions, memorising all her tells. Her fingers threaded into his hair, her lips parting on gasps that weren't frantic but trusting.

He kissed her between her thighs, slow, deep, and patient. Not claiming. Learning.

"Jamie, I need you…"

"Not yet." His voice was steel wrapped in gravel, holding her right there, on the knife's edge. His eyes flicked up, locked on hers, and the sheer control in his expression nearly undid her. "I'm going to know every single way your body breaks before I'm inside you. Every tell. Every sound. Every weakness. That's the map."

She tried to bite back a sound, but the moan ripped out anyway, her head falling back into the pillow.

He took his time, utterly undoing her until his own desire finally made him stop. Evelyn looked beautiful and wrecked, which made his soul ache.

James hovered above her, his dark eyes burning into hers.

"Are you sure you want this?"

Her hands slid down to the back of his neck, pulling him closer, her voice low but certain.

"I need you. I need this."

That was all she needed to say. With steady, practiced hands he slid a condom on, his gaze locked to hers, not leaving her for a second.

When his body returned to hers, he paused only long enough to rest his forehead against hers, their breath mingling in total anticipation. Then he pushed inside, slow and sure, his body joining hers like it was always meant to be.

Evelyn arched up to meet him without fear as James groaned low, the sound reverent, grounding himself in her warmth.

"God, Ev…" His voice was rough and unsteady. "You feel like home."

The rhythm between them built, not rushed but certain. These were two bodies who had fought side by side long enough to know exactly how to move together. Every touch was power and devotion; every kiss a promise that, whatever came, they were in it together.

Her lips brushed his ear.

"Don't hold back…"

And in return, he gave her everything. It was strong, controlled, overwhelming in the way only James Reaves could be. Every movement was intentional, tuned to her, for her.

He held her as if the world would burn if he let go, and she met him with equal fire and devotion. When their release came, it wasn't chaos, instead it was intimate, inevitable, like gravity.

They stayed locked together, two savage souls who had finally found peace. His head tilted as he gently kissed the edge of her lips, sealing the moment with utter adoration.

"You okay?"

She burrowed against him, whispering so softly he almost missed it.

"Thank you. I needed to feel something real."

"Always, Red." His voice was grounding, his thumb brushing across her face. "Ev, we are the most real thing I've ever had."

They shared one last kiss, tasting the truth in each other's words, for once all their bravado gone.

"No matter what happens next… you and me. I love you."

The room was hushed. James shifted only enough to pull her tighter into his chest, their legs tangled, their bodies utterly exhausted. Evelyn rested her cheek against his heartbeat; it was steady and strong beneath her ear. For the first time in years, neither of them felt like they were free-falling. Both souls were tethered together, anchoring each other in the moment.

The horrors of the last mission were briefly put on hold as they let themselves believe in something more than just death and violence. Neither of them spoke again, but the silence wasn't empty. It was full. Full of the weight of everything unspoken and the certainty that, whatever battles lay ahead, they had already claimed this moment as theirs."

Chapter 19

James woke with a start at the sound of the front door unlocking, instinct snapping him upright before his brain caught up.

"Yo, James," Mack's voice rang out casually from the hall. "You left your shit in my…"

Boots clunked closer. James barely had time to move before the bedroom door swung open.

"…car."

Mack froze.

Eyes went wide.

The scene was undeniable.

Clothes were scattered like a grenade had gone off. A condom wrapper glinting in the morning light. James, stark naked on the edge of the bed, hair a mess, chest still rising heavily. Evelyn starfish-faced face-down across the sheets, gloriously naked, her hair a wild halo, one arm hanging limp off the side, dead to the world.

Mack's eyebrows shot so high they nearly cleared the doorframe.

"Jesus, Mary and Joseph!" He barked, then clapped a hand over his mouth. "Sorry!"

James was already moving, yanking the duvet up over Evelyn and shoving Mack bodily out into the hallway.

"What the fuck, Mack!" he hissed.

"I didn't…" Mack stammered, a smirk tugging at his mouth despite the words. "I just… fuck, I'm sorry…."

"Out. Now!" James slammed the door in his face and leaned against it, eyes squeezed shut, dragging air through his teeth.

From the bed came a muffled groan. "Was that Mack?"

James groaned right back. "Go back to sleep, Valkyrie."

Two minutes later, James was stalking out to the garden in nothing but boxers, a cigarette already between his lips. Mack followed, hands shoved deep in his pockets, grinning like a cat that had raided the cream.

James lit up, dragged deep, and exhaled hard. "Not. A. Word."

"Oh, I'm saying something," Mack said, rocking on his heels. "Ten years of unresolved tension, bickering like an old married couple, sneaking off after ops… And the reveal is me walking in on full-frontal Paladin, with Valkyrie starfished like she's gone twelve rounds with Tyson Fury. That's cinema, mate. Pure cinema."

James cut him a glare sharp enough to kill. "You done?"

"Not a chance. Was it good?"

James's jaw flexed. He dragged deep on the cigarette, deliberately silent.

Mack lifted his palms, mock-innocent. "Relax, I'm happy for you. Just saying… if that was a one-off, you're an idiot. I know a guy, less of a cunt, one who doesn't smoke like a chimney… great teeth.."

James looked like he was about to kill his best friend, slowly and painfully "Shut the fuck up!"

Mack grinned like a twat "A woman like that in your bed? That's not casual. That's biblical."

James pinched the bridge of his nose.

"Oh, and next time?" Mack added, leaning in. "Maybe tidy up the evidence. The condom on the side, you filthy bastard. And as for the condom wrapper… was practically waving a flag saying, "Congratulations, they finally fucked.""

The screen door creaked.

Evelyn padded out barefoot, hair a glorious mess, one of James's T-shirts hanging loose on her frame. Two mugs in her hands. She passed one to Mack and the other to James, like she hadn't just been starfish-naked twenty minutes earlier.

"Morning," she rasped.

James grunted his thanks, grateful to hide his red face behind the mug.

Then, without ceremony, Evelyn plucked the cigarette from his fingers, took a slow drag, and exhaled like it was hers to begin with.

Mack froze mid-sip, eyes ping-ponging between them like he'd just witnessed the second coming. "Ohhh my God."

James growled. "Don't."

"Oh, I'm doing." Mack pointed at the cigarette. "That right there wasn't casual. That was a claim. She just marked you, mate. Like a dog on a lamppost."

Evelyn handed it back to James, unbothered. "He was hogging it."

Mack slapped the porch rail, wheezing. "Hogging it! Jesus Christ. I'm gonna need popcorn when the others find out."

James muttered, "Should've changed the fucking locks."

Evelyn sipped her coffee, calm as a saint. "You writing a field report, Mack, or just standing there flapping your mouth?"

"Oh, there'll be a report," Mack said, still grinning. "And when the others read it? They'll need binoculars to see how far over the line you two just crossed."

James dragged his hand down his face. "I fucking hate you."

"No, you don't," Mack shot back, smug as sin. "But I do love being right. And I've been calling this for a decade."

The smell of bacon and coffee clung to the air like a peace offering James hadn't meant to make. He stood at the stove in sweatpants, flipping bacon with all the grim focus of a man preparing for war. The sizzle and pop filled the silence.

Evelyn leaned against the counter, barefoot, drowned in one of his shirts, coffee in hand. Her hair was a halo of chaos, her expression unreadable but steady.

The front door swung open without so much as a knock.

"Morning…!" Irish's voice rang out as he strolled in, Rose at his side with a big pink box of doughnuts. Behind them came Selena, Bullet, AJ, and Frost, the whole pack cramming into the kitchen like it was a briefing room.

James didn't turn. "What the actual fuck! You're all trespassing."

164

"Relax," Selena said, sliding onto a stool. "Mack texted Bullet, then Bullet sent the bat signal. You had to know this was coming."

Rose's face split into a grin the second she clocked Evelyn. "Well, well. Finally. How was the debriefing, love?"

Evelyn took a long sip of coffee. "Classified."

The room erupted. Mack was doubled over on a chair, Bullet pounding the table, and AJ wheezing like he couldn't breathe.

Frost, deadpan as ever, just said, "My money was on Reaves breaking first."

"Mine too," Irish cut in, but his voice wasn't playful. He leaned against the counter, arms folded, eyes locked on James. "And I'll be honest... I'm not sure I'm celebrating."

That stopped the laughter cold.

James finally turned from the stove, spatula in hand, meeting Irish's stare. "You got a problem?"

Irish's jaw flexed. "Aye. My problem is I've been cleaning her blood off my hands for a decade. Holding her together while you were both too stubborn to admit what everyone else could see. And now I walk in and she's barefoot in your shirt, looking like she just walked through fire on that mission, and you expect me to laugh about it?"

The silence was sharp and uncomfortable. Evelyn's eyes flicked between them, but she stayed quiet.

James's voice was low. "You think I don't know what she's been through? You think I haven't carried it just as much?"

Irish leaned forward, bracing on the counter. "You hurt her, James… If you so much as crack her in ways I can't fix, there isn't a team, a mission, or a god alive that'll stop me breaking you in two."

The air was heavy enough to choke on.

Bullet cleared his throat, desperate to cut it. "Sooo… we're skipping straight to the champagne toast then?"

AJ smirked nervously. "Or doughnuts. Doughnuts feel safer."

Selena slid the pink box onto the table. "Eat before this turns into a homicide."

Evelyn finally broke the silence with a smirk, sipping her coffee. "You boys keep talking like this and I'll start a pay per view channel. Pack it in."

The laughter crept back in, shaky but present. Mack slapped the table, roaring again. "She's right! You're all bloody pathetic."

James just shoved the plate of bacon into the middle of the table, and pancakes for AJ, but his jaw remained tight. "Eat. And keep your mouths shut."

Evelyn brushed past him, her bare thigh against his joggers, and whispered just loud enough for him to hear, "They'll calm down eventually."

He smirked, eyes on the pan. "Not Irish."

Irish was sitting back in his chair with that medic's calm that meant he'd been reading the room since the moment he walked in, finally cut through the noise.

"So… is this real?" He looked between them. "You two finally doing it? Or you both fucking about?"

The whole kitchen seemed to still for a beat, eyes flicking between James and Evelyn like they'd just been caught holding a detonator.

James glanced at her.

Evelyn, mid-sip of coffee, gave the smallest, almost imperceptible nod, not a sheepish one, not embarrassed. Just sure.

James set down the spatula, leaning his hip on the counter.

"Yeah," he said, voice even but carrying a weight that shut everyone up. "It's real. I love her. Always have."

There was a muttered, "No shit Sherlock" from Frost, deadpan from his corner as he reached for the toast.

Bullet grinned like Christmas had come early. "And here I thought we'd have to put you two in a supply closet with a bottle of whisky to make it happen."

Mack raised his coffee. "Finally. Now maybe we can all stop betting on when it'd happen."

Selena smirked. "Oh, don't worry. The new bet is on how long before one of you drives the other insane."

Evelyn arched an eyebrow, lips quirking. "That's adorable. You think we're not already insane."

James just reached for her coffee cup, took a sip without asking, and handed it back like it was the most natural thing in the world, and in that tiny, casual move, the whole team clocked it. This wasn't a fling. This was them.

Twenty minutes later, James finally pushed himself off the counter, waving a hand like he was shooing feral cats.

"Right… get the fuck out of my house. Go terrorise someone else. Re-meet at thirteen hundred hours. Black Swan. Irish pub in Norfolk."

A mix of groans and laughter followed as chairs scraped back.

"Irish, Rose… stay a bit, yeah? Need your help with something," Evelyn said, stretching like the morning hadn't been pure chaos.

Bullet was halfway through the door but whipped back, grin wicked.

"Ohhh, the girl needs medical after last night!"

"Fuck off, Bullet!" Evelyn snapped, flinging a tea towel at his head.

He ducked it, still laughing. "I'm just saying, Paladin's a bloody unit. Might be internal damage."

"Out!" James barked, but the smirk tugging at his mouth betrayed him.

Bullet backed out with both hands raised. "See you at one, boss. Don't wear her out before then."

Evelyn muttered just loud enough for James to catch it: "No promises."

His eyebrow shot up, sharp and loaded, and she knew damn well he'd carry that line in his head until the next time they were alone.

Chapter 20

The door shut with a solid thunk. James leaned against it for a beat, as if he could keep the night and everything they'd just done sealed away.

Irish was already moving, his eyes scanning Evelyn with the clinical sharpness of a man who had patched her up more times than anyone dared to count.

"Alright, Ev. Talk to me."

Her throat tightened. The warmth from before was gone, replaced by something heavier. She glanced at James, then back at Irish.

"I need your opinion on… a scar."

James's smirk vanished like smoke. His whole body went still.

Irish frowned, pausing mid-step. "You don't know what it's from?"

She shook her head. "Got shot in Colombia in my leg. Went under. Woke up with it."

"No entry in the report?"

"Nothing."

Irish's voice dropped low. "Bathroom. More light."

James straightened from the door. "I'm coming."

"You're not my assistant."

"I'm not letting her walk in there without me."

Irish finally met his eyes. "Then stay the fuck out of my way."

The air snapped tight between them, but Evelyn was already moving. The bathroom was small and bright, with sunlight cutting sharply through half-open blinds. She pulled her shirt over her head without hesitation.

James filled the doorway with his arms crossed and the heat rolling off him. Irish crouched close, his fingers ghosting over the pale, jagged scar running diagonally across her back.

It wasn't surgical. It wasn't shrapnel. It looked embedded.

Irish's face hardened. "This wasn't battlefield work. This is deliberate. Precise. Like something was put in, not taken out."

Her stomach plummeted. "So… not just a scar."

"No." His voice was iron. "This is biotech insertion work. And it's tied to what happened in that Revenant lab."

James's jaw flexed. "Then we scan her. Today."

Irish's eyes didn't leave the scar. "Fine. But nothing goes into the records. Not a word. Whoever did this will come looking."

Her pulse hammered. "You saw the lab?"

Irish's composure cracked, anger leaking through. "Saw you lit up like lightning. Saw him"—he jerked his chin toward James—"holding your neck like it was the only thing tethering you to life. I'm not blind, Ev. But Christ, you should've come to me."

James pushed off the wall, voice like gravel. "She did come to me."

Irish spun on him. "And instead of taking her to a med bay, you took her to your fucking bed?" The word cut like a blade. "Tell me, Commander, how do you justify that?"

James's reply was measured, lethal. "Because I wasn't handing her to anyone until I knew she was safe. The only safe place is with me. You've got a problem with that? You bring it to me. Not her."

Irish stepped in, nose to nose, his voice low and venomous. "Safe? You fucked her when she was vulnerable. Tell me how that's protection."

James surged forward, voice rough. "You don't know a damn thing about last night. Ten years, McBride. Ten years I held that line. She came to me. She chose me. So don't you ever question my respect for her."

Irish jabbed a finger into his chest. "Respect doesn't keep her alive. You're thinking with your cock, not your head."

James caught his wrist, shoving it down hard enough to rattle the floorboards. "Watch yourself."

That was when Evelyn snapped.

"Enough!" Her voice cut sharp, shaking but dangerous. She shoved between them with her chest heaving. "James didn't take anything from me I didn't want to give. And Irish, don't you ever suggest I can't make my own choices again. You got me?"

The room froze. Both men glared over her shoulders, breathing hard, neither willing to blink first. Evelyn stood between them, the scar burning hot on her back, the air thick with the kind of tension that could shatter bone if it broke.

Irish's jaw was locked so tight a vein stood out at his temple.

"Outside. Now." He pointed at the door, his eyes never leaving James. "You better start talking, proper talking… before I knock this cunt out."

James stepped forward like a strike. "Say that again."

"Fucking stop!" Evelyn's voice cracked as she shoved James back. Rose's arms hooked tight around Irish, dragging him half a step back.

Evelyn was shaking with fury and desperation bleeding together.

"I've had enough of you two measuring dicks. Irish, fine. You want answers? You and me, outside. I'll tell you everything."

Irish's glare never left James, but his shoulders eased just enough for her to shove him toward the door. His boots thudded on the floorboards like warnings.

"Let's go," she muttered, flinging the door open. Cold air rushed in.

Irish stepped out without hesitation, but not before throwing James one last deliberate death stare, the kind that promised this wasn't over.

James stayed in the kitchen doorway, fists balled, chest heaving, with a cigarette burning slowly between his fingers, like it was the only thing keeping him still.

The garden was damp from last night's rain, the air sharp in her lungs. Irish stopped halfway across the lawn, spinning on his heel so fast she nearly collided with him.

"Start talking, Ev. No dodging. Straight answers."

She folded her arms. "You saw what happened in the lab."

173

"I saw a lot of shit in that lab." Irish's voice was fire and ice. "I saw James grab you like you were about to blow; your skin lit up like a fucking Tesla coil, him covering you like the whole world couldn't see. And now there's a scar you can't explain. And that look in your eye? It says you're holding back."

"I couldn't tell you...."

"Bullshit." His finger jabbed at her chest. "You didn't tell me. Big difference."

From the kitchen window, James was just a shadow in the glass with his Shoulders squared. Watching like a guard dog on a short chain.

Evelyn raked a hand through her hair. "Colombia. Gaza. Libya. Every op I walked away from with more than I went in with...and I don't mean scars. The lightning? Not new. The scar? Didn't have it before Colombia. Woke up from surgery, and there it was. No record. No explanation. I had to be smuggled out, and I think someone called Ghost pulled it off."

Irish's eyes narrowed. "You fucking what! You got fucking smuggled.... And Ghost is...?"

"He's not the threat I thought. He's been following me for years. Protecting me. I think he knew my dad. Knew what I was before I did."

Irish swore under his breath, pacing hard across the grass before wheeling back on her.

"You think? Christ, Ev. You get cut open in cartel country and don't tell me? Ghost? Any of this? I'm your medic. Your best fucking mate. Day one, it should've been me... not James. Not Selena. Me."

174

Her voice cracked low. "I went to James because I needed him. And before you lose your shit, it wasn't about sleeping with him. That happened after. I was falling apart. He stopped me from breaking."

Irish's tone was raw fury. "So you let him fuck you instead of getting medical help? And I'm meant to be fine with that?" His gaze lifted past her, locking through the glass. "No, Ev. Just... no. I have known you do some stupid shit in your time, but this!"

James didn't look away. He flicked his cigarette to the ground, grounding it out with his heel, and stepped through the door slowly, deliberately, every movement a warning.

The back door slammed closed hard enough to rattle the frame.

James stepped out barefoot, jeans low on his hips, hair still wrecked from her hands. No shirt. No attempt to hide the bruise blooming high on his collarbone.

"Alright," he said, voice low but carrying. "Enough of the covert backyard grilling. If you've got something to say about me, Irish, say it to my face."

Irish squared up instantly, that half-smile dark and dangerous.

"You really want me to, Commander? Fine. You're supposed to keep her alive as part of Obsidian, and instead you've been balls-deep in her while she's lit up like a science experiment. That what passes for duty in Detroit?"

James didn't flinch. "She's alive because of me. You weren't there when she came apart in my hands. You didn't see what it

175

cost her to hold on. I made the call to keep her safe, and I'd make it again."

Irish closed the gap, boots sinking into the wet grass. "Safe? You think you're her safe place? You've been dancing around her for a decade, letting her bleed because you were too scared to hold on. Don't talk to me about safe. I've been stitching her back together since long before she ever looked at you."

Evelyn slid between them, palms out, but neither man's eyes shifted.

James's voice dropped to a growl. "And all that time, you've been waiting. Waiting for me to screw up. Waiting for her to choose you. Don't think I don't see it…you're in love with her. Married or not, you can't stand that she picked me."

Irish's jaw ticked, his voice breaking sharply.

"This isn't about me, and it's sure as fuck not about you winning some prize. She's my sister… nothing more, nothing less, you utter gobshite. And this?" He jabbed a finger between them. "This is about her. If you can't see that, step aside before you break her… or I break you."

Evelyn shoved them both, her voice cutting like glass.

"Enough! This isn't a pissing contest over who gets to save me. I'm not a prize. I'm not a damsel. And if either of you forget that again, I'll walk. Right now."

But the air between them stayed molten, the two men who would burn the world for her, chest to chest, neither willing to step back.

Evelyn's voice cut through the tension like a blade.

"You know what... fuck the both of you."

They froze.

She was already storming back inside, snatching her clothes off the back of a chair and shoving them on with furious, jerking movements. James and Irish barrelled in after her like shadows chasing a fire.

"I can take care of my fucking self. Been doing it for thirty-four years." She jabbed a finger hard at James. "You... don't get to play savior one minute and act like you own me the next."

She spun on Irish, eyes blazing. "And you... don't get to treat me like some kid you're babysitting. I'm not nineteen anymore."

Her voice rose, gathering force like artillery.

"Let me remind you... I am Evelyn Blackthorn. A decorated, highly trained operative with a Conspicuous Gallantry Cross. Do either of you have one? No? Didn't think so."

She advanced a step, fury sharpening every word.

"I've been in every war zone in the last fifteen years. Helmand, Waziristan, Baghdad, Raqqa, Donbas, Benghazi, Mali, Yemen, Kyiv... want me to keep going?"

"I've led infiltrations, hostage rescues, weapons disarmament, Intel recovery, extractions, and biohazard containment. I've pulled civilians out of hellholes while under fire."

"I've earned eleven commendations... including a UN Humanitarian Service Medal and a Queen's Commendation for Bravery."

Her voice cracked, but it only made the words hit harder.

"And just sixteen months ago, I carried you, James... all six-plus feet of you... bleeding and half-dead, over my shoulder through a fucking firestorm. So don't either of you ever forget who the fuck I am."

James reached for her arm. "Ev..."

"Don't." She ripped free, eyes burning. "Just don't."

Irish's jaw slackened, his voice softer. "Ev, I'm sorry..."

"Just fuck off!" Her voice shook now, rage barely holding it together. "I don't belong to either of you."

She shoved past them, boots clutched in one hand, storming for the door.

Rose leaned against the wall with a mug of coffee, calm as a sniper on overwatch. She didn't move as Evelyn blew past, she just watched the two men standing stunned in the wreckage.

"Well, gents," she said, taking a slow sip, "you royally fucked that one up."

The porch boards thudded under Evelyn's boots, and then ...

BANG. The front door slammed hard enough to shake the frame.

James stood rooted where Evelyn had left him, chest tight, fists flexing at his sides. Irish's breathing was ragged, like he'd just walked away from a fight he still wanted to finish.

The only sound was the soft clink of Rose setting her mug down. The echo seemed louder than it should've been. She looked between them slowly, her stare level and merciless, stripping away whatever rank or ego they thought they still had.

"You two are unbelievable," her voice was calm but sharp enough to cut glass. "I've seen pissing contests before, but this? You took a woman who's been to hell and back, who only just started letting her guard down…and you made it all about you."

Irish opened his mouth, but Rose's hand snapped up.

"No. You don't get to talk yet."

Her gaze shifted to James first, unflinching.

"You. You know exactly how hard it is for her to trust. You had that trust… and instead of protecting it, you used it as ammo in the middle of your testosterone parade."

Then she turned to Irish, her tone colder.

"And you. Don't even start. You charged in like you had the moral high ground, but all you did was make her feel like she had to justify herself to you. You know her history. You know her pride. And you bulldozed her anyway."

James exhaled sharply, jaw tight. "Rose …"

"No." She cut him off like a whip crack, lifting her mug again for a measured sip. "You think either of you 'won' something here? She walked out. That's what you won. Right now she's halfway down the street convincing herself she doesn't need either of you. And she'd be right."

Irish's shoulders sagged, his eyes dropping. James stared at the floor, jaw locked.

Rose gave a short, humorless laugh as she pushed away from the counter.

"You two love her so much you can't even see you're playing the same game. And newsflash …" She picked up her mug, shaking her head. "…you're both losing."

Chapter 21

Evelyn's boots hammered the pavement, each step harder than the last. Her chest was tight, her throat raw, with rage burning hot enough to keep the hurt from spilling over. She fumbled a cigarette out of the crumpled pack in her pocket, lit it with shaking hands, and dragged deep until the smoke scalded her lungs.

"Fuck this," she muttered, exhaling hard through her nose.

The street was quiet, the damp air clinging to her skin, but she couldn't stop moving. She couldn't stop pacing like she was being hunted by her own thoughts. Her phone was in her hand before she even realised she'd pulled it out. She didn't think; she just hit Bullet's number.

He answered on the third ring, voice lazy, grin practically audible.

"Red. Didn't think I'd hear from you this early. What's up, trouble?"

She took another drag and blew the smoke at the night sky.

"You know if there's anything going down tonight?"

"Going down?" Bullet chuckled. "Ev, it's Norfolk. You want me to Google if the local knitting club's kicking off?"

Her silence stretched, sharp, and when she spoke again, her voice was flat.

"I mean fights. Cage, pit, doesn't matter. Somewhere I can bleed this shit out before I burn the whole house down."

That sobered him. Bullet whistled low.

"…Alright. Yeah. I'll make a call. Don't do anything until I ring you back, yeah?"

"Too late," she muttered, already flicking her cigarette butt into the gutter.

Evelyn was pacing outside the corner store, another cigarette almost burnt to the filter, when the roar of a familiar engine cut through the quiet. A battered black Camaro skidded to the kerb, paint scuffed, one headlight taped, music blasting heavy bass. Bullet leaned across the passenger seat, his grin wide and wolfish.

"Get in, Red. You look like you're about to strangle God himself."

She ground the cigarette under her boot and slid in, slamming the door behind her. The car smelt of leather, gun oil, and cheap aftershave.

"Where we going?" she asked, voice low.

Bullet flicked his eyes to her, still grinning.

"You called me, chica. That means I get to choose the therapy. And luckily for you, Norfolk's got a nice little underground setup tonight. Proper pit, no rules, cash on the table."

Her fingers drummed on her thigh, restless. "So, you watching or fighting?"

Bullet barked a laugh, taking a sharp corner like the laws of physics didn't apply.

"Ev, when have I ever taken you to watch anything?"

She finally cracked a smile, sharp and dangerous. "Good. Because I need to hit something before I start breaking furniture back at my flat."

Bullet slapped the wheel, whooping. "That's my girl! Alright then, Red, let's get you bloody."

The Camaro shot down the wet streets, neon bleeding across the windscreen, the night buzzing with the promise of violence.

The club reeked of stale beer, sweat, and smoke, the kind of place where fights broke out even before the cage opened. Neon strips flickered above, sticky floors pulling at boots. Bullet led the way through the crowd, shouldering aside drunks and punters until they hit the back stairwell.

Down the stairs it got darker, hotter, and louder. The bass from upstairs bled into the roar of voices below. The pit was under the club, half-basement, half-dungeon, with caged chain-link bolted to cracked concrete, and bloodstains old and new smeared across the floor.

At the edge, a thick-necked man with tattoos up to his ears took one look at Bullet and grinned.

"Diego Zavala. You still alive, cabrón?"

"Barely," Bullet shot back, clapping his hand. "Pawel, got a fighter for you." He jerked a thumb at Evelyn, who was peeling off her jacket.

Pawel's brows shot up. "She's half the size of my usual boys."

Bullet's grin turned feral. "Put your money on her. Trust me."

Evelyn stripped down to her vest, boots kicked aside, and her hair tied back roughly. She climbed into the cage with no hesitation, rolling her shoulders like a predator stretching. The crowd jeered and whistled, some laughing already at the thought of her getting crushed.

Then her opponent stepped in.

A wall of muscle. Six-six easy. Bald head, nose already broken twice, fists like mallets. The crowd went wild.

Bullet cupped his hands around his mouth. "Hey, big guy! Don't blink!"

The bell rang.

The man charged. Evelyn moved.

Not just fast, but inhumanly fast. She slid under his swing, drove an elbow into his ribs hard enough to make him grunt, then pivoted and cracked him across the jaw with a hook that snapped his head sideways. He staggered.

The crowd gasped.

He came at her harder, throwing wild punches, but she was already inside his guard, ducking, weaving, and slamming knee after knee into his midsection. The sound of each hit echoed off the walls, dull thuds that made stomachs turn."

Blood sprayed as she smashed her forehead into his nose, then spun behind him, one arm wrapping around his throat. Her legs kicked off the cage for leverage, dragging the giant down like a collapsing tower.

He hit the mat with a crash. She didn't let go. Her bicep flexed, face twisted, and the chokehold tightened until his

184

thrashing slowed. Pawel shouted for her to stop, but Evelyn's eyes burnt, teeth gritted, feral.

Bullet vaulted the barrier, banging on the mat. "Ev! Enough! He's done!"

She held a beat longer, then shoved the man's head down and stood, chest heaving, arms glistening with sweat and blood that wasn't hers.

The cage shook with the sound of the crowd losing their minds. Pawel was already counting cash, barking at bookies who hadn't backed her.

Bullet jumped in, grabbed her wrist, and held it high like she'd just won a title fight. "That's my girl! Told you, never bet against Red!"

Evelyn's eyes scanned the crowd, wild, alive, and more electric than any battlefield. For the first time all day, she wasn't angry. She was free.

Bullet's phone lit up. James. He swiped immediately.

"You with Ev? You were both supposed to be at the Irish pub twenty minutes ago."

On the other end came a roar of background noise: cheering, chanting, and the clang of metal on metal. Bullet's laugh cut through, smug as hell.

"Yeah, boss. I'm with her."

James's brows snapped down. "Where the fuck are you?"

"She's busy, mi amigo." Bullet chuckled, and James could hear the grin. "Currently punching a bloke in a cage while picturing your face."

James's voice straightened like he'd been shot. "What?"

"Relax. She's fine. Better than fine. Winning me some serious cash."

"Bullet..." James's voice dropped into command steel. "...don't make me pull rank. Where?"

A pause. Then a muttered, "Fuckin' kill me later... under Club Viper. Ask for Pawel."

Fifteen minutes later, the basement cage was already roaring when James shoved his way through the crowd. He was fuming, ready to tear the whole place apart. Then he saw her.

Evelyn.

Sweat-soaked, wild-eyed, fists flying faster than his eyes could follow. She ducked under a haymaker, drove her knee up, and sent a man twice her size crumpling against the fence. The crowd went feral.

James froze, anger bleeding into something else. Something hotter. Pride. Possession. His chest swelled, jaw flexing, watching her move like a weapon forged from every scar and every fight they'd survived.

Bullet spotted him through the cage mesh, grinning like the devil. "Oi! Paladin! Took you long enough!" He shoved a wad of cash at a bookie. "Get your money in before she finishes him!"

James didn't even think. He pulled out a roll and slammed it down. "All on her."

When the bell rang, Evelyn launched forward like she was born for this. James found himself at the cage edge, his fists

186

gripping the chain, yelling over the chaos. "Come on, Valkyrie! Drop him!"

The crowd barely mattered anymore. She fought like fire, and he was right there with her, not as her commander, not even as her lover, but as the only man alive who could match her feral heartbeat beat for beat.

When her opponent finally collapsed and the ref waved it off, the basement exploded in sound. Evelyn stood in the center of the cage, with her chest heaving, eyes finding James through the mesh.

His rage was gone. All that was left was pride. Wild, raw and undeniable. He grinned at her, with his teeth bared like an animal. And for the first time since the fight in the kitchen, they were on the same side again.

Evelyn dropped from the cage with the grace of someone who had no business being that bloodied and that beautiful. Sweat clung to her temples, her knuckles raw and her adrenaline still crackling in the air around her like a storm that hadn't quite passed.

James stepped forward with his hands out like he might catch her if she stumbled, but she didn't. She stood tall, chest heaving, eyes blazing.

"I get it, Red," he said, voice rough but steady. "You don't need saving. You're not my possession. You are brilliant, and fucking mental, and terrifying…" His mouth kicked into a grin he couldn't hide. "…and you just won me a ton of cash."

For a beat she just stared at him, feral and alive. Then she burst out laughing, loud and unrestrained with her head tipping back with it. The crowd's noise faded; it was just the two of them in that moment.

"Come on, you gobshite," she teased, still breathless from the fight. She hooked an arm through his, tugging him toward the bar. "Bullet... bar?"

Bullet was already halfway there, with his fist in the air and a grin from ear to ear. "Fucking yes! First round's on me. Actually... no, it's not; Red just paid for the night!"

James shook his head, still grinning like a lunatic as Evelyn dragged him through the crowd. For once, there was no fight left between them, only fire.

The club's upstairs bar was all grime and neon, with sticky floors, bad vodka, and music vibrating through the walls like the fight pit was still rumbling beneath their feet. Evelyn leaned against the counter with her cheeks flushed and her hair sticking damp to her temples. A pint was shoved into her hand before she could even ask.

"Fucking champion," Bullet crowed, slapping her on the back hard enough to make her stumble. "That wall of meat didn't know what hit him. You're like..." He mimed quick punches in the air, sound effects and all "rat-tat-tat, boom! Night-night."

Evelyn laughed so hard she nearly spat her drink. James stood close, half-guarding, half-buzzing with pride, his eyes flicking to the scrape on her shoulder and the raw skin over her knuckles. She caught him looking and rolled her eyes.

"Don't you dare start patching me up in the middle of a club, Paladin."

"Wasn't gonna," he muttered, though he'd already clocked where the med tape would need to go.

Bullet dropped onto a barstool, propped his boots on a bar stool, and leaned back, fixing James with that lazy grin of his. "You want to lose her, Hamito? Clip her wings. Our Valkyrie needs to fly… and she doesn't need permission. Sure, be there when she's in the shit, pick her up when she falls, but don't patronise her like a kid."

James's ground his teeth, but Bullet didn't stop.

"She outranks all of us, whether there's brass on her shoulders or not. And you need to remember who the fuck she is." He raised his glass in a toast. "Blue sparkles and all."

Evelyn blinked at him, caught between being touched and amused. "Blue sparkles?"

Bullet smirked. "You know. That thing you do when you light up like a rave mid-fight. Thought we didn't notice?"

Her laugh cut through the noise, real and unguarded. James's eyes softened, pride settling deeper than his earlier anger. He raised his glass too, meeting hers.

"To the Valkyrie," he said.

"Damn right," Bullet added, downing his shot.

And for the first time all night, Evelyn felt like she wasn't caught between two men pulling her apart. She was exactly where she belonged: wild, free, and untouchable.

The bar noise blurred into a dull roar by the time Evelyn slipped outside. The air was cool and damp, the street slick with rain, neon reflections stretching in broken colours across the pavement. She leaned back against the brick wall, her pint long finished, the fight adrenaline finally bleeding away.

James followed a minute later with his hands shoved into his jacket pockets. He didn't crowd her this time, he just stood close enough that she could feel the quiet steadiness rolling off him. For once, he wasn't trying to fix or contain her. Just... there.

Her arms crossed over her chest, a shiver running through despite the heat still clinging to her skin. "I'm fine," she muttered automatically.

He huffed a laugh, shaking his head. "Didn't say you weren't." His eyes softened, tracing the faint bruises already darkening along her jaw. "You were... fucking incredible in there, Red."

That tugged a real smile out of her, tired but genuine. "Yeah, well. Needed to blow off steam couple of egotistical wankers really pissed me off today."

James nodded, letting the silence hang, his gaze steady on her like he was trying to memorise the shape of her standing there: wild, proud, and untouchable, even with scraped knuckles and a split lip.

She finally tilted her head, studying him. The soldier, the man who'd just cheered her on like an animal from the sidelines, the one who wasn't trying to cage her after all.

"You wanna stay over at at mine?" she asked, casual, as though it wasn't the most intimate thing she'd ever offered.

James's throat worked, his jaw tightening for a second like he had to stop himself from saying "fuck yes" too fast. Instead, he just nodded, voice low. "Yeah. I'd like that."

For the first time that night, her shoulders dropped, the fight leaving her completely. She pushed off the wall, slipped her hand into his like it wasn't a big deal, and led him down the rain-slick street.

Chapter 22

The next morning, quiet didn't last. It never did.

Twenty minutes of peace tangled in each other's arms were dissolved the second a sharp knock rattled the door.

James cursed under his breath, pulling free from Evelyn's arm and yanking on his joggers. His hair was a mess, his eyes still heavy, but the tension in his shoulders was already back. He cracked the door.

Selena. Two coffees in hand. Smile soft, eyes hard.

Behind her, AJ, and within seconds he was already setting up camp at the kitchen island: screens flickering, burner phones stacked, and the hum of tech filling the air like static.

"Morning, boss. Didn't expect you here," Selena said mildly. But her tone carried weight. Urgent weight. "Sorry to break in, but you'll both want to see this. Irish is on the breakfast run."

James rubbed a hand over his face. "Ev, get up," he called back. "Guests."

By the time Evelyn padded in barefoot, her hair wild and James's shirt hanging loose over her frame, the kitchen looked more like an ops room than a home.

AJ didn't waste time. "Intel out of Colombia. Hospital. The Intel, it just reemerged, I don't understand it, but someone made access easy, like I was supposed to find it, and I am glad I did." His eyes flicked up. "It's rotten. Embedded doctors on the Revenant payroll. They scan trauma patients for survivability. If you're strong enough, they implant this…" He tapped a key, and an image popped up: a grainy x-ray, Evelyn's spine lit with something alien, "…biotech plate. If the body takes it, you get flagged for serum compatibility."

James felt something burn low in his chest. He didn't ask where the Intel had come from, he knew the answer already. Evelyn didn't move, didn't blink. Still unreadable.

Selena's voice dipped. "They were grooming you, Ev. Setting you up for the program before you even knew it."

James's jaw tightened. The muscles in his arms flexed like he was holding back from smashing the table.

"There's more," AJ said, voice clipped. "Records show fourteen vials of your blood were harvested during surgery. All sold. Every last drop."

James's head snapped towards him. "To who?"

AJ's hands hovered, then tapped. "Shell corps, ex-lab heads, and traffickers. Some of the worst operators in biotech. Private militaries. People who buy nightmares and rent them out."

AJ could see tension crawl over both Evelyn's and James's bodies, the shift so sharp it seemed to electrify the air. His throat worked as he swallowed, his fingers twitching against the edge of his laptop. When he finally spoke, his voice was raw and strained.

"I'm sorry, boss. There's more."

He dragged his hand down his face, his eyes burning with something between fury and sickness.

"These people, the buyers, the sellers, the traffickers… they're not just filth on the fringes. They're organised. A network. On the dark web, they call themselves the Aegis Consortium."

His words came faster now, tumbling out like he couldn't hold them back.

"They are funded… by men who play god in butcher's coats. Labs where bodies are carved up and rewritten, where people are nothing but parts to be tested, spliced, broken, and rebuilt. Supremacy at any cost. Flesh. Bone. Nerves. They cut until there's nothing left human."

He shut his eyes for a second, fighting his own disgust.

"And my Intel—Ya Allah—my Intel says this Consortium? They're behind the labs we've been tearing apart. Every cage we opened, every experiment we thought we stopped. That was theirs. All of it."

AJ's gaze locked onto Evelyn now, the weight of it nearly buckling him. His voice cracked, just once.

"And, Ev… They've marked you. You're on their list. You've been targeted."

The silence that followed was worse than shouting. James just leaned over the table, eyes crawling across the list like he was carving names into his skull.

Selena spoke carefully. "These aren't back-alley crews. They erase whole groups, vulnerable ones, refuges… prisoners of war unlawfully held in captivity."

194

Finally, James looked up. His eyes had gone black.

"Then we erase them first."

No heat. No bluster. Just certainly.

The door swung again. Irish stepped in with a cardboard tray of coffees. He froze mid-stride when he clocked the screens. His gaze flicked to Evelyn, then James. Slowly, he offered one out.

"A peace offering," he said. "And an apology."

James took it. No hesitation. "No apologies needed, brother. Wouldn't be the first time we punched each other bloody after a shit storm of a mission. Emotions ran high."

They clasped hands, a firm grip that turned into a shoulder-clap.

Evelyn's voice cut sharp. "I'll take your apology, you absolute cockend." Then she hugged him anyway.

Irish's expression sobered as his eyes tracked back to the screen. The x-ray glowed pale. The thing in her back looked like it didn't belong to a human body. He spoke lower.

"Selena filled me in. That plate comes out today. Before it starts transmitting something we can't undo."

James's rolled the tension out his shoulders. "Agreed. But no hospitals. No records."

Selena zoomed in. The image filled the screen: a hexagonal slab fused to Evelyn's spine. Black lines ran outward like veins.

"Biotech composite. Micro-lines are a transmitter grid. Right now passive. But it can be switched. Remote activation. Trackers.

Vitals. Maybe more. This is likely to be the consortiums handy work."

"Active?" Irish asked.

"Not on any open net," Selena said. "Could still be pinging somewhere closed."

James's voice was flat. "We cut it out. Today."

"On the kitchen counter," Irish snapped. "We keep it sterile. Frost will be here in twenty, keep you calm. Selena scrubs in if I need her. I lead."

Evelyn, who'd been silent until now, walked up barefoot. Looked at the scan.

Her eyes went flat. Cold. She stood weighing up her fate.

Then she left the room abruptly without an explanation.

When she came back, Bella, was in her hand. She flipped the blade once and held it out to James.

"Cut it out."

The kitchen went deathly quiet.

James took the knife, but his voice stayed steady. "Ev, this isn't a splinter. If I fuck this up…"

"Now." Her eyes locked on his. Calm. Absolute. "I am not dying like one of them!"

Irish's voice cut sharp. "No. You want it out? Fine, but we're not butchering your spine with a combat knife. We wait for Frost, and we do it clean."

Her eyes darted from the screen to Irish, she twitched like she wanted to argue. Instead, she nodded to James who set Bella on the counter with a soft clink.

Minutes later, Frost came through the door, silent as his namesake. He didn't ask, just looked at the scan, then at Evelyn.

"Selena says you're doing this. You need me to hold her?"

Evelyn stripped James's shirt off like it was nothing. "Damn right."

Irish laid the sterile kit open. His eyes locked to Frosts; his voice was clipped with command. "She jolts once; she's paralysed. Hold her still."

"This is going to hurt," Irish warned.

"Then make it quick," she said, teeth bared.

The kitchen reeked of bleach, iodine, and metal. Every surface was stripped, counters gleaming under the harsh bulb that buzzed above them like a dying fly.

Evelyn lay face-down across the table, shirt off and her skin already slick with sweat. Her eyes were wide and fixed, her breathing shallow, and her hands clawed white against the wood grain.

Irish's voice was low, almost apologetic. "Locals in. Give it a minute."

Evelyn's lips twisted into a bitter smile. "Won't work. Already feeling it burning off. Do it."

James's head snapped toward her. "No. We wait…"

Her gaze speared him. "Do it."

Irish didn't argue again. The scalpel bit into her flesh.

She screamed, not a cry, not pain alone but something primal that rattled the glass in the cupboards. Her whole body arched violently before Frost bore down on her, pinning her chest and shoulders with his full weight.

"Don't move," Frost whispered, voice steady and close against her ear. "I gotcha, Red. Stay with me. Breathe with me. Don't move."

Blood sheeted out fast, pooling under her ribs. But it wasn't just blood, it sizzled, acrid smoke rising as the scalpel touched the alloy. Irish froze. The metal lit up. Blue lines spider-webbed under Evelyn's skin, racing outward like veins alive with lightning. She convulsed hard, choking on another scream.

"Jesus Christ..." Irish's knuckles whitened around the scalpel. "It's fucking wired into her nervous system."

Evelyn slammed her head against the counter, muffling a guttural roar. Her teeth bit into her other forearm hard, blood mixing with spit.

James lurched forward. "You're frying her alive!"

Irish snarled back without looking up. "If I stop, it digs deeper. It's fighting me."

And it was. The plate pulsed under her skin, writhing, edges flexing like it was alive. Sparks crackled off the incision, the smell of burnt flesh rising sharp and sweet. Evelyn bucked, but Frost didn't move, arms caging her in.

"I gotcha, breathe with me." he whispered again, steady as a heartbeat. "Stay with me, Red. Don't give it the satisfaction."

AJ's voice cut through from the laptop in the corner, wired into scanners. "Holy shit… I'm reading signals. It's transmitting. It knows. I can't find where its transmitting to…"

"Cut it the fuck out!" Evelyn rasped, her voice shredded with every word torn from her throat.

Irish hooked the forceps and drove them under the plate. The second he levered it up, Evelyn screamed so violently her body snapped rigid. The lights overhead flickered.

Then it fought back.

The plate's edges curled like claws, embedding deeper into the muscle, black tendrils sparking through tissue. Her back lit up with fractal blue fire, veins bursting against her skin.

"Hold her!" Irish roared.

Frost bore down, his mouth to her ear, whispering steadily, relentlessly. "Don't move. I gotcha."

Evelyn's nails tore through the wood, blood soaking her palms, but she stayed pinned under him as Irish wrenched. The metal screamed with a shrill, electronic shriek that made every nerve in the room jolt. With a wet, tearing pop, it came free. The plate writhed in the forceps, still sparking, still pulsing. Irish slammed it into the lead-lined tin, and the moment the lid snapped shut, the screaming cut off.

Silence. Just Evelyn's ragged, broken sobs against the blood-slick counter.

Irish stitched with hands steady, sweat dripping into the wound. Frost finally eased off, but only enough to cradle her carefully, whispering, "It's out. You're safe. I gotcha."

James stood frozen, chest heaving, every muscle trembling with rage and awe. His eyes burned on the sealed tin where the plate twitched faintly against the lid, like something still alive, still wanting her.

Frost lifted her like she weighed nothing, careful but quick, her blood soaking through his shirt. Evelyn didn't even fight him with her normal bravado was fully gone. She just hung there against his chest, face slack, and body trembling. He carried her down the hall and laid her face-down on the bed, the sheets were already pulled back.

Irish was right on his heels, with his kit clattering. He drove the morphine into her hip without hesitation. Evelyn hissed and tried to turn her head, but her voice cracked into a slurred laugh.

"Christ, McBride… ginger, sexy… giraffe."

Irish shook his head, his lips pressed thin, but his eyes softened. "You're trouble, you know that?"

James knelt by the bedside, brushing her damp hair from her face. His voice was quiet, almost reverent.

"Christ, Ev… You're brave."

Her eyelids fluttered, a crooked grin pulling at her lips even as the drugs dragged her under.

"Please… I've had worse tattoos. You pulled bigger shrapnel out of my arse in Baghdad…"

Her eyes slid shut before she could finish.

The room went still, only the sound of her breathing evening out. Frost tucked the blanket over her shoulders, then slipped out without a word.

James lingered, with his hand still resting against her hair for a moment longer before he forced himself up. He padded back to the kitchen, where Irish was already elbow-deep in bleach and boiling water, scrubbing down steel and wood until it looked like nothing had happened.

James leaned against the doorway, his body wound tight. For a beat, he just watched. Then it snapped.

"You knew," he hissed, voice low and sharp as broken glass. "You knew it wasn't just metal."

Irish didn't look up. "I suspected."

"Suspected?" James's whisper came out as a snarl, his veins standing out in his neck. "She was screaming like she was on fire, and you suspected?"

Irish finally set the scalpel down, shoulders taut. "And if I'd told her it was fused to her nervous system, she'd have let it sit there. Fester. Spread. You think she'd ever ask for help if she knew what it meant. You know her better than that."

James took a step closer with his fists flexing. "You should've told me."

Irish met his glare now, blue eyes like ice. "And what would you have done? Locked her down? Caged her? You'd have torn this whole team apart trying to keep her safe. She doesn't need a warden, James. She needs brothers who'll get her through the fire. Even if it burns us too."

The two men stared at each other across the blood-scrubbed counter, the silence heavy with everything neither of them wanted to say out loud.

The kitchen was quiet and still, a stark contrast to the earlier screams. Blood still clung to the air, copper and sharp, mixed with the faint sting of antiseptic and bleach. Every creak in the wood sounded louder than it should have, every breath heavy in the silence.

Then it came.

A jagged, electronic ring that was too raw, too harsh to be anything normal. Not a mobile, not a house phone. Alien. Abrasive.

The sound tore through the room.

Irish froze mid-scrub with water dripping down his arms. Frost who had been on watch straightened in the doorway with his rifle slung low and eyes narrowing. AJ padded in, barefoot but sharp, his head tilted like he was already decoding the pattern of the noise.

The sound wailed again: shrill, insistent.

James was moving before he thought. Slow. Calculated. He swept the room like a battlefield. All counters were clear. The table drawers were empty. He dropped low, scanning beneath cabinets, back against the grain of the noise. It wasn't just sound anymore; it was vibration, rattling in the walls and the boards, like the whole fucking flat had swallowed something alive.

He pressed his hand flat against the wood. He felt it.

A tremor. A pulse.

Another burst cut through, louder, reverberating in his chest.

"Where the fuck is it?" Irish muttered, the rag twisting in his fist like he wanted to wring the air itself.

James traced the tremor, his palm moving across a panel seams until his nails scraped a warped edge. A lip. Hidden. Wrong.

He yanked. Wood splintered. Dust coughed out into his face. And there it was.

A burner, black and ugly, taped into the skeleton of the cabinet. Slim. Angular. Plastic hot to the touch, the edges marked like it had been used too often, too hard. Charging wires drilled into the wood like roots, so it would always be operational. The sound cut the second it was exposed. The silence it left behind felt worse. Heavy. Expectant.

James stared at it, chest tight.

"Christ…" 'Irish', whispered, like the word itself was dangerous.

James tore it free. It sat heavy in his hand, alive. Wrong. Screen black. Call missed. No name. No number. Just a blinking cursor, pulsing like a heartbeat.

The room held its breath.

James glanced towards the bedroom, where Evelyn lay unconscious, sweat still damp on her temple. His jaw locked. Slowly and gently, he crouched by her side. Her hand was limp and soft in his grip, but her fingers were still smudged with blood. He pressed her thumb to the scanner.

The phone hissed awake.

Green light bled across the screen, too bright and too sharp. For a second, nothing. Then: a missed call notification, the number scrambled nonsense.

The device screamed again.

James's heart lurched. He hit accept, lifting it to his ear.

A voice crashed through, frantic, the Glaswegian accent was thick and the words sounded slurred by panic.

"Evelyn! I know you're home… are you safe?"

James froze. His throat dried out. "Who is this?"

Silence. Just a breath on the line. Then:

"Burn the tech. Destroy it. Dispose of the ashes in different places… far from Ghent."

James's knuckles whitened around the phone. "Who is this?" he snapped, low and dangerous.

The voice came back, slower now. Steady.

"You know who I am. And I know who you are. James Reaves. Born November twelfth, nineteen eighty-seven. St Michael's tattoo on your chest. Townhouse on West Street, Virginia Beach. Black Ford Raptor. Triumph Bonneville T120 locked in your garage. Favorite table at Casa Mia. Care, kid. One sister… Ruby Reaves."

James's stomach dropped, cold bleeding into his veins. His eyes flicked to Evelyn who still lay out cold, unaware.

The voice pressed closer.

"If you don't do as I tell you, I'll use that information and do it myself. Do you understand, Commander?"

James swallowed hard, the word tearing from him before he could stop it.

"Ghost…"

Chapter 23

The morning light bled pale through the curtains when Evelyn stirred. Her body felt heavy, cotton-stuffed, but wrong too; her back wasn't screaming in pain the way it should have been after last night. She dragged herself upright, blinking hard, half-expecting the sharp burn of stitches every time she moved. Instead, there was just a dull ache, almost muted. That unsettled her more than the pain would have.

She swung her legs over the bed and braced herself against the wall, her boots were waiting where she had dropped them the night before. Pulling them on was slow work, her muscles felt tight, her ribs were still sore, but manageable in a way that felt unnatural. The flat was too quiet as she hobbled into the hall, every step steady, waiting for Irish's voice to come barking at her to get back to bed. But nothing came.

The kitchen door stood open, and when she stepped inside, she stopped dead. James, Irish, Selena, Frost and AJ were all seated around the table. None of them spoke, none of them moved; they just stared at her like she had walked in with blood on her hands.

James slammed something onto the table with enough force to make her flinch: a phone. Black, burner, ugly.

Her stomach lurched the second she saw it.

James's voice was low, his control far more dangerous than a shout. "You've been lying to me, Captain Blackthorn. Withholding Intel that could destroy my team."

Evelyn drew in a sharp breath, trying to steady herself. "Okay… your team?" She shot back, her tone sharpening like a blade.

James leaned across the table he was braced on his palms with his eyes boring into hers. "Don't do that, you're not changing the subject with your bullshit. You want to tell me about Ghost?"

The flicker in his jaw told her exactly how close he was to exploding, but before the spark caught, Selena's mug landed softly on the counter.

"Sit down," she said evenly. "No jokes. No dancing around it. Start at the beginning."

Evelyn dropped into the chair with a sigh and a coffee clutched between her hands. "Fine. But you're not going to like it."

She looked each of them over, James burning hot, Frost unreadable, Irish stirring his tea like nothing rattled him and AJ, who was clearly uncomfortable. Then she drew in a long breath.

"Here's the truth. I can't tell you. And that's not me dodging; it's literal. If I give you names, times, details… anything… you'll all be targets. Ghost is being hunted by governments, agencies, traffickers, cartels, arms dealers, and every bastard with a secret worth killing for. If he's exposed, he's dead. And probably so are we."

Her tone was steady, her eyes locked on James. "He only ever shows when something happens to me, when he thinks I need protecting. And every single time he does, he risks being caught. He has dirt on people you couldn't even imagine: politicians, generals, mob bosses, presidents. He's a loaded gun pointed at half the world, and my duty is to keep him hidden. I protect him as much as he protects me."

James's jaw flexed hard, the muscle ticking. "Ev, you've lied to me. You made me think you were trying to figure him out too...you made me think I was helping you work out his agenda...and you knew... you feed me bullshit...Did you sleep with me to stop me asking questions... did you play me... fuck Ev!"

"No... Fuck Jamie no! That was real... that part wasn't a lie. I don't know who he is. I didn't know who smuggled me out."

His voice sharpened. "And I'm supposed to trust you after finding a burner taped into the kitchen walls? He's been near you, he's watching you, and you didn't think I needed to know?"

She shook her head slowly. "No."

"Don't do that," James snapped, stepping closer. "Don't shut me out."

Her gaze didn't waver. "James, you cannot know the rest."

He stared her down. "Ev..."

"No." Her voice cracked like a whip, sharp and final. "You'd have to torture me, Jamie. And I mean really torture me—cut me, bleed me, break me—and I still wouldn't talk. Because the second you know too much, you're in danger. And I won't carry your body because of him."

She gave a bitter laugh, drained of humor. "Besides, trust me... you don't want to see what I look like when I'm keeping secrets under duress. It's not sexy. Lots of blood. Bad hair day."

The kitchen went silent. Even Irish stopped stirring. Frost's arms folded tighter, his eyes burning into her. Selena sat forward slightly, but her expression didn't change.

Evelyn's voice softened, but the words landed heavier than a blade. "If any of you so much as hinted you knew about him, they'd put you on a slab and cut you apart until you gave him up. That's why I carry this alone. It's not martyrdom; it's maths. My life for yours. Always."

James's knuckles went white where he braced against the table. "You think I won't push?"

"I think you'll try," she said quietly. "But you won't win. Not this time."

The words hung like frost in the air.

Finally, Frost broke it. "She's right."

James's head whipped toward him. "Excuse me?"

Frost didn't blink. "If Ghost is what she says, poking at him brings the wolves with him. You don't just drag one ghost out of the dark. You drag everything chasing him too. And we all burn in the fallout."

Selena added, voice calm but carrying steel. "And if they even suspect we made contact, they don't just come for him. They erase us. All of us. No questions asked."

That silenced James, but only in volume. His whole body was still a storm barely held together. He turned back to Evelyn, his voice low and bitter. "You're a liability. You could've told me sooner."

"No," she said simply. "I couldn't. And if you think for a second I'll risk your life, or theirs, for answers you want but don't need, then you don't know me at all."

The silence stretched. James looked at her like she'd just slammed a steel door in his face.

Finally, he broke, turning to Selena. "Fine. Bury and burn everything you've got on Ghost. AJ too. No files, no chatter, nothing. Make it vanish."

Selena gave a short nod. "Done."

James's gaze snapped back to Evelyn. "That good enough for you, Blackthorn?"

She studied him for a beat, undecipherable, then gave the smallest nod. "Almost." She sipped her coffee again and muttered, "But if anyone wants to make themselves useful, they could at least bring me a bloody croissant."

That tiny crack of humor barely lightened the mood, but it was Evelyn's way of showing she was still herself. Still standing. Still holding the line.

Selena clocked it instantly with the shift. This wasn't trust. This was James acknowledging, maybe for the first time, that there was a line Evelyn could draw that even he wouldn't cross. And that changed everything.

The silence sat heavy, the kind that usually ended with someone storming out or a door slamming. But instead of exploding, James exhaled through his nose, a low, ragged breath. His fists unclenched, his shoulders dropped just a fraction. He looked at her like a man torn in two—furious and proud in the same heartbeat.

"You're impossible," he muttered, and for once it didn't sound like an insult.

Evelyn arched a brow, sipping her coffee. "Thank you."

James shook his head, the ghost of a smile tugging at his mouth even as the storm still raged in his chest. He turned, eyes flicking to AJ, who was leaning against the counter, hands buried deep in his hoodie pockets.

"You destroyed it? The plate, the chip…scattered it?" James asked, his voice steady now, softer, but carrying weight.

AJ nodded once, cool as ever. "Yeah. Burnt to nothing. Bullet and Mack helped me scatter the ashes…different containers, different ships. Some heading east, some west. Half the world won't even know what cargo they're carrying."

Selena gave a small, approving hum. "Smart."

Evelyn let out a long breath, shoulders loosening for the first time since she had walked in. "See? Family business handled. And you didn't even have to break my fingers to get it done."

James leaned against the table, studying her, every line of his face still taut but softer now, almost reverent. "You fucking terrify me, you know that?"

Her smirk was tired but sharp. "Good. Means you're paying attention."

Irish clapped his hands, trying to shake the tension from the room.

"Right. Someone make her a coffee. And you…" he pointed at Evelyn, "…should still be in bed."

Evelyn rolled her shoulders with deliberate nonchalance. "Nah. I'm fine."

Irish's brow furrowed. "Fine? You've got a high threshold, sure, but there's no way in hell you're fine after what you went through last night."

She tilted her head, voice flat but edged with that sharp defiance only she could pull off. "Honestly. All good. Look."

Before anyone could stop her, she grabbed the hem of her top and peeled it off in one sharp, unceremonious movement.

The room stilled.

Irish was on his feet in an instant his scowl deepening and hands already reaching. He tugged at the dressing across her back, irritation muttering through him... until the gauze came away.

The hiss he let out wasn't irritation anymore.

Underneath wasn't a fresh wound. It wasn't even a neat line of stitches. The flesh was wrong. It had knitted in on itself too quickly, puckered in strange raised ridges that spiraled out from the center like something had burnt itself into her skin from the inside out. Veins darkened around it, branching like black lightning beneath the surface, fading and vanishing as though chased by something alive.

It looked less like a scar and more like something had claimed her.

Irish staggered back, his hand fell instinctively to the counter to steady himself.

"What the fuck..."

AJ choked on his coffee. Selena's hand went straight to her mouth, with her eyes wide but calculating as they traced the strange, unnatural weave of tissue. Frost didn't move, but the muscle in his jaw ticked like a drumbeat.

Evelyn leaned back, utterly unbothered, her eyes flicking between them like she'd just won a bet.

"See?" she said, voice steady, almost mocking. "Fit for service, Commander Reaves."

James hadn't breathed. His fingers laced around his dog tags to ground himself, his face was pale. He stared at the mark on her like it might start moving, like it might split open and reveal something not meant for this world. His throat worked, but no sound came out. When his eyes finally lifted to hers, they were raw, stricken… shaken in a way no battlefield had ever left him.

It wasn't anger anymore. It was fear.

Chapter 24

The HQ hummed low that morning, with the usual mix of clicking keyboards, burnt coffee hanging in the air, and Frost muttering to himself over comms calibration. Evelyn leaned back at the briefing table with her boots kicked up, pen spinning between her fingers, pretending not to notice James pacing as he skimmed the latest SITREP from Syria.

The secure comms line on the wall chirped, sharp and urgent. Selena's eyes flicked to James, who was already crossing the room. He tapped the panel and leaned in. The voice that came through was clipped and official. Not NATO. Not American military. Afghan clearance codes rattled off like gunfire, followed by a name and a location: Korangal Valley.

Evelyn froze mid-spin. Everyone knew that place. Death Valley. The voice continued, listing the details without inflection. Hostages. Taliban splinter cell. Active minefield. They needed operators who could both extract and defuse, a rare combination. James cut the line, stood still for a beat with his back to the room, shoulders set like a man bracing for impact. When he finally turned, his face gave nothing away, but the temperature in the room seemed to drop.

"Briefing room. "Five minutes." He walked out without another word.

No one moved at first. Frost glanced at Selena, who glanced at Irish. Evelyn dropped her boots to the floor with a dull thud. "Death Valley," she muttered. "That's not exactly a casual Tuesday."

Ten minutes later, the war room door clicked shut behind James. He dropped a file on the table stamped 'CLASSIFIED' in red. "Afghanistan," he began, voice steady but clipped. "Korangal Valley. You all know the nickname." Silence answered him. He flicked the file open and slid drone shots across the table with grainy sweeps of green cut by jagged rock and narrow dirt tracks.

"Splinter cell. Five Afghan hostages. Terrain wired with Soviet mines and fresh IEDs. That's why they want us; they need a team who can move fast and disarm on the ground." His eyes moved from face to face as he spoke. "Mack, you're staying here. You've got point if this goes sideways." Mack looked ready to argue but held it in and nodded once.

"Bullet, AJ... you're out. "Too green for this one." Both started to protest, but James's look shut them down. "Selena, it's not your wheelhouse. Comms and logistics are covered. Frost, you back up Mack in our absence... This needs hands on the ground." Finally, his gaze landed on Evelyn. "That leaves two of us. Me. And her."

The room went silent. "Eighteen percent chance of success," James added flatly. "And that's being generous. No air cover. In and out before they know we're there." Evelyn leaned back in her chair with a smirk just sharp enough to cut the tension. "So... standard odds for us then?" James didn't smile. "Pack light. Wheels up in four hours."

The briefing room door had barely closed before Mack caught James by the arm, pulling him up short in the narrow hallway. His voice was low but edged sharp enough to cut.

"You've lost your damn mind. Eighteen percent chance, no cover, and you're taking her?"

James jerked free but didn't break stride, his boots hit hard against the linoleum. His tone was tight and controlled with fury simmering just below the surface.

"You think I'm taking her because I want to? She's the only one in this building who's walked that valley and made it back."

Mack kept pace, shaking his head. "That was years ago…"

"And she did it three times," James snapped, rounding on him now. His eyes burned, with every word a hammer blow. "Three tours in Afghanistan before Obsidian. Two of them in the Korangal. She speaks Pashto like she was born there. She knows every goat trail, every choke point, every line in the dirt that could get us killed. And you know how many people in the world can look at the casing of a mine and tell you if it's a Soviet PMN from the eighties or a fresh IED planted last week? One. And she's sitting in that room."

Mack's jaw tightened, but James didn't give him air to argue.

"She's pulled legacy mines that had been buried twenty years before she set foot there. She's walked terrain the locals won't touch. She's lifted hostages out from under armed cells without losing a single civilian. If I take anyone else with me, they'll slow us down… or worse, they'll get us both killed."

For a long moment, the only sound was the low hum of the fluorescent lights above them. Mack's shoulders shifted like he wanted to push back, but all he managed was a flat, hard question.

"And if you don't come back?"

216

James's voice dropped, rough and certain, with his gaze unflinching.

"Then I went in with the only person who gave us a fighting chance."

Mack exhaled hard through his nose, the weight of it dragging his shoulders down. He stepped back at last, conceding ground with a mutter.

"You're both out of your damn minds."

James's mouth twitched with the faintest ghost of a smirk.

"Yeah. But that's why we come back."

The kit room filled with the clink of buckles and the rasp of webbing. Evelyn unpacked gear that looked like relics from another life: sand-worn gloves, a faded keffiyeh, and a battered minesweeper head still scarred from a blast wave. She checked each piece with calm precision and laid them out in a neat line. Beside her, James moved just as methodically, loading his carrier and sliding extra mags into pouches. For a long while, the only sounds were gear shifting and straps tightening.

Eventually, Evelyn broke the silence. "Who are we meeting out there?"

"Afghan SOU," James answered without looking up. "Half seasoned, half green. The rookies carry weight and stay quiet."

She clipped her folding shovel into her pack. "Medics?"

"Two locals, NATO-trained. They've never set foot in Korangal. Don't rely on them."

Her eyes flicked to him, sharp. "Extraction route?"

"North Ridge. Fastest, but mined. The safe path's six hours with no cover. That's why it's us."

She held his gaze for a moment. "So we move, I cut, you cover?"

"Exactly. No improvising."

Her mouth curved slightly. "You've learned."

James holstered his sidearm, finally meeting her eyes. "I learn fast when you're the one holding the cutters."

She slung her pack over her shoulder, brushing against him as she passed toward the door. "Then let's go remind Death Valley why it hates us."

Chapter 25

Afghanistan – Forward Operating Base, Desert Perimeter

The air inside the briefing tent was stifling, canvas walls trapping the dry heat. Dust and sweat clung to the air like a second skin. A map of the Korangal Valley lay spread across a folding table, dotted with red circles and black Xs. Outside, the steady thump of helicopter rotors underscored every word.

James stood at the head of the table, with his finger stabbing toward the satellite feed glowing on his laptop.

"We insert here. Extraction's here. Mine is between both points. Eighteen percent chance of pulling this off without losing half the team. So…."

He broke off when movement snagged his eye. Evelyn, three seats down, slid a burner phone out of her cargo pocket. She glanced at the screen with her jaw tight.

"One minute, Commander," she murmured.

James's gaze stayed on her longer than it should have, but he gave a curt nod. She rose, ducking out of the tent without explanation.

He carried on, briefing terrain choke points, probable sniper nests, and extraction windows, but his mind kept drifting to where she'd gone and why.

Two minutes later, the flap lifted. Evelyn strode back in, all business. She didn't sit. Instead, she crossed straight to the table, pulled the laptop from under his hands, and set it in front of herself.

The burner was still pressed to her ear, her free hand flying across the keys, entering coordinates and strings of data no one else in the room recognised.

"Copy," she said at last, voice flat and clipped. "Roger that."

She killed the call, tossed the phone back into her pocket, and slid the laptop toward James. Then she dropped the sentence that froze the room.

"Ghost sent us extra Intel. Should push our odds higher."

Silence. Even the distant choppers felt muted.

James's eyes snapped to hers, with so many questions burning through him. How the hell does Ghost know where we are? What we're doing? And why is she the one holding his line?

Evelyn just met his stare, unreadable. "You're welcome."

When the rest of the team filed out of the tent, James caught her arm. She braced for him to drag her somewhere private and rip her apart for going off-script.

Instead, he just stood there with the desert sun carving hard lines across his face. Dust had already gathered on the shoulders of his sand-coloured combat shirt. His sleeves were rolled to the forearms, with sweat darkened at the creases. His plate carrier sat tight against his chest, MOLLE webbing heavy with spare mags, and a hydration tube over one shoulder. A tan sidearm rode low on his thigh, blending into the camo. His shemagh shifted in the hot breeze, the fabric dark against the grit shadowing his jaw.

She looked no less battle-carved. Desert fatigues worn in but clean, her sleeves tight around lean muscle. Her carrier was lighter, built for speed, and loaded with charges, snips, and a slim med roll. The sun and sand had kissed the edges of her hair where it broke free of her helmet, sticking damp to her temples. Dust streaked her cheeks, but her eyes were sharp, calm in the way of someone who'd survived this ground too many times. Her rifle hung low, the grip loose but ready, and her boots scarred from years of the same terrain.

James's stare didn't waver. His voice was low, stripped of anything but iron.

"Thank Ghost for me. Next time, he comes out of the shadows. That Intel just saved us—exit point we planned on was wired with IEDs."

Her brow ticked upward, surprise shading into something closer to relief. "Noted."

For half a heartbeat his mouth threatened a fuller truth, but he swallowed it back. He just shifted his rifle, gave her a sharp nod, and turned toward the waiting convoy.

Evelyn fell in behind him, her boots crunching in the grit, both of them moving toward a mission with only an eighteen-per cent chance of survival, carrying secrets heavier than any pack.

The Humvees growled in the heat, engines rumbling beneath the drone of cicadas and the distant wash of rotors. Heat waves shimmered above the sand, distorting jagged ridgelines into wavering ghosts.

James hauled himself into the lead vehicle. Headset on. Mic live. His voice cut through the engine roar, sharp and uncompromising.

"Convoy, lock it up. First and last vehicle on overwatch. Everyone else, hold arcs. Move on my call."

Evelyn slid in beside him, rifle across her lap. Posture loose. Eyes sharp. She looked like the valley hadn't earned the right to make her tense.

The radio spat a burst of Pashto, fast and clipped. Evelyn didn't flinch.

"Road ahead's quiet since dawn," she translated, calm as a heartbeat. "Could mean nothing. Could mean they're waiting."

James gave a single nod, his jaw tight. He keyed his mic.

"Copy. All callsigns, close gaps. Nobody relaxes."

Another transmission, layered in static. Evelyn tilted her head, listening.

"Checkpoint three reporting movement in the wadi," she said. "Kids playing… or recon. Not clear."

James shifted in his seat, eyes sweeping the horizon through dust-streaked glass.

"Gunner, lock that wadi. If it moves like a fighter, treat it like one. No chances."

The convoy rattled forward, its suspension groaning over rutted ground.

Every so often, Evelyn spoke; short and precise translations dropped into the comms like scalpel cuts. She didn't raise her voice. She didn't need to.

James was steel, carrying command like a weight on his chest. Evelyn was ice, cutting clean through the noise with the right words at the right time.

The valley rose ahead. A dark cut of rock and shadow. Sound warped strangely here. The air tasted of dust and old iron.

Evelyn's eyes flicked sideways.

"Feels like the kind of day Death Valley earns its name."

James didn't look at her.

"Then let's make sure it's not ours carved on the list."

The convoy ground to a halt at the edge of the wadi. The heat here was different—heavier. It pressed into their skin and lungs like it wanted to slow them down before the fight even began.

James was out first, boots sinking into powdery sand. His voice carried low and sharp.

"Dismount. Keep it quiet."

Evelyn swung down after him, pulling her scarf across her mouth. A hot wind shifted and carried the stench of burning diesel, mixed with something coppery and metallic. Older. Blood baked into the earth.

The ground was a graveyard. Just past the first cluster of rocks, cracked clay showed the faded, half-buried discs of Russian mines left decades ago. Some were rusted open; jagged teeth of metal curled outward where shrapnel had torn them apart. A few still bore the outline of boots that had stepped wrong years ago, blackened leather fused into clay. The wind exposed scraps of bone, pale and brittle, tangled with fabric that had once been a uniform.

And then—fresh steel. Plates that hadn't yet weathered. Wires too clean, too new.

James lifted a fist, halting the line. His jaw flexed tight.

223

"Whole stretch is laced. Valkyrie, you're up."

She moved past him without hesitation. Each step deliberate, her mine probe sliding into the dirt at precise angles. Sunlight glanced off the sweat beading down her temple, but her hands never shook.

The team followed her steps exactly. Nobody wanted to test the ground outside her path.

She marked the safe route with faded red cloth tied to rocks, muttering warnings in Pashto when she spotted pressure plates locals hadn't seen. The scouts hung back. They could see she'd done this dance before.

Halfway across, gunfire ripped from the ridge.

"Contact left!" James barked, dropping to a knee and firing back. The team scattered low, rifles cracking.

Sand and dust kicked into Evelyn's face, bullets whizzing past her head. She didn't stop.

"Valkyrie!" James roared.

"I've got it!" she snapped, ripping a fresh plate out of the dirt and tossing it clear.

The firefight bled on. Minutes dragged, echoes rattling the valley. Then silence. Just ringing ears and heart hammering.

"All accounted for?" James called.

"All here," voices answered.

Not a single man down.

They pushed forward, the path narrowing into a twisted gash of stone. The air cooled, funneling between sheer walls, but no one relaxed. Every man knew this was a killing ground. Evelyn's stride didn't falter, and James's orders never paused.

By the time they reached the extraction zone, sweat had soaked through every shirt, gear was streaked grey with dust, and adrenaline gnawed at their veins like fire. The hostages were there: three civilians and a fourth, barely conscious, half-buried in a collapsed goat pen. They dragged them out quickly. A young Afghan soldier, broad-shouldered and calm-eyed, lifted the wounded man onto his back without breaking stride.

"Let's move," James ordered, his voice raspy but steady. "Same path back. No detours." Step by step, the unit traced Evelyn's red-marked trail. Boots fell into silence. Only the crunch of gravel, the rasp of breath, and the hiss of comms static broke the quiet.

Then the wadi opened, and blinding sunlight slammed into them, the wide desert spilling out in every direction. The chokehold of stone was gone. Every chest loosened at once. James looked at Evelyn. Dust caked her plate carrier, sweat darkened the edges of her scarf, but her eyes never rested. Always sweeping the ridges.

"You did good," he said, his voice meant only for her.

Her smirk was small and sharp. "Told you. I know this valley."

When the convoy rolled out and the valley shrank in the mirrors, James keyed the mic. "Mission complete. No losses. Repeat… no losses."

The reply from base wasn't just relief. It was reverence.

The Humvee rocked over ruts and sand, with its suspension groaning, the convoy dragging itself back toward base. Dust poured in through the half-open hatch, sticking to their lips and the sweat solidified on their skin. Inside, the air was thick with engine heat, with faint traces of cordite still clinging to their clothes.

Evelyn sat beside James, her rifle balanced across her lap, her scarf pulled high across her face. She looked like she hadn't even blinked since they'd left the wadi, her eyes remained sharp and restless, scanning out the window as if the desert itself might rise up and ambush them. James watched her for a moment too long, then leaned in. His gloved fingers tugged gently at the edge of her shemagh, pulling it down just enough to see her mouth.

She turned to him, with a question in her eyes, but before she could speak, he dipped in close, aiming for a kiss. Their helmets clashed with a hard crack. Both of them froze, then she gave the faintest huff of a laugh and lifted her hand, starting to unbuckle her chin strap.

Before she could, James caught her wrist, his grip firm but not harsh. His voice was low, pitched just for her over the rattle of the Humvee. "Don't do that... Knowing our luck, that's how we die."

She smirked, eyes gleaming under her dust-caked lashes, and let her hand fall. Neither of them moved closer again, but the charge in the space between them said enough.

Chapter 26

The base was quiet except for the steady hum of a generator somewhere outside, a low thrum that filled the silence between words. They'd both showered, quick and perfunctory, the kind of rinse that left streaks of grit circling the drain. Now they sat cross-legged on the floor of James's quarters, with their backs propped against the bedframe and their boots abandoned by the door. Between them, two cold bottles sweated onto the dusty floorboards.

For almost an hour they'd been swapping war stories, trading those sharp-edged moments from the op that still spiked your pulse even after the danger was over. James was mid-sentence when Evelyn's voice shifted, quieter, her gaze dipping toward the bottle in her hand.

"Ghost was right," she murmured, more like she was reminding herself than telling him. "He's always right."

James stilled, bottle halfway to his lips. His eyes cut to her, wary. "How did he know where we were, Ev?"

She didn't flinch; she just met his stare head-on, steady as stone, like the question didn't deserve to rattle her.

"I told him before we left," she said simply. "Figured we might need a hand on this one."

James blinked, the words sinking in like a slow hit to the ribs. Then a short, disbelieving laugh broke out of him, low in his chest, equal parts exasperation and reluctant admiration. "I'll be damned…"

The obvious questions pressed hard against his tongue. How much had she told him? When? Did Ghost know more than even he did about their op, about her? But then he caught something in her eyes, a quiet steel, conviction unshaken. The look of someone who'd already weighed out every angle and decided.

James gave a long exhale, then a nod that felt like letting go of something heavy. "Alright," he said, with his voice steady. "If you trust him, I trust you."

Her mouth curved into that faint, knowing smirk, but she didn't answer. Instead she just tipped her bottle back for another swig, then leaned her shoulder against his as if it were the most natural thing in the world.

For once, James didn't push. He let the silence settle, carrying with it a strange, uneasy warmth, the kind that felt like trust, even when you weren't sure it should. Somewhere in the back of his mind, though, the thought flickered like static: Ghost hadn't just been right. He'd been ready. Like a man already moving pieces on a board they hadn't even seen yet.

Evelyn leaned her head back against the bed, studying him with lazy curiosity. The quiet between them wasn't awkward; it was thick, alive, humming with everything they'd just survived.

Then, out of nowhere, she tilted her head and asked, "You ever had sex in a desert camp?"

James's eyes snapped up from his bottle so fast she almost laughed. "Nope. Can't say I have," he said, cautious, like he wasn't sure if this was a trap.

Her grin was slow, wicked, and unrepentant. "You wanna change that?"

His mouth opened and closed. "Jesus Christ, Ev…"

Her laugh was low and warm, curling around him like smoke. That was it. Whatever restraint he'd been clinging to snapped clean in two. One second they were sitting there; the next he was on her, their bottles forgotten, hands in her hair, her back hitting the floor in a tangle of knees and laughter.

"Messy start or not," she breathed against his mouth, "tomorrow isn't a given. Come on… danger shag."

James groaned into her lips, her laughter vibrating through him as his weight settled over hers. The scent of dust, sweat, and heat clung to both of them. The air was suffocating, but neither cared.

Then he froze just long enough to mutter, "Shit. I don't have a rubber."

She smirked, brushing her nose against his. "I'm on the pill."

That bought him two seconds of hesitation, his eyes searching hers for any flicker of doubt. There wasn't one.

"Fuck it," he growled, voice low and dangerous.

Her answer was to hook her fingers into his shirt and drag him down, kissing him like she'd been waiting for this exact moment since boots hit Afghan soil.

The heat snapped from simmer to white-hot. Gear half-pulled, half-ripped away. His hands skimmed her scars like they were battle honors. Her back arched, legs tangled in his, with the canvas creaking beneath them as the camp outside carried on oblivious.

The first thrust punched the air from both of them, not from pain, but from the shock of how much closer, how much more it was without the barrier.

"Jesus..." James's voice was ragged, forehead pressed to hers.

Her nails scraped the back of his neck. "Different, isn't it?"

A dark laugh rattled out of him, hips grinding deeper. "Different's one word for it..."

Everything was sharper—the heat, the friction, the sound of her breath catching when she clenched around him. The thin canvas walls may as well not have existed; the only world was the space between their bodies.

"You're... insane," he muttered against her mouth.

"Good thing you like crazy," she shot back, biting his lip.

He groaned, thrusting harder. She moaned, with her head tipping back, and he pressed his mouth to her throat. "Keep it down, Ev..."

Her wicked grin flared. "Make me."

Those two words broke him. His pace grew brutal, his hand slipping between her thighs to work her clit, driving her over the edge until her muffled groan vibrated against his palm. She came hard, dragging him with her, both of them covering each other's mouths as the climax tore through.

They collapsed, tangled, slick with heat, a breathless laughter spilling into the heavy dark. Neither moved for a long moment, just taking in the wreckage of what they'd done.

James finally lifted his head, brushing a kiss over her forehead. "Next time, we're doing that in a bed."

She smirked. "Next time, I'm picking the desert again."

Evelyn wriggled under him suddenly, making a face. "Fuck, I'm covered in you. Grab my T-shirt!"

He fumbled for it, still pressed against her. She winced. "Jesus Christ... I think I've got sand in my butt crack."

James broke. He laughed so hard his forehead dropped to her shoulder. "You're such a menace."

"Don't laugh at me! This is a tactical hazard!" She shot back, shoving at his chest.

"Hazard?" His grin was wicked, still breathless. "Ev, it's like sandpaper."

She groaned dramatically. "See? Exactly why people don't have sex in the desert!"

"Yeah," he murmured, kissing her anyway, "but I'm not complaining."

"You will when you've got sand rash in places you don't wanna explain to the medics."

He poured water into her mouth, then his, then over both their chests until it ran cool between them.

"Worth it," he said without missing a beat. The look in his eyes made her bite back a smile, feral and unrepentant.

The following morning the sun was already burning through the thin canvas of the tent when Evelyn stirred. Every muscle protested, from the mission and from the night before. She stretched, wincing at the grit on her skin, and rolled over to find James sitting cross-legged at the tent's entrance, sipping coffee and scanning a map.

He glanced back at her, and for the briefest second, that hard commander's edge softened into something warmer. "Mornin', trouble."

"Ugh," she groaned, rubbing her eyes. "My mouth tastes like desert and bad decisions."

He smirked. "You're the one who said, 'you wanna change that?'"

"Yeah, well," she sat up, hair a mess, "we're not dead yet."

After the debrief with the local unit, one of the Afghan commanders approached Evelyn, speaking quietly in Pashto. James watched her switch languages effortlessly, her tone steady, calm, and authoritative.

When she turned back to him, there was a spark in her eyes. "They're asking if I can stay a couple of weeks. Train their sappers on defusing the old Soviet mines still in the valley. Most of them are kids, James; they've been losing legs out here for decades."

He didn't even hesitate. "Then we stay. I'll help their infantry while you work with their engineers."

It was slow work, patient and meticulous, the kind of thing that built trust without them even realising it. Evelyn knelt in the dirt, guiding a young soldier's hands as he probed the earth for pressure plates. James was often just a few metres away, drilling the rifle teams, translating her safety warnings when her hands were too busy to sign or gesture.

They ate together in the shade between sessions, trading bites of ration packs and laughing about nothing. She fixed his busted watch strap with a scrap of paracord; he patched a tear in her fatigues without a word.

At night, they'd sit just outside camp, boots kicked off, watching the valley fade into blue shadow. Sometimes they talked about places they'd been, stupid ops gone wrong, and the people they'd lost. Sometimes they didn't talk at all. Some nights they made love, while others they just slept in each other's arms.

On their last evening, she caught him looking at her, not like a commander watching his operative, but like a man who'd just realised he couldn't picture his life without her.

"You're staring," she teased.

"Yeah," he said quietly, not looking away. "Guess I am."

For the first time, she didn't deflect. "Good. I like it when you look at me like that."

Chapter 27

The next morning came too fast. Word spread through the valley long before they'd even packed their gear. The young sappers clustered around Evelyn, dirt still under their nails, trying to hide the pride on their faces as they showed her clean, marked fields that had been deadly just days before. She corrected one grip, ruffled another's hair, and her voice was patient but firm.

James stood a few paces off, finishing with the infantry squad. They wouldn't say it out loud, but they carried themselves differently now, with their shoulders squared, eyes sharper, a little less reckless.

When the vehicles finally rumbled into camp, the air shifted. Reluctance hung heavy, like the dust refusing to settle. The Afghan commander pressed James's hand in both of his, then turned to Evelyn with words that needed no translation: gratitude, respect, and a promise.

She answered in Pashto, her tone softer this time, then glanced back at James as if to say, "That's enough. Time to move."

They climbed into the transport together, with their dirty boots thudding against the metal floor. As the convoy pulled away, the valley opened out behind them with rolling stone, sun-bleached ridges, and the faint shapes of young soldiers still standing watch.

Evelyn leaned her head back, closing her eyes for a moment. James watched her, with the dust rising in the mirrors until the valley blurred and disappeared.

"You'll miss it," he said quietly.

"Not the place," she murmured, without opening her eyes. "The people."

He didn't argue. He just reached across the space between them and laced his fingers with hers, the gesture hidden from everyone else in the transport.

For once, she didn't pull away.

The hum of the C-17 was a low, steady backdrop as they sat shoulder to shoulder in the dimly lit troop bay. Most of the soldiers around them were already asleep, with their helmets tipped forward and rifles balanced against their knees. Evelyn had her knees drawn up, boots hooked on the edge of the bench, and her head tipped toward James.

They'd been talking since wheels-up, conversation weaving through mission chatter, sarcastic jabs, and something far more personal.

"She's called Ruby," James said, a small smile tugging at his mouth. "My kid sister. Works for Amnesty International now. Spends her days ripping into human rights abusers, writing up briefs that scare the hell out of people who think they're untouchable."

Evelyn tilted her head. "Sounds like she's got your bite."

"She's got my stubborn," he corrected. "But she's smarter than me. It's why I joined the military: to get her through uni. Had some side hustles when I was on leave as well, you know the type, security and some stuff I can't exactly put on a CV. Worth every minute."

Evelyn's gaze softened. "You never really talk about your family."

He shrugged, eyes on the deck. "Didn't want them in the crosshairs. Didn't want you in them either."

She nudged his boot with hers. "Bit late for that, Paladin."

When he looked back at her, she was already launching into her own story about Liverpool, the council estate where everyone knew everyone's business, sneaking into pubs at fifteen, and learning to fight in a boxing gym because it was easier than crying when the world kicked her.

"Lived in a flat over a chippy," she said with a grin. "Whole place smelt like salt and vinegar. Mum used to joke I'd come out of the womb with batter in my hair."

James chuckled. "Explains a lot."

They kept talking for hours, not the way operatives swap Intel, but like two people peeling away layers they'd been holding onto for years. The flight was hours long, but it didn't feel like it.

By the time the cabin lights dimmed further, their shoulders were pressed together, not quite by accident anymore. Every so often she caught his eyes flicking to her profile in the half-light, and instead of deflecting with a quip, she let him look. Let him see.

For once, there was no battlefield between them. Just the steady drone of the engines, the weight of the dark sky outside, and the quiet pull of something neither of them was ready to name, yet both of them felt.

The drone of the engines was almost hypnotic; most of the soldiers around them had long since fallen asleep. James leaned back against the cold bulkhead, one knee brushing hers. Evelyn slipped one AirPod out and offered it without a word.

The Killers kicked in with *Hot Fuss*, the opening chords of *Mr. Brightside*.

They mouthed the lyrics silently, careful not to wake anyone.

By the second chorus they were grinning, shoulders shaking with suppressed laughter. When the bridge hit, Evelyn noticed the way he kept rolling his neck like something was bothering him.

She leaned closer, her breath warm at his ear. "You wanna learn a secret?"

James arched a brow, that ghost of a smile tugging at his mouth.

She held out her hands. "Shield me."

Curious, he leaned in, his broad frame blocking her from view of the rows. He watched as she closed her eyes, focused, and then her fingertips glowed, faint and blue, like moonlight trapped under skin.

She pressed them lightly against the tense muscle at the base of his neck. The warmth of her touch carried a subtle hum, like distant electricity. Heat spread through him, chasing the ache down his spine until it dissolved into nothing.

His eyes widened a fraction, but he didn't move away.

When she finally pulled back, with the glow fading, she flashed a cheeky grin. "Cool, huh? You're the only one who knows I can do that. It's why I don't get hangovers. Why my back healed. That plate they put in? Didn't do shit. I fixed it myself."

James just stared at her, absolutely stunned into silence for a moment, that rare softness breaking through. "My god, Ev... That's magic. And I promise, I'll keep it that way. But... the whole time we've been away, you haven't shimmered once. Not once."

Her smile faltered, just slightly. "Ironically, it's probably 'cause I felt safe. I knew what I was doing. And I had the best man covering me."

He shook his head, almost disbelieving. "Can you feel landmines like you do biotech weapons?"

She exhaled a quiet laugh. "No. They're too old. Dead tech."

He studied her like she was something he'd never be able to categorise. "You're magic. Or inhuman. Or both."

Evelyn leaned back against the bulkhead, close enough that their shoulders brushed. "Yeah," she said softly. "Tell me something I don't know."

Evelyn nodded off not long after, with her head resting lightly against his shoulder, her AirPod still in. James sat there with the other one in his ear, letting the last tracks roll through while the low cabin lights painted her face in soft gold.

But he couldn't stop thinking about that blue light.

Not just what it was, whatever strange, impossible thing lived under her skin. But what it meant that she'd shown him. Evelyn Blackthorn didn't give away pieces of herself for free. She guarded them like classified Intel, and most people didn't even know the vault existed.

Tonight, she'd handed him a key.

He shifted slightly, careful not to wake her, pulling the blanket higher over her shoulders. His eyes traced the faint scar along her temple and the steady rise and fall of her breathing, and something deep in his chest tightened like a wire pulled taut.

This wasn't just about missions anymore.

It wasn't just about having her on his team.

He thought about all the times in the past year she'd slipped out of reach, wrapped herself in barbed jokes to keep people at a distance. And now here she was, sleeping against him like he was the safest place in the world.

James wasn't sure what the hell he'd done to earn that kind of trust, but he knew one thing with absolute clarity: he was never going to lose it.

Not now.

Not ever.

He leaned his head against hers, letting the hum of the engines drown out everything else, and he surrendered to the exhaustion running deep in his bones. Somewhere in the quiet, the decision settled inside him, solid, unshakeable: if she wanted all in for life, so did he.

Chapter 28

The C-17's wheels screamed against the tarmac, with dawn bleeding across the Virginia sky in streaks of orange and pink. Soldiers filed out in silence, their boots crunching on the frost and their shoulders slumped with exhaustion.

Evelyn stretched, her cap pulled low and her hair sticking out at wild angles.

"You look like hell," James murmured as they walked side by side across the airstrip.

She smirked. "Good thing I don't get paid for my looks then."

The quiet between them wasn't defensive anymore. It was easy. Warm. The kind that didn't need filling.

Inside Obsidian HQ, Mack was already in the Ops chair, with a fresh coffee steaming in his hand. His eyes flicked over them with their matching pace, relaxed shoulders, and the subtle smile Evelyn didn't even try to hide.

"Well, look at you two," he drawled. "Guess Death Valley's good for something after all."

Evelyn raised a brow. "Not even gonna ask if we made it back in one piece?"

"Don't have to." Mack tipped his mug in a lazy toast. "I can see it."

James just shook his head, but there was no bite in it. "No debrief. Three weeks in the dirt earns us seventy-two hours off."

They didn't head for the barracks. James slung his pack higher and led her to the lot. No questions needed to be asked, there was no hesitation. She already knew the answer.

By the time they reached his place, the sun was climbing higher with light spilling through the blinds. Evelyn dropped her bag by the door, kicked her boots off, and padded inside like she'd been there a hundred times before.

"You know," she said, sinking into the couch, "if every mission was like that, I might actually stick around."

"That sounded dangerously like commitment."

She smirked. "Guess you're growing on me."

He sat beside her, her hand finding his without her looking.

"Good," he murmured. "I was hoping I was."

They collapsed onto his bed, with their boots gone and jackets abandoned. Evelyn curled against his chest, his heartbeat steady beneath her ear. The weight of the world eased off in the quiet—until her pack buzzed faintly against the floor.

She reached lazily for it, the burner phone screen glowing pale blue. Normally she'd leave the room. This time she didn't. She unlocked it right in front of him.

One new message.

You did good, kids.

Evelyn huffed a laugh. "Ghost."

James raised a brow. "Yeah?"

She tilted the phone so he could see. "Yeah."

For a long beat, they just looked at it together. There was so little written, yet it carried the weight of everything unsaid. Evelyn set the phone aside, her eyes falling shut again with utter exhaustion, her hand stilled on his chest like she was anchoring herself to him. Then a small smile tugged at her lips.

"You know," James murmured, raw with fatigue and warm, "for a guy who's supposed to be a ghost, he's got a hell of a way of showing up."

"Mm." She didn't open her eyes. "Guess I'm not the only one who looks out for you. I think he knows I love you."

The air shifted, it was no longer heavy with questions and distrust. Now the air was full of trust and respect. The room cocooned them with the promise of safety and grounding, the atmosphere felt settled. She had trusted him with everything. And James knew he would never let it slip.

He leaned his forehead against hers. "Then I guess I'd better not fuck it up."

Her smile widened, whisper soft.

"Guess you'd better not."

Later that night the firepit popped and spat sparks into the warm Virginia night. Mack crouched over it like an orchestra conductor, coaxing the flames higher. Smoke curled up through his garden, with the aroma sharp and sweet.

James and Evelyn wandered in from the house, hand in hand. No tension. No sharp edges. Just an ease you couldn't fake.

Irish spotted it instantly, mid-swig from his beer.

"What the fuck happened to you two? You look… disturbingly civilised."

Evelyn smirked, stealing his bottle. "We've ascended."

"To what?" AJ asked from his perch on the deck rail. "Smug coupledom?"

"Enlightenment." Her reply was deadpan. She took a swig.

Mack tossed a log onto the fire. "More like she's finally house-trained him."

"Oi," James pointed at him. "I was always house-trained."

"Mi amego", Bullet cut in, grinning, "You didn't even own matching plates until Ev moved back."

"That's strategy," James shot back. "Less to wash."

The laughter rolled easily across the yard.

Selena drifted in behind them, pressing a kiss to the top of each of their heads. "You both look happy."

Evelyn's grin softened. "We are."

Selena squeezed her shoulders and moved off. James and Evelyn shared a glance that said they didn't need to explain a damn thing.

Frost, guitar across his lap, started picking. "Enough soppy shit. Bass, Blackthorn. Prove you haven't gone soft."

Evelyn dropped into a chair, taking the battered bass. She tuned it with a twist of her wrist. "You remember how to play The Chain?"

The iconic bassline hit, and the firepit exploded into chaos. AJ drummed on a crate, Bullet danced like a man possessed, and

243

Mack slapped the side of the cooler for rhythm. Evelyn belted out lyrics, with her bass guitar resting on her lap, laughing through her best Stevie Nicks impression. James didn't take his eyes off her once.

By the final chorus, she was grinning so wide her cheeks hurt. The fire roared bright, faces bathed in flickering gold. Smoke. Music. The kind of contentment that only came when no one had anywhere else to be.

Evelyn leaned back, bass still in hand, cheeks flushed. James sprawled next to her, his arm over her chair and fingers brushing her shoulder like it was muscle memory.

Then he gave her that quiet look. The one she could read without a word. She nodded. Handed the bass back to Frost. They stood together.

"Right," James said, stretching. "We're calling it."

That was all it took.

Irish pointed with his beer. "Aye, there it is!"

Bullet clutched his chest in mock agony. "The domestication of Paladin! Tragic!"

AJ hopped down from the railing. "It's like a nature documentary… the alpha pair breaking away from the pack to, y'know… mate."

"Christ, AJ," Mack groaned, but he was grinning. "About bloody time. You two circled each other for years. Sharks in heat. Glad you stopped trying to kill each other to establish dominance."

Selena smirked over her glass. "Guess we'll need noise-cancelling headphones at HQ now."

Frost, still tuning his guitar, didn't even glance up. "Told you all. It'd happen after a firepit night. No more one-offs followed by cage fights."

The chorus of whistles, cackles, and cheers chased them across the yard. Evelyn laughed so hard she nearly tripped on the decking, James catching her hand to steady her.

By the time the front door shut behind them, the firepit was still roaring with laughter.

Chapter 29

Obsidian HQ buzzed with the low hum of machines and boots drumming across concrete. The briefing room screens glared white-blue, spilling grainy satellite images of a snow-dusted compound across the table.

Selena tapped the display, zooming in on a rusted perimeter fence half-buried in frost.

"Ex-Revenant facility. Aegis Consortium has been linked to movement there. Officially decommissioned three years ago. Unofficially? Someone's squatting in the comms wing. Power grid's live. Encrypted chatter on low-bandwidth channels."

"Which means," AJ said, leaning on the table, "either someone's recycling old code... or they've got something worth guarding."

James stood at the head of the table with his arms folded, his gaze hard. "We're not leaving it standing. Two objectives: Intel and demolition. Comms wing gets stripped—drives, servers, anything that hums—and comes home with us. Then we flatten the place."

He split the map into two sectors with a swipe.

"Team One: Selena, AJ, Bullet. You're with me. We breach comms, pull hardware, sweep for hidden storage. Team Two..."

His eyes didn't move on. They held steady. On her.

Evelyn.

She leaned back in her chair, calm but sharp, surprise flickering across her face.

"You're running it," James said. "Frost, Mack, Irish. You're with her. Perimeter control, outer sweep, and plant the charges. Make sure we've got a clean exit."

For a second, the room held its breath. No doubt. Obsidian didn't doubt. It was recognition. James Reaves didn't hand over half a mission lightly, not on a Revenant site.

Evelyn's brow arched. "That's you letting go of the leash, Paladin."

"That's me trusting you to hold the line." His voice was steady, sure.

Her lips curved, just a fraction. "Then I'll hold it."

Mack let out a low whistle. "Well, shit. Guess we're in the big leagues tonight."

The tension broke. Chairs scraped back. Boots hit the floor. Banter sparked as the team split. But under it all ran a new current. Evelyn wasn't just on the mission. She was running half of it. And James had just made damn sure everyone knew.

The hum of HQ sharpened into the rhythm of metal on metal, Velcro ripping, and zippers closing. The armoury lit up with motion.

Evelyn pulled her plate carrier on in one smooth move, slotting mags like she'd never stopped. Frost checked detonators, and Mack racked his rifle with a heavy clack.

"You know," Mack said, glancing at her, "if you fuck this up, we're all gonna die."

Evelyn smirked, adjusting a strap. "Good thing I don't fuck up, then."

247

Across the room, James's half of the team moved faster and tighter. Selena stacked shockproof cases, and AJ hunched over a portable rig, fingers flying. Bullet spun a suppressed pistol in lazy circles until James's voice cut sharp:

"Save the tricks for the bad guys, Zavala."

Bullet grinned, holstering with a flourish. "Yes, Dad."

Two blades, honed for different cuts, one heavy, one fast.

At the bay doors, James paused long enough to press a comm bead into Evelyn's hand.

"Channel three for me. Keep me updated."

She brushed his fingers on purpose as she slipped it in. "You'll hear me before you see me."

His look was half-warning, half-pride. "Good. I want the bastards to hear you coming."

Engines roared. One convoy peeled for the perimeter, the other for the heart of the compound.

In the back of her truck, Evelyn checked her rifle, glanced at Frost and Mack, and grinned.

"Alright, boys. Let's go hold the line."

The Alaskan night bit deep, with the wind cutting through the treeline as Evelyn led her unit down toward the valley. The facility crouched in the snow like a carcass left to rot, half-buried, half-awake. Light pulsed faintly from the comms wing windows, pale and sickly, like breath fogging from a corpse.

"Intel says minimal guards," Frost whispered, scanning through glass. His tone was low, too low, like the trees might listen.

Evelyn lowered her binoculars, her mouth set tight. "And I say Intel doesn't smell the air. This place isn't dead. It's feeding. North side… roving pairs. South side? Footprints. Too many."

Mack shifted his rifle, shoulders bunched. "Think Paladin's picked it up yet?"

Her jaw flexed. "He'll know soon enough. Question is if he's still breathing when he does."

Inside the comms wing, James's team breached clean. Disturbingly clean. The hall was stripped bare, no echo, no dust. And then the shadows moved.

The first burst of gunfire wasn't from a rifle; it was from something deeper. A staccato rattle, guttural, like bone splitting against steel. Figures spilt from the corners and shadows, creatures with armor half-welded to their flesh, their helmets fused into skulls, and eyes burning with chemical glow.

Selena dived behind a console, hissing curses as sparks rained down. Bullet snapped off two rounds, dropping one of them, but when it hit the ground, it didn't stop moving. The finger clawed through the tiles, dragging its body forward until a second shot blew out what was left of its head.

"Where the hell did these come from?!" AJ whispered into the comms, shoving the decryption rig across the floor toward cover.

"Doesn't matter," James growled, blade-edge sharp. "Oracle… get the drive. Rook… keep it breathing. We hold, or we don't leave."

Then the comms lit with static, his voice breaking across the tree line like thunder:

"Paladin to Valkyrie… Multiple hostiles, Revenant class. We're compromised. Need support now."

Evelyn didn't wait. "Zero. Grim. With me. We burn this place down. Wrath stay here cover us, casualties are probable."

Snow churned red where James dropped down hard, a deafening crack split the night as a round tore into his side. He didn't fall clean; he twisted, with his body shielding AJ instinctively. James dragged him into cover as more creatures immerged with their claws scraping through metal just inches away.

Evelyn rounded the breach, with her shots destroying any threats, then her heart stopped.

James was down, firing one-handed, his blood pooling dark into the snow. AJ crouched behind him, wide-eyed, as something crawled through the smoke with its jaw unhinged, its teeth were metal, and its chest glowing like a furnace that refused to die.

"Cover me!" Evelyn commed, she advanced with her rifel singing, as she sprinted through the fire. She was engulfed with bullets, sparks, claws, but it didn't matter. She slammed down beside her paladin, pressing her hand hard against his side. "You stubborn son of a…"

"Get him out," Paladin rasped, voice breaking. "Save our AJ."

"You're delusional if you think I'm leaving you." She hauled him up, ignoring the tremor in his frame.

Frost and Mack stormed in, with their rifles cracking, muzzle flashes lighting glimpses of nightmares stitched from dead flesh. The air reeked of copper and decay, the smoke thick with the stink of meat that never should've lived.

Evelyn dragged James step by step through the churn, with her boots slipping in blood and ice.

"Valkyrie, go…I'll cover!" Frost snapped, his rifle barking controlled fury.

"Copy, Zero," Evelyn spat, shoving James into Mack's grip. "Get him to the LZ. That's an order."

James's hand shot up, locking on her wrist with an iron grip despite the blood slicking his fingers. "Valkyrie…"

She leaned in, fierce, eyes burning. "Trust me."

Then she was gone.

The halls inside stank of things long dead. Bodies were suspended frozen upright against the walls, with dirty tubes still feeding into them. One stirred when she passed, its jaw twitching, eyes rolling white. The noise from its shattered jaw sounded like twisted agony. Evelyn didn't look twice; she put two rounds through its skull and kept moving.

She moved with stealth as she planted charges at every load-bearing beam she could reach. Her hands were steady, but her heart pounded, not from fear, but from the sound of movement behind her. Too many. Too close.

She felt her body ignite, blue pulses ripped up her body making her movements quicker, her eyes sharpened and she could see with enhanced clarity through the dust and smoke. Every sense heightened as she felt something rip through her, evolving her into the creatures equals. Fast. Strong. Violent. One creature lunged out of the dark, with its mouth full of shattered glass. She dropped low with inhuman speed, and fired point-blank, it fold backward and melted into the metal floor. Her last charge was locked in. Her fingers flew as the timer primed.

Evelyn sprinted, with inhuman speed.

The facility screamed around her. The walls shuddered as if the building itself knew what she'd done. She broke through the final door, stumbled into the snow, and slammed the detonator.

The earth split around her. A wall of fire roared upward, swallowing the complex in a bloom of light and bone. The shockwave rolled over the valley, scattering snow and smoke like ash from a burning grave.

When the haze cleared, James was there. Pale. Bleeding. Upright. But barely. His arm was locked painfully over Mack's shoulder while Irish patched him with hands slick in red. His eyes locked on hers like nothing else existed.

"You're insane," he rasped, voice shredded raw.

Evelyn dropped to a crouch in front of him, lightning disappearing from her veins, her hair damp with sweat, and with blood streaking her cheek. She grinned like the devil herself.

"Yeah," she said. "But you're alive. And I just buried their fucking ghosts."

Six hours later, Obsidian HQ smelt of antiseptic and smoke.

James sat on the edge of the medbay cot, with his shirt peeled halfway down, fresh stitches glaring against the torn skin at his ribs. He wasn't looking at the wound. He wasn't even looking at the medic scribbling notes at the terminal. He was staring at the floor, rage coursing through his body, his fists braced against his thighs.

Evelyn leaned against the doorway, still in half-melted snow gear, with streaks of soot and blood smeared on her cheek. She'd washed her hands, but blood still clung beneath her nails. She didn't speak at first, just watched him breathe like each inhale was another battle he might lose.

"You're supposed to be in bed," she said at last, her voice softer than she meant it to be.

His eyes lifted, sharp, cutting right through her. "You went back in."

She folded her arms, feigning nonchalance. "You were bleeding out."

"That's not the damn point, Ev." He pushed upright, the movement dragging a wince out of him, though he bit it back like he'd rather choke than show it. "You had a clean exit. My team was clear. And you still ran back into a collapsing hellhole full of monsters."

Her boots scraped against the floor as she crossed to him, her chin held high, not flinching from the storm in his eyes. "Because the job wasn't finished. Because if I hadn't gone, someone else would've, and they wouldn't have come out. Did you not see

253

them, James? The concept is no longer a concept. Those weren't people anymore. They were weapons. Breathing prototypes for an army. If I'd left them standing, the consortium would have their assets, and we'd all be corpses next winter."

His voice cracked low and dangerous. "I know what I saw. But whatever the hell we're walking into, you never slow down because of me. And you never go dark on me again."

That hit harder than a shout.

She froze, with her breath caught, because the edge in his voice wasn't command. It was fear.

James leaned forward, elbows digging into his knees, his eyes burning into hers. "You think I didn't hear you drop off comms? Thirty-eight seconds, Ev. Thirty-eight seconds where your voice wasn't there. Do you have any idea what that did to me?"

Her throat tightened, but she forced a smirk anyway, armor laced with defiance. "Yeh I lit up… it blew the coms out. I was quick Jamie, and strong… they had no chance against me. And as if I'd ever leave you behind, soft lad. And that place had to be blown sky-high. End of."

His hand flexed at his side, the tremor betraying him. "You finish it, fine. But you don't make me stand there and listen to you vanish while you do it."

They were toe-to-toe now. She could see the fury in his eyes, but underneath it, a crack. The part of him that was shaking.

Her mouth twitched, caught between a smirk and the tremble she didn't want him to see. "You're really wrecking your whole broody-commander thing right now, you know that?"

"Good," he muttered, and before she could fire back, he hauled her into him. His arms locked around her like he was afraid physics might steal her if he let go.

Her cheek pressed to his chest. Beneath the sweat and smoke, his heartbeat thundered steady and unyielding. She closed her eyes, letting it anchor her.

"Next time," he murmured into her hair, rough and low, "we both walk out. Or neither of us goes in."

Her lips curved faintly against his chest where he couldn't see. "Deal," she whispered.

But they would break that rule if it meant saving the others life.

She leaned into him tentatively, with her arms loose around his shoulders, the medbay thick with antiseptic and humming air vents.

"I've got..." she murmured, teasing around the edges, "...five weeks left on my Obsidian contract." She tipped her head back just enough to catch his eye. "What you gonna do without me, Paladin?"

His mouth curved, but his stare was iron. "Not happening."

Her brow arched. "Not happening?"

"You think I'm letting you walk after this?" He caught her hand, rough and firm. "Five weeks, five years, you're still here. With me."

"Big talk, commander," she said, her voice stayed low, but there was a crack of vulnerability within it.

"Not talk," he muttered.

255

Before she could answer, she kissed him quick and sharp, then leaned back with a smirk. "Seven years you've been nagging me to go permanent. Offer still on the table?"

His frown deepened with suspicion flickering before she dropped it, flat and sure:

"I want to stay. With the team. With you."

He stared at her, with his throat working, then he cupped her face like he didn't trust his own hands. "Ev, I'd take you any way I could get you."

She glanced around and shifted her body to block the nearest camera. "Hold still."

"Ev…"

Her fingers lit faint blue, pressing against his wound. A low hum ran through him, his pain started dissolving, while every muscle knitted beneath her touch.

He hissed out a breath, his eyes sharp. "The hell was that?"

"Something I can do. Something no one sees. I can heal more than just my own pain and your muscle aches." Her mouth twisted. "And for whatever reason, it only works on you."

Silence. His jaw flexed. "If the wrong people…"

"They won't," she cut in, reassuringly steady. "Only you know."

His gaze locked with hers; no argument was left. Just a nod. "Then I'm taking that secret to my grave."

She smirked, brushing grime off his cheek. "Not letting you die. Not until we're old and shouting at grandkids."

Her words hit him like a shot. They didn't talk about the future. The future was not a given didn't dare tempt fate with such hope. Not normally.

He covered it with a crooked grin. "Grandkids, huh? Planning on outliving me?"

"No, James." Her voice sharpened. "Planning on us surviving. Together."

That made him falter, with his grip tightening at her hip. "You don't say things like that."

"Guess I just did."

The world shrank down to her breath, his heartbeat under her palm. He pressed his forehead to hers, voice gravelly. "Mean it, Ev."

"I've never meant anything more."

His hand slid to her jaw, his thumb brushed her mouth. "Come here."

She did. The kiss wasn't battle-born, it wasn't desperate. It was raw, unguarded. A vow.

When they broke apart, she smiled faintly. "So… old and grandkids?"

His grin cracked through. "Yeah, Blackthorn. That's the mission."

Chapter 30

The Forge common room was all hum and low chatter until Evelyn strode in, James at her back. Her boots were heavy, with dirt and ash still streaking her field kit, her hair yanked into a knot that had half fallen out. She stopped dead centre, with her thumbs hooked in her vest straps.

"I'm staying," she said, calm and clipped. "No more contracts. Obsidian's it. I'm yours."

The silence fell just for a heartbeat.

Then Bullet detonated.

"WHAT—holy fuck! Mack, get tequila, champagne, a smoke machine, something! This is history!" He bolted toward the kitchen, doubled back, pointing both hands at her. "T-shirts. No… tattoos. Foreheads. Someone hold her down."

Mack barked a raw and rough laugh, then sauntered over and ruffled her hair. "About bloody time, kid. Thought we'd have to chain you up to keep you."

Irish didn't even hesitate… He grabbed her off the floor in a bear hug that made her yelp. "Knew it! One of us. Always were."

Before her boots touched the ground, AJ launched at her like a missile, with his arms locked tight.

"Finally! Do you know how many bribes I paid just to keep you around? Do you?!"

"Two, and they were shit bribes!" Bullet yelled from the kitchen, like a child who had devoured a Red Bull.

Selena glided in, calm and glowing, pressing kisses to both her cheeks. "Welcome home, sister," she said warmly, squeezing her shoulders.

Frost came last with no words, just a brutal slap between her shoulder blades and a mutter: "'Bout time."

Evelyn stood in the middle of it, chaos erupting around her, a smirk tugging at her lips. "Alright, alright… Calm the fuck down. Someone's gotta keep you idiots alive. Might as well be me."

"Bullshit," Bullet crowed, reappearing with a half-empty tequila bottle. "We are going out! You're buying the first round; that's the tax for finally admitting you love us!"

"Tax?" Mack snorted. "Nah… initiation. She's gotta beat Bullet at pool. Loser shaves their head."

"Oi!" Bullet yelped, clutching his hair. "That's slander!"

Irish pointed his mug at her, grinning wide. "She'll thrash him. Worth it just to watch."

James? He was still in the doorway, arms folded, with a quiet grin tucked under the storm like he'd known this would happen all along.

Irish hauled James back by the wrist as he stepped out of the war room into the low hum of the corridor. "Oi! You got shot. You need to be in bed, Commander." The words were half-order, half-plea.

James hesitated and looked like he had been caught out. "No. I'm fine. Surface scratch."

"Bullshit," Irish snapped. "It was deep. I treated you on sight. Back to medical."

Slowly, like he was showing a relic, James lifted his top. There was no fresh wound, only a pale, puckered scar running like a seam across his ribs. The light caught it and made it look impossible. "How the fuck... did Red do that?" His voice was small and stunned.

Irish's hands trembled for a second, not with fear, but disbelief. "Right. I'll scrub the medical reports, wipe them clean." He swallowed and looked at James properly, the medic's calm broken by something else. "James, this is... this is incredible."

James closed his eyes for one beat. "I know. I'm lucky to have her. Promise me you'll say nothing."

Irish straightened, shoulders square. "It's Ev. I'll guard her with my life."

In the club the bass didn't just hit, it punched through bone. Trance music cracked open the floor, with strobes splitting the dark into shards of silver and smoke. The crowd was one organism, moving, screaming the lyrics like gospel.

Evelyn had ditched her boots for black leather heels, with her hair down and eyes lined in gold dust that caught every flash. Bullet didn't even give her a chance to breathe; he hauled her straight into the pit, with AJ sliding in at her back with a grin sharp enough to cut glass.

In the crush of bodies, the three of them became their own storm. Bullet locked her hips to his, nose to nose, grinning like the devil's favorite son just got a hall pass. Evelyn curled her arms around his neck, swaying into him, matching chaos for chaos.

260

AJ's hand slid against the small of her back, his other fist punching the air as the bass rattled the walls. Together they moved like a pack. They were wild, lawless, untouchable. Evelyn was laughing, with her head tipped back, onto AJ's shoulders, her hair whipping free like the music itself had claimed her soul.

Across the floor, Selena and Frost were a different fire. Selena leaned back seductively into him, her wrists caught in his hands, her hips rolling slowly and deliberate as the beat burnt through them. Frost bent to murmur against her ear; whatever he said made her laugh, her head tipping, his eyes locked on her like she was the only thing alive. The shadow and the mystic belonged together, as clear as night and day.

And above it all, the balcony was command central. James stood with his sleeves rolled, watching with the quiet intensity of a soldier off duty but never off guard. Mack lounged with a beer; Irish was already shouting over his second whisky; the three of them were kings over a kingdom of noise.

Irish lifted his glass toward the chaos below, his voice like thunder over the track:

"The Queen is dead!"

Mack and James didn't miss a beat. They roared back in unison, the balcony shaking with it:

"LONG LIVE THE QUEEN!"

Down below, Evelyn spun under Bullet's arm, AJ catching her on the turn, her laughter cutting through the beat.

"Never leve us again sister." AJ beathed the words more like a vow than a question.

She Kissed his cheek then glanced up at the balcony and caught the eyes of the steely entourage and playfully flipped them off without breaking stride.

The crowd swallowed her whole again, a living myth written in strobes and sweat.

By the time they stumbled into Mack's, the night hadn't lost a drop of heat.

The fridge had been raided. Rum was flowing like water. The speakers in the corner were blaring Mr Brightside loud enough to rattle the cupboards.

The kitchen was packed to the rafters. AJ was standing up on a chair, fists pumping in the air, screaming every lyric. Bullet had Selena were spinning in a dizzy blur; Frost bent double with laughter as beer sloshed down his sleeve. Mack leaned against the counter, grinning, letting the chaos burn itself alive inside his four walls.

And right in the middle. James and Evelyn.

They weren't dancing anymore, not really. His hands stayed locked low on her hips. Hers hooked possessively around his neck. They were kissing eachother like it was oxygen. Messy, hungry, like they were still twenty and drunk in some dive bar, nothing left but want.

The chorus his … Evelyn broke just enough to mouth the words against his lips, with her wicked grin flashing, before dragging him back down. He laughed unapologetically into her mouth, spun her sloppily so her back hit the counter, and kissed her like the world outside didn't exist.

Irish sauntered past them, smirking. "Christ, get a room, you two."

"Already in one," James shot back without looking up.

The kitchen howled as they watched their commander. This was the man who grew up thinking that everyone would leave him eventually. This was the man who never let himself hope for something as pure and beautiful as being unconditionally loved. But her he was, being wrapped in adoration from the love of his life. And it was beautiful.

"Jesus," Frost muttered, shaking his head. "I miss the days when he was brooding, not acting like a lovesick teenager."

"You're a fine one to talk!" James shot back without a beat.

The music rolled on, louder, dirtier.

Bullet grabbed Evelyn's bass from the corner, hammering out 'Seven Nation Army', weven though he didn't know the cords. AJ turned the table into a drum kit and commandeered chopsticks to hit the beat, They eventually snook off for a phone call that left his face smitten. Evelyn cheered him on, still tangled in James's arms, her hair a riotous crown from hours of dancing.

Selena and Frost claimed a corner by the pantry, her head tipped back, laughing at something he whispered low, his forehead nearly pressed to hers.

Irish held court by the fridge, retelling some battlefield crawl with enough arm-flailing to knock over half the glassware. Mack just played traffic control. He was refilling drinks, cramming crisps into hands, and cracking windows when the air got too hot. Every so often, he'd catch James's eye across the chaos and give him a nod. She's home now. She's safe.

And still, in the center, James and Evelyn.

They hadn't let go since the club. His hand anchored at the small of her back, the other brushing hair from her face. They weren't just kissing, they were speaking in kisses. Slow ones between verses. Quick ones when the beat surged. Laughing into each other's mouths.

At one point, she leaned up and whispered something that made his eyes go sharp and his laugh drop low and dangerous. The kind of sound that promised trouble later. Bullet caught it, grinning like a devil.

"Oi! At least warn us before you fog up the windows."

Evelyn threw her head back, laughed, and pulled James back in, her fists curling tight in his shirt.

No one stopped them.

No one wanted to.

Because it wasn't just drunk kissing in a crowded kitchen.

It was proof. Proof they'd lived, proof they'd made it home, proof that for one rare night, the war could wait outside.

Chapter 31

James's Townhouse wasn't quiet anymore.

There was always music: vinyl crackling, something old and raw, or Evelyn barefoot in the kitchen, with her hair down, swaying like she had a secret only the beat could hear. Laughter lived here now, like dust in the corners. And he hated how much he needed it.

It started small. A sketchbook, battered, sitting on the coffee table where kitbags were usually dumped. He flipped it open out of habit and found faces, hands, places he knew. His places. Her pencil caught them like ghosts. She didn't flinch when he looked.

"Better than therapy," she muttered. "Costs less too."

He didn't argue. He just sat back, unsettled, because he couldn't remember the last time someone had left pieces of themselves lying around like they weren't planning on leaving.

Then the new record player, replacing his cheep one that barely worked. One evening it was just there, the needle dropping before he could question it. She pressed a sleeve into his hands.

"You need something to play this on. Don't wreck it, it's original."

The Clash filled the room, jagged and alive. That night they drank on the floor until two in the morning, laughing at nothing. And he thought, 'Christ, she's going to ruin me.'

The clothes came next. A plastic container shoved by the wardrobe. It contained folded T-shirts and vintage jeans, worn memories from her youth. She never asked for space, she was far

265

too stubborn for that. But later, when fatigue hit her and she was out cold on his sofa, he built her a drawer. Cleared half his wardrobe. No note, no fuss. Just… space.

The next morning she froze dead.

"You cleared your wardrobe."

"Needed the space."

Her face shifted, softer than he'd ever seen it. And something in his chest gave way.

After that, the invasion was steady. Crystals glinting on the bedside table. Her blanket, the lucky red Liverpool one she carried through warzones, was draped over his sofa like it was claiming territory. The way she rewired his nights without trying: sitting beside him, sketching while he worked; reading over his shoulder, marking typos in his reports with smug little notes; or, on the bad nights, cooking tea like she had always belonged here, calling it 'tea' like only someone from Liverpool would. He stopped correcting her. He liked knowing her language.

The final blow came on a Sunday. He was pulling on his boots when she handed him a shopping list. Paper crumpled, doodles scrawled in the margins, a lopsided heart at the bottom.

"Anything else?" he asked.

"Yeah. Tampons."

No hesitation. No shame. Just handed him her need like it was nothing. And right then, he knew.

This wasn't his flat anymore.

It was theirs.

She'd carved herself into the walls, into the silence, into him. No speeches. No asking. Just existing until he couldn't imagine her not being here.

And he was done pretending he didn't want it. He was done pretending he wasn't already hers.

Five months later, their lives had found a rhythm: missions that broke them down, nights that pieced them back together. His flat had become the refuge in between, with records spinning low and food cooking slow. It wasn't peace, not really, but it was as close as either of them ever got.

Then came the night fate shoved him forward.

HQ was heavy with the drag of a post-op comedown adrenalin. Evelyn sat hunched at one of the long tables, scrolling on her phone, with her eyes focused and her jaw tight with stress. The team circled her, all talking at once trying to help her with her predicament.

"No, not that one," AJ said, craning over her shoulder. "Too much traffic. You'd lose your mind in a week. You would never get rest after a mission. Mamma needs her sleep"

"Not there either," Bullet added. "Street's known for dealing. The hard stuff. You'd hate it."

Evelyn blew out a sharp breath. "Fuck… there's got to be something I can afford."

Selena slid a mug of tea in front of her, her fingers gently brushing her back. "We'll sort it. I've got a spare room."

"Mine's bigger," Mack offered casually, leaning against the table.

That was when James walked in, peeling off his gloves, his eyes narrowing at the huddle. "What's this impromptu operations meeting about?"

"Landlord's selling her place," Bullet answered for her. "She's got to move."

Evelyn muttered without looking up, "Fuck it. I'll go back to barracks until I sort it."

The word hit him like a dart in his chest. Barracks. Like she hadn't spent months making his space her own. Like she wasn't already home.

Mack's eyes flicked knowingly to his for a second, silent and heavy with meaning. You know what you need to do.

James didn't reply instead he just pulled his jacket back on and left HQ without a word of explanation.

Evelyn barely noticed him go. She was still absorbed in her scrolling, still cursing rent.

Half an hour later, the door swung open. James's boots hit the floor heavy but steady. He didn't stop to speak to anyone, he was far to nervous for small talk. He made a b line straight to her, stopped behind her chair, and let something metal fall onto the table.

A key. Silver, with a red ring glinting under the strip lights.

"You've got a home if you want it," His voice came out calm, but his chest was tight, his hand flexing loosely at his side. "You practically live with me anyway."

The room went still. The air felt loaded, all eyes were watching Evelyn, the one who never stayed anywhere too long, who lived out of kitbags and safehouses, now confront the one thing she'd never let herself have: permanence.

She lifted her eyes slowly, locking onto his. Her voice was soft, but it cut straight through him in a way he never expected.

"Is this what you want?"

His breath stuck. Because he knew what she was asking wasn't about space or walls or drawers. It was about the future. It was about the line between survival and belonging.

He thought about the sketchbook left on his coffee table. The records she'd slipped into his shelves. The blanket with '*You'll Never Walk Alone*' stitched across it. The crystals are on her bedside. The way her laughter had soaked into his walls until the place felt alive.

He thought about how, before her, his flat had been four walls and silence. And now it was a home. He thought about how for the first time in his life he welcomed the evenings, looked forward to down time and loved the silliness she brought into his world.

"Yes," he said, steady, certain. "If you're happy, then I'm happy, Ev. Even with your millions of plants."

For a moment she didn't move. Didn't blink. The air was thick with it. Then her mouth twitched, with the faintest ghost of a smile, and she slipped the key into her pocket like she was just humouring him.

But everyone in the room knew better.

She was his now. And he'd never let her go.

The choice had been made.

269

Two days later, James was hauling the third box up the stairs, muttering under his breath about "three bloody outfits" somehow multiplying into half a greenhouse.

Evelyn followed with a laundry basket, smirking. "You said make it home, Paladin. Don't whinge when the jungle arrives."

He shot her a look over his shoulder. "One more fern and I'm charging the fucking thing rent."

"Then I'm charging you for emotional labour, I should be getting overtime now. Listening to you moan." she fired back, brushing past him into the townhouse like she'd always lived there.

They started with the shelves. The old planks he'd had for years but never had reason to hang. She steadied them while he drilled, and when he muttered something about "bloody crooked studs", she snorted.

"You know, for a soldier, your lines are shit."

"Careful, or you'll be hanging off them when they collapse."

But when the books went up, she didn't just place them, she claimed the space. *Gatsby. Fight Club. Animal Farm.* Dog-eared, warped, with covers bent like they'd survived wars of their own.

He picked one up, turning it over in his hands. "You read them or just use them as plant coasters?"

She rolled her eyes, sliding another into place. "They're lived in, Jamie. Like me. Battle worn and loved like you. Try not to fuck the corners."

Then she shoved two into his chest without warning: *Fight Club* and *Fear and Loathing in Las Vegas.*

270

"These ones, you will love them." she said flatly. "Take them, read them, but don't lose them, or I'll skin you."

He almost smirked, tucking them under his arm. "Figures you'd hand me a manual for your chaos."

Next came the tin. She tipped it onto the table which sent photos clattering out in a mess of corners and bent edges. Mack with a swollen black eye, grinning like an idiot. Selena passed out in a deckchair, a book sliding off her chest. Bullet crouched at a barbecue, looking like he was about to declare war on a packet of sausages.

Evelyn sifted through them quickly and sharply, pinning them to walls, frames, and corkboards like she was marking territory. Every now and then she shoved one into his hand with a muttered "that goes there", brushing his fingers like it meant nothing.

He leaned over one photo, her half-hanging out of a helicopter door, goggles pushed up, grin wide enough to split her face. "Christ. You look like a lunatic."

"I was," she said simply, pinning another shot up high. "Still am."

Some were funny enough to make him bark out a laugh; others were quieter and softer, her voice dipping low when the memory that cut too close. He didn't push, didn't ask, instead he just listened.

By the time they were done, the flat wasn't his anymore. Books were stacked, boots by the door, photos cluttering the walls like graffiti. Plants everywhere. Her everywhere.

He leaned back against the doorframe, arms folded, watching her shove the last picture into the mirror's edge.

"You've redecorated," he smiled.

She glanced over her shoulder, chin lifting, smirk curling.

"You're welcome."

By the time they were down to the last box, James figured he'd survived it all, the jungle of plants, the mountain of vinyl, and the avalanche of art supplies.

Then Evelyn heaved the final crate onto the table with a grunt.

He popped the lid.

And froze.

Inside was enough firepower to overthrow a small government. Bella and Bertie, her twin blades, gleamed on top like smug sentries. Beneath them: two custom pistols engraved with her initials and the blackbird, rows of knives, C4 bricks, detonators. This was basically a love letter to chaos and violence.

"Ev…" James blinked, dragging a hand down his face in pure disbalife. "Is there anything you don't have in here?"

She shrugged, deadpan.

"Didn't bring the grenade launcher. Didn't want you to think I was moving too fast."

He closed his eyes. "Christ almighty." Then he casually jerked his chin toward the hallway. "Come on."

She followed him, curious, until he keyed in a code on what she thought was his office wall. A hidden door hissed open.

Her eyes widened.

Inside was a cathedral of steel and wrath. Each wall was adorned with mounted weapons; every piece meticulously placed under strip lights. Rifles, sidearms, combat knives, grenades. A perfect arsenal so neatly arranged it looked like it should have its own museum plaque. And right in the centre, a swathe of empty hooks and shelves.

James gestured like it was no big deal.

"Made you some space. Figured you wouldn't be happy keeping this lot under the bed."

Evelyn stepped in slowly, reverently, her fingertips grazing a rifle barrel. "James…" She breathed it out like a prayer. "This is… obscene."

"You like it?"

"Like it?" She picked up Bella in one fluid motion, weighing the blade like it belonged in her hand. "Jamie… I'm turned on."

He huffed out a laugh, rubbing the back of his neck. "Knew it. I spend half my life trying to keep you alive, and all it takes is a tidy weapons wall to get you going."

She turned like a predator, with her dangerous eyes surveying the space. "Not just tidy. Sexy. Look at this spacing. These mounts. I've seen less precision in heart surgery."

"Ev, for fuck's sake…"

"No, really. Symmetry? Perfect. Lighting? Moody, but flattering. If you'd had this setup when we first met, I'd have jumped you two years earlier."

James pressed his lips together, trying—and failing—not to grin. He nodded at the blades in her hands.

"Ev. Why the hell are they called Bella and Bertie? Why not, I dunno, Skullcracker and Widowmaker?"

She smirked, flipping Bella with a flourish.

"They're named after the Liver Birds. Bella watches the sea; Bertie watches the city. Legend says if they ever fly away together, Liverpool floods and the world ends. Until then… they protect."

James tilted his head, taking her in, the way her fingers lingered on the hilts like they were blood and bone.

"You do realise you've just made mythical birds sound like Scouse guard dogs."

"Exactly." She smirked, sliding Bella back into place with a soft click. "My city. My rules."

James shook his head, but something warm settled in his chest. Watching her there, in his armory—their armory now—laughing, smirking, and alive. And it hit him, sudden and solid.

She wasn't just in his life.

She was his life.

Chapter 32

The flat was quiet, with Netflix droning in the background and takeaway cartons half-finished on the coffee table. Evelyn had her book open, feet tucked under her, already sinking into the kind of night that felt almost normal.

Then James's personal phone rang.

She barely glanced up until she noticed the way his head snapped up, sharp and wary. That phone never rang. He checked the screen, and just like that, his whole face softened.

"Hey, Rubes," he said, and Evelyn heard the smile in his voice from across the room.

Her book was still.

"Yeah… I am. Officially. It's Evelyn."

He leaned back in his chair, the low chuckle carrying across the flat. "Mm-hm. Yeah, we've finally got our shit together. Made it official."

Evelyn tried to read her page, but his words pulled at her.

"She's a Scouser, by the way. Proper Liverpool. Means she'll tell you your hair looks shite and then make you a brew in the same breath." His grin was audible now. "Half the time I don't know if she's flirting with me or threatening me. Sometimes both. Calls me 'Paladin' when she's taking the piss… 'Jamie' when she wants to win an argument. Which, for the record, she always does. Have you any idea how many different ways that British people use the word piss! Out on the piss, Piss taker, pissing me off, pot to piss in, pissing in the wind… yeh that means pointless, who knew!"

Ruby must've teased him, because his laugh came easy, warm and unguarded. "She'll steal my hoodie, swear it's hers, then tell me I've lost weight like she's doing me a favor. And don't even get me started on the football. Liverpool FC till she dies. I've learnt not to schedule missions on match days."

Silence for a beat. His voice dropped, softer, almost reverent.

"She's… it for me, Rubes."

The ache hit Evelyn low in her chest, dangerous and slow, the kind that threatened to pull her walls down brick by brick.

James listened a moment longer, then chuckled again, lighter. "Yeah, I'd love that. We've got a week coming up, rostered leave. I'll ask her."

He hung up, still smiling to himself. Evelyn didn't look away fast enough when his eyes found her.

James slid the phone into his pocket, his thumb grazing the seam of his trousers like he wasn't sure if he should speak. Finally, he did.

"My sister's home," his voice was rougher than it needed to be. "Do you… want to fly to New York with me to meet her?"

That wasn't a casual ask. Not from him.

Evelyn raised an eyebrow, a smirk tugging. "You asking me on a holiday, Reaves?"

He huffed, lasing his fingers into his dog tags like he always did when he was anxious. "Don't let it go to your head. Just

276

rostered leave. But yeah… I want you to meet Ruby. She already knows you're a Scouser and thinks it's hilarious."

Evelyn's grin spread slowly, wickedly. "She's not wrong."

The flight to New York was uneventful, except for the way James kept glancing at her over in-flight coffee, like he was braced for her to vanish before they landed. Evelyn didn't. "Meeting family" wasn't something she'd ever been good at, most of hers had burnt those bridges long before she could walk across them. But the fact that he wanted her here, that was enough.

A cab carried them through winter-slick streets, with rain painting the asphalt gold under the lights. The driver pulled up outside a tall brownstone in a neighborhood that smelt faintly of bakeries and old money. James stepped out, his expression showing a flicker of nerves she almost never saw.

"She's going to love you," he muttered, like he was reminding himself.

The door opened before they knocked.

"Jamie!"

The woman who burst out was small compared to him, but the resemblance was immediate: same warm brown skin, same dark eyes, and same smile like sunlight cutting through cloud. Black curls framed her face in glossy spirals. Her dress looked as if it had been pulled straight from *Vogue*, not a Monday afternoon.

She crushed James in a hug that looked painful.

"You didn't tell me she was gorgeous," Ruby said over his shoulder, eyes flicking to Evelyn with an approving once-over.

"Didn't think I needed to," James said, his voice lighter than Evelyn had heard in weeks.

Ruby let him go and held her hand out to Evelyn, which was warm, open and definitely not testing. "Ruby. And you must be the Scouser. I've been warned."

Evelyn smirked. "All lies, I'm sure."

Ruby laughed, champagne-bright. "Doubt it. Come on. Bottle's open, fridge is full of cheese."

Inside, Ruby's flat was exactly what Evelyn expected, huge high ceilings, soft bohemian textiles against sunlit walls, and expensive art that somehow worked with it. A record player spun low jazz in the corner.

James glanced around, shaking his head. "You've gone full boho princess."

"And you've gone full sap," Ruby shot back, pouring champagne. She handed Evelyn a glass. "He was all gruff when I knew him in care. Now look at him…smiling, introducing me to women he actually likes."

"Don't ruin my reputation," James muttered.

Ruby stage-whispered to Evelyn, "He pretends he's unshakeable, but really he's just a Labrador with a gun."

Evelyn laughed into her drink. For the first time, she felt like maybe she was being folded into a different kind of family.

They sprawled across Ruby's overstuffed sofa, Ruby curled in one corner, James stretched out in the mustard-yellow armchair, and Evelyn tucked into the middle. Banter flowed: Marmite spoons and sugar-packet hoards from their children's home days, arguments about which of them was the psychopath. For every sharp memory, there was an equal warmth: they had survived together, and it showed.

Later, with the champagne gone and wine softening the edges of the night, Evelyn perched on the coffee table in front of James, folder in hand.

"I've got something for you both," she said, sliding it across. His name was scrawled on the front in her handwriting.

Inside was a clean genealogy report. Percentages, maps, a history that had been blank until now.

"Mediterranean…" James murmured. "Christ, Spanish/Portuguese, Italian, specifically Sicilian… Greek… Oh wow, 15% West African… Hey Ev, 5% Irish and even a trace of Middle Eastern… That's crazy, Ruby."

Ruby leaned over, wide-eyed. "You always said you didn't look like a Detroit boy."

His head snapped up. "How did you…"

"I stole your toothbrush," she said, deadpan.

Ruby burst out laughing. James just stared, scandalised and smiling despite himself.

The next page froze him. A black-and-white photograph: LUCA PETROSINI, 1918–1944. WWII partisan. Resistance fighter. Escaped twice. Died diverting German forces to save six men. Buried with honor. Forgotten by blood. Until now.

Evelyn's voice softened. "He was your great-grandfather. Your mum never knew him. But I found him. You said when you saw my grandads medals that you wanted to know... now you do."

The paper trembled in his hands. Ruby rested hers on his arm. "We came from someone, Jamie."

His voice was rough velvet. "I never thought there'd be a 'who'. Just empty space."

"Not empty," Evelyn said, laying her hand on his knee. "Just waiting for you to come home to it."

He pressed his forehead to hers, with the folder still between them like a fragile thread finally tied. Ruby smiled faintly. "She's a keeper, Jamie."

Later, the fire was low in the hearth, Evelyn leaned forward, her voice shifting. "Permission to speak to Ruby about Revenant Intel?"

James stilled, caught off guard by the formality. "Is it relevant, Valkyrie?"

"It is."

After a beat, he nodded.

Evelyn studied Ruby's face, her voice was low.

"Have you ever heard of a group called the Aegis Consortium?"

Ruby froze. Not just surprise, something older, heavier. Her expression shut down, the way it did in court when she had to guard herself.

"Yes," she said at last. "I've worked with families of victims. Women trafficked, soldiers who disappeared, prisoners of war who never came home. Their files… ended in silence. They were believed to have been taken into Revenant-linked facilities, but no bodies were ever recovered. No admissible evidence. Just absence. Just grief."

Evelyn leaned forward. "What are they?"

Ruby's tone shifted, precise now, like she was building a case before a judge.

"They are not a cartel. They're not mercenaries. They are scientists—funded and shielded—operating as a consortium. Their work has always centred on biotechnical enhancement. In plain English? They use people as raw material. Predominantly women. Predominantly soldiers or prisoners of war. With the world as it is now, they have even started taking refugee children. Their objective is fixed: create a Revenant soldier. The records I've traced point back to the 1980s, a Russian facility. The project was codenamed Chimera. Only two individuals are thought to have survived those trials. Rumour suggests they escaped before the procedures killed them. Their identities were buried. No trace."

She drew a steadying breath, her gaze cutting to James. "When James told me about Libya, I opened a file. I reached out to colleagues. We cross-referenced movements, witness statements, banking trails. The victims you encountered, you were right, they were targeted assets, pre-cleared for sale on the American market. James broke protocol by disclosing it, but because he did, my team and others intervened. We intercepted, extracted, got them safe. And yes, what we uncovered pointed to deep connections. The Consortium has reach into government, corporate defence, private biotech. They have capital on a scale that bends oversight. It's… frightening."

Evelyn turned on James, her voice taut.

"You never told me about the Libyan victims. Why?"

His jaw locked. "Same reason you don't tell me about Ghost. To keep you safe."

And she understood—too well.

Ruby's eyes flicked between them, her voice quieter now. "Why are you asking me about Revenant and the Consortium?"

Evelyn exhaled, the sound ragged, heavy.

"Because I've been identified as a target. After Colombia… they flagged me. I'm compatible with nanite-infused biotech."

Ruby went utterly still. For a solicitor, silence was rare, but this confession stole her words. When she finally spoke, her voice was stripped bare.

"Jay…"

"I know," James said quietly.

Ruby's gaze hardened, grief and fury burning behind it.

"Then you know exactly how bad this can get."

By midnight, Ruby had kissed Evelyn goodnight and vanished to her room. The flat was quiet, with the city hum faint through the windows.

James sprawled on the sofa; Evelyn curled beside him with two mugs of coffee. For a while, they said nothing.

"Ev, you cant tell anyone about me leaking the Libyan Intel" he said, finally.

"I know, but I am so fucking proud of you, you know that?" Evelyn replied.

He nodded, staring into the dark liquid. "And no one will touch you... ever... not why I am breathing... not this consortium... not some trafficker... ever... I promise..."

Evelyn bumped her knee against his, defusing his apprehension and torment. "Pretty sure your sister likes me."

"I think she's already planning Christmas," he said with a faint smile.

Silence again—warm this time.

"Ev," James said at last, low and certain. "Thanks for that report... your gift... you gave us something we have never had... You showed us we matter."

She smirked. "Your grandad sounds like a lionheart, a freedom fighter, like both Ruby and you."

He brushed a strand of hair behind her ear, his hand lingering, "And you don't need to thank me for loving you, and your sister."

His gaze shifted, closer to a confession and a question that he'd never dared to ask.

But not yet.

Chapter 33

The call came just after midnight.

James was still at the war table, staring at a half-finished rotation plan, when Selena handed him the sat phone. He listened in silence, his posture stiffened immediately, before cutting the line with a clipped "Copy."

When he turned, Evelyn was already there with her boots laced and her hair braided back, like she'd felt the shift in the air.

"What?" she asked, her voice steady, but her eyes already sharp.

He didn't answer straight away, instead she led her down the hall, past the mess of voices and maps, until they were in the shadowed corner of the briefing room. Only then did he speak.

"They've asked for you. Death Valley. Afghan clearance teams. Eighteen days. They want a clean path… mines, IEDs, the whole fucking desert."

Her chest rose, slow and deliberate, with no fear and full resolve. "Yes."

"Ev…"

"No." She cut him off, stepping closer to him, with her voice fierce but calm. "If I can clear ground and keep those lads alive, if I can stop one kid from walking over a bomb… then I'm going. You know I am."

He stared at her, his chest tight with equal parts pride and trepidation. He'd seen that fire before, the one that made her run towards the danger while everyone else ran away. It was what made her who she was. It was also what had nearly broken him, over and over again.

Finally, he exhaled, his voice low and rough. "Fine. Then I'm going with you. I'll cover you. Every step."

That's when it happened.

The faint hum under her skin, the flicker of blue light threading across her collarbones like ghost veins. The nanites stirred, restless, shimmering to life as if his words had triggered them into action.

"Ev…" His voice cracked.

She froze and tried to tuck her arms against herself, but it was too late. He reached for her wrist, just to steady her…

And the light jumped abruptly.

The shimmer crawled onto his olive skin, lightning up his veins, racing from her pulse to his hand, up his arm, flowing across his chest. He staggered back, gasping as the sensation ignited him, his vision fracturing with flashes that weren't his. It was overwhelming and suffocating. It was her cold, blind and soul crushing fear. Fear of losing him. Fear of him falling.

It was not abstract. Not imagined. He felt it, raw and jagged.

The future fear of steel tables. The smell of antiseptic and blood. The bone-deep terror of him lying broken in the dirt, of hearing his voice go silent over comms, of losing him the way she'd lost everyone else she'd ever tried to love.

It hit him like shrapnel. His knees nearly buckled.

"Jesus Christ, Ev…" He ripped his hand back, clutching his chest like the air had been punched out of him. "What the fuck was that?"

Her face was pale, eyes wide with something worse than fear. Shame. "I… I don't know."

"Don't lie to me," he snapped, but his voice cracked. "I felt it. I felt you. Your fear… of me. Of losing me."

She shook her head hard, tears brimming but unshed. "Jamie, I don't understand it. Sometimes they flare, sometimes they burn. But that…" Her voice broke. "… That's never happened before."

He paced once, raking a hand through his hair, breath ragged. Then he turned back, crouched in front of her, forcing her eyes to meet his. His voice dropped to something raw, something she'd only heard from him once or twice before.

"You're terrified of me going with you. But I'm going anyway. You hear me? Because I don't let you walk into hell on your own. If I die so be it. I die protecting you."

She shook her head. She was desperate to fight him, to argue, but the words wouldn't come.

He reached for her again, slower this time, his palm open, deliberate. His touch on her hand was steady, no matter how his heart thundered. The nanites shimmered faintly, but they didn't surge. They pulsed, low and quiet, like they were listening.

"We face it together," he said, his voice like an oath. "Mines, warzones, Revenant… whatever the fuck comes. Together. And nothing, not even whatever's inside you, is going to scare me off. Im Your Red. Everything I am is yours. Always."

286

She leaned into his palm and let her eyes close against his hand. "Then don't die on me, Jamie. Baby."

He pulled her in, forehead to forehead, and his voice rough against her skin.

"Not a chance."

And though the hum still vibrated faintly under her skin, for the first time it felt less like a curse and more like a bond neither of them could break.

Later the kitchen smelt of the HQ's signature scent, gun oil and strong coffee. Both their kitbags where lined up and expertly packed by the door. Evelyn sat at the table tightening straps on her vest while James double-checked the gear list on his tablet, already in travel mode.

Rose had turned up unexpectedly the night before they were due to travel, much to Irishes delight. She had not been due back for three weeks but had been able to take early leave. She had been helping Irish pack medical supplies for James and Evelyn when she bustled in, with a canvas washbag in hand. She set it on the table with a brisk little thump.

"Right. "Medic duty," she said, flipping the zip open. "You two don't look after yourselves worth a damn, so I've done it for you."

One by one, she lined items on the table. "Painkillers. Antibiotics. Electrolytes. Anti-nausea tablets. Gauze. Saline sachets. Antiseptic wipes." Each placed with care, her voice light but efficient.

Then she held up a blister pack. "And the pill. Checked with Irish." She set it squarely in the center between them. "Three months' worth. Split them between your kits… just in case one gets lost."

Evelyn groaned under her breath, "Bloody hell, Rose…" but zipped the washbag closed all the same.

James gave a quiet huff, not looking up. "She's right. The last thing you need is more weight to carry out there." His hand brushed Evelyn's shoulder, protective, oblivious.

Rose's smile softened as she patted the bag. "Promise me you'll use them. Both of you have enough on your plates."

"Yeah, yeah." Evelyn smirked tiredly. "Yes, Mum."

Rose chuckled, turning away. But her fingers lingered on the table for half a beat longer than necessary, her eyes flicking once, sharp, towards the washbag before smoothing her face back into something sisterly. Safe.

Chapter 34

The transport ride was quieter than usual without the rest of Obsidian. Just the two of them in the back, the drone of the engines filling the space between clipped conversations about terrain, weather and expected contact.

When the bird dropped into the small, dust-choked airstrip, the heat was already brutal. It rolled off the tarmac in shimmering waves, carrying the smell of fuel and sand. It was utterly suffocating, burning their lungs, as they moved with precision and purpose.

They were met at the camp gates by Captain Daoud, his face breaking into a broad and welcoming smile the second he spotted Evelyn. He clasped her hand like an old friend, his Pashto warm and rapid. She answered without hesitation, her voice carrying the easy authority of someone who belonged there.

James stayed a step behind, letting her lead. In the Korangal, she wasn't his second. He was hers.

Their tent was small, with two cots, a battered desk and a fan that barely turned, but it was theirs for the next however long. He tossed his bag on his bed while she started laying out kit, already slotting detonator tools into her vest.

"You realise," he said, "this is where it all started. When we stopped dicking around and became something real."

She glanced over, a small smirk tugging at her mouth.

"You mean when you started following me around like a lost dog? Yeah, I remember."

He grunted, but there was no heat in it. Their first time here had been weeks of dust, danger and something neither of them had wanted to name at the time. A future together. And now here they were, the very future they had fought so hard to Invision was now in jeopardy.

This time, the stakes were higher. The Afghan army had already marked three active danger zones in the valley. The mines were older than some of the soldiers in the unit but still deadly, and there were whispers about insurgent patrols pushing closer to the routes they'd need to clear.

That night, they joined Daoud's officers for a map briefing. Evelyn handled most of it in Pashto, the local commanders nodding as she marked hazard lines and choke points. James listened, watching the way her focus sharpened, her hands sure over the map.

When she was done, Daoud clapped him on the shoulder.

"You are here to protect her, yes?"

James didn't blink.

"Always."

That night, the camp was still but for the low hum of the generators and the occasional crack of distant gunfire. Heat clung stubbornly to the air, even in the dark. James was stretched out on his cot, boots still on, kit bag open at his feet. Evelyn sat at the battered desk, she was ritually stripping and cleaning her favored blade Bella with slow, deliberate movements.

He'd seen her in every mood: sharp, cocky, playful and defiantly stubborn: but this was different. Her shoulders were set just a little tighter, her movements a fraction more deliberate, like she was keeping her hands busy to quiet the churn in her head.

It wasn't much. Most people wouldn't have caught it. But he'd been watching her for a decade. He knew.

"You alright?"

She glanced up, the easy smile she usually threw back at him absent. Instead her face was etched with something he couldn't read.

"Fine."

He sat up, resting his forearms on his knees.

"Ev."

She set Bella down, leaning back in the chair, exhaling through her nose.

"It's not the work. The work I can do in my sleep. It's…" She trailed off, eyes flicking to the tent flap, toward the valley beyond. "It's different this time. Hotter. Louder. More eyes on us. And it's just you and me."

He stood, crossing the space between them, and rested his hands on the back of her chair.

"We've done this before. You've done this more than anyone I know. And I'm not going anywhere. You know I'll be on your six every second we're out there."

Her lips twitched, not quite a smile, but close.

"Yeah. I know."

He stayed there a moment longer, close enough to feel the heat radiating off her skin, before he moved back to his cot. She picked up Bella again, her hands steadier now, and he knew that tomorrow, when they stepped out into the valley, the nerves would be buried deep under the armor she wore so well.

The air in the tent was thick, the kind that clung to skin and made the world outside feel a million miles away. Evelyn sat back in the chair, Bella lying across her knees, the cleaning cloth limp in her hand. She'd gone quiet, that rare kind of quiet that James didn't hear often, the kind that meant something was gnawing at her edges.

She turned slowly, her eyes locking on him in the dim light.

No armour. No deflection. Just Evelyn.

"Make love to me like it's our last night on earth, Jamie baby…Just in case…"

His pulse kicked in hard. Not because she'd never asked before, but because of the way she said it with no teasing smirk and no dare in her voice. This was just needed.

He didn't hesitate, and within two seconds he was there, pulling her up from the chair, his hands sliding around her waist. She rose into him like she'd been waiting all night for this, her mouth finding his with a hunger that was all devotion and heat.

They stumbled back toward the cot, tangled in each other, boots half-undone, kit abandoned in their wake. His fingers threaded into her hair, tilting her head so he could taste every kiss like it might be the last. She tugged his shirt over his head, her nails scraping over the scars on his chest, pausing on the ones she'd seen him earn.

When his hands slipped under her top, he mapped every inch like it was sacred ground: the curve of her spine, the dip of her waist, and the steady beat of her heart under his palm. She gasped into his mouth when he lifted her, setting her down on the cot without breaking contact, his weight pressing into hers.

Outside, the muffled voices of the camp faded. In here, the only sound was her breath as he set his fingers to work with the confidence of a man who knew every single perfect spot of her that he had taken time to study and memorise. Her breath was fast and uneven as he made her come on his fingers, followed by the soft rustle of sheets as he slid his hands down her thighs, pulling her closer. She hooked her legs around his hips, pulling him in until there was nothing left between them but heat and the unspoken knowledge of everything they'd survived together.

He moved like a man who knew every contour of her body by heart but still found something new in the way she arched under him, in the way her fingers dug into his back. She met him with equal urgency, hips rising, lips finding his ear to whisper things that made his blood run hot.

Every kiss, every touch was a defiant vow neither of them said out loud: *I'm here. I've got you. We make it through this; we make it through anything.*

When release finally came, it wasn't just heat, it was a breaking point, a flood of everything they'd been holding back since the moment that they knew tomorrow could be their last day on earth. He stayed inside her, with his broad chest pressing to hers, their heartbeats pounding in sync, both of them breathing like they'd just run through gunfire.

Her hands slid up into his hair, and with his forehead resting on hers, she was holding him there in their chaotic yet perfect moment.

"Not our last night," he murmured against her skin. "Not by a long shot."

She smiled faintly, with her eyes half-closed, not knowing—neither of them knowing—that somewhere in that tangled moment, in the shadow of Death Valley, they had just made their legacy.

Chapter 35

They woke by the faint call to prayer drifting from the village below. The air was already warm, promising the kind of heat that made metal burn to the touch.

James moved first.

Evelyn was half on her side, with the sheet tangled around her hips, one arm flung over his stomach like she owned the space, and she did. Her hair was a mess, the golden strands catching in the slant of early light filtering through the canvas. She looked uncharacteristically unguarded. He didn't see that often. How beautiful she was when she was at peace. His heart ached to savor this moment, to keep the image etched in his memory for eternity.

For a moment, he let himself just watch her breathe, the steady rise and fall against his chest. There was a pull in him he couldn't name, something deeper than the usual war-born urgency. Something that made him want to keep her here, safe, for the rest of their lives.

But the day didn't wait for anyone.

By the time she stirred, he was sitting on the edge of the cot, lacing his boots. She pushed herself up, with her hair falling and sticking to the sweat on her face. She reached for her vest without a word, slipping straight back into mission mode. The softness from the night before was tucked away behind her usual composure.

They moved around each other in the cramped tent with the rhythm of two people who'd shared a thousand mornings in the field, both passing gear, checking weapons, and securing straps.

Evelyn slung Bella across her back, gave the hilt a habitual pat, and adjusted the strap of her detonator kit.

"You ready, Paladin?"

He looked at her for a beat longer than he meant to, catching the faintest hint of a smile tugging at her mouth.

"Always."

They stepped out into the glaring morning sun, the camp already alive with shouts in Pashto and the metallic clatter of kit. Captain Daoud was waiting by the gate, with maps tucked under his arm.

Evelyn switched seamlessly into the language, exchanging quick greetings and handshakes with the soldiers she'd trained before. James hung back half a step, letting her lead, as that was his role here, and it was simple: cover her six.

And as they headed toward the valley's edge, with their boots crunching over the dry earth, neither of them knew that the night before had already changed everything. They had more than each other to protect while walking through the gates of hell.

The sun was barely up when they set out, but the heat already pressed down like an oppressive weight. The valley stretched ahead in sharp ridges and narrow passes, the kind of terrain that made every shadow a possible threat.

Their Afghan team fell into formation easily, consisting of six soldiers James knew by sight if not by name. Evelyn, however, knew every one of them. She greeted them in Pashto, trading quick, warm words that made hardened faces crack into grins. A few of them had trained under her years ago, and two had trained with her the last time James and Evelyn were in Afghanistan, and she was very happy to see them still alive. Now they stood armed and ready, trusting her to walk them through it again.

James hung a half step behind her, his eyes moving constantly over the ridgelines, fingers loose on his rifle. This was her mission, her expertise, and his job was simple: keep her alive.

They reached the first flagged section within an hour. The markers from previous patrols fluttered faintly in the breeze, faded by the sun. Evelyn crouched low, running her gloved fingers over the dirt until she found the faint outline of an old pressure plate.

"Anti-tank mine," she called in Pashto, her tone calm and instructive. She talked the nearest soldier through identifying the trigger, showing him the safest angles to approach. Her hands were steady, movements unhurried, even with the occasional crack of distant gunfire bouncing off the valley walls.

James kept his eyes up, scanning the ridges, every nerve on alert. The Afghan soldiers were good, disciplined and experts in their own right, but the Korangal had a way of hiding danger until it was breathing down your neck.

When she finished disarming the first mine, she sat back on her heels and gave the soldier a nod.

"Your turn next time," she said in Pashto, with a grin flashing quickly before she stood and dusted off her gloves.

They moved on.

The heat climbed higher, the air hung thick with the smell of dust and hot metal. Twice, James caught movement on the ridge, but the shapes were gone as soon as he locked eyes, and both times, the Afghan rear guard tightened their formation without needing a word from him.

By midday, they'd cleared three sections. Evelyn never faltered, her focus narrowing to the mine in front of her, the next safe step, and the safety of the men behind her. But James caught the sweat beading on her neck, the subtle drag in her shoulders as the day wore on.

When they finally called a halt in the thin shade of a rock overhang, she dropped her pack with a grunt and took the canteen he offered. Their eyes met for a moment, a silent check-in, a pulse of reassurance neither needed to put into words.

The valley was already trying to test them. And it was only day one.

They were halfway through clearing the fourth section when the first shot cracked across the valley.

It came from high on the ridgeline, the sound carrying a split second before the bullet pinged off a rock two feet from the Afghan point man. The team dropped instantly, rifles up, scanning the ridge.

James was already moving.

"Contact, one o'clock!"

Another shot rang out, then another, and then the valley came alive with the echo of small arms fire. Dust kicked up around them as rounds chewed into the dirt.

Evelyn was crouched over a half-exposed anti-personnel mine, her hands already inside the perimeter she'd just cleared. She didn't even flinch.

"I've got it. Cover me!"

James didn't argue. He swung to the ridge, shouldering his rifle and letting off controlled bursts, pinning the shooters down. Two Afghan soldiers shifted to give him overlapping fire, with the rest scanning for flankers.

The heat was blinding, with sweat running into his eyes, but his focus stayed locked, counting her breaths, the movement of her shoulders, and the angle of her hands.

"Thirty seconds," she called, her voice calm like she was reading from a recipe.

A round smacked into the dirt a foot from her boot. James snapped off a burst in reply, sending one of the shooters rolling out of sight.

"Make it twenty!"

The Afghan rearguard barked a warning in Pashto about movement on the left flank. James shifted his aim, laying down suppressive fire. He could hear the metallic click of her tools and the faint grind of metal being eased out of the dirt.

Then her voice, steady and sure:

"Clear!"

She slid the disarmed mine into her satchel and was on her feet in a heartbeat, sprinting low to the overhang where the team had regrouped. James was right behind her, firing in short bursts until they were both under cover.

They caught their breath in the brief lull, with dust clinging to their sweat, the air still buzzing with adrenaline. Evelyn gave him a crooked grin.

"Just like old times."

He shook his head, a wry half-smile tugging at his mouth.

"Except you're even more insane now."

She just laughed, checking the satchel like she hadn't just been working a live mine under fire.

The Afghan captain leaned in.

"We move now, before they regroup."

Evelyn nodded, already shouldering her pack.

James fell in beside her, his rifle up, his eyes on the ridge, knowing the valley was far from done with them.

The camp was quiet when they got back, but it wasn't peaceful, it was the brittle stillness that comes after a day spent on the edge. The air still carried the faint tang of cordite and dust, the kind that clung to skin no matter how many times you scrubbed.

Evelyn stripped her vest off the second they stepped into the tent, dropping it onto her cot with a heavy thud. She peeled her gloves off next, flexing her fingers, the skin underneath was raw from hours in the heat. James watched her for a moment, taking in the way her shoulders rolled, loosening muscles that had been locked since the first shot was fired.

"You good?" he asked.

She gave a half-smile, running a hand through her bedraggled hair.

"We cleared three sections, pulled the trigger wires from four more, and got shot at twice. Yeah, I'm good."

But he could see it, the lingering adrenaline, the edge that wouldn't fade on its own.

He crossed the space between them, cupping the back of her neck rubbing small circles to ease the tension. She leaned into him almost immediately, her forehead pressing to his chest like she'd been holding herself upright all day just to get here.

"You're a bloody terror out there," he murmured into her hair.

"Takes one to know one," she shot back, but her voice was softer now.

When she tilted her head up, he caught the glint in her eyes, and it was not just from the fight but from the way she looked at him after a day like this. It was the same look she'd given him earlier that year, the first time the valley had nearly chewed them up and spat them out.

The first kiss was hard and hungry, born out of knowing tomorrow could be worse; tomorrow could be the end. Their boots scraped against the floor as they moved, with his hands finding her hips, hers pushing his shirt up over his head. The cot creaked under their combined weight as they fell into it, the heat between them snapping like livewire.

Every touch was rougher than the night before, fuelled by the memory of bullets cracking off rocks and the taste of dust in their mouths. She tugged him closer with her legs hooked around his hips, nails biting into his back. He moved like a man who refused to waste a second, anchoring her to him with every kiss, every press of his body to hers.

Outside, the valley kept its own vigil with the distant crack of a rifle and the low murmur of guards on the perimeter, but in here, time narrowed down to the sound of their breath and the feel of skin against skin.

When it was over, she lay sprawled across him, their bodies slick with heat, her fingers lazily tracing along his ribs.

"If every day's like this," she murmured, "I might not survive this mission."

He brushed a damp strand of hair from her face.

"We'll survive. Together. Like always."

Her smile was small, but it reached her eyes, the same eyes that would be sharp and unflinching again by morning.

Chapter 36

Day Two

The second day started before the sun had fully cleared the ridge. Heat pooled in the valley even at dawn, the air already heavy. The Afghan team fell in without question, Evelyn at the point, James half a step behind, rifle up.

By mid-morning, they'd found two more mines, one buried so deep it took her forty minutes to work it free. Sporadic fire came from the ridges twice, both times driven back by James and the rear guard. Sweat soaked through their shirts, and dust ground into every crease of skin.

When they got back to camp, there was no debrief, as they didn't need one. Evelyn dumped her satchel by the cot, drank half a canteen in one go, and shot James a look that said she wasn't interested in food, showers, or talking.

That night, they barely made it to the cot before they were on each other, with their mouths urgent and hands stripping away the day's grit. The cot groaned under their weight as he pressed her down, her legs wrapping around his waist, pulling him closer. Every touch was raw, every kiss edged with the day's danger. It wasn't gentle. It wasn't meant to be. It was survival in another form. It was their silent vow, we made it through today. We will make it through tomorrow.

Day Three

The valley hit back harder. They were halfway through clearing a narrow pass when gunfire erupted from both sides. The Afghan team split with two laying down covering fire while the others scrambled to keep the ridge clear. Evelyn stayed on her knees over a mine, her voice steady in Pashto as she directed one of the soldiers through securing a tripwire. James's rifle barked over her shoulder, dropping a figure that had crept too close.

They made it back to camp with three confirmed kills and a dozen near misses.

The desert wind rattled the canvas walls, carrying dust through the cracks like whispers of every ghost they'd left outside. Evelyn sat cross-legged on her cot, her boots still on, her bra unhooked but shirt buttoned back up. Her hair was plastered with sand, her hands raw from hours of defusing landmines under a sun that wanted to kill them all.

James ducked inside, his helmet under his arm and his steady eyes already locked on her.

Evelyn tilted her head suspiciously. "What?"

He hesitated just for a moment, then sat down across from her, with heavy silence pressing in. Finally, he exhaled.

"Marry me."

Her brows shot up in total shock. "You serious, Jamie?"

He nodded once, jaw tight. "Life's short. We've practically been married for years. I don't want to wait. Our life is beyond dangerous and if anything happens to me, I want to die your husband. And if nothing happens…. I want to live, as your husband."

She stared at him, then let out a half-delirious laugh. "Romantic as ever. You've still got dirt onn your face and you're talking about me being a war widow.

He reached for her hand anyway. "Ev, I'm not talking about fairy lights and champagne, I'm talking about you and me. Before something takes us out."

Her chest tightened. Because he wasn't wrong.

She leaned back against the cot pole, eyes burning, then grinned sharply. "Fuck it. Yeah. Let's do it."

"Yeah???"

"Yeah. And not because I think we're gonna die… yeah, because I want to spend the rest of my life tripping over your size 12 boots, and cursing you for it!"

James pulled his phone out, thumbs already moving.

"Im not fucking about, I will text Sel and Rose. Tell them it's happening. Mack can get eyes on something for me to wear. Normal. No bullshit. If you want a dress, I'll pay. Sorry, Ev. Not romantic."

She burst out laughing. "Jamie, baby, since when have we ever been romantic? We fuck in desert camps between getting shot at… and that's a good date."

James smirked and dropped the hammer in the group chat:

James:

Sel, Rose – wedding in 3 weeks when we're wheels down. Mack, find me something normal to wear. DO NOT let Bullet pick. Somebody tell my sister Ruby, number to follow. Don't hit Ev with a million choices — she's got Death Valley on her plate. Make calls on her behalf. Oh, and somebody get her white Doc Martens, or she'll wear her combat boots. AJ—you're not DJing. Your music sounds like two tanks shagging in a scrapyard.

Evelyn groaned.

"I don't care what I wear. Just make sure it isn't plastic or black. I'm trying to keep us all out of body bags, so dress shopping isn't top of my list."

Bullet: EX-FUCKING-CUSE ME I was literally born to DJ this wedding. I already got the playlist: "Enter Sandman" for walking down the aisle. You're welcome.

AJ: Oi. My music slaps. And it's art, thank you very much. Two tanks shagging in a scrapyard = METAL POETRY.

Mack: Settle down, children. I'll handle the suit. James, do you even know what your size is outside of "combat issue"?

Irish: I'll sort the whisky. None of that American pisswater. Proper Irish stuff. If you're getting married in 3 weeks, you'll need it.

Rose: Already on dresses. Don't worry, Ev, we'll keep it simple. And yes, James, WHITE DOCS. Consider it done.

Selena: Noted. Logistics underway. Evelyn — I will require your shoe size and preferred shade of white.

Evelyn: Preferred shade of white?? Sel, it's not a bloody paint swatch. Just… not shiny.

Bullet: Oi, shiny boots would look sick. Disco ball bride!!

Evelyn: Diego, I swear to god.

AJ: No, no, let him. Imagine Ev stomping down the aisle in sequin Docs. ICONIC.

James: No.

Mack: That was the fastest "no" I've ever seen typed. Man's sweating bullets already.

Irish: He'll be sweating more when Ev sees the bill for all this.

Evelyn: Not if we keep it cheap. I literally don't care. I'd marry him in a bloody poncho.

Bullet: SAY. LESS. I know a guy. Poncho, sombrero, maracas…

James: I will end you.

AJ: Oh my god, this is the best group chat ever.

James: OK, so no one seems surprised.

Evelyn: …and none of you ballbags said congratulations. How rude.

Bullet: Congrats—you absolute lunatics. There, happy now??

AJ: I was too busy crying over not being allowed to DJ… but yeah… congrats, Mum and Dad.

Mack: Congratulations, you stubborn idiots. We've only been waiting a decade.

Irish: Aye. Congrats. Now don't fuck it up.

Rose: (heart emoji) Couldn't be happier for you both.

Selena: Congratulations. And don't worry, Evelyn.—I'll handle details. You focus on staying alive.

Evelyn: Right, I'm gonna make sure it's a wedding and not a double funeral… It's mental out here.

Bullet: Wow. Way to kill the mood, Ev.

(Ruby gets added to the chat by James.)

Ruby: …wait. WAIT. Did I just read "wedding"?? James Reaves. You're telling me you finally pulled your head out of your arse?!

Bullet: WELCOME RUBES—pour yourself a drink; you're gonna need it.

Mack: She took that well.

AJ: Better than James did when she joined last Christmas's Zoom.

Ruby: Congrats, you two. Keep each other safe, yeah?

Evelyn: Always.

James: Always.

(Two minutes of chaos scroll by — Bullet dropping memes, AJ arguing about the playlist, Mack trying to keep everyone on task… (Then finally Frost chimes in.)

Frost: … Congratulations.

(Dead silence for a second in the chat. Then—)

AJ: Frame it. First time Frost's ever sent more than an emoji.

Mack: That's practically a poem coming from him.

Evelyn: Thanks, Malik. Means a lot. Ignore the ballbags.

Frost: Always.

Day Six – The Hit

The sun was high and merciless, baking the rocks until the air shimmered like heat haze off a barrel. Evelyn was knee-deep in the dirt, working on the final mine in a section that had already taken most of the morning to clear. The Afghan team held the perimeter, with their eyes on the ridgelines. James stayed low behind a crumbling wall, rifle ready, scanning the high ground.

The first shot came without warning, the sharp crack echoing off the valley walls, followed by a hiss as the bullet ricocheted off a rock to her left. The Afghan team shouted, rifles barking in reply. James dropped to a firing crouch, sweeping the ridge.

"Contact, ten o'clock!" he shouted, the words swallowed by the sudden roar of gunfire.

Evelyn didn't look up.

"Almost there, give me thirty seconds!" she yelled back, her voice steady despite the chaos.

Then the second shot came, and this one found its mark.

She jerked, the breath knocked out of her, but her hands didn't leave the mine. The round had torn through the outside of her upper arm, just below the shoulder. Blood blossomed instantly, dripping down into the dust.

James's gut tightened.

"Valkyrie, you're hit!"

"I'm fine!" she snapped, not breaking focus. Her hands kept working, her movements precise even as her sleeve darkened. "Get them off the ridge!"

He swore under his breath and pivoted, letting off a burst that dropped one shooter and drove another back into cover. The Afghan captain moved his men up, laying suppressive fire.

"Fifteen seconds!" Evelyn called, her voice a notch tighter now.

Bullets smacked into the dirt around them. James took down another figure moving along the ridgeline, then risked a glance back. She was tightening the last clamp, pulling the mine free with a smooth motion like the pain was just background noise.

"Clear!" she shouted, standing and slinging the satchel over her good shoulder.

James was at her side instantly, one hand pressed to her arm, steering her toward the nearest cover as the Afghan team pulled back in formation.

They made it to a cluster of boulders, where the gunfire finally began to fade. Evelyn slid down against the rock, breathing hard, with blood running freely down to her elbow. She gritted her teeth but grinned up at him.

"The route's safe. You're welcome."

He shook his head, torn between admiration and wanting to wring her neck.

"You're out of your damn mind."

"No shit."

The Afghan captain knelt beside them, checking her arm with quick efficiency, muttering something in Pashto that made Evelyn snort. James didn't understand all of it, but he caught "stubborn woman" and "good soldier".

As the adrenaline bled away, the ache in her arm deepened, but she never once let it show on her face. The mine was disarmed, the route cleared, and that was all that mattered.

Day Ten

The valley was awake before the sun, the air sharp and restless. By the time they reached the first flagged zone, the heat was already building, baking the rocks under their boots. The Afghan team spread out to secure the perimeter, their movements quick and practiced.

Evelyn dropped to one knee in the dust without hesitation, her gloves on, her eyes scanning the ground. James took position two paces back and slightly to her left, his rifle sweeping the ridgeline. He didn't need to look to know exactly what she was doing, as he could read her now by the angle of her shoulders and the way her weight shifted when she'd found something worth digging into.

She was talking quietly to one of the Afghan soldiers in Pashto, pointing to a barely visible seam in the dirt. The man nodded, moving to mark it while she began the slow, deliberate process of uncovering the mine.

James's eyes kept sweeping the valley, but they came back to her more than usual. Not just out of habit, but because something in him was keyed tighter today. Every time she leaned forward, every time her gloved fingers disappeared into the dirt, his chest tightened just slightly.

Two shots cracked from the ridge, sharp and sudden. James was already pivoting, firing back in short bursts, and barking a warning in English and Pashto. The Afghan team returned fire, pushing the shooters back into cover.

Evelyn didn't even glance up.

"The wire's still live. Give me twenty seconds!"

He kept firing and reloading, with his stance shifting to put more of himself between her and the ridge. It was instinct, not strategy.

By the time she called,

"Clear!"

The valley had gone quiet again. She sat back, brushing dust from her gloves, her face flushed from the heat.

James moved to help her up without thinking, his hand steady under her uninjured arm. She gave him a quick grin, grabbing her satchel.

"You're fussing, Paladin."

"Maybe," he said, scanning the ridges again. "Let's keep moving."

They cleared two more sections before the sun reached its peak, sweat streaking the dust on their faces. Back at camp, she slung her kit down and reached for her canteen, and he caught himself watching her again, the way she moved, the set of her jaw, something he couldn't quite name.

He didn't know what it was. Not yet. But the thought that she'd be walking into fire again tomorrow sat heavier on him than it ever had before.

That night, the camp was quieter than usual, the earlier heat having bled out into a cool, dry night. James had been running a last weapons check with Daoud's men when he ducked back into their tent, expecting to find Evelyn pacing or fussing with her kit like she always did before they crashed.

Instead, she was sitting on the floor by her cot, one boot off, the other half-laced, head tipped back against the wall. Her eyes were closed, her braid loose over one shoulder, and her breathing was slow, and not the light, alert kind that could turn sharp in an instant, but the deep, heavy pull of someone truly asleep.

He froze in the doorway.

Evelyn didn't do this.

She didn't stop mid-routine. She didn't fall asleep without meaning to. She didn't leave herself halfway between dressed and undressed.

James crouched beside her, brushing the stray strands of hair from her face. Her skin was warm, flushed from the day's work, and when he slid her other boot off, she barely stirred.

"Ev," he said quietly, just to see if she'd wake.

Her lashes fluttered, but her eyes didn't open.

"Mm… just… five minutes."

He smiled faintly, even as something in his chest tightened. He got her up gently, one arm around her waist, guiding her onto the cot. She curled toward him the moment she hit the mattress, her hand resting on his thigh like she didn't want him going anywhere.

James sat with her until her breathing evened again, the dim lantern light catching the curve of her cheek. He told himself it was just exhaustion, the heat, the gunfire, and the endless hours in the dirt. But a quiet thought whispered in the back of his head that there was more to it.

He didn't know. Neither of them knew. But that night, something about her stillness stayed with him.

Chapter 37

Day Eighteen in the Valley

The sun hadn't even cleared the ridge when the camp began to stir. This was it, their final day in the Korangal. Eighteen straight days of crawling through dust and heat, hands in the dirt, every muscle aching.

The kind of work that stripped you down to the core and left only the stubborn standing.

Evelyn pushed out of the tent, hair tied back, sleeves rolled. She looked leaner than when they'd arrived, with her skin darkened by the sun, her eyes still sharp, but her shoulders carried a weight he could see even before she spoke.

She reached for her canteen before she even greeted him, tipping it back and draining nearly half in one go.

"Thirsty?" James asked, arching a brow.

She wiped her mouth with the back of her hand, nodding.

"Like I could drink the whole river dry. Guess my body's finally realising how much I've been sweating out here."

He watched her a beat longer than necessary, the faintest flicker of concern crossing his mind. Evelyn never let herself get to the point of gulping water like that unless she was already running on empty.

But she was already moving, grabbing Bella, and checking her detonator tools with the same precision as day one.

"Let's get this last section done and get the hell out of here."

They joined the Afghan team for the final push, the air thick with dust that clung to sweat and grit. Evelyn led them out, crouched over the flagged zone before anyone else had even unshouldered their rifles. James took his position a step behind, rifle sweeping the ridge like always, but his eyes kept darting back to her.

She worked fast, too fast, like she could outrun the heat, the fatigue, and the end of the mission itself. By midday, the last mine was in her satchel, and the valley was quiet again.

When they headed back to camp, the Afghan soldiers clapped them both on the back, their thanks warm and genuine. Evelyn just grinned, accepting their praise in Pashto, but James could see it by the way her grip tightened on her canteen as soon as they were alone.

Tomorrow they'd be wheels-up, heading home. The valley was behind them. But James knew the valley never truly let go, and this time, it had left him with something he couldn't quite name.

The Last Night

The camp was quiet, the air cooling just enough to make the night bearable. Their tent was dim, lit only by the low glow of a lantern on the desk. The muffled sounds of the Afghan night were distant conversation and the occasional metallic clink, which faded into the background.

Evelyn sat on the edge of the cot, her hair loose, damp from running a wet cloth over her skin. She was in one of his shirts, sleeves rolled, the hem brushing her thighs. When he stepped inside, she looked up at him, and it wasn't the usual post-mission challenge in her eyes. It was something steadier.

Without a word, she reached for him, fingers curling into his vest to pull him closer. The kiss was slow at first, deliberate, her mouth soft but insistent. When she pushed him back onto the cot, straddling his hips, he let her set the pace.

She moved over him with purpose, her palms braced on his chest, her eyes locked to his. James had seen her in every mode: deadly, cocky, and wild; but this was different. There was no hurry, no frantic edge. Every movement was controlled, like she was memorising him as much as he was her.

His hands traced up her thighs, gripping her hips, guiding her just enough to feel her shiver. She rolled her hips slowly, drawing out each wave until his jaw clenched, his focus narrowing entirely to the woman above him.

She didn't look away, not once. And he couldn't either.

Every flicker of light caught in her hair, every hitch of her breath, every shift of her weight, he took it in like it was the only thing he'd ever need to remember.

When she leaned down, her forehead resting against his, he could feel her smile against his lips.

"What?" he murmured.

"Just... you."

It hit him harder than he'd ever admit.

The rhythm built, her hands sliding up to cup his jaw as she kissed him again, deeper this time. The heat between them was enough to make the air feel thick, but there was no rush to get anywhere, just the slow, steady climb until neither of them could keep their breathing even.

When they finally broke, she stayed on top of him, her head dropping to his shoulder, their bodies still tangled and slick with heat. His hands stayed on her hips, thumbs stroking the curve of her waist without thinking.

It was hot as hell. It was intense. But it was also something else, a deeper connection, something neither of them could quite understand. But they both felt it.

Departure – Wheels Up

Dawn broke pale and sharp over the valley, the mountains cutting hard lines into the horizon. The air was cool enough to bite, but James knew it wouldn't last, and by mid-morning the heat would turn the rocks to griddles again.

They moved through the camp without fuss. No speeches, no send-off. Just the quiet nods and firm handshakes of people who understood the weight of shared danger. Captain Daoud clasped Evelyn's hand in both of his, murmuring something in Pashto that made her smile and answer softly. James didn't catch all the words, but he knew the tone: it was gratitude and respect, the kind you didn't earn without spilling blood and sweat together.

Their packs were lighter now, but the eighteen days they'd spent here felt like they'd been stitched into their skin. Evelyn's bandaged arm was a faint reminder of just how close the valley had come to taking more from them.

They walked side by side to the waiting transport, with their boots crunching over dry earth, the Afghan team watching from the perimeter. Evelyn glanced over her shoulder once, taking in the ridges, the dust, and the narrow passes she'd walked again and again. There was no sentiment in her eyes, just the quiet acknowledgement of a place that had tested her and, somehow, still given something back.

James caught her hand before they stepped up the ramp. She didn't pull away.

"You ready to get home, fiancée?"

Her smirk was faint but real.

"Thought you'd never ask."

The transport's engines roared to life, drowning out the valley. As the ground fell away beneath them, the Korangal shrank into a scatter of green and brown, the scars of their work just visible from above.

Neither of them knew it yet, but they weren't leaving the valley empty-handed. Somewhere deep inside her, quiet and unseen, the first flicker of life was coming with them, and a part of the Korangal they'd never forget.

Chapter 38

The plane lurched to a stop with a groan of metal, the stink of jet fuel bleeding into the stale cabin air. James and Evelyn slumped like corpses on parade, weeks of Afghanistan carved into their faces. Dust in their hair. Boots cracked. Every bruise and scar was caught in the harsh fluorescent light.

The hatch dropped. Cold air rushed in.

James stepped down first, shoulders squared out of habit, though his body moved like it had forgotten how to rest. Evelyn followed, her jacket hanging loose, pallor stark beneath the dirt. Behind them, the rest of the soldiers off the flight filed down in silence, one exhausted shadow after another.

And waiting at the bottom of the stairs: Mack, Irish, and Rose.

With her coat cinched tight, clipboard in hand, phone tucked under her arm, Rose radiated an energy that hit like a slap of cold water.

"Well, it's about bloody time you two!" She called, grin wide. "Three weeks you've had me sweating this thing...now you're home and we've got one week to pull a wedding out of nothing, so let's move!"

Mack groaned audibly, shaking his head in a silent apology to James. He was a man who understood post mission fatigue, and he was quietly pissed off that Rose didn't offer them a moment to just breathe.

Irish just shook his head, grinning despite himself. He had not seen his wife this content since their wedding.

Rose swept into them like a storm, hugging Evelyn first, quick and firm, before holding her at arm's length. Her eyes narrowed, scanning with the precision of someone who noticed too much. Evelyn presented with pale skin. Slumped shoulders. That faint green tinge wasn't just exhaustion.

"Evie… You're lighter than a feather. And your skin…" her voice dipped low and sharp "have you been sick?"

Evelyn exhaled hard, rolling her eyes in frustration. "Just let me sleep first, Rose. I'm knackered."

She pulled away, already moving past, one hand absently brushing across her abdomen as she shifted her weight. A fleeting touch. Unconscious. Gone in a blink.

But not unseen.

Rose's eyes flicked down, sharp and assessing, before her face smoothed back into its bright grin. She turned to James, clapping his shoulder with practised ease.

"Don't let her skip meals. I'll have your head if she walks down the aisle half-starved."

James only nodded, too bone-weary to notice the way Rose's gaze lingered on Evelyn a beat too long.

Falling into step beside Evelyn, Rose launched into cheerful chatter about dresses and flowers. Too many questions. Too much detail.

"Colours are sorted, the venue is booked, food organised… You don't need to lift a finger. Just tell me one thing: silk or something more practical?"

321

Evelyn blew out a sharp breath. "Just let me sleep first, Rose. I'm feeling rough, flight took it out of me."

Her tone slammed the door on it. Final. She pulled free, already moving past.

Rose's smile held, but her eyes followed the faint shadows under Evelyn's gaze. The hand that kept hovering, without her noticing, over her abdomen. She said nothing, just filed it away.

James only nodded, still too exhausted to notice the way Rose's was studying his fiancée.

As the team trudged across the tarmac toward the waiting transport, Rose drifted a step behind. Her hand slipped into her coat pocket, phone sliding free. The glow lit her face in ghostly paleness.

One quick message, tapped out with her thumb.

Encrypted. Silent.

Confirmed: signs of pregnancy. She doesn't know yet.

The reply came almost instantly.

Just one symbol.

A single green dot.

Rose's expression flickered, sharp, clinical, utterly at odds with the grin she'd worn seconds ago. Then the phone vanished back into her pocket.

By the time she caught up with the others, her mask was perfect again. Bright smile, cheerful chatter, arm hooked through Evelyn's like any doting sister-in-law would.

"Now, about those flower colours…" she sang, as if nothing at all had happened.

That Night

Their home was quiet, a rare, welcome kind of quiet.

After weeks of the desert's chaos and the deafening, back-slapping welcome from Obsidian, the stillness felt almost alien.

Here, it was just them.

The door clicked shut behind them, and Evelyn didn't bother with lights. She threw her jacket off as she walked. Boots were kicked in opposite directions. The kitbag dropped by the door with a dull thud. Every movement was mechanical, drained.

She grabbed a bottle of water from the counter, unscrewed it with shaky fingers, and drained it in one pull. The plastic crumpled in her hand before she let it fall to the floor.

Without a word, she stripped the rest of her clothes on the way to the bathroom, leaving a trail like shed skin. The shower hissed alive, with steam swallowing the mirror instantly.

She peeled the dressing from her arm. James was already there, moving to help.

"It's okay," she muttered. "It healed straight away. Didn't want to take it off in camp… too many questions."

He studied her arm. Angry red, nothing more.

"Shit, Ev… That's dangerous. What if someone catches on to this…"

"They won't." Her tone cut sharp and final. "Don't tell anyone I got shot out there. Ghost already purged the record."

She stepped under the spray and stayed there until the water ran cold, her forehead pressed to the cold tiles, letting grit and blood sluice away. When she finally shut it off, she didn't bother with her hair, instead she just dragged the towel halfheartedly once over herself. Her skin still felt damp as she blindly stumbled to bed.

She collapsed face-first onto the sheets. No food. No words. No shits given. Just gone.

James was already there, propped against the headboard in his own dusty clothes. He watched her fold into the mattress like gravity was pulling her down into surrender. James watched her as concern overcome him. This was not her, not her routine, she normally had a big spoon of peanut butter if she was that exhausted, just for sustenance.

"Ev… You okay?" His voice was soft, almost tentative.

She mumbled into the pillow with half laugh, half groan. "Just need to sleep, Jamie. I'm absolutely ruined."

He reached out, brushed damp strands of hair from her face, and pressed a kiss to the back of her head. His hand stayed there. Grounding her. Guarding her. Then her breathing slowed into the heavy rhythm of someone too exhausted to dream.

James lay restlessly on his back beside her, wide awake, staring at the ceiling. The war was still on his skin, still in his blood, but what terrified him most was the thought of how close her was of losing the only thing that ever made him feel human.

The following afternoon, James and Evelyn stepped into Obsidian HQ, only to find it transformed. Maps and weapons boards had been replaced by swatches of fabric, flower samples, and catering spreadsheets. The War Room was now Wedding HQ.

Selena stood at the front like a mission commander, her arms folded, and notes projected across the holo-display.

"Right. Timeline is tight. Venue secured, food ordered, legal documentation in progress. We'll run two rehearsals: one tomorrow and one the day before. Dress fitting is scheduled for 0800 sharp. Do not be late, Evelyn. Security sweep is ongoing, but I want a final lockdown by Friday."

Her tone was pure operations briefing and logistics. No one dared interrupt.

For a full five seconds.

Then Mack leaned back in his chair, arms folded behind his head, grin spreading. "Christ, Red. You survived Afghanistan only to sign your life away to *him*? Should've waited for the post-mission debrief before making that kind of tactical error."

Irish snorted. "Aye, she could've done better. Plenty of us were available."

Bullet slapped the table. "Correction, *I* was available. And unlike Paladin here, I'd have given her a rock big enough to signal aircraft."

James sat up straighter, jaw tightening. "The ring's fine."

AJ nearly fell out of his chair laughing. "Fine? She's Valkyrie, mate. That stone should be blinding satellites from orbit."

The whole room broke into cackles. Even Frost's lips twitched where he sat in the corner, arms crossed.

Selena didn't so much as blink. She flicked to the next slide: a seating chart rendered in cold military precision. "Phase Two: placement of assets. Irish and Rose, front flank. Mack, best man duties—you'll survive. Bullet, Rook, Zero—you're ushers. Don't flirt with the civilians. James, your only task is to turn up on time and refrain from scowling in the photographs."

That set them off again.

"Refrain from scowling?" Mack roared, slapping James on the back. "Selena, you might as well tell him to sprout wings."

"Oi," James growled, but Evelyn only leaned back in her chair, smirking as if she had already won the op.

Then Rose swept in behind her like the opposite storm, all warmth and chatter, arms full of fabric swatches and flower photos.

"Evie, darling, you're going to love this. Sunflowers for the bouquet, they're strong and wild... just like you. Bridesmaids are in green, nothing too shiny, I promise. Oh, and there's this adorable little arch we can..."

Evelyn yawned. Loud.

Rose froze mid-sentence. Selena's brows flicked up. James's head snapped toward her instantly.

Evelyn held her hands up. "Sorry. I'm not bored. Honest. I think I've picked up some kind of bug. Just... bone tired..."

Another yawn cracked her jaw.

"Make the decisions for me," she added, sinking deeper into her chair. "I trust you with it. Just don't make me wear lace or heels."

Rose pressed her lips together but nodded, already scribbling notes. Selena's gaze lingered on her for a moment, sharp, but she moved briskly on.

James, though, didn't look away from Evelyn once. His arms were folded tight and garding, his teeth grinding and his eyes hawk-sharp on every twitch of her face, every sag in her posture.

Bullet leaned over to AJ and muttered, "Man, it looks like he's about to throw hands with a chair if she sneezes."

Evelyn cracked one eye open. "I heard that."

"Good," James said flatly, still watching her.

The room rippled with muffled laughter, but the undercurrent stayed with James tracking her every move, Rose filing things away behind that smile, Selena already recalculating timelines in her head.

Wedding HQ buzzed on, but the weight of something unsaid hung like static in the air.

It had only been two days since Hell Valley, and Evelyn still hadn't bounced. Normally she'd be sparring, cracking jokes, riding adrenaline far past reason. But now? She was pale and sluggish, stretched out on one of the couches with her boots still on. An untouched mug of tea cooled on the table beside her.

Later, Selena found Evelyn sitting alone with her shoulders hunched, the strain of Afghanistan still etched into her face.

Without a word, she set a steaming mug down in front of her. The faint scent of cardamom and mint curled through the air.

"I brewed this the way my grandmother used to," Selena said softly, settling beside her. "Good for the body... better for the spirit."

Evelyn managed a tired smile. "You didn't have to."

"I know," Selena replied, nudging the cup closer. "But you're not just Ev to me. You're my sister. And sisters look after each other."

Evelyn's throat tightened. She picked up the mug with both hands, letting the warmth seep into her bones, and for the first time since returning home, she allowed herself to lean on someone else.

James had been watching for hours, his brow creasing each time she reached for another bottle of water. She downed them like she'd crossed a desert, then winced, hand brushing her stomach.

Finally, he couldn't stand it. He caught Irish by the triage cabinet.

"Con, I need you to check on her." His voice was low, firm, and brooking no argument. "She's been off since Hell Valley. She says it's a bug, but she looks like shit. Drinking nonstop. Not herself. She has not taken the piss out of anyone since she has been home."

Irish followed his line of sight, with his eyes narrowing at the sight of Evelyn half-curled under a blanket. He opened his mouth, and Rose cut in. Sharp. Almost too quick.

"Oh, for God's sake, leave the girl alone."

Both men turned. She stood at the kitchen hatch, arms folded, her apron dusted with flour like she'd just stepped out of some cosy domestic scene. Her smile was thin.

"She's exhausted, James. Same as the rest of us. You think she's indestructible, but she's human. She's allowed to feel it without you boys turning it into a medical mystery."

James's jaw flexed.

"She's not just tired, Rose. I know her tells."

Rose softened, her voice slipping into the cadence of reassurance, like she was soothing a child.

"And I know women's bodies better than you do. She's fine. What she needs is sleep, food, and to be left the hell alone without you hovering like a vulture. Poor lamb can't even blink without someone writing her obituary."

Irish hesitated, caught squarely in the crossfire. James's stare was unyielding, suspicion carved deep, but Rose's words landed like oil on water. Smoothing. Silencing. Covering.

Evelyn shifted then, muttering from under the blanket, half-asleep.

"Bloody hell, can you all stop fussing…"

That was enough to make James fall quiet. He dragged a hand over his face, muttering under his breath.

"Bug. Right."

Rose gave a satisfied nod and turned back to her flour-dusted apron, the picture of domestic ease with the matter, to anyone else's eyes, neatly settled.

Chapter 39

The following day the door slammed open, and Selena swept in with a zipped garment bag slung over one arm. Rose followed close, juggling a box of shoes and pins like she was storming a salon.

"Right," Selena barked, crisp as a commander. "Boys out."

James looked up from where he was lacing his boots. "It's my home."

Selena's dark brows arched. "And this is her dress, boss. So… off you fuck."

James blinked, then slowly raised both hands in mock surrender.

Mack appeared, leaning against the wall with a protein bar, barked a laugh.

"Scatter! Boss." he shouted, already dragging James off his couch like an extraction operation.

Within seconds, the flat was a mess of retreating boots and muttered complaints. James lingered longest, with his protective eyes still fixed on Evelyn, before finally ducking out with the door clicking behind him.

Evelyn padded barefoot from the bathroom, her hair damp, the garment clutched awkwardly in her hands. Selena grinned as she tugged the zipper down and eased the lace over her shoulders. The fabric slid like water, pooling against her skin with weightless shimmer.

When Evelyn turned toward the mirror, she froze in disbelief.

The dress clung to her in all the right places, plunging lace framing her collarbone, bell sleeves dripping with fringe like spells spun into thread. She let out a shaky laugh.

"Wow... my boobs look massive. This is very me... Thank you so so much girls, its mint!"

Rose cut in fast, stepping close with pins already in hand.

"Yes, I had a little uplift built in," she said too brightly, smoothing the bodice as though it were nothing more than fuss. "Trust me, it's perfect."

Evelyn snorted. "Christ, if James sees me in this he'll combust."

Selena giggled at the sight of Evelyn flouncing about doing her best Stevie Nicks impersonation. She shook her head. "He is going to be a mess, lets break that commander right open. I want tears from that emotional rock. That's the point."

Evelyn gave one last spin in the mirror, bare feet tangling slightly in the fringe hem. She grinned wide, radiant, glowing...

...utterly unaware of the tracker sewn into the seams.

Dinner had been soft and rare. James took her to her favorite brasserie, ordered without looking at the menu, as he knew by now what she wanted. For once, there was laughter without sand, wine without gunfire. Afterward, they walked home through quiet streets, his arm brushing hers, her head tilted against his shoulder.

He teased her, trying to wring a detail about the dress out of her.

"Alright, c'mon, give me something. Colour, shape, I don't care. I'm going in blind here, Ev."

"Fine," she grinned. "it's cham…" she broke off mischievously, "champagne. With a Liver Bird in gold across the back, tacky vest sewn into the lining, and…"

She swayed suddenly, her fingers suddenly gripping his forearm. Her face turned pale, as sweat beaded on her forehead.

James was all hands immediately, steadying her, scanning. "Hey. Ev. Easy, I've got you… easy baby."

She waved him off with a breathless laugh. "Relax, Jamie. Just lightheaded. Running on fumes. Get me home before I drop."

He kept his arm around her the whole walk back, pulling her close and on total alert.

By the time they reached home, she was already muttering about needing a big bottle of water. She downed half a bottle in almost one. Then she showered quickly and roughly, on date nights they usually got a shower together, but not tonight. Tonight, she was in full survival mode, and he could see it etched into her as she crawled into bed still damp. Her hair curled wet against the pillow, breathing heavy before he'd even joined her.

James brushed a strand from her cheek, his thumb grazed her skin, which felt far too hot, too fragile but not quite full feverish. She barely stirred, but her lips parted on a sigh as she curled deeper.

He lay back beside her, with his strong arm draped across her shoulders, counting each breath. He saw the hollows in her cheeks, the way her collarbone cut sharp beneath her skin, bruises blooming dark over her ribs.

She's just run down, he told himself, with his body wound tight. Rest. Food. A week away from bullets. That's all.

But his hand stayed on her back, fingers tracing circles through the towel she hadn't even changed out of. She didn't move. Didn't stir. Not once.

James pressed his lips to her damp hair and whispered into the dark:

"I've got you, Ev. You'll be alright. Just sleep."

Her breathing deepened, with the heavy rhythm of someone too exhausted to function. James stayed awake long after, with every nerve screaming to keep watch.

Hours later, he woke with a start. The room was wrong, everything looked far too bright.

It wasn't the TV. Not a lamp.

Her.

Light stirred beneath Evelyn's skin. At first it was faint, a ghostly shimmer under the delicate curve of her collarbone, like moonlight caught in veins. Then it moved and spread like liquid mercury.

Threads of silver lit up across her arms, her chest, her stomach. Not still, not mechanical. They moved. Fluid and alive, weaving and unweaving into patterns that shifted with her every breath.

James's gut clenched. It was like watching galaxies bloom beneath her skin, constellations sparking into being, dissolving, and sparking again. Rivers of liquid silver curled around her ribs, across her hips, and up the line of her throat. Every flicker painted her body in starlight.

And with the light came the sound.

Soft at first, almost imagined: a faint crackle, like static electricity skating over glass. Then a low hum, steady as a second heartbeat. James realised it wasn't in the room; it was in her. A rhythm that pulsed through every vein, rising and falling like a breath. Like a heartbeat.

"Ev…" His voice cracked. His hand shook slightly as he touched her shoulder, terrified and reverent all at once. "Ev, wake up!"

She stirred slowly breaking through the layers of fatigue. Her lids were heavy, her voice slurred. "Mmh? Jamie?"

"Look at you," he whispered, awe tangled with fear. His hand hovered above her stomach, close enough to feel the warmth radiating from her skin. "It's everywhere… Ev, you're lit up."

She looked at the shock and confusion in his face, she was still sleep drunk, but as she broke through, she look down. And froze.

And there it was, her own body glowed beneath her eyes. Ethereal bule liquid light moved with fluid pulses, crawling under her flesh, then spilling like silver rivers. She pressed a palm to her belly. The glow flared beneath her touch, brighter, with the hum deepening as though answering her heartbeat.

Then, as suddenly as it had begun, it ebbed. The constellations collapsed inward, its threads shrinking back into her veins. The hum stuttered and faded until there was only silence. Her skin was bare again in the cold moonlight. Human. Fragile.

Evelyn exhaled, too sharp, too quick, then forced a smirk. "You've finally lost it. Or I'm radioactive. Either way, nothing to worry about."

James didn't smile. He cupped her face, thumb brushing over her cheekbone as if to remind himself she was flesh, not starlight. "That wasn't nothing."

The silence between them pressed heavy.

Finally, she rolled back into the pillow with a sigh. "Then it's stress. Don't make it more than it is, Jamie. Please."

But James lay rigid beside her, his heart hammering with fear, and his ears remained ringing with the phantom hum. He didn't argue. Couldn't. He couldn't explain what he had just seen. It looked beautiful and yet disturbing in a way that made him feel utterly uneasy.

Because the sight of her lit from within, the sound of that second heartbeat thrumming under her skin, was seared into him. And he knew, as surely as a soldier knows a battlefield, that it wasn't stress.

Morning light bled through the blinds in thin gold slats. James had been awake for hours, staring at the ceiling, the memory of her body lit from within still burning across his mind. Every time he closed his eyes, he saw it again: constellations crawling her skin, that strange hum in her veins.

Beside him, Evelyn stirred at last, stretching like someone who'd carried the weight of the world in her sleep. She rubbed at her face absentmindedly, her hair sticking out in damp tangles, and she sat up with a groan.

James followed, jaw set, eyes fixed on her.

336

"Ev…" His voice was low and steady but edged. "I want Irish to have a look at you. Something's not right."

She froze halfway through twisting her hair into a messy knot. Her reflection in the mirror stilled.

"No, Jamie."

His brows drew tight. "Ev…"

"No." She turned on him, sharp, but the exhaustion dragged at her words. "We get married in two days. Can't we just… just have a couple of days with no drama?"

Her voice cracked. Frustration blending into it, raw.

"We've just come out of a war zone. I was responsible for keeping everyone alive twelve hours a day for weeks. Crawling through dirt, wires, and mines. My nervous system's shot to hell. And now this wedding circus on top of it… its hard going Jamie, and everyone is doing my head in."

She stopped, her breath ragged and her shoulders rising and falling. Then softer, almost breaking:

"I wish we'd just gone away and done it quietly. I'm just… strung out, Jamie."

James sat there, staring at her, her words caught hard in his chest. Finally, his words broke out, rough and unsteady:

"I need to know… I know we got engaged in the most fuck-it way. I know it hasn't been romantic, that everything feels rushed. And I've failed you. I should have treated you like a queen, Ev. If you don't want this, if this wedding stuff isn't for you, it's okay. We stop. No pressure. None."

Her head whipped toward him, eyes wide, soft and fierce all at once.

"You messing Jamie…" She reached across the sheets, catching his hand, squeezing hard enough to ground him. Her lips pressed into a faint, weary smile. "I do want it. I want you. I just don't want all the noise that comes with it. I'm not backing out, so don't you dare think it. I just… need you to back off a bit while I get my head straight, alright?"

James's jaw flexed, every instinct screaming to push, to argue, to protect. But he let her hand anchor him, curled his palm around hers, and nodded slowly.

"Alright."

But even as he said it, his eyes never lost their weight. And inside, he was already planning: if she wouldn't go to Irish, then he'd damn well keep watch himself. Every breath. Every flicker. Every shadow.

Chapter 40

The day before the wedding was carnage. Obsidian could run black ops in their sleep, but flowers and seating plans? Chaos. Rose stormed the house with lists in hand, Bullet hid twice, and Mack threatened desertion.

The madness broke when Ruby stepped through the door. "Bloody hell," she said, curls wild from the cold. "Feels like NATO HQ in here."

James's shoulders dropped the second he saw her. "Rubes."

She hugged him tight, grounding him, then spotted Evelyn pinned under Rose's interrogation of veils and flower colours. Ruby slid onto the sofa beside her, calm as tidewater.

"Ev. You holding up?"

Evelyn gave a tight laugh. "Trying. Rose is running this like an op… its wrecking my head mate."

Ruby plucked a swatch from the table. "Rose, love, give us a breather. Go boss the others around."

With Rose gone, Evelyn sagged. "Ta love."

"Don't mention it," Ruby smiled. "My superpower's keeping women like Rose from driving women like you insane."

Later, over tea, Evelyn's guard cracked. "I wanna marry James. God, I do. But the wedding… it just reminds me I've got fuck all family. No one to give me away. I miss my mum and dad so much; it feels like a big arse hole I can't fill."

Ruby squeezed her hand, but a floorboard creaked. James stood in the doorway, with his jaw tight, then turned away fast.

Outside, the cold bit as he faced Irish. "Ev would never ask. She's too proud. But I heard her. She's breaking inside, Con. She feels like she's got no one. So I'm asking... will you give her away?"

Irish's expression softened. "Aye. No questions there, lad. It'd be an honor."

When they came back in, Irish didn't hesitate.

"Ev," he said, grinning. "Bad news. You're stuck with me tomorrow. I'm giving you away. If ya will have me."

She froze, then laughed, suddenly and brightly. "Jesus, poor James. He's marrying two of us now." She launched into his arms, nearly winding him.

"Careful, woman. Break my ribs and I'll limp you down that aisle."

She grinned. "Iconic. People would talk for years."

Her laughter filled the kitchen, but as Irish kissed the back of her hand in mock ceremony, a faint shimmer of blue rippled beneath her skin.

He froze. Ruby's eyes caught it too, the reflection dancing in her teacup. Evelyn, grinning, whipped her hand back. "Oi, none of that, Con. I know I'm radiant, but you don't have to kiss me like Cleopatra. Save it for tomorrow."

Irish laughed, but his eyes lingered. Ruby only sipped her tea, expression unreadable.

Later, when the house finally settled, Rose slipped into the hall, phone in hand. The message she typed was clinical, cold.

Maternal nanites active. Confirm package ready for interception. Op Eve green.

Send.

Her face was calm when she tucked the phone away, but in the kitchen Evelyn's laugh still echoed unknowing, unguarded, radiant blue.

The last night before the wedding was theirs. No stag, no hen, no chaos in city bars. Just a firepit out back, Macks garden lit by fairy lights and the glow of coals from the barbecue. The air smelt of charred meat and woodsmoke, laughter threading through the night like a song.

Plates balanced on knees, boots up on logs, no one drinking more than they could handle, but just enough to take the edge off.

Evelyn leaned back in her chair, with the firelight licking across her face and her eyes glinting. "I'm a bit disappointed, you know," she said, loud enough to get the whole circle's attention.

James looked up mid-bite of steak. "At what?"

"That you haven't had a stag night, Jamie. I would have loved to see you stripped bollock naked, mousetraps on your bollocks, tied to a lamppost while these idiots are dressed as Teletubbies…"

The firepit went silent for one beat, then it exploded into hysterical laughter.

"What the fuck, Ev…?" James choked, with his eyes wide and a fork frozen halfway to his mouth.

"What?" Evelyn said innocently, hands spread. "That's how we roll in the UK. Am I right?"

Her gaze slid to Rose and Irish.

Irish raised his beer, smirking. "Aye, she's not wrong."

Rose nodded, grinning wickedly. "Sounds about right. You'd never live it down."

"See?" Evelyn crowed, pointing around the circle. "Americans are just boring. No sense of tradition."

That set Bullet off into wheezing laughter, AJ almost dropping his plate. Mack shook his head, muttering, "Jesus Christ," while Frost just smirked into his drink.

James groaned, scrubbing a hand over his face as the laughter rolled on. "I think I like my testicles intact, thanks."

"Boring," Evelyn shot back, grinning imitating a yawn.

He leaned over, caught her hand under the firelight, and murmured just loud enough for her, "Not boring tomorrow, angel."

She rolled her eyes, but her smile softened as she squeezed his hand back, firelight reflecting in her wicked smile.

The fire in Mack's garden burnt low; glowing embers cracked beneath the faint hiss of cooling wood. Smoke and charred meat still clung to the air, and the grass was littered with bottles catching the low amber light.

James and Evelyn sat back-to-back in the centre of the circle, her spine pressed against his, their warmth shared like a silent pact. Around them, the rest of Obsidian sprawled in mismatched chairs or cross-legged in the grass, the earlier chaos distilled into a quieter, more deliberate kind of intimacy.

Irish leaned forward, with his elbows braced on his knees, his gaze sweeping the circle.

"All right. You know the rules. No jokes, no sass. Tonight's for the stuff you actually carry. One question each from us; you both answer. Honest. Deal?"

"Deal," James said immediately, eyes fixed on the fire. His voice was flat and steady.

Evelyn smirked. "Yeah, all right. But I can't promise no sass."

Irish started. "Did you ever think you'd get here? This… about to get married?"

"No." James didn't even pause. "Figured I'd be dead long before I had the chance."

Evelyn tipped her head back against his shoulder, lips twitching. "Didn't think I'd see thirty, so yeah. Marriage wasn't exactly on the cards."

Bullet grinned, raising his bottle. "When did you know it was love?"

James's jaw flexed, eyes still on the flames. "When she found out I grew up with nothing. No birthday parties. No toys. No books. And on my thirtieth… she brought me a copy of *Alice in Wonderland* and *Wind in the Willows*. Got me a *Star Wars* Lego set. Then she set up this kids' party in the mess hall — jelly, ice cream, balloons. Invited everyone on base. Thirty grown men, some of them SEALs, playing musical chairs and battering a piñata. First time I'd proper belly-laughed in years."

343

The circle broke into laughter. Bullet nearly spat his drink, AJ wheezed, and Mack shook his head with a grin.

Evelyn smirked, lifting her glass. "You're welcome. Best bloody party you'll ever have."

James finally glanced at her, the firelight softening the steel in his eyes. "That was when I knew. No doubt. She was it."

A hush followed, broken only by the crack of wood.

Evelyn rolled her eyes like she couldn't stand the weight of it. "Afghanistan. First tour with him. Mortars dropping all around, and he just planted himself in front of me. No shield. No cover. Just him and his thick skull. The dumbest thing I'd ever seen. And I thought, if he's gonna be that reckless, I might as well keep him."

The circle laughed again, easing the moment.

Selena's voice came quietly. "What are you most scared about tomorrow?"

James didn't hesitate. "That I'll choke. That I won't get the words out."

Evelyn swirled her drink. "That something'll happen before we even get to the 'I do.' Never trusted the world to give me an easy day."

Mack leaned forward, unusually serious. "Hardest thing you've had to forgive each other for?"

James's reply was low. "When she shut me out. I knew she was hurting, and I couldn't reach her. Forgiving that..." His throat tightened. "It was the hardest thing I've ever done."

344

Evelyn's grin faltered but didn't vanish. "When he keeps walking into fire without thinking what it'll do to me if I lose him. Still working on forgiving that one."

Frost's voice was steady. "What's the thing you've never said out loud?"

Evelyn tilted her head, a cheeky smirk tugging despite the heaviness. "That half the time I think I don't deserve him. But if he ever realises it, I'll deny I said that."

James's voice roughened. "That she's the only reason I'm still here. And if she ever walked away, I'd let her. Rather she were free than trapped by me."

The fire popped, sparks kicking into the dark. No one moved.

Ruby broke it softly. "If you strip away the work, the team, the adrenaline… If there were no wars left to fight, who are you to each other then?"

Evelyn blinked, then raised a brow. "Jesus, Rubes, you don't mess around." She leaned back, eyes closing briefly. "He'd still be the one I want to drink coffee with every morning. The one I'd still argue about music with. If there was nothing left to fight, I'd just… love him."

James shifted against her back, voice quieter now. "She'd still be the one I'd look for in a crowded room. Always."

Ruby gave a single nod. "Then you're fine."

Irish leaned forward, breaking the moment with a grin. "Last rule. One question each. Just you two."

Evelyn twisted, meeting James's eyes over her shoulder. "If tomorrow didn't happen… if it all went to hell… What's the one thing you'd want me to know?"

James didn't blink. "That loving you was the only thing I ever got completely right."

He leaned back, meeting her stare head-on. "My turn. If you could change one thing about the path we took to get here, would you?"

Evelyn's smile trembled at the edges but held. "No. Not one bloody thing. Every scar, every fuck-up, every close call dragged me here. To you. So you're stuck with me."

Silence settled again, but this time it was warm.

Irish grinned, easing back. "All right. Enough feelings before Bullet starts bawling into his beer."

Bullet sniffed loudly, glaring at the bottle in his hand. "I'm not crying, you're crying."

Evelyn barked a laugh, tipping her head back until it rested against James's shoulder. He reached behind, found her hand, and laced his fingers with hers. She squeezed once, cheeky and soft all at once, her silent thank-you.

The fire burnt lower, the circle of Obsidian tight around them, the night thick with smoke and warmth. Tomorrow would change everything. But here, now, they had laid their truth bare — and found it more than enough.

They left the laughter and glow of Mack's firepit behind them, slipping out together once the others were deep into their stories and bickering. The walk home was quiet, the kind of silence that didn't need filling. James carried their jackets slung over his arm, Evelyn's hand tucked into his, like she belonged there.

Their home was warm when they stepped inside, the hush of the city muffled by drawn curtains. No team, no chaos, no war talk. Just them.

James locked the door out of habit, then turned to find Evelyn already undoing the buttons of her shirt, smirking at him over her shoulder. "One more night and you're stuck with me for life."

He caught her waist, drew her close. "Best deal I ever made."

She laughed, soft and low, before pushing him gently back onto the bed. She climbed astride him, her palms braced against his chest, her hair tumbling loose around her face. The weight of tomorrow pressed at the edges, but right here, right now, there was only them.

Her movements were unhurried, every shift a slow claiming. His hands gripped her hips, holding her steady, his eyes locked on hers like he could drink her in whole. She bent to kiss him, deep and lingering, her lips tasting of smoke and wine.

"Christ, Ev…" he groaned against her mouth, her fingers tracing the curve of her spine.

Then it happened.

Her body lit up.

Not a faint shimmer this time, a full constellation bursting to life beneath her skin. Rivers of blue light unfurled across her shoulders, her breasts, and her stomach, pulsing in time with her movements. Galaxies spun beneath her flesh, stars blooming and fading with every ragged breath.

Evelyn gasped, freezing mid-motion. "Jamie…" Her wide eyes flicked down at herself, panic threatening to crack through.

James's grip tightened. His voice came hoarse, reverent. "Don't stop." His eyes drank her in, raw and awed. "You look… beautiful."

She searched his face, and what she found there steadied her. Slowly, cautiously, she began to move again. The light surged brighter, cascading like starlight across her skin. Every rise, every arch of her body sent new constellations pulsing into being, painting the room in a soft blue glow.

His hands roamed her, reverent, like he was charting the heavens. "My God, Ev…" His words were breathless, worshipful. "You're the whole universe."

Her lips crashed into his, silencing him, hair falling around them in a golden halo. The glow flared where their bodies met, every kiss, every touch amplifying the light until they were drenched in it, two bodies, one orbit, burning together.

When it was over, she collapsed onto his chest, the glow fading slowly until it left only the faint hum of warmth in her skin. James held her tight, one arm banded across her back, the other stroking damp hair from her face.

"Tomorrow belongs to vows and rings. Tonight, you were starlight in my arms."

Her breath trembled against his throat. She closed her eyes, and for the first time in weeks, let herself believe tomorrow might really come.

Chapter 41

The morning light spilt through the curtains in a soft, golden wash, and Evelyn stirred against the warmth of James's chest. His arm was looped around her, holding her so close like he was an extension of her, their legs were tangled tight beneath the sheets. He breathed her in like he was memorising the way she smelt; the way her hair tickled his chin.

"I can't believe", he murmured, voice still rough with sleep, "that in less than twenty-four hours, you'll be my wife."

Her lips curved as she traced a hand along his jaw. "Believe it, Paladin. I'm all yours. You're gonna be stuck to this little chaos gremlin... FOR...EVER!"

He leaned in and kissed her slowly, unhurried, the kind that made the world drop away. Somewhere deep in his chest, that protective instinct stirred, the one that whispered, "Hold on to this...You don't know how many more mornings you get." He kissed her harder for it.

The faint rattle of keys at the door broke the moment.

James groaned. "Oh, for…"

The door swung opened like the flat was being breached by a SEAL team. Mack's voice boomed from the hall with zero chill. "Morning, lovebirds!"

A split second later, a bang, the bedroom door flew open and a spray of coloured paper erupted over their bed. Confetti fluttered down like a cheap Vegas snowstorm.

"For fuck's sake, Mack! I am gonna have to clear this up!" James growled.

Mack, grinning like a wolf, sauntered to the foot of the bed with no sense of boundaries. "Right, up you get…" He yanked the duvet back with a theatrical flourish and froze for half a beat. "Christ, you two smell like sin. Paladin, up. Shower. Now."

Rose appeared behind him, her coffee cup in hand, and promptly stopped dead in the doorway. "Oh my…" Her eyes flicked from James's very naked form, with everything hanging out, then to Evelyn. "Ev, my love, I can see why you're marrying him."

James arched a brow. "Do you mind?"

Evelyn only smirked and stood, gloriously unbothered, not even reaching for the sheets. Mack's laugh broke into a full-blown cackle. "Jesus Christ girl, don't start my day like that. I will have a heart attack!"

"Alright, no time for gawking," Rose said, tossing something in Evelyn's direction. "Get into this bride!"

Evelyn caught a pair of silky white satin pajamas and a matching robe, the back embroidered in gold: "*Mrs Reaves*". She slipped into them with a cheeky grin.

James's gaze swept over her, slow and hungry. Something in his chest ached, half from wanting her, half from the sharp, unspoken knowledge that nothing in their world was ever truly safe.

"Dressed like that…" he began.

"Boss, you're feral," Mack cut in. "Rose, get her out of here before they savage each other."

350

James sighed deep, grabbing a sheet and wrapping it around his waist. He stepped closer to Evelyn, tilting her chin up between his fingers. His voice dropped low and gravely, meant for her alone. "See you in a few hours. Don't be late, Blackthorn."

She rose on her toes and brushed her lips against his. "I love you, Jamie baby."

As she left, he let his eyes linger on her one last time before the door shut, willing the universe to give them the day they deserved, and trying to ignore the quiet voice that said it never worked that way.

Irish and Rose's house had always been a sanctuary for Evelyn, a place layered with memories, both kind and unkind. It was where she went when the world roared too loud, when her heart felt heavy, when she needed straight-talking advice served with Rose's calm voice and a mug of herbal tea.

But today, the house was different.

She arrived early with Selena, stepping into a space that felt warm and sacred, alive with the quiet rustle of satin bridesmaids' dresses and whispered laughter. Somewhere upstairs, hairpins clinked into place. Mascara wands hovered nervously over fluttering lashes and champagne was drunk.

Two hours later, she was ready.

Irish stood in the hallway, half-dressed in his suit, turning a small sunflower pin over in his fingers as though it were something holy.

Footsteps thundered on the stairs.

"Irish!" Selena's voice rang out, gleeful and breathless. "You're gonna freakkk!"

She bounded down the last steps barefoot, her emerald dress trailing like a forest fire. The colour made her dark eyes burn brighter. "Okay, okay... close your eyes."

Irish gave her a skeptical look but obeyed. "This better not be a prank. If you've put her in a mankini..."

"Shut up," Selena laughed, smoothing his lapel with the easy familiarity of a sister. "It's not a prank. It's her."

He froze.

Then came the soft footsteps. Slower now. Measured. Each one pressing down on a thousand shared memories of scraped knees, firelit talks, her shuffling into the safehouse kitchen in combat boots and bed hair.

And now...

"Open them," Selena whispered.

He did.

And there she was.

Evelyn stood at the top of the stairs like something pulled from a dream he didn't know he'd had. Sunlight kissed the golden crown in her hair, slid over the fine vintage lace of her dress, the plunging neckline, the Stevie Nicks-style fringed bell sleeves. The sunflower bouquet trembled slightly in her hand, but her face... her face was steady. Brave. His girl.

Irish's breath caught. And for the first time in years, he cried.

"Ahh, mate, don't start," she said softly, blinking fast herself as she came down toward him. "You messing? You'll wreck my makeup."

"I'm not ready for this, Red," he murmured, smiling through the tears. "You're so grown. You're… Evelyn. You're a bride."

"I'm still your nightmare in boots," she teased, touching his arm. "I just clean up really well."

He laughed. It was broken but proud. "You look fucking beautiful. Who knew there was all this under that war paint? James has no idea what's about to hit him."

And in that perfect moment, held together by sunlight and unspoken love, nothing else in the world mattered.

The ceremony hall was a cathedral of light. Gold poured through the tall windows in warm sheets, dust motes drifting like tiny ghosts in the still air. Marble pillars rose high, carved like the gods themselves had built this place for his goddess. Old oil paintings lined the walls, their faded eyes watching over him.

James would never have picked somewhere like this; it was too grand, too polished, but for her? For her, it was perfect.

He stood at the front, hands clasped behind his back, staring at the arched doorway like it was a fight he intended to win. The dark suit fit him like it had been cut in defiance of his usual armour, showing his perfect broad shoulders with crisp lines, and a white shirt open at the collar just enough to remind the world he was still him.

He'd refused a tie, saying he couldn't breathe in one.

Bullet, Frost and AJ arrived first, all looking unbelievably handsome in their unique ways. Their eyes locked on to James, he could feel the mischief rising in them before they even opened their mouths.

AJ was the first to break. He sauntered forward, grin broad and lethal. "Oi...would you look at him. Someone give that man a warning label: 'May cause spontaneous pregnancies.'"

Bullet chuckled, leaning against a pew. "Save some of that radiance for the rest of us, Paladin. We're trying to do a job here, not melt into a puddle."

James's voice was flat and deliberately unimpressed. "Eyes on the aisle. Don't get distracted; we're not here to audition for romance novels."

Bullet elbowed him. "Says the man who practices brooding in the mirror." He waggled his eyebrows at James. "You trying to make the explosives jealous? Because that suit's about to out-blow everything in this room."

Bullet pushed off the pew and strolled up behind James, close enough for a teasing whisper. "Sweet Jesus, that suit's doing things to me I'm not allowed to admit in public."

James turned, a slow smile that didn't reach his eyes at first, then softened when he saw them. "Shut up," he said, voice low. "You lot acting like I dressed up for you."

AJ made a show of wiping an imaginary tear. "No, no. We dressed up for you. We're the supporting cast. Don't steal the spotlight; we get jealous. But Baba you're dangerously dressed. I'm volunteering as tribute."

Frost allowed the barest of half-smiles. "Try not to faint in front of the guests, James. Put a lid on whatever that is." He jerked his chin toward the door. "Evelyn's going to be here any second. Don't go full statue."

Bullet clapped James on the shoulder. "Do the thing where you look like you're waiting for a war briefing and a romance headline at the same time. It's very you."

James rolled his shoulders, the tension shifting into something like ease. "If I survive the vows," he said, eyes flicking to the doorway, "there's a beer with my name on it later."

AJ grinned. "Make it two. And get us front-row seats for the bit where she punches you in the face for stealing the wedding playlist."

They fell into a loose, familiar cadence—teasing, warm, a small island of levity before the march began. Outside the doors, footsteps slowed. James squared his shoulders and exhaled. The grin he gave them then was private and fierce. "Alright then. Save the theatrics for after."

"Always," Bullet said. "But if you keel over from being that handsome, we're naming the funeral playlist after you."

The space around him hummed faintly with the soft echo of music drifting from the rafters. It was beautiful, but it barely registered. All he could think about was the next few minutes. The steps. The moment.

"Jesus Christ," Mack's voice came from behind, low and laced with something between disbelief and a grin. "I leave you alone for one morning and you turn into a GQ spread."

James glanced over his shoulder. "You saying I clean up well?"

"I'm saying you look like the cover of a military romance novel, and I hate it," Mack replied, clapping a hand to his shoulder. "Where's the guy who wore combat boots to Christmas dinner?"

"Buried under three layers of tailor's regret," James muttered, adjusting his cuff.

Mack studied him. "Nervous?"

James exhaled slowly. "She's late."

"She's a bride. They're meant to be late; it's dramatic."

"She's never late," James said quietly, eyes fixed back on the doorway. "Even on missions, with bullets flying, she's always right on time."

Mack's voice softened. "You're not worried, are you?"

"No," James said too fast. Then again, lower: "No. I just... don't want to blink and miss it."

That was the truth of it. The edge beneath his calm. The man who'd survived every battlefield but still feared missing the moment she walked in.

"You're not gonna miss it," Mack said, straightening his sleeve. "She's gonna walk in, see you in that suit, and forget her own name. Hell, I nearly did."

James cracked the smallest smile. "Don't start crying."

"I only cry at war films and when Irish sing folk songs on whisky," Mack smirked. "You've got this."

James nodded once. Back straight. Shoulders squared. Heart absolutely wrecked.

And then…

The music shifted.

The room stilled.

Mack stepped back.

James looked toward the doors. The opening notes curled into the air — soft and familiar, carried by piano. And it took him a moment to recognise them.

When he did, he couldn't help himself, and he laughed under his breath, the sound low, raw, and almost disbelieving.

You'll Never Walk Alone.

It wasn't a wedding march. It was her song. Her gift to him. The one that had carried her through impossible nights and war zones. The song she'd told him meant love, loyalty, commitment, and home. The song that said, *I am just a girl from Liverpool, and now, you are my home.*

His throat tightened. Of course she'd chosen it. Of course, it would be the one thing that could steady him and undo him all at once.

The doors opened.

Selena came first, radiant in emerald, her dress clinging and flowing like ivy in the wind. She walked up to James, grinning like the cat who'd orchestrated the whole thing, rose on her toes, and kissed his cheek.

"You're welcome," she whispered.

Then came Rose, barefoot elegance, red curls spilling over her shoulders, a sunflower tucked behind her ear. She caught his gaze and made a heart with her hands. His smile broke wide before she winked and took her place.

Then Ruby, his only blood, his little sister, the one who had been family when there was no one else. Calm. Beautiful. Steady. Her gown shimmered in the light, and she walked up like the moment belonged to her too.

She stopped beside him, eyes bright. "You look amazing," she said. Then, softer, "Wait till you see her."

James swallowed.

His heart pounded hard enough to shake his chest. Somewhere behind him, he could feel the others watching, Mack a steady presence, Irish hidden beyond the door, and Bullet probably pretending not to wipe away a smug tear.

And still… he hadn't seen her.

The music rolled on, building toward something inevitable. James braced himself for the sight of the woman who had survived every war with him, the woman who was about to make him hers.

And he waited.

Irish stood tall and elegant, with the kind of pride that didn't fit into words. His shoulders were straight, his dark navy shirt rolled at the sleeves in quiet defiance of formality, with a sunflower pinned neatly to his chest by Rose's hand earlier that morning.

Beside him, Evelyn glowed.

The lace of her dress moved with her like wind over water, the fringe swaying around her wrists and hemline, giving her that wild, gipsy-soul edge. Her crown sat low across her forehead, delicate gold catching the light in soft waves of blonde. A sunflower bouquet rested easily in her hand. She didn't fidget. She didn't flinch. But when her eyes met his, really met his, they were glassy.

Irish blinked hard, his jaw tightening before he looked away. Then he turned back, letting out a breath that seemed to carry every year of their history.

"I love you, Red," he said quietly.

Her hand slid into the crook of his arm. "I love you too, brother."

They weren't family by blood, but no one alive would dare question it. Not after the battles and firepit nights, the grief shared and carried across borders. He had held her through near-deaths and bad dreams, and she had pulled him out of his own darkness just as often. Now, he would walk her into the arms of the only man he trusted to take over that duty.

She gave him a small nod. He lowered his head, resting it briefly against hers. Together, they stepped through the doors.

The room stilled.

Even the air seemed to pause, caught between the echo of the last piano note and the golden hush that followed, before the first chords of an acoustic *Everlong* began to play.

James had trained his whole life to read the sound of footsteps, the breath before an ambush, and the click of a safety being released.

But he wasn't ready for this.

Evelyn stepped into the light.

And he forgot how to breathe.

The lace shimmered like starlight woven by human hands. Sunlight spilt through the arched windows, gilding her skin in warmth. The gold banded crown in her hair flared like fire when it caught the light. But none of it—not the dress, not the music, not the light—was what undid him.

It was her.

The way she looked at him.

No fear. No hesitation. Just a love that was steady and endless. Like she had always belonged to him and always would.

Behind him, Mack leaned in and whispered, his voice cracking, "You're done for."

James didn't blink. Didn't move. His jaw flexed, fighting to hold something — emotion, pride, maybe a tear — inside. His hands stayed clenched at his sides, resisting the urge to close the distance. Every nerve in his body screamed, *'Go to her,'* but he held his ground. This was her walk, her light, her moment.

Selena, Rose, and Ruby turned slightly, each glancing back. Bullet swiped at a tear, smudging his eyeliner and instantly denying it. Frost stood like carved stone, but his eyes had softened. AJ's smile was quiet and reverent, his hand pressed over his heart.

And James, James felt every scar he'd ever earned protecting her.

He watched his girl walk toward him and knew, with perfect clarity:

He'd burn the world down just to make her smile like that again.

When Evelyn reached him, the rest of the world fell away. The music blurred into silence. The crowd's breathless hush softened into something close to prayer. Even the light seemed to dim everywhere except around her.

She stepped up beside him, her eyes piercing blue and bright, that spark — the Evelyn fire — still burning under all the emotion.

And with the widest, warmest grin, she said:

"Hello, Jamie baby."

His breath hitched, then he laughed. Just once. Just enough. The room shifted with it, soft chuckles rippling through the air like tension breaking.

He shook his head, eyes locked on her. "You look beautiful," he said, his voice thick. "You're killing me."

"Not yet," she murmured back, a smirk tugging at her lips. "I still have vows to read."

The officiant stepped back a little, giving them space.

James went first. Of course he didn't hold a paper; this was James Reaves. He didn't need notes. He was cool and calm, the man who always knew what to say when it mattered.

"I never believed in fate," he began, voice low and steady. "Not until I met you. I believed in strategy. Timing. Discipline. Not miracles. But then you came in... boots, fury, fire... and rewrote everything I knew about love. About loyalty. About what it means to come home."

He looked at her like the rest of the room had ceased to exist.

"You are my safe place in a world that never gave me one. You are the only promise I will ever make that I want to keep. And I swear, Evelyn Blackthorn... I will love you in every life we live and I will protect you with everything I have in this life and the next. Always."

Her lip trembled, but she smiled. Of course she did.

Then Evelyn reached into her bouquet and pulled out a slightly crumpled scrap of paper. It was tattered, dog-eared, with words scribbled and crossed out. Chaos to his calm. She opened it with exaggerated ceremony, sending a little puff of fake dust into the air, which she blew dramatically toward the congregation.

"Sorry," she said. "It's been waiting a while... for him to pull his finger out."

James couldn't help but laugh.

"Okay," she sniffed. "I'm gonna try not to swear."

The room chuckled.

"I once told Mack I'd never fall in love with a man who wore tactical boots in the shower."

James blinked. "You're leading with that!"

"True story!" Mack stage-whispered to Bullet, who grinned.

"But then I met you," she went on. "And you were... annoying. Broody. Barely spoke. Built like a wall. Like a really big wall covered in razor wire and broken glass at the top. Absolutely no sense of humor. And somehow... completely perfect."

He laughed loudly. Everyone did.

"It took you ten years, but you broke through every wall I built around myself. You saw the parts of me I was too scared to show anyone else... And you stayed. You've held me through nightmares, danced with me in kitchens, and once kissed me on a roof during a gunfight."

She grinned. "So obviously, I had to marry you."

Her voice softened.

"I vow to keep choosing you. Even on the days we're tired. Even in the storms. Even when we argue about who left the gear bag out."

"I never leave it out," he murmured automatically.

"You always leave it out," she shot back, prompting another ripple of laughter.

"I love you, Jamie baby," she finished. "And I will love you until the stars stop burning."

The silence that followed was heavy and sacred.

Then...

"Shall we?" she whispered.

He nodded once.

The officiant stepped forward, voice warm and reverent. "I now pronounce you—"

But James didn't wait. He kissed her like they had survived everything together, because they had.

The cheers rose like thunder, chairs scraping, applause echoing off marble and glass. But James only felt her lips, her breath, and the soft weight of the vows she'd just given him.

The kiss was still lingering, their lips parted, when…

BOOM.

Chapter 42

The kiss hadn't even ended when the world tore apart.

The multiple explosions hit like a hammer. The marble floor buckled with the strain, as the stained-glass windows shrieked as they blew into shards as red and gold rained down like knives. Plaster snowed from the ceiling and large chunks fell heavy onto the congregation. A sea of screams rose in terror where only moments ago there had been laughter.

James didn't think. He dragged Evelyn down, covering her body with his own as splinters and dust scythed past.

The chapel doors blasted inward with another deafening explosion. Hinges tore loose, brass botls shrieked, and wood disintegrated into shrapnel. Black-masked men surged through the smoke, with their combat boots smacking through the debris, their rifles already raised.

Another blast gutted the rear. More shadows poured in emerging through the rain of coloured glass.

For a fraction of a second, everyone froze. Then the gunmen opened fire.

James roared above it all, voice raw: "DOWN!" His pistol was pulled from the back of his suit and was in his hand before most had even registered the ambush. He pressed Evelyn harder to the marble as bullets shredded pews and carved the sunflowers into mulch.

The team responded as one. Ruby vanished under Mack's bulk. AJ rolled for the altar's cache, twin pistols flashing into his grip, his fire clean and surgical. Frost appeared beside him,

365

stripping one weapon and moving with glacial precision. Bullet's rage rang feral as he hammered shots from behind a crumbling pillar. Irish stormed through the chaos, shoving civilians down and dragging them out of the line of fire.

But Evelyn never stayed down. She should have stayed down.

James felt her body coil and twist beneath his, and then she was gone, rising like a blade, the hem of her dress tearing, and her crown slipping. One gunman lunged, and she broke his jaw with a hook, stole his rifle, and shot two more before the first had fallen. Another closed in, she hurled the dead body into him, then tore up a jagged chair leg and rammed it through his skull. It only took seconds before the hum of blue lightning started moving through her veins, this time it was not peaceful, it was fury incarnate.

With that a surge of masked operatives moved for her, she had just lit up and signed her death warrant. There was no hiding, she was the target.

Her voice was a snarl. "Come on, fuckers! Not my family. Not today!"

"Valkyrie, FALL BACK!" James barked, firing over her shoulder.

But nothing in the world would stop her. This was her family. Her fight.

Five men swarmed her. She dropped one with a brutal knee strike, forcing his kneecap to snap backwards. But the second slammed his pistol butt hard into her temple. The crack was sickening. Blood sprayed across her face and van violently down her white dress. For a moment she staggered, then as unconsciousness her, her body buckled into the sunflower arch, collapsing in a shower of petals that fell like sparks.

James's roar ripped through the air. He lunged recklessly, but Frost locked onto his arm, firing past him to hold the corridor, before a stream of bullets screamed in their direction.

Masked hands seized Evelyn's limp form, dragging her like she was a lump of meat and headed toward the doors.

Selena's voice was sharp and furious cutting through the chaos. "NO SHOT! They're using her as cover!"

Rose screamed, a sound that shredded the chaos.

The flashbang hit.

Blinding white light consumed and engulfed everything. The sound collapsed into a brutal, ringing void.

When the world cleared again, the doors were blown wide. Black SUVs skidded to a halt outside, engines howling, with motorbikes circling like wolves. Suppression fire poured in, pinning the team, forcing them to watch.

James ripped free of Frost's grip. His voice was raw, breaking with desperation. "TAKE ME! TAKE ME INSTEAD, YOU FUCKING COWARDS!"

They didn't even turn their heads.

He saw the attackers throw Evelyns limp body violently inside the SUV, her hair was tangled, her temple slick with blood, her body slack and lifeless in the back seat. The doors slammed. Engines roared to life.

James bolted, reckless, charging through smoke, but the pillions pivoted as one, with bullets slicing the air. One skimmed his skull, another tore across his arm. Mack dropped from the loft mid-run, tackling him to the marble before the third shot could cut him down.

"You'll die!" Mack roared in his ear. "We lose you too; we're finished!"

The convoy tore away in a storm of tyres and gunfire. Smoke and dust swallowed the chapel, choking every breath.

James staggered to his feet, his gun trembling in his hand for the first time in years. At his boots lay a single sunflower pin from his lapel, the petals were battered and soaked crimson.

Her blood.

His eyes flashed around the wreckage, "Ruby!! Where is she?"

"I'm here... Jay... I'm safe." She appeared bedraggled from behind Irish who looked like rage had crawled into his very soul and had overtaken it.

Inside the chapel stank of plaster, dust and cordite; flowers were crushed into filth. Without hesitation the team snapped into action surrounded by pure carnage. For a brief moment, this was just another mission before the cold hard reality hit in.

AJ crouched by a broken pew, his face was carved with focus, his tablet already pulled and glowing faintly. But his eyes betrayed him. This was his sister, his mother, his family. The only woman who knew everything about him and loved him through every hurt. As his eyes flicked up, he cleared the grief from is voice as best as he could. "Perimeter feeds went dead before the breach. Street cameras cut clean. They knew exactly how to blind us."

Mack sifted splinters by the rear. You could see the cogs turning in his head as he was trying to come to terms with what had just happened, eventually he chocked out a reply. "Satellite?"

"Fifteen-minute lag," AJ snapped. "Worthless."

Irish smashed a chair leg into splinters. His anger bubbled over like lava as Rose just watched on offering no comfort. "This was no merc raid. It was precision."

Frost knelt at the altar, even his usual cool and calm composure was cracking, his breathing was heavier as he tried to hold himself stable. He stopped for a moment, turning a casing in his glove. "Formations were military-precise. Flashbangs arc to herd civilians, not kill. Coordinated flanks. But no insignia, no comms, no chatter."

Bullet's voice cracked, the young man face was laced in confusion and pain as he stood in the wreckage. "Then who the fuck were they?"

Selena stepped into the aisle. Her hands shook at her side as she surveyed the damage. Frost saw the ache in her soul and slowly approached, placing his hand on the base of her back to ground her. She didn't need comfort, she didn't need his touch, she needed answers. Her heals pressed through petals matted with blood and blue shimmer. Her gaze swept the ruin. "Not military."

James's head turned, unreadable.

"They didn't come to negotiate," she said. "No demands. No message. They knew who was here, and they hit anyway."

Bullet-paced, fists flexing. "Then what was it?"

369

Selena's voice cut sharp. "A hit."

The word landed like a body.

Rose whispered it back, pale and shaking. "A hit... on Evie?"

Frost stood slowly, casing in hand. "So who orders a hit on a decorated operative, in front of her team, on her wedding day?"

Silence pressed in.

James crouched again. Her blood streaked the marble, thick and black-red, threaded with faint blue veins that pulsed like veins of light under stone. He felt a pull, like it was dragging his hand in, needing him to touch it. Against every instinct, he pressed his fingers into it.

Warm. Wet. Hers.

And then it moved.

Static tore up his arm, crawling under his skin. His vision seared white. His chest locked.

He felt her.

Pain slammed into his skull, the crack of the pistol butt, the drag of marble under her spine, smoke scalding her lungs. Fear pressed sharp against his chest. Don't panic. Never panic. But a cold, merciless fear.

James gasped, staggering back, bracing himself against the broken pew. The world dissolved. All he could hear was her.

And then, a whisper in his blood.

"Jamie..."

Not in his ears. Inside him.

His heart tore against his ribs. "Ev?" he rasped, voice raw.

Frost caught his arm. "James, what is it?"

But James couldn't answer. The blue shimmer writhed across his fingers, tiny constellations crawling over his skin like they were alive, like they recognised him. For a heartbeat, he was tethered. Linked. And then the bond snapped away.

The glow dulled. The blood lay still.

James dragged in air like a drowning man. "She's alive." His voice was shredded. "I felt her. Pain. Fear. But she's alive."

The others froze. They had seen the light on his hand. None of them doubted what he felt.

Selena's voice was grave. "Her blood…it's linked to you."

James rose slowly, his eyes locked on the ruined doors. Every line of his body trembled with the promise of violence. His voice was steady, lethal. "They took her from me. And they'll bleed for it."

At the breach, Mack sifted through debris with tight hands. Frost examined a torn vest — carbon weave, prototype grade, not on any market. Mack lifted a cracked earpiece, its channel dead.

"They were listening," Selena said quietly.

Ruby crouched beside Bullet resting her hand on his trembling back, her eyes tracing the shimmer on the marble. "Jay… you know who is hunting her... They have found her."

James's didn't respond. He couldn't. There were no words. Instead, his boots crunched on glass as he stepped in. His voice was flat. "What've we got?"

371

Frost handed him the vest. "Custom. Experimental. Not military. Classified design."

AJ hurried up, pale, with a casing in his hand. "And this."

James took it between his still-stained fingers. A tiny engraving: three curved slashes across a diamond.

"What is it?" he asked.

"Nothing on record," AJ said. "Not military. Not PMC. Not cartel. Doesn't exist."

Selena's jaw set. "Then what the hell is it?"

Frost's tone was final. "That's not a symbol, that's a treat...I have seen this before."

James rolled the casing in his palm, the faint blue still smearing his skin. His eyes burnt cold. "The bullet doesn't matter. It's not about what they used. It's about who let them use it."

Selena's gaze was sharp. "Then we find who greenlit this. That's our way in."

James turned toward his pack. His chest heaved, but his voice was calm as death.

"Zero—trace the casings. Supplier, chain of hands, everyone who touched them. Rook — sound map of the retreat, exact route, exact exit points. Wrath—I want a civilian headcount. Survivors, wounded, and dead. Nothing goes unlogged. Oracle — scrub for chatter. Not open comms — hidden frequencies, ghost bands. Mack — find me a vehicle database. SUVs, plates, tyre chains, anything."

He turned to his sister, "Ruby, get me everything you know about Aegis Consortium, facts, rumors… Anything… please… I need you."

He turned back to the ruined aisle, his boots leaving blue-smeared tracks on the marble. His voice dropped lower, every word deliberate.

"We follow the tech." His eyes were glacial. "And then we find the bastards who have her. I will fucking end them. If my wife hasn't already done it."

No one moved. No one spoke. They felt the air changing, the shift from soldier to weapon. Paladin was awake.

The light from their makeshift lanterns threw jagged shadows across broken marbel. Wind pushed through the gaps in the roof, rattling loose panes of stained glass like bones knocking together.

Frost could see the heartache around him; he knew that the best chance of finding Ev was to keep a cool head while the others were in various stages of pain. The weight of the last few hours was dropping heavy on the team, and Frost knew well enough that the time they had to claim her back was already slipping. He crouched near the cracked altar, laptop propped on a pack, bullet casings lined neatly on a strip of cloth in front of him. His gloved fingers moved with slow precision as he fed another casing into the scanner. The machine hummed, its green bar crawling forward.

The team held their silence. Only James moved. He paced the length of the chapel, boots grinding across grit, jaw locked, hands flexing like he needed something, anything, to break.

Irish hadn't spoken. Grief sat heavy in his chest, but duty gave his hands something to do. He moved through the team one by one, pressing bottles of water into palms, checking them like soldiers, not friends. When he reached James, he crouched, hand half-raised for his shoulder.

James looked up, eyes bloodshot, hollowed.

Yeh, you fucking bastard, Irish thought. *You could have stopped this.*

His hand recoiled before it touched him, as though James's skin was hells inferno itself. Comfort was useless here. In Irish's eyes, James had failed her and nothing could mend that.

Through the silence the laptop pinged. Frost's face drained of colour. "Oh fuck. Oh mon dieu, que Dieu sauve son âme" (ow God save her soul)

Every head turned. James stopped dead. "What?"

Frost didn't look up, his voice low and deliberate. "These casings aren't Russian. Not NATO. Not cartel. They're tagged. The digital signature is buried in the alloy itself. Look."

He spun the laptop so the screen's glow spilt across the cracked stone. The archive spat out a match — Facility IX.

"Facility IX", Frost said, the name tasting like poison. "Bioweapons division. It's rumored to be one of the developmental sights for the Aegis Consortium. Ruby was right. Supposed to be myth. But this… this is live." He clicked deeper, scrolling through encrypted archives and mirrored sites. "The dark web's flooded with whispers. Bids. Trades. IX produces bioweapons, designer ammunition, hybrid payloads. They're

374

moving product to the worst of the worst... cartels, mafia syndicates, black armies, and even rogue states. And the casings we picked up?" He tapped the cloth, the spent brass lined like relics. "Identical. Same markers. Same source."

Selena's voice cracked the silence, sharp with disbelief. "Facility IX, It was supposed to be shut down in the nineties. It's just a myth."

Frost finally looked up, dark eyes cold. "It's not. It's alive. And it's feeding the world."

The words sat heavy, the ruined chapel suddenly smaller, suffocating.

The wind moaned through the broken rafters, carrying the smell of damp stone and burnt wax. The laptop's glow lit Frost's face from below, making his expression look carved from shadow.

"There's more," he said, his voice flat but heavy enough to cut through the silence.

Everyone stilled. James's pacing stopped mid-stride.

Frost scrolled deeper, encrypted threads blooming across the screen — screenshots, auction listings, fragments of medical reports. "Facility IX isn't just making weapons. It's been linked to Revenant trials. Same strain we've seen rip people apart in the field." He clicked another file, his mouth tightening. "And it's not just tech. They're selling people. Prisoners. Civilians. Even kids. Bodies and blood. Tissue samples auctioned to whoever can pay — cartels, mercenary armies, states with no flag."

Ruby looked over his shoulder "Its definitely Aegis territory J, it matches all the Intel that I have seen while working with victims trafficked and found before being lost to Revenant integration."

Selena's face drained. "Revenant labs don't exist outside black budgets. If this Aegis is running them, it means the myth was covered. They've been building it under our feet this whole time."

Frost's fingers lingered on one image, an invoice string, blurred names, and a line that read: Subject transfer: live – viable nanite reaction expected.

Bullet swore viciously, punching the stone wall so hard his knuckles split. "They're fucking selling people like lab rats? They are selling innocents. Malditos bastardos."

AJ went pale, swallowing hard. His voice cracked but was steady enough to carry. "That means... that means... they don't want her dead."

James's jaw worked like it might shatter his teeth. His voice, when it came, was a low growl that carried through the ruined chapel.

"They know...They fucking know."

The words fell like a verdict.

Frost's words still echoed off the broken stone, the hum of his laptop the only sound against the silence of the ruined chapel.

AJ hunched over his own screen, fingers flying across the keys. "It's worse than that," he muttered, eyes narrowed. "Facility IX isn't a single site. There are multiple installations — some active, some decommissioned — but they move. Constantly. One day it's in America, the next it's Venezuela, then it's gone. Whole labs vanish and reappear halfway across the world. No fixed

376

footprint, no permanent coordinates. They're designed to stay ahead of anyone trying to track them."

Selena's voice was tight. "Mobile black sites…"

AJ swallowed nodding, his face pale in the glow of the monitor. "Not just labs. People. I've been scraping chatter off darknet auctions. They're selling blood, tissue samples… and people. Survivors, operatives, test subjects. Moved like cargo between IX hubs."

The silence thickened.

James stopped pacing, his eyes drilling into AJ. "Say it plain."

AJ hesitated, then forced it out. "If they've taken her… she might not be close for long. They could already be moving her. She could be on the circuit, listed, traded…"

"Enough." James's voice cracked out like a gunshot, but his pacing had turned into full strides, back and forth, boots grinding against stone. His jaw was clenched so hard it looked like it might shatter.

Bullet swore under his breath, as fear hit him like a sledge hammer. "Jesucristo, necesitamos encontrarla... ¡Ahora!" (Jesus Christ, we need to find her, Now)

Selena's face had gone pale, her hands tightening on her prayer beads as her tears began to fall. Bullet locked his trembling arms around her, pulling her into him, as she was overcome with guilt and grief. "Facility IX is active… I missed it… and Ev..."

Frost voice stayed quiet, closing the casing box with a hollow click. "Lina, Ce n'est pas ta faute, mon amour…. But it's real. And they've got her."

Chapter 43

They tore back to Obsidian HQ in silence, the convoy cutting through streets like a blade. The war room doors opened wide, and chaos poured in, emerald silk and tailored suits colliding with black steel, wedding colours bleeding into the cold light of the war room. What should have been a night of champagne and photographs now looked like a funeral march.

The table was a sprawl of open laptops, burner phones and mugs of coffee supplied by Rose that had long gone cold. AJ's monitors spat data like rain, code streaming down their faces in jittering light. Frost leaned against the far wall, arms folded, eyes narrowed; his stillness was its own threat. Mack paced in a tight circle, all restless muscle. Irish planted himself by the door, a wall of quiet fury, daring anyone to breach. Ruby hovered near the whiteboard with a pen poised in her fingers, calm but sharp-eyed, ready to catch every thread before it slipped. Her phone always close. And Rose stayed quiet. Watching.

James entered last. He didn't shout. He didn't need to. His voice was low and lethal, carrying enough weight to still the air.

"Listen up. We're done reacting. From here on… we hunt."

He pointed at AJ first. "Fourteen buyers tied to her blood out of Colombia. I want everything. Handles. Wallets. Proxies. If their cousin's dog has a digital footprint, I want it. Track the flow from venipuncture to vial to vault. If there's a ledger, crack it. If there's a dead drop, map it."

AJ's fingers were already moving; eyes locked on his screens. "Yalla."

379

James turned to Frost. "I need info on Ghost. Every fallback, every half-burnt route he's ever used. I need to know who had access to Evelyn's medical folders before he torched them. Who mirrored them, even for a second. Where they landed, who looked, who copied."

Frost's expression tightened, a dangerous glint in his eyes. "Copy."

"Handlers, traffickers, shell companies, clinics, logistics fronts," James pressed on. "Anyone who has ever touched Revenant air. Names and addresses I can break."

Mack stopped pacing, jaw tight. "Why the hell are we talking like Evelyn's a Revenant asset? Why didn't you tell us her blood was taken? Sold? And why the fuck are we talking about Ghost like he's in play?"

The room froze. It became very clear only a select few knew everything, and Mack was not one of them. The cold feeling of betrayal started creeping through him.

"Just do it," James snapped.

Mack didn't flinch. "No. You don't get to pull Paladin's voice without explaining why you're tasking us like she's property. Irish… Sel… AJ…Frost…what do you know that I don't?"

"You're not to ask them, that's a fucking order Mack! Someone out there is treating her like a Revenant asset," James cut in, clean and hard. His eyes burnt like ice. "And if we don't think like the scumbags who trade and traffic, we'll never find her."

The silence that followed was a live thing, coiled and dangerous.

Selena broke it first, her voice cool and precise. "He's right. Whoever took her knows what she is. What she can do. That changes the profile. It changes the price. And it changes how fast her and her blood moves through the market."

Bullet's head jerked up, his voice unsteady. "What she is? What can she do? I have seen that blue lightning in battle... that's not a Revenant quirk... James... COMMANDER..."

Mack's eyes narrowed. "What aren't we being told?"

James didn't blink. "Need-to-know. And right now, what you need to know is this: the buyers aren't medics or scientists. They're engineers of people. And they've been circling for months. Years maybe."

Ruby placed her pen flat on the whiteboard ledge. Her voice was steady. "Then we plan like they know everything. And we act like we're already out of time."

James gave a single nod and moved forward, slamming his palm against the whiteboard before scrawling dark lines across it. Lanes. Targets. Orders.

"Frost—squeeze your brokers. Three names for every alias tied to Revenant. If they hedge, lean harder."

Frost gave a curt nod. "On it."

"Irish — ports and private airfields. Night manifests. Unlogged charters. Medical coolers shipped in unmarked crates. Anything moving bio off-paper."

Irish's jaw flexed. "Moving."

381

"Bullet — street-level. Clinics buying centrifuges they don't know how to use, saline showing up in the wrong districts, ex-mil medics suddenly flush with cash. You talk to the people who don't talk to cops."

Bullet's eyes were feral, his nod tight. "Roger."

"AJ—dark forums, invite-only markets, closed biohacker servers. Watch for keywords: 'accelerant', 'adaptive serum', and 'self-repair'. I want a heat map of every buyer desperate enough to whisper it."

AJ was already coding, face lit by blue light. "Parsing now."

"Rose — Look after the teams welfare."

Rose nodded In acknowledgement, she was more than happy to stay close.

James's gaze locked on Selena. Their eyes met, and a conversation passed in silence.

"You and me," he said. "Med pipeline. Cross-match black-bag trial sites with Revenant subcontractors. If they're building a cage, we find the blueprint."

Selena inclined her head. "Yes, sir."

Mack still hadn't moved. His stare was iron. "You really not going to tell us why this smells like state secrets?"

James stepped in close enough that only the first ring could hear. His voice dropped, velvet wrapped around iron.

"Because if this room leaks, she dies. That's why."

He straightened and swept his gaze across the table. His tone was final, brooking no argument. "You want more than that? Then find her with me."

For a beat, Mack held his stare. Then he flicked his eyes toward the rest of the team, his shoulders loosening. One sharp nod.

"Alright, you don't trust me fine… I do this for her." he spat the words in frustration. "But, Commander, I will have answers."

Selena caught James in the corridor outside comms. Her voice was low, but it cut like glass.

"James, this is more than Colombia. I've seen the way you're moving on this. What is she?"

He froze, then shook his head hard. "I don't know, Sel…" His voice cracked, frustration spilling raw. "I don't fucking know, and neither does she."

Selena's gaze never wavered. "Then tell me what you do know."

James dragged a hand down his face, as if he could scrape the truth out through his skin. "She can do things…" His chest heaved. "She can heal. You have seen it. But there is more, she can heal me. She healed my bullet wound. My flesh knitted together… like nothing happened."

Selena's brows pulled tight. "Biotech?"

"No!... I don't know!" His voice slammed against the concrete walls. "No mods. No implants. Nothing since that shit we pulled out of her. But since Afghanistan…" His hands cut the air, searching for words. "Her skin lights up. Like stars under it.

Like… she's burning from the inside out. No pain. And I don't know why."

The hum of the overhead lights filled the silence. James's voice fell to something raw and hollow. "All I know is whatever she is, they want it. This Aegis Consortium has been watching her…Fuck!! Ghost warned me… Ruby warned me… and I just kept putting her in danger just so I could keep her about.." He broke off, swallowing hard. "They have been watching her… they know what she is… I fucked up… Why else take her?"

His fist slammed into the wall, rattling the frame. "Why else?"

He spun, eyes burning. "And where the hell is Ghost? He gave her a burner straight to him. No contact, nothing. If he's alive, he's hiding. And if he knows something and isn't here…" James's voice dropped into venom. "Fuck she trusted him, what if he sold her out?"

Selena stepped closer, steady, her tone firm. "Breathe James. We will find her."

James began pacing like a caged animal. "We have to. Because if they test her, if they figure out what she can do… we don't get her back the same, or she dies."

Selena's eyes sharpened. "There is something else, isn't there."

James's hands scraped his face again. His voice was barely a whisper. "She can feel biotech weapons. She can interact with it. And with people who have been given the Revenant strain, like the children we found in Libya. But with the weapons, she can

384

integrate with them… she can fucking disarm them Sel... she can almost talk to them… understand them…"

Selena froze. Her words came out like a verdict. "If she can disarm them… then she can arm them. Remotely?"

The weight of it hit them both. James staggered as if the idea itself was poison. Bile climbed his throat, burning him "Fuck, Sel…" He raked both hands through his hair. "If they find that out…" His voice broke. "We don't get her back."

A voice cut through the corridor. "How long have you been sitting on this?"

Frost stood in the doorway, a file in his hand, his face carved from stone.

Selena tried to soften him. "Don't my love…"

"No." His tone snapped like ice. He stepped forward, closing the space. "You've had us chasing shadows without telling us why. Now I hear Evelyn Blackthorn might be the most valuable thing every sick bastard in the world wants, and you're hiding it?"

The air thickened.

James's jaw tightened. "This isn't your business."

"The hell it isn't!" Frost closed in. "You put us in the field blind. And now I find out Evelyn isn't just a target; she's an asset. A weapon."

James's roar ripped through the corridor. "She's not a fucking weapon! You saw what they pulled from her back. You held her down. It changed her, yeh, but she is not a weapon; she's my wife! She is your friend… fuck… she loves you… both of you."

Frost's reply cut clean. "And you've been hiding what she is from the people now risking their lives to try and locate her. That's not leadership. That's betrayal."

Selena shoved herself between them, a hand against each chest. "Enough."

But Frost's voice was still hot. "They will use her James... to arm everything we fight to stop..."

James's eyes blazed. "Shut the fuck up. She is not a bioweapon."

Another voice slipped in from the doorway. "Back up."

Bullet leaned there, a Red Bull can dangling from his fingers, his usual grin gone. "Did I just hear my CO say Ev can disarm and arm biotech like it's nothing?" His gaze locked on James. "Qué demonios?"

"Bullet..." Selena began.

"No." Bullet stepped forward. "If she can do what you're saying, that makes her the hottest asset on the planet. And we are digging through the darkest info... you're risking our lives with fuck all trust. I am not a kid anymore... you let me be your weapon... brought me out of my own country... I left my family for you Reaves and you can't trust me with this... its fucked..."

James's chest rose, fell, then snapped. "Enough!"

The word cracked the corridor open.

"We don't know any of this for a fact," he thundered. "She feels bioweapons. That doesn't mean she can switch them on and off. What I do know is this... when she's happy, her skin lights up like stars. When she feels safe, there is something in her body,

386

in her fingertips. And she can heal." His voice grew hoarse, breaking, but unyielding. "Does that sound like a weapon to you? I have never seen her use it for violence. Not once. She is not a Revenant experiment. She is my wife. So back. The fuck. Off."

Silence pressed the air thin.

The door creaked open again. Mack stood there, arms folded, his gaze sweeping the wreck. "So… the rest of us just heard that."

James's head snapped toward him.

Mack raised both hands. "Not saying a word. But maybe it's time we all got on the same page before we start poking around in places we can't crawl out of. Because if half of what you just said is true, they didn't just take a random operative. They took her. And that means we're already in the deep end."

James' hands violently shook as the gravity of the situation smacked him hard. "We don't have time for this. Every second we're standing here, she's in hell."

He slammed his fist into the wall hard enough to rattle the frame. "So, unless you've got something that gets me closer to her, shut your mouths, dig deeper, and move now."

The corridor locked into silence. Mack muttered dryly, "Guess that's the briefing," and reached for the nearest file.

But Frost's voice cut through, softer now and far more chilling. "That isn't healing, James. Not really. Healing means restoring what it was. What she does… it's rewriting. Biology reprogramming itself in real time. That isn't human."

The words landed like a shadow crawling across their faces. Nobody moved. Nobody spoke.

For the first time since the abduction, it wasn't just fear of losing Evelyn that filled the corridor. It was the deeper terror of what they might bring back if they found her.

Chapter 44

The war room stank of burnt coffee and electronics running too hot. Old fluorescent tubes buzzed overhead, throwing pale light over maps, scattered Intel and the loaded silence of a team living on four hours' sleep and caffeine fumes.

James stood over the table, eyes fixed on the evidence bag in front of him, the three-slashed diamond bullet catching light every time he shifted. The others worked in their corners, a restless hum of movement without conversation.

The door hissed open. Selena strode in, a tablet clamped under one arm, her jaw tight like she'd walked through fire to get here.

"I've got something."

James's head snapped up. "Talk."

She dropped the tablet onto the table, the screen already alive with grainy overhead stills. "Hamburg. North dock district. Industrial on paper with freight warehouses, customs checkpoints, nothing special. But in the last seventy-two hours…" She swiped through the images, her voice flat but loaded. "…security tripled. Not local police but private contractors have—contractors that can be linked to high-value asset trafficking. They're carrying suppressed carbines and thermal optics. They're running infrared sweeps every half-hour. They are preparing for a new arrival."

Frost leaned over her shoulder, his gaze narrowing. "Too heavy for import freight."

"Exactly. And it gets worse." She tapped again. Satellite overlay bled into a web of utility readouts. "Power draws up thirty per cent across the block. Underground water usage has doubled. Enough to run climate control for a medical facility... or a lab that doesn't want to exist on paper."

Mack's eyes were locked on the tablet. "What about supply routes?"

"Two unmarked trucks in every night, one out. No manifests, no GPS pings. Drivers are all ex-military, mostly Balkans and Eastern Bloc. And the shipments going in? Manifested as 'refrigeration units.'"

Irish exhaled through his teeth. "That's not a warehouse. That's a holding site."

Selena's eyes found James's, steady and unblinking. "The security, the utilities, the supply pattern, it fits IX methodology. No proof yet, but if we wait, we lose the trail."

James stopped dead in the centre of the room, fear was etched on every part of his normal stern face, his voice came out low, steady but dangerous.

"Facility IX. Who runs them?"

Frost and AJ exchanged a look. Neither spoke.

Finally, Frost shut the laptop with a snap. "Your worst nightmare."

The silence was thick enough to choke on.

Selena's voice cut through it, quiet but razor-sharp. "There are rumours. One name keeps surfacing in whispers across

390

darknet boards, black ops back channels, and even intelligence chatter that no one wants to put in writing."

James's eyes narrowed. "Say it."

"Kashir."

The name hit the air like a drop of blood in water. Roses eyes darted up too quickly.

Selena didn't stop. "He's not a commander. Not a general. He's something worse. A shadow operator, British-born, or so the whispers say. No confirmed identity. Kashir is a code name. He doesn't just run Facility IX. He is Facility IX. The labs, the auctions, the bioweapon development — they all trace back to him. Likelihood is, he is a key player in the consortium's supply chain, if not the leader. He is thought to be a billionaire so can buy silence and pay for key players in the biotechnical world, and enough money to pay off anyone who stands in his way. He is a supremacist."

She stepped closer to the main screen that was now covered in data, her eyes hard. "Kashir doesn't kill for power or politics. He breaks people apart to see how they work. He sells blood and bone to the highest bidder, governments and cartels alike. Revenant nanotech, human tissue, whole operatives cut into samples, he'll trade it all. And those who disappear into his labs…" Her voice dipped. "…don't come back."

James's pulse thundered in his ears. "And he knows already what Evelyn is."

Selena's face was pale, but her words were flat, merciless. "If Facility IX traffickers already have her, then yes, second they test her, Kashir will know." She trailed off for just a moment, the weight of it crushing the space between them.

"Our worst nightmare just became hers."

James didn't even blink. "We'd better pray that he is just a ghost story. We go now."

The room erupted into motion.

Chairs scraped back. Lockers slammed open. Wedding gear was replaced with technical gear. The air went from tense stillness to the metallic clatter of weapons and the sharp hiss of Velcro tearing as vests went on.

Mack threw open the steel arms rack, pulling rifles from the rack and tossing them down the line without looking. "Primary on the left, secondary on the right… move."

Bullet stripped and cleaned his sidearm in thirty seconds flat, the clack-clack of the slide loud in the tight room. "Coyote locked," he muttered, holstering in one smooth motion before pulling extra mags from the crate.

Frost was methodical, adjusting his optic until it clicked into perfect focus, loading each mag with a mechanical rhythm. "Zero set."

Irish raided the med locker, stuffing his trauma bag with chest seals, tourniquets and enough morphine to quiet an army. "Wrath ready."

Selena synced her comms rig with a speed that bordered on violent, her fingers flying over the keyboard. "Oracle live."

AJ shoved a flash drive into his pocket before slinging his carbine over his shoulder. "Rook green."

Mack grabbed the nearest dry-erase marker and began scrawling on the mission board as fast as James spoke:

"Dockside two entry. Frost and Mack… breach. Bullet and AJ… flank sweep. Irish… med sweep and evac channel. Selena… control room, lock down comms, burn their eyes and ears."

"And you?" Mack asked without looking up.

James slid a mag home with a decisive click. "I'm going for her."

No one argued.

Rose placed a hand on James's shoulder "I will come with you… keep the team cared for."

James replied with a weary nod. "Roger that."

AJ made an excuse to buy him a few minutes alone and sat alone in a bunk room, the screen glow painting his face pale. His stomach twisted with the weight of everything, then his phone buzzed – it was Ryan. He hesitated, thumb trembling, and then answered.

"Habibi?" Ryan's voice was soft, but AJ could hear the worry beneath it. "You don't sound okay."

AJ forced a smile into his tone. "I'm fine. Just… gonna be away with work for a while."

A pause. Then Ryan's voice sharpened. "Let me help you. Is this about that Revenant stuff you hinted at?"

The words hit like a knife. AJ's chest tightened, throat burning.

"No. Ryan…no. I don't want you anywhere near this. We're digging in dark places. I don't want to lose you." His voice cracked, raw. "There'll be bounties on our heads already. You can't even imagine what we're walking into."

Ryan exhaled, shakily. "And what if I lose you? Please, it took me so long to find you. You're my everything."

AJ's hand curled into a fist. His voice dropped to a whisper.

"If that happens… just know I died fighting for someone I love, someone who has been a mother to me. Someone who held me through grief and loved me and us for who we are…."

Silence. Then Ryan's voice, low and broken: "So it's Ev, then."

AJ shut his eyes. The truth weighed heavy, but there was nothing to say. Only silence, his breath uneven in the dark. Finally, in a voice barely audible, he let it slip free in the only words that ever felt big enough:

"بحبك من كل قلبي"

(I love you with all my heart.)

Ryan's breath caught on the other end. Neither spoke again, but the connection between them thrummed with everything left unsaid.

AJ sat frozen on his bed absolutely devastated as the call ended, his phone was still in his hand, screen gone black. His chest ached like someone had driven a knife straight through it.

The door creaked open. Mack leaned on the frame, a bottle of water in one hand that was intended for AJ. He didn't say anything at first, just took in the sight—AJ hunched, eyes red from fatigue and grief, his knuckles white around the phone.

"Just checking in on you, kid, we gotta go soon..." Mack said softly.

That broke him. AJ shoved the phone into his pocket and got up fast, head ducked, but the tears came anyway. He crashed straight into Mack's chest, with his fists gripping the front of his hoodie.

"I just had to say goodbye to my boyfriend," AJ whispered hoarsely, the words spilling out like blood from a wound. "In case we die hunting this. In case I don't come back."

Mack froze only a heartbeat before his arms wrapped around him, tight and steady. He didn't flinch at the word 'boyfriend'. Didn't joke. Didn't pry. He just held him.

"Jesus, AJ..." Mack murmured, placing his hand steady between his shoulders. "That's one hell of a goodbye."

AJ pressed his face into Mack's chest, trembling. "He doesn't belong in this. He's light. He's good. And I love him. But if I bring him anywhere near this war, I'll lose him."

Mack tightened his hold, his voice gruff but gentle. "Then you did right by him. And for the record, you don't have to hide that from me. Not from any of us. You hear me?"

AJ gave a shaky nod against him.

"Good," Mack said, rocking him just slightly the way he might with a younger brother. "Now, you've got me in your corner. No matter what. We'll carry this together. I know how much you love Red, and you know what, if you need a hug, while you're away from your man, you have me."

395

For the first time since the call, AJ let out a broken little laugh. "You're gonna make a shit big brother speech about this, aren't you? If we don't get Ev back. Will you be my brother?"

"Damn right, already am kid." Mack said, kissing the top of his head without hesitation. "Because you're family. And that means your boyfriend just got himself one very overprotective brother-in-law, whether he likes it or not. We will get your Red back buddy, she will meet this man of yours."

For a moment they both looked into each other's eyes, both knowing that her retrieval was against the odds, but they will die trying.

Half an hour later, the safehouse was a ghost with its lights off and tables cleared, the echo of boots fading into the night. Outside, the convoy idled in silence, matte-black vehicles rolling one after another into the dark.

The following day docks of Hamburg waited, cold and wet, and smelling of diesel and rain, and somewhere in that maze of corrugated steel and shadow, there might be a door that led to her.

Chapter 45

The Ghost Trail – Hamburg

The storm over northern Germany had teeth.

Cold rain hissed through the skeletal branches, drumming against rotting bark and pooling in black water that slicked the roots. Wind tore through the trees in ragged gusts, bending them until they groaned like old bones.

And in the middle of that ruin stood something older and uglier than the storm.

A bunker. Squat, windowless, half-swallowed by the earth. Its concrete skin was blotched with moss and algae, seams soft with decades of rot. A relic from a war the world liked to pretend was finished.

James halted at the perimeter fence, boots sinking into a bed of sodden leaves. The chain-link rattled in the wind like teeth chattering in a skull. He stared at the structure beyond and felt his stomach tighten. The air around it was colder and heavier, as though the forest itself leaned back from the thing buried there. Predatory.

Official records swore this place had been decommissioned, stripped, and demolished. Erased.

But AJ's drone sweep had caught the lie: infrared images showed the faint pulse of power, stubborn and steady, deep under the concrete. A heartbeat where none should be.

Mack and Frost were already at the rusted hatch, crowbars biting into warped steel, every pull sending rust screaming into the rain. AJ crouched on a slick boulder, laptop balanced on his knees, its glow painting his face a ghostly blue. Selena's scanner bled a thin electronic whine as she studied the readout, her breath steaming in the cold.

"This was a Facility IX satellite," she said. Her tone was clinical, but her eyes never left the bunker. "Seven years abandoned. Shut down in a hurry. No reason on record. But recently activated."

James's voice was quiet, but the conviction in it snapped like bone. "She could've been routed through here."

Not speculation. Certainty.

The hatch gave with a metallic groan, the lock surrendering like a rib snapping. A breath of air exhaled up into the storm. Not rot, not mould, but something worse. A dry chemical sting that clung to the tongue, sharp enough to burn the nose. Preservatives. Like a mortuary where the bodies had been sealed too tight.

The storm hissed harder through the trees, rain hammering the roof of the bunker, but it didn't mute the sound from below: the hollow groan of old pipes, the faint tick of dripping water, and beneath it all, a vibration too regular to be natural. Machinery. Still alive in the dark.

James's hand tightened on his rifle. "We go in."

The others fell silent, the storm at their backs, the black throat of the hatch yawning wide in front of them.

And then they descended.

The descent was narrow and steep, the stairwell a throat of rusted iron. Each step groaned under their weight, slick with condensation. The air grew colder the deeper they went, squeezing their lungs; the storm above swallowed them whole.

Then the first light flickered.

A failing strip, wired into some ancient emergency grid, blinked in a three-second pulse. Each flash revealed walls stained a colour that might once have been white and pipes streaked with brown rivulets like dried arteries.

AJ's voice was thin. "No vermin. No mould. This place isn't rotting. It's… curated."

Irish brushed his fingertips across the concrete, then rubbed them together, his nose wrinkling. "Bleach. Disinfectant. But under it? Iron. Blood. Old."

They passed door after door, each with a narrow viewing slit fogged on the inside. One cleared just enough to glimpse a room lined with stainless steel gurneys. The straps were buckled neatly, waiting. The leather was cracked with sweat stains and fluids long dried had seeped into them like shadows that wouldn't wash out.

Mack pushed into a larger chamber and froze. His breath caught.

The floor was white tile, the kind found in operating theatres, but too clean, as if scrubbed obsessively. Surgical trays lay waiting, each containing selections of their scalpels and bone saws dulled beneath a film of dust, lined in perfect symmetry.

From the ceiling, rigs hung like carcass hooks. Cuffs and chains suspended at wrong angles, twisted configurations that made the imagination recoil. They swayed faintly in the stale air, as though they still remembered the bodies they once held.

The smell here wasn't rot. It was sharper. The stench was overwhelming of antiseptic gone sour, undercut with the tang of copper that bleach could never mask.

At the far wall, a bank of monitors sat black. All but one.

Green text bled across the screen, jittering in the dark.

SUBJECT: R—BLA_KTHORN

STATUS: TRANSFERRED

Selena's whisper barely rose above the hum. "She's been here."

James stepped closer, his boots scuffing tile, with every sound too loud. Frost slid beside him, his fingers flying across a dead keyboard until a video stuttered alive.

Grainy, colourless footage: Evelyn. Bound. Unconscious. Her head lolled between two masked guards as they dragged her down this very corridor. Her wedding gown was torn at the shoulder, with blood smeared from temple to jaw. Her legs trailed limp, too still. She carried the marks of someone who had taken punches across her body.

James's hands flexed until his gloves creaked. His jaw locked hard enough to ache, but he said nothing.

AJ's voice came quick and brittle with fear. "Logs show... subject testing. Neural reactivity. Compatibility indices..."

He froze, with a cold chill creeping up his body.

Mack snapped his head around. "What?"

AJ swallowed, eyes wide. "She tripped a dormant genetic flag. Subroutine designation... Revenant."

The word hit like ice water.

Bullet's frown twisted. "Shit... those labs we've been busting, the ones where people don't die, they just... keep going? They're gonna do that to Ev?"

Frost's voice was flat, merciless. "Not here, Bullet. Don't lose it. Stay sharp. I need you."

Selena's gaze cut like flint. "This says she is Revenant... Clear as day. She can't be, but all the markers are here. We've already seen glimpses of what she can do."

Irish's whisper cracked as he reads the medical readouts, almost a prayer. "Jesus, look at the markers, they are sky high. How the fuck did I not see this, I would have seen this."

AJ's knuckles were white on the terminal. "They're activating her. Turning her on. Look at the level of Revenant serum they are pumping into her... Its unprecedented amounts... she should be dead... this should have killed her."

The overhead strip light flickered again, shadows rolling across the rigs and restraints like they were moving on their own. Surgical steel caught the dull glow. The monitor scrolled Evelyn's name in phosphor green; her limp body burnt behind James's eyes.

The walls felt closer. Complicit. As if they had been waiting years for her return.

James's voice finally broke the silence, stripped bare to steel. "Burn it. Files. Drives. Every inch of this place."

Mack's throat worked. "Where next?"

James turned, the afterimage of her bloodied temple carved into him. His voice was quiet, but it shook the room.

"We find the next Facility IX. We get her out. And then we ignite it."

The silence cracked with a sound, soft, wet, and wrong.

From the far side of the chamber, one of the doors rattled faintly. A dragging scrape echoed inside, metal against tile.

Bullet's rifle was up first. "Movement."

Frost yanked the door. It opened onto a small holding cell, lit only by the pulse of the failing strip light.

On the floor lay a man. Or what had once been one. His body was wasted, skin stretched thin over bones, his veins spiderwebbed with dark tracks. His chest rose and fell shallowly, a grotesque parody of breathing. One arm twitched with each pulse of the light, spasms jerking the fingers like a puppet's strings.

His eyes rolled toward them, glazed and unfocused, yet somehow aware. His lips cracked and bled as they parted.

A rasping whisper clawed the air.

"Kill… me."

The team froze in unison. The horror of the poor man's body hit them like a freight train as the realistion hits, this will be Red.

James stepped forward. He didn't hesitate. He didn't look away. With mercy, his came gun came up, muzzle steady. He whispered a words under his breath, low enough for anyone to hear, maybe an apology, but maybe a last prayer for the dammed man's soul.

The man twitched again, one last spasm, and repeated in a broken whine, "Kill… me…"

The shot echoed through the chamber, deafening against the tile.

The body stilled.

James lowered the weapon, his face carved from stone. His voice was hoarse when he spoke.

"That's what they'll make of her if we don't move. That was a message."

No one argued.

They worked in silence.

Frost and Selena gutted the servers like a butcher, pulling drives and memory banks out in wet, metallic jerks. AJ fed them into the crusher, the soft hum obscene against the violence of erasure.

Irish moved methodically, soaking files in solvent until the ink bled, then striking a match. Pages curled to black, coughing acrid smoke that stung the throat.

Mack sloshed fuel across the operating theatre, the liquid streaming into tile seams and dripping from the cuffs and chains overhead. A bullet followed, ripping cameras from the walls, wires snapping like tendons.

James didn't move. He stood in the centre of it all, staring at the surgical trays, at the glint of scalpels waiting for a body. His hands shook. He clenched them tight, but the tremor crawled through him like insects under the skin.

Selena appeared at his side, silent. She pressed the detonator into his palm. It felt heavier than it should, like it carried the weight of her blood.

"Clear," Frost called.

The team pulled back through the tunnel, with their boots ringing on iron. Cold rain swept in through the hatch, merciful against the reek of bleach and rot.

James was last up the ladder. He looked back one final time. The straps in the theatre still swayed faintly, as though something down there was breathing.

He pressed the trigger.

The blast went deep, swallowed by the earth. Heat roared up the shaft, carrying the stink of burning chemicals, scorched steel, and melting straps. The ground trembled beneath their boots, then fell still.

Smoke curled into the rain, pale and thin, vanishing into the storm.

No one spoke on the walk back. Mud sprayed under the tyres as AJ reversed them onto the track.

James sat rigid in the passenger seat, his eyes fixed on the trees until the ruin was gone. The image still played behind his eyes: Evelyn's head lolling, blood drying on her skin, swallowed whole by a room that wanted her to stay.

Mack caught his reflection in the mirror. James didn't blink. His voice was iron when it came.

"We find the next site."

Not a request.

A Vow.

Chapter 46

Week 2 – False Lead, Near Collapse

The call hit like a gut punch. It came through a friend at Interpol.

A Jane Doe was found in a shipping container on the Marseille docks. Female. Blonde. Same height. Tattooed. Bloodied. Straps, needle marks, surgical interference, the same signatures Revenant Labs left behind.

Close enough that AJ's voice broke when he read the morgue file.

Close enough to drag James across a continent without a second thought.

The morgue light was surgical white, it was cruel in its clarity. Refrigeration hummed beneath it, with the air heavy with steel and disinfectant.

The zip rasped open.

Blonde hair spilled out, matted and dark with blood. James's heart stopped. For a breath, the room closed in, and all he saw was her. Evelyn. Broken. Cold.

Then the face. Swollen, one eye sealed shut, her lips split and raw. Her arms where littered with punctures. The chest was opened and sewn back in a Y-cut, the stitches were neat, mechanical, and careless.

Frost had come with him to help translate, when he saw the face even he flinched and turned away.

James leaned in like a man reading coordinates under fire, eyes dragging across every inch. Searching. Hoping. Dreading.

His breath caught.

But then…

"The scar's wrong." His voice rasped, raw, breaking as it left him. "Her tattoos are missing. And the finger… no. It's not her."

Relief should have come. It didn't.

It felt like nothing. Like stepping off a ledge and finding no ground beneath him. His knuckles whitened on the steel. Frost steadied him without a word.

James wrenched his gaze away at last, the effort brutal. Frost's voice cut the silence, steady but quiet. "I'll take it from here."

James nodded once, short and sharp, and turned for the door.

Chapter 47

Week 3 – The Handler

AJ found him.

The handler. The shadow they'd been chasing for weeks. The man who had moved Evelyn. Who had delivered her into the hands of something worse than death.

Tonight, he was flesh and blood.

James hadn't slept more than scraps since the wedding. His body was stripped lean, carved down to fury and caffeine, but his eyes—his eyes were fire. He was less a man than a blade, wound far too tight to last.

The handler sat strapped to a steel chair, his face was pulped, his lip was fully split, sweat streaking down his body with grime and blood. The warehouse burnt slowly around them, with hot flames gnawing at the rafters, and smoke twisting through the air like a funeral shroud.

James crouched low, that voice of his was calm enough to kill.

"Tell me again."

The handler's good eye twitched. "I—I don't know…"

"Facility IX. Where is it?"

"I don't—he only uses cut-outs…"

"Who?" James's tone was stripped down to wire.

The man's mouth opened, and for a second, nothing came, then it ripped out like shrapnel.

"Kashir!"

The sound froze the room.

James didn't blink. Didn't breathe. His face went still, he looked like he had been possessed by the grim reaper, poised and ready to execute.

The handler scrambled, words spilling. "He doesn't use names! We only see terminals… tech, shipments, subjects…the screaming…"

Selena's voice sliced through, cold and sharp, interrogation was not her usual remit, but someone had to stop James falling into the abyss.

"Evelyn was tagged in your logs. Live inventory."

The man shook his head violently, with terror leaking out of him. "That was code! I never touched her…. I just moved shipments!"

Frost stepped forward, quiet as a scalpel.

"What shipments?"

The handler's voice broke. "Neural prep kits. Genetic isolators. Blood samples. I didn't ask… I didn't want to know…"

James stood, slowly rising, like something volcanic, forcing its way to the surface. His voice once sterile and cold erupted and shook with rage.

"IS SHE FUCKING DEAD?"

The handler's nod was frantic. "No. Not dead. Not yet."

Something detonated in James, like an inferno rising from his fractured soul.

His fist snapped the man's jaw sideways with a sickening crack like bone splintering under his artillery. The chair collapsed, with the mans battered body and metal smashing into the floor. Whether he still breathed was irrelevant. James had absolutely no morality left as the monster within him released itself with zero fucks given.

James didn't stop. He couldn't.

He drove a boot into the wreck of the chair, both man and metal screamed as bones gave in under the relentless impacts. He hauled the handler upright with one hand like he weighed nothing, with thick blood pouring between James's knuckles, his face twisted into something primal. Lethal. Murderous.

"You gave her to him!" James's roar tore the room apart, spit flying, veins standing out along his neck. "You delivered my wife to Kashir! She is my fucking wife… and you just…Just…"

His voice broke, with his fury splintering into raw horror. "Do you have any idea what he does? What he is?!"

The handler sobbed through broken teeth, but James slammed him back down so hard the floor rattled. His fists kept coming—left, right, bone against flesh—until Mack's arms locked around him from behind, dragging him back.

"Jamie…stop!" Mack's voice was ragged. "He's done! He's done…"

James thrashed like a wild animal, dragging Mack a full step before the others moved. Frost braced his weight against James's shoulder, AJ gripping his arm, Selena shouting over the chaos.

"He has Evelyn!" James bellowed, his eyes were pained and bloodshot, spittle clung and solidified on his chin. "Kashir has her... He'll tear her apart... He'll cut her to pieces!"

The handler's broken body slumped against the ruined chair, blood ran thick dripping onto the concrete, his breaths rattling shallow, if at all.

James shook them all off, his chest was heaving like he'd run a marathon, firelight from the burning building was carving his face into something raw and demonic.

His voice came hoarse, ripped apart at the edges:

"Every route. Every lab. Every fucking facility with a Revenant signature. I don't care if we burn the world...we find her... we have to fucking find her."

The team looked on with exhaustion, watching their commanders' mind and morality crumbling In front of them. James used to be just, he was named Paladin as he was the shield. And here he was, beating a man to death, without hesitation.

AJ's laptop then lit, his pale face looked destroyed after witnessing the demise of James. His voice cracked, then reluctantly he spoke, landing another hammer blow.

"Ok, I have a lead...Moldova. A cold facility just went dark. Possible IX satellite."

James's head snapped toward him, eyes burning through smoke.

"MOVE. Now."

The room stank of blood and fire. And in James's chest, the only truth left was molten and absolute:

411

Kashir was real. And he had Evelyn. Anyone standing in his way would die.

Moldova Burn Site

The plane touched down on a strip of frostbitten earth an hour outside Chişinău. No customs. No signatures. Just silence under a low, heavy sky that pressed the hills flat. The cold bit deep, the kind that didn't sting; it sank straight to the bone.

James stood at the loading ramp, visor down, combat jacket thrown over the same filthy T-shirt that he had worn for weeks. He stank of smoke and sweat. He hadn't noticed. He didn't care.

Behind him, Mack, Selena, AJ, Frost, and Bullet disembarked without a word. Conversation had

Two dead border posts approached.

Up through black pines where frost turned to hard snow.

They reached it at dusk.

A Soviet lab, half-buried in the mountain. No markings. No signs. Just stone and steel chewed by decades of winter, with a single reinforced door set deep into the rock. Wind tore across the valley and then fell still, as though the mountain itself was holding its breath.

AJ swept the treeline with his wrist pad, his face lit blue. "Thermals are flat. But there's power. Internal."

"No guards?" Mack asked.

AJ's mouth was tight. "No life."

Frost crouched, with the wand sweeping the frame. The readout hissed. "Dead. But not abandoned. Someone scrubbed it clean."

James's jaw locked under the visor. His voice was stripped raw.

"Then let's see what they left behind."

Interior: Sublevel 3 – 43 Minutes Later

The corridor pulsed with the dying rhythm of backup red strobes, each flash washing the walls in blood-coloured light. Wet metal glinted in the half-dark, and shards of glass crunched under their boots. The air was damp and chemical-sharp, laced with the bitter tang of scorched flesh that clung to the back of the throat.

They moved carefully through the ruin. Overturned stretchers lay in their path, surgical trays bent and twisted, and datapads melted into slag that still stank of burnt circuitry. Every surface was marked with rust-coloured smears that looked too much like blood.

Selena stopped at a door, its Cyrillic lettering buried under layers of grime. She wiped it clear with her sleeve and read aloud, her voice tight. "Subject Isolation—Batch 9." AJ stepped forward with his bypass kit. The magnetic seal gave with a tired hiss, and the door groaned open like it was reluctant to show them what lay inside.

The lab beyond was a massacre. Containment pods were shattered, their thick glass spiderwebbed and dripping with congealed fluid that had dried in dark rivulets across the floor. Blood had pooled in the uneven tiles, turning black under the strobe light. Bullet holes riddled the walls, some rimmed with plasma burns where the steel had boiled and blistered. What had once been a lab had become a battlefield, and what was left of the battlefield had been purged in a hurry.

"Jesus Christ," Bullet muttered under his breath. "What the fuck happened here?"

Mack scanned the destruction, his face hardening. "This was a wipe. They pulled out and cleaned house, fast and brutal."

Frost crouched by a half-burnt tablet, his gloves brushing soot from the surface. "No drives. No cores. Anything with data's been ripped or torched."

On the far wall, Selena crouched, her hand brushing over something burnt into the steel. She rubbed until the outline emerged: a diamond, slashed through with three jagged lines scorched deep into the metal. AJ's breath caught when he saw it. "Same mark as the bullet," he said quietly.

James didn't respond. He moved through the wreckage slowly, each step deliberate, with his boots grinding glass. His hands stayed loose, but his shoulders were drawn so tight they shook, as though he was forcing himself to keep control. Then he stopped.

Near the back wall, buried under a collapsed shelving unit, a broken IV stand jutted from the debris. Dangling from its base was a small tag, stained with dried fluid. James knelt, lifted it, and read the words.

SUBJECT: E. BLACKTHORN

STATUS: TRANSFERRED

His breath hitched, audible even through the silence. He turned it over in his hand, and on the reverse side, written in a rushed, uneven scrawl, was a single word:

IX

James stood, the tag crumpling in his fist. His visor hid his eyes, but the silence that followed was enough to make the rest of the team shift uneasily.

"She was here," he said finally.

Selena's voice came out strained. "And they moved her."

The weight of it hit all of them. The realisation that they were always just one step behind, that whoever held her knew they were coming and had cleared the board before they arrived.

Frost swore under his breath. Bullet lashed out and kicked a tray until the metal bent. AJ stared down at the floor, jaw clenched. Mack only watched James, as if bracing himself for something to break.

When James spoke again, his voice was low and cold enough to frost the air. "Someone is watching us... Someone knows our movements."

This time the silence that followed wasn't tactical. It was deep soul gutting despair.

The cold was sharper outside. Snow hissed against the pines, with wind tearing down from the ridge. James walked until the broken lab was only a shadow behind him, then ripped off his visor and hurled it into the snow. His breath came ragged, with clouds breaking in the frozen air.

Mack waited by the convoy, his arms folded concealing his emotion. Bullet stood off to the side, cigarette glowing between his shacking fingers. Both were braced for the hit.

James stopped, with his jaw tight and his hands flexing like he was trying to crush something that wasn't there.

"She was here, it almost came out as a desperate plea. "Hours. Maybe less. Right here. And we…" His voice tore out, then broke, strangled into silence. He pressed his palms into his eyes as if he could grind the image away.

Mack stepped forward, steady but careful. As if he was approaching a wounded wolf. "Brother…"

"They're ahead of us every damn time," James snapped, his voice cutting at the trees, the snow, and the ghosts in his head. "Every time we get close, they move her. Like they're toying with us."

James looked up. His eyes were glassy but burning, his voice cracked in anguish as it slipped out.

"We didn't even get to dance…"

The words hung in the air, jagged as shrapnel. Mack's expression broke as he watched the strongest man he knew crumble into grief and desperation. He put a heavy hand on James's shoulder, desperately trying to anchor him. "We'll get her, brother. No matter how many bastards we've got to burn to ash."

James stood still, head bowed under the weight. Then he shoved it back down, scooped his visor from the snow, and snapped it into place.

"Load up," he said, voice flat. "We move now."

416

He climbed into the lead vehicle, the engine snarling to life, the mountain disappearing in the mirrors.

The mobile HQ thundered through a frozen pass near the Romanian border, with its tyres grinding over ice. Outside was a smear of black and snow. Inside felt like a coffin: too warm, heavy with sweat, shit coffee, and the chemical tang of overheated circuits. Red emergency bulbs flickered low, washing the cramped space in the same blood-glow that haunted the labs.

James sat at the front, visor pushed high, staring into the dark road like he could bore through mountains. His frame was rigid, every muscle braced, his hands raw and split where he'd driven them into the wall hours earlier. The blood had soaked into his gloves, the leather held black patches that hadn't dried. He hadn't spoken since.

The team behind him looked half-dead. AJ crouched behind a barricade of screens, with blue light cutting hollows into his face, his lips were chewed raw, his jaw ticking whenever static spat across a feed. Mack slumped with manifests balanced on his knee. His once alive mischievous eyes now were stained with exhaustion, he had a tremor in his hand every time he turned a page. Frost worked in silence, assembling and disassembling a pistol in endless rhythm, each metallic snap too sharp in the stagnant air. Selena couldn't stop pacing, her boots hitting the steel floor in sync with the engine, arms locked tight across her chest. Bullet hunched at the back with his head lowered, shoulders bowed like the weight of it all was crushing him down.

The hum of the engine filled the silence until James's voice cut through, low and jagged.

"She was there."

Every head lifted.

"The tag was fresh," he went on. "No dust. No rot. She'd been moved within hours. And they knew we were coming."

"They had an automated burn," Mack muttered, not looking up.

Frost's tone was flat. "We tripped a sensor the second we breached."

Selena stopped pacing, her voice sharp. "We are being tracked. In real time. I have checked no trackers, no coms in or out. We are flying blind."

AJ didn't raise his eyes, only spoke through clenched teeth. "The leak's in the Intel chain. Whoever we're pulling from is watching the same feeds we are."

James's jaw flexed. "What's still active?"

AJ's hands froze over the keys. "One site. Poland–Ukraine border. Listed as chemical storage, but satellite feed shows deep heat underground. Movement. Last forty-eight hours."

James pulled over and jumped in the back. The motion was sharp and final, like a guillotine falling. "Prep to roll. Six hours."

Selena's voice softened, breaking the silence. "We haven't slept, James."

He didn't turn. Didn't even blink.

"She hasn't either."

The words hung there in the red-lit coffin of the HQ, heavy as a curse.

418

Border Run – Poland–Ukraine Line

The convoy pushed east through the night. Snow hammered against the windscreen, a steady hiss like static swallowing the dark. The engine's growl never changed, a monotone vibration that made the team's eyelids heavy and breath shallow.

Inside the mobile HQ, the air was thick with fatigue. The red bulbs overhead flickered in irregular bursts, washing the cabin in pulses of bloody light that made every shadow twitch. The heater ran too hot, filling the space with recycled sweat and burnt plastic.

Exhaustion had all but broken the team.

AJ's head kept dipping over his keyboard, the screens blurring in front of him until a sharp buzz or static jolt yanked him awake again. The young man's face looked gaunt and fingers twitching from too much caffeine and not enough food.

Mack sat hunched with a manifest slipping from his grip, with his chin nearly on his chest before he snapped himself upright again, muttering curses under his breath. Frost's eyelids drooped even as his hands moved over weapon parts, clicking them together on pure muscle memory. Selena leaned against the bulkhead with her arms folded, with the steady rhythm of her pacing finally broken by exhaustion—now she just stood, with her eyes half-lidded but jaw locked. Bullet sprawled on the bench, a cigarette stubbed between his fingers letting it burn his skin to keep him awake. He wasn't sleeping, but he wasn't fully alert either.

Only James hadn't moved.

He sat rigid in the front seat, his visor shoved high, his raw knuckles clenched against the wheel frame like he could choke

419

answers from it. His eyes burnt red-rimmed, staring through the windscreen as though sheer will could punch through the night and find her.

Every time one of them stirred, James's voice cut the silence—low, cracked, and half-delirious.

"They moved her hours before we got there."

"They know when we're coming. They're laughing at us."

"She's still alive. I can feel her. I can feel her hurting."

At first they thought he was talking to them, but after the third time it was clear he wasn't. He was talking to himself. To her. To ghosts.

Mack finally shifted forward, voice rough. "Brother, you need to rest. Even ten minutes. We can cover the drive."

James didn't blink. His voice was flat, cold.

"If I close my eyes, I'll see her on that table. You want that image in your head, Mack? Because it doesn't leave."

No one answered. The silence pressed heavier than the snow outside.

AJ rubbed his temples, muttering, "We're running on fumes. All of us. If we go in like this…" He didn't finish.

James finally tore his eyes from the road long enough to glance back. The red light made his face look hollow, skin stretched tight over bone, his eyes dark pits burning in their sockets.

"If you're tired," he rasped, "then stay in the truck. I'll burn the site myself."

No one spoke after that.

The convoy kept rolling, engines eating the miles, snow hissing against the glass. And in the cramped, suffocating dark, every one of them felt it—the spiral had begun.

James wasn't leading them anymore. He was dragging them into the abyss with him.

Irish gripped the wheel like it was the only thing left anchored to him. The second convoy hugged the tarmac close behind the lead; his hands trembled but he kept them steady, his fingers were lazy from fatigue and too many cans of Monster crushed at his feet. Rose sat beside him, her hand warm on his knee like an anchor he couldn't feel.

"He's losing it, Con." Her voice trembled and tried to sound steady. "He'll get you all killed. She's gone, he needs to stop chasing shadows. You need to talk to him. Please."

Irish tasted bile. *Tell him. Tell him to stop killing himself for ghosts.* He wanted to scream it at the road. Wanted to wrench the wheel and drive straight into whatever hole James had jumped into and drag him out by his collar. Instead he kept his jaw clenched, voice low and rough.

"You shouldn't have come, Rose." His words came out brittle. "What good is this doing you… to us? The team's fraying at the seams."

"I should be with them," she said, sharp. "Helping them through this."

"You're not going in that vehicle. I don't trust James not to crash it." The lie tasted like ash. He did trust James, full stop. That was the worst of it."

"But I could help him come to terms with this," Rose pleaded. "She's gone. He needs to understand that."

She's gone. The thought made something inside him clench and unspool. "Just stop, Rose. Stop." He dragged his knuckles over his face. "She's not gone. She's lost."

"You always put her before me. Before you. You'll die, Con." Her voice cracked.

He should have felt anger. Instead, everything in him went sideways and soft. "I would happily die for her." It slipped out before he could stop it, a stupid, true confession.

"And there it is," Rose spat, stunned and cruel. "You're in love with her."

"No I'm not." He snapped, because the truth hurt too much. "You're telling me you'd let her go through that and walk away? I've told you everything, Rose. All of it. Do you want that for her? You know dam well what she is, I have been honest with you from the start."

"She's probably already dead. Let her go." The words were a blade.

"Never," Irish said, the sound tearing out of his chest. "I'm never giving up on her."

"So you're giving up on us?" Her voice rose into something raw. "You'll leave me a widow for her? Christ, Con, think about what you're doing. Get James to stop."

He laughed then, a short, broken sound. "I have no power over him." The admission knocked the air from him. "If he's walking into hell to find her... I'm going with him."

The road blurred. His hands shook. He wasn't proud of the words. He didn't want to be the man who would follow a ghost into the dark, but he would. If James burned, he'd stand in the flames beside him. That's what loyalty did to a man like him.

Chapter 48

Week 5 – The Breaking Point

The OTF bunker in rural Slovakia stank of wet concrete, rust, and old mildew that clung to walls no one had cared for in years. Rain hammered the corrugated roof in a relentless drumbeat, the sound burrowing into the skull. The generator whined, strip lights flickering so the war room strobe sickly, like a morgue.

The Poland site map was spread across the table, pinned open like a body waiting to be cut.

James stood over it, one hand braced on the steel, the other resting on his holstered sidearm. He still hadn't changed his t-shirt; it was dirty with the edges stiff with dried blood. His face was hollow, skin gone grey beneath the unkept beard, his eyes ringed black as bruises.

AJ sat hunched at the far end, tablet in his hands. His knuckles were split from hitting walls, his eyes shadowed deep enough to make him look a decade older. He slammed the tablet down, the crack of plastic against steel jolting the room.

"We're getting nothing."

The words cut sharp. Mack froze mid-weapon check. Bullet stood still with a mag in hand. Frost's gaze flicked up from his rifle, unreadable.

AJ's voice frayed higher. "Every time we get close, it's gone. Burnt out. We're not saving her… we're just logging what's been done to her." He pushed off the table, pacing tight, his boots loud in the dead air. "We're chasing ghosts."

"Watch it," Frost warned, quiet but edged.

"No," AJ snapped, his voice breaking. "Moldova proved it. The blood was still wet. The restraints still warm. She was there, James. And we lost her."

James finally lifted his head. His eyes were bloodshot, rimmed with sleepless red, but his voice came out steady—razor-sharp from sheer will.

"We didn't lose her."

"You don't know that!" AJ barked.

Bullet shoved his chair back hard. "We know she's out there."

AJ let out a laugh with no humour in it. "Do we? Or are we chasing a woman who's already…"

"Don't." Mack's voice cracked like gunfire.

James circled the table, slow and deliberate. He didn't need to raise his voice. His presence carried enough violence to fill the room.

"You don't get to finish that sentence," he said, low and raw. "Not while I'm breathing."

AJ's chest heaved once before the fight bled out of him. He turned, kicked a can that was thrown on the floor, then he slid down it until he sat on the floor, head in his hands. Selena crouched beside him, one hand gripping the back of his neck. Her voice was soft but cut through.

"You're not the only one breaking boss."

Bullet leaned forward, with his forearms braced on his knees. "Haven't slept in four days."

Mack stared at nothing, his voice flat. "Feels like we're always late. Like they're already writing the ending without us."

Even Frost sat back a fraction, silence shifting from steel to stone.

James looked at each of them. At the cracks spreading through the only people he trusted. And then his own fracture showed.

"I haven't breathed since she was taken."

The words detonated in the bunker, louder than rain, louder than the generator's dying whine.

He dropped onto the edge of the table, elbows on his knees, head bowed. His voice was barely a whisper.

"I keep hearing her. 'Jamie, baby.' Like she's right behind me."

No one spoke. Only the hammer of rain and the whining generator filled the void.

At last, Selena's voice broke the silence, quiet but firm. "We stop. One night. Eat. Sleep. Or we'll lose more than her."

James didn't argue. Didn't lift his head. He just gave one slow nod.

"Four hours," he said. "Then we move."

The bunker slept fitfully. Four hours. That was all James had given them, and even then most lay awake staring at the ceiling, too wired, too raw.

James didn't sleep at all.

He sat in the corridor outside the makeshift war room, his back against the wall, a pistol balanced across his thigh. The strip lights buzzed overhead, flickering in time with the generator's tired whine. Rain seeped through the cracks in the roof, dripping in slow taps into rusted buckets.

His eyes burnt, dry and red, but every time they closed he saw her. The video feed from Moldova. Head lolling. Blood on her skin. Every time he blinked, it was waiting.

At first, he thought the voice was a memory.

Jamie, baby...

So faint he barely registered it. Just another echo.

But then it came again, closer this time, warm at his ear.

Jamie, wake up...

His head snapped up. The corridor was empty. Just rain, shadows, and the endless hum of the generator. His pulse pounded in his throat.

He dragged a hand over his face, muttering, "You're losing it."

Still, he stood. He walked the corridor in silence, with his boots echoing on damp concrete. And there, in the reflection of a cracked observation window, he swore he saw her. A blur of blonde hair. Her hand brushed over his shoulder the way she always did when she wanted him to breathe.

He spun. Nothing. Just mildew-stained walls and the sickly strobe of failing lights.

His breath came hard, ragged. His fingers flexed around the pistol grip like he was bracing to shoot at shadows.

From the barracks, a door creaked open. Mack stepped out, with a rifle slung loose across his chest, blinking blearily. His eyes narrowed when he saw James standing rigid in the dark.

"You alright, brother?"

James forced himself to nod. "Fine."

But Mack didn't buy it. His gaze lingered on James's shaking hands, the raw split knuckles, and the feverish gleam in his eyes. He opened his mouth to say more, then thought better of it. He just gave a grunt and moved on.

When the door clicked shut again, James whispered into the silence.

"I'll find you, Ev." His voice broke. "Just... don't stop talking to me."

The shadows pressed closer. For a moment, he could swear they breathed with her voice.

Chapter 49

Day 53 – Ghost Feed

The bunker was dead quiet.

Not the easy quiet of rest, but the brittle kind that came when exhaustion had stripped everyone down to the bone. AJ had passed out in a chair, his jacket over his head. Mack stretched across a bench, one arm over his eyes. Bullet and Rose were curled against the wall, boots touching, leaning unconsciously into each other. Even Frost had surrendered, dozing upright, arms folded like a barricade.

James was the only one still awake.

He sat at the far table, were his elbows dug into the steel, staring at a monitor that hadn't flickered in hours. Evelyn's name — E. BLACKTHORN — burnt in green on the frozen screen. His coffee sat cold and untouched, the air thick with the stink of it, mixed with sweat, mildew, and rain hammering the roof. His jaw worked until the metallic tang of blood sat copper-sharp on his tongue.

Then it came.

A ping. Sharp. Loud.

James's head snapped toward AJ's backup terminal, half-buried under ration wrappers and crumpled maps. Static hissed from the tiny speaker, faint but alive. He crossed the room in three strides, sweeping junk to the floor. The screen bloomed weakly to life.

Incoming Feed — Node 617-Delta

429

Source: Discontinued Satellite Uplink

Integrity: 19%

Encryption: Breached

Identifier: Ghost → Paladin

His chest tightened. Ghost.

The feed crawled forward, jagged and broken, fighting to push through. Then the data spat onto the screen.

SUBJECT: E. BLACKTHORN

Status: Stabilised

Location: CLASSIFIED (IX)

Biometric Scan: Active

Heart Rate: 59 BPM

Blood Pressure: 128/84

Neural Oscillation: Elevated

Genetic Response: Revenant Positive

Alive.

James's knees nearly buckled, and he gripped the table hard enough to make the steel groan. She was alive.

But before the thought could take root, another panel flickered up.

Anomalous Data Detected

Vital Pattern: Non-Human Spikes

Nanite Presence: Confirmed

Subject Class: Revenant – Stage 3

Note: Genetic Activation Occurring Spontaneously

The words pulsed, green and merciless.

Selena stirred, dragged from shallow sleep by the light. She blinked, then froze when she saw the feed. Her face drained of colour. "James... this isn't stasis. This is transformation."

Irish pushed upright, his voice low and grim. "Stage 3 it's a prototype. They're turning her into one of them."

Bullet's cigarette slipped between his fingers, forgotten. "Revenants? Fuck no. That's—those things we've been putting down in cages. They don't talk. They don't think. They just scream."

Mack slammed his fist against the wall, plaster dust rattling loose. "That's Evelyn. She's not some lab rat. Don't you dare put her in the same breath as those things."

"Don't romanticise it," Frost cut in, flat, precise. He gestured to the screen. "This isn't poetry. It's metrics. She's already changing. And if they've pushed her to Stage three..." He didn't finish. He didn't need to.

Selena's gaze didn't leave the feed. Her voice was sharp but softer at the edges, like she was forcing herself to say it. "We need to consider what happens if we find her and she isn't her anymore."

The words landed like a detonation.

James's head snapped up. His stare hit her like a blade. He moved, slow and deliberate, until he stood in front of the screen, shielding Evelyn's name like a shield.

"No," he rasped. His voice was wrecked, raw, but absolute. "She is her. She is Evelyn. And we are bringing her back. No matter what."

"James…" Selena began.

"She's not gone!" he roared.

The bunker shook with the force of it. The sound rang off wet concrete, reverberated through the rusted beams, leaving the silence after thick enough to choke on.

James braced both hands on the table, leaning over the glow of her name, every muscle coiled so tight it looked like he might shatter. His voice dropped to a whisper, hoarse but burning. "She's alive. I don't care what they've done. I don't care what the screen says. She's mine. She's my wife. And I'll tear the world apart before I let them keep her."

No one breathed.

Then, in the dying static, the final line typed itself across the feed, broken and distorted, crawling letter by letter.

EXTRACTION WINDOW: 72 HOURS. FAILURE = PERMANENT LOSS.

The screen flickered once. Then it died.

The strip lights buzzed overhead, sick and unsteady. Nobody spoke. Not because there was nothing left to say, but because every one of them was thinking the same thing.

If she came back at all… she will be nightmare fuel.

Rose had gone quiet the second Irish started looking at the trigger data and the reams of outputs from her medical files. He deciphered medical data that no one else could understand. He hadn't said much, but it was enough. Rose knew that look. The measured tone. The way his words stepped like boots over a minefield.

When James turned back to the terminal, all fury and focus, Rose touched Irish's arm.

"Bathroom. Now."

He frowned, but she was already moving, weaving through crates and cables toward the back hall.

Inside, the yellow light was harsh, making the hollows under their eyes deeper and sharper. Rose shut the door hard enough to kill the hum of the war room.

Her voice came low, urgent.

"You think she's pregnant, don't you?"

Irish's jaw flexed. "Rose…"

"Don't stall me, Conall. I've seen that look before. I can read the data just like you. You've had it since you opened your mouth about activation triggers."

He braced both hands on the sink, leaning until his head hung low. His breath fogged the cracked mirror.

"I don't know for sure."

"That's not a no."

He let out a long breath, the sound scraping raw. "If she is… it changes everything. Nanotechnology tied to hormonal surges… progesterone, oxytocin… pregnancy would be the perfect storm to force them awake. Whoever's running IX would know it."

Rose's chest tightened like a fist around her ribs. "Ow god, you can't say anything, it will break him."

Irish nodded once, grim, eyes on the porcelain. "That's why I didn't say it out there. If James hears it now, he'll burn Hamburg to the ground before we even land. We need a plan, not a funeral pyre."

Silence stretched between them, filled with the drip of water from a rusted pipe. Rose stepped closer, pressing her hand to his arm, her voice soft but hard at the edges.

"Then you keep that thought to yourself until we have her in our hands. And pray to God you're wrong."

The Mouth of the Mountain

They hit the site under moonlight.

An Activated Facility IX wasn't a rumour anymore; it wasn't a ghost story traded in black corridors. It was there in the flesh, carved into the spine of the Carpathians, hidden under decades of reinforced steel and buried files.

But the doors were open. Not breached. Not blasted. Just... open.

James didn't like gifts. Not from people like this.

They moved fast, rifles raised, eyes cutting every shadow. No guards. No alarms. Not even a scavenger left to strip copper. The emptiness was worse than a firefight.

James felt it in his chest before they cleared the first hallway.

"Stay sharp," he murmured into comms, voice low and coiled. "They've already moved her."

Frost fell in beside him, scanning each corner. "Feels wrong."

"Not wrong," Selena said from the rear, her scanner whispering static in her hand. "Scrubbed."

The elevator groaned as it took them down into the mountain's gut. With every metre, the air grew heavier, pressing against their lungs. It stank of ozone and of rusted metal, and underneath it all, something sweet and putrid that clung to the back of the throat.

Gooseflesh prickled under tactical sleeves. Not one of them spoke.

The lights buzzed and flickered overhead with the sick hum of dying fluorescents. Each second dragged, elastic and wrong, like time itself wanted James to turn back.

The doors slid open.

Nothing waited but silence.

Not stillness. Not peace. The kind of silence left when something had been erased completely, scrubbed out of existence.

Silence that breathed.

The Corridor of the Dead

The walls were scorched, with the cells yawning open like broken mouths. Each one barely large enough for a dog, let alone a human. Surgical lamps swayed faintly overhead as if something had brushed them and left. A single latex glove had melted into the floor beside a collapsed gurney, which was fused into the concrete like a fossil.

AJ's whisper barely carried. "They cleared it."

Selena's scanner clicked in her hands. "Residual vitals. Heart rate logs. Neural spikes. Two days ago." She stared at the static, jaw tight. "And then nothing. Left here on purpose."

James moved deeper, boots echoing too loudly. He stopped dead. His breath caught.

Twelve black body bags lay in perfect formation across the corridor. Uniform. Precise. Each one large enough to hold Evelyn. Lined up like a guard of honour from hell.

He knew what it meant before he touched the first zip.

"Oracle, Coyote, Rook… Hold position. Wrath, 7KB. Now."

Irish arrived to find James already on his knees, Frost and Mack kneeled beside him, slowly unsealing the bags one by one.

The smell hit first. Sweet rot. Chemicals. The unmistakable reek of death.

The bodies were in varying ruin: skin stretched too tight, eyes clouded and sunken. Some weren't entirely human anymore. One corpse was blackened, as though burnt from the inside out. Another's chest cavity had collapsed inward, their ribs snapped like cage bars. A woman's jaw hung unhinged, metal tubing was still bolted into her throat.

James forced himself to look. He checked every wrist, every scrap of skin for tattoos. He had no choice but to look, because one of them might have been her.

Irish crouched, his voice slipping into a medic's cold register. "These three… Revenant rejection. That one—overdose. Those burns? Internal combustion, maybe nanite failure. Two from sepsis. Two executed." His eyes flicked across the remains. "The rest… torture."

James bowed his head. "All women?"

Irish didn't answer. He didn't need to.

James's voice was gravelly. "They're not just taunting us. They want me to see her like this. They want me to imagine her zipped into one of these bags if I move wrong."

At the corridor's end stood one door. Unlike the others, it was untouched. Clean. Waiting.

The pull in his gut left no room for hesitation. James pushed it open.

Inside, his stomach dropped as vomit surged up his throat.

A sterile restraint table sat beneath a surgical lamp. The cuffs still glistened with dried blood. The copper stench clung through the heavy tang of bleach. Scratches scarred the wall, deep grooves clawed into metal. He leaned closer. Fingernail fragments clung to the scores.

Then he saw it.

Her wedding dress. Draped across the table like an offering, stiff with blood. Her blood.

And resting on top — her wedding ring.

Above it, scrawled in jagged letters, smeared in what could only be blood:

GAME OVER, PALADIN.

Mack froze in the doorway. "James…"

James didn't answer. He lifted the ring as though it were a relic, kissed it, and slid it onto his little finger. His voice rasped out raw and hollow.

"They kept her in her wedding dress. They made her bleed in it. They're taunting me."

Selena appeared, face pale but unshaken, datapad in hand. "I know you said don't come, but AJ cracked the corridor log."

Selena's eyes locked on the bloodied wedding dress and the bloody message scrawled crudely across the wall. "Ow! my sister…." Her knees buckled as frost surged forward to catch her.

James didn't even acknowledge Selenas grief instead he took the data pad, his body and mind in automatic pilot, and he scanned it.

SUBJECT: E. BLACKTHORN

Status: TRANSFERRED

Reason: CLASSIFIED

Last Entry: ESCORTED VIA LEVEL 7 TUNNEL — K-HANDLER CLEARANCE

"No location?"

"Wiped," Selena whispered through broken words. "But within the last seventy-two hours."

Frost's voice was cold steel. "K-handler?"

Selena's reply was a whisper edged in venom. "Kashir."

James nodded once. Then again, slower, letting the name sink into his bones like a brand.

"She was here," he said. His voice cracked, then hardened. "They hurt my girl. Our Red."

He pressed his hand to the restraint table, fingers curling over bloodstained steel. That's when it hit him — faint under the copper, under the bleach — a ghost of perfume clinging to the fabric. Her perfume. Vanilla and smoke, the scent she wore the day she walked to him.

His throat locked. His eyes burnt.

His whisper was low and feral, the sound of a man already halfway to war.

"I will kill everyone to bring her back."

Chapter 50

Somewhere Else — Kashir Watching

The room was warm. Luxurious. A deliberate contrast to the steel and rot James waded through on the other side of the feed.

Kashir sat alone at a polished mahogany desk, the glow of multiple monitors casting pale light over sharp, angular features. He was in his early sixties, but age had not softened him; instead, it had honed him. Every line of his face was cut with precision, like a blade sharpened over decades. His hair, silver threaded through iron grey, was combed back so precisely that not a single strand dared to move. The clean-shaven jaw, the perfectly pressed grey suit, and the cufflinks that caught the light allspoke of a man who never allowed himself to be anything less than immaculate.

His ice-blue eyes were the only thing alive about him, and even they held no warmth. Just cold, sadistic calculation.

In his right hand, a crystal glass of whisky. Two fingers, no more, the amber catching the light with every slow swirl. The scent of expensive peat smoke hung faintly in the air.

On the central monitor, James was on his knees in IX's lower levels, opening body bag after body bag. Frost's broad frame loomed nearby, Mack's face grim, and Irish moved like a silent shadow at his side.

Kashir leaned back, one ankle resting over his knee, sipping as if watching the theatre.

He saw the tremor in James's hands. He could see the way that this hardened war dog's shoulder tensed when a body inside looked too similar to Evelyn's frame, the raw flicker in his eyes when Irish muttered another cause of death.

Kashir smiled faintly, but this was not out of joy but out of satisfaction. This was precisely the pain-ridden reaction he'd wanted.

On another monitor, he pulled up the later footage of the restraint room. Evelyn's wedding dress in blood, the ring laid out like an offering, and the words "GAME OVER, PALADIN" freshly painted. He let it play side-by-side with both recorded feeds, enjoying the full impact of a decorated soldier breaking.

As he watched James reaching for the ring, Kashir smiled at his own memory of pulling it from Evelyn's bloody fingers and placing it there.

The whisky touched his lips again, and his voice was little more than a whisper to the empty room.

"Run faster, Paladin."

He set the glass down gently, never taking his eyes off the screen, watching as James stood again, rage tightening every muscle in his body.

"You'll never find her," Kashir murmured, almost to himself. "You will try and fail... She'll be something you won't recognise."

He tapped the edge of the monitor with one manicured finger, marking the moment James's eyes locked on the last unopened door.

The smile returned, thin with cold malice.

"Perfect."

Somewhere Else — Reds cell

The air in the cell reeked of bleach and iron. The kind of sterile, chemical tang meant to mask the truth, but the copper bite of blood lingered beneath it, stubborn and unwashed. Evelyn lay chained to a cold metal slab, her wrists bound in steel cuffs so tight they'd rubbed her skin raw and swollen. The thin, blood-stained medical gown clung to her frame, offering no warmth against the freezing bite of the reinforced room.

Her face was a map of violence, with one eye swollen shut, the other barely able to open beneath a bloom of purple and black. Her lips were split, and a thin trickle of blood crusted at the corner of her mouth. Her blonde hair, matted with dried blood and sweat, clung to her temples in uneven clumps. The rest of her body was wasted, the sharp edges of bone pushing against pale skin, each mark telling its own story of the last thirty-two days.

The heavy steel door groaned as it opened.

Kashir stepped inside, his presence sucking the air out of the room. Immaculate as always, with a perfectly tailored grey suit, silk tie, and shoes polished to a mirror shine. His ice-blue eyes swept over her with the detached precision of a collector inspecting a prized piece, not a human being.

He took his time crossing the distance, the click of his shoes echoing against the walls. When he finally spoke, his voice was calm. Smooth. British. The tone of a man who never raised it unless it was to kill.

"Do you not find it strange," he said softly, almost like a confidant, "that your husband is not looking for you?"

Evelyn didn't move. Her breathing was slow and ragged, with each inhale a knife in her ribs.

"He mustn't love you after all," he continued, the faint curl of a smile touching the corner of his mouth.

Her throat worked, straining to form the word. Her lips trembled hard, but she forced it out. One word escaped her lips in utter defiance, so small yet so sharp it cut the air between them.

"Liar. He will find you. He will fucking kill you."

Kashir's jaw twitched. He moved in close, leaning over her, the scent of expensive cologne ghosting her battered skin. His hand shot to the back of her head, tangling in her bloody hair, and he yanked it back until her face was angled up toward his. Pain lanced down her neck, but she refused to flinch.

"You know, don't you?" His voice was quieter now, almost intimate. "You feel it. The change. The weight." His ice-blue eyes bored into hers. "You're carrying a life."

Evelyn's pulse spiked.

He leaned closer, his words now a knife's whisper. "He won't love you when he finds out you are carrying my child. My legacy. You will help me build the future… one child at a time." His grip tightened, forcing her to hold his gaze. "You are mine now."

Her lips curled in disgust. She gathered what little strength she had left, enough to spit at him, with a wet, blood-tinged fleck catching his cheek.

He only smiled. Slowly. Like she had given him exactly what he wanted.

The door behind him opened again, and the room began to fill. Doctors in sterile gowns, scientists with data pads, and heavy-set guards with expressionless faces took their positions around the slab.

Kashir released her head, stepping back toward the door, smoothing his suit sleeve with a casual tug.

"Begin," he said, his voice flat and final.

One of the doctors stepped forward with a syringe containing a thick, black, oil-like fluid that glistened under the overhead light. Without hesitation, he plunged it into the side of her neck, with no care or compassion that you would expect of a doctor.

The effect was instant. Her back arched violently, every muscle locking as the serum tore through her bloodstream like fire. Her breath became ragged, her teeth clenching so hard she thought they might shatter.

The heavies closed in on her, their fists and boots landing in savage, clinical succession; the aim was simple: to kill her, to break her, to weaken her body while the injection did its work. Her body convulsed, head slamming against the metal, a guttural sound ripping from her throat before her eyes rolled back and her chest stilled.

The heart monitor flatlined.

"Vitals?" Kashir asked.

One of the doctors worked fast over her abdomen with a portable scanner. "Maternal vitals are gone…" A pause. "…but the foetal heartbeat is strong. Steady. Completely unaffected."

Kashir's lips curved, and for the first time there was something in his eyes: not warmth, not humanity, but hunger.

"She dies," he murmured, "and the child survives. Even in death, her body protects it."

Then…

A flicker.

The monitor for Evelyn's own vitals jumped.

It began in her womb, a faint golden glow beneath the skin, pulsing once, then again, stronger. The light spread like fire through veins, along her ribs, and into her neck until her whole body burnt with that strange, living luminescence. The restraints rattled under a sudden surge of strength as her chest heaved, and she dragged in a breath that sounded more like a growl than air.

Kashir watched, fascinated, as her eyes snapped open with the faint metallic glint of nanites swarming in her irises before the glow faded back into her skin.

He took a slow sip of the whisky in his hand, savouring it like the moment itself.

"Repeat the process," he said calmly, setting the glass down. "Do it again."

Chapter 51

The safe house felt like it was holding its breath.

It was an old farmhouse buried in the mountains, its stone walls swallowed the wind and dulled the sound of boots on warped boards. The air smelt of damp timber and gun oil, with gear stacked in every corner. A place built to keep the world out and the pain in.

Selena paced the length of the room, each clipped step controlled but brittle. AJ sat cross-legged on the floor, his face lit cold blue by his laptop, cables spilling like veins. Mack leaned against a support beam, arms locked across his chest as if holding himself together.

James hadn't spoken in an hour. He sat at the head of the table, hunched forward, twisting Evelyn's ring on the chain with his tags. His thumb brushed the metal again and again, like it was the only thing keeping him anchored.

In the middle of the table lay what was left of her file: blacked-out documents, stripped biometrics, and the single blood-stained tag from the Facility. No images. No updated scans. Just the record of a table she'd been strapped to—and the knowledge that if they failed, she would vanish forever.

Mack broke first. She slammed a folder down, paperclips rattling.

"Why her?"

No one answered.

"Why her?" The voice grew louder and sharper. "They didn't ransom her. Didn't kill her. They cleared an entire facility to move her and handed her to Kashir. They scrubbed IX clean. So tell me, Jamie. If she's nanotech, then this isn't kidnapping; it's acquisition. Why?"

AJ's voice was thin. "Macks right. They purged everything… for one person."

Irish's jaw tightened. "I am here medic. She's not Revenant. Not before this… She never registered."

Selena's eyes cut like blades. "Then why does she react to their tech like it belongs to her?"

James finally looked up. His voice was low, like snapping wire.

"What if it does?"

The room stilled.

"You're saying she's engineered?" AJ asked.

"No." James's voice was deep. "I'm saying she is naturally compatible. We all know she is something else."

Bullet shoved off the wall. "Ev's human. She's us."

"Your right, we have all seen it." Selena countered. "Almost six weeks forcing a Revenant reaction, look at the data, anyone else would be dead."

James shoved his chair back, standing hard. "She's surviving what no one else did. Every subject in those trials died. She is Kashirs fantasy of supremacy."

Selena leaned in. "We saw how the Revenant plate from Colombia bound to her. That should've been impossible. James, she is more than human. Has to be"

"She's adapting." AJ murmured. "Like the code recognises her."

Bullet's voice broke. "So the woman who stitched me up in the field, who danced barefoot in the kitchen… they're turning her into one of those people we found fucked up in Libya…. No… James… No?"

James cut in, steel in his tone. "No. She won't be one of them, she is subject A. Something new."

The silence that followed was different. Heavier.

Mack's voice was grim. "She's evolving."

And James, almost to himself: "They don't know who and what they are dealing with."

The safe house sank into stillness, like the walls themselves were listening.

AJ's laptop hummed, a blue glow stuttering across his hollow face. The facility's last ping—her vitals, a spike of agony, then flatline static. His fingers blurred across the keys, chasing dead servers and shadow networks. Each slammed shut faster than the last until the feed stuttered, collapsed…

NO DATA AVAILABLE. SOURCE DISCONNECTED. TRACE EXPIRED.

The words blinked back like a tombstone.

AJ's breath hitched. He leaned back slowly, the colour draining out of him. "It's gone," he rasped. "Not lost. Not corrupted. Wiped."

Selena's voice was sharp, panicked. "How clean?"

AJ's voice cracked. "Dead. Every node, every echo. They didn't just cut her off—they killed the line, burnt the backups, and torched the archives. There's nothing left." His throat closed around the words. "…It's like she was never there."

The room froze.

Mack swore under his breath, but even anger sounded small here.

James sat motionless at the head of the table, eyes locked on the ring threaded through his tags. His thumb pressed so hard against the scratches that they drew blood.

Frost's voice was stone as his hands slammed keys. "She's gone cold. Buried."

The silence was suffocating. Then AJ's laptop flickered. He frowned and dived back into the code. His voice came out thin, horrified. "It's spreading."

Selena's head snapped around. "What do you mean, spreading?"

"They're not just wiping Facility IX data," AJ whispered. His screen flashed lines of collapsing directories, entire datasets folding in on themselves. "They're pulling her everywhere. Military logs. Personnel records. DNA banks. Black web blood banks. Even comm archives." His fingers trembled on the keys. "Every record that Evelyn Blackthorn ever existed… it's vanishing in real time."

Selena grabbed her phone, thumbing fast. Her face drained white. "Her socials… they're gone." She swallowed hard. "Every post. Every picture. Every trace." She lifted her eyes, dark and wide. "It's like she never lived."

Bullet swore, the sound jagged and desperate. "No… no, that's bullshit. She's real, she's…" He broke off, fists clenching uselessly at his sides as the tears threatened to come.

Irish whispered to Rose, "Jesus Christ, they're erasing her."

AJ's voice was a rasp. "Give it another day, and the only proof she ever existed will be in this room."

That was when James broke.

The ring slid from his hand with a clink. His palms pressed over his face as if he could stop the world from collapsing. His breath tore ragged from his chest, the sound raw and unbearable.

"I failed her."

The words didn't echo. They sank, finally.

"I was supposed to keep her safe." His voice cracked wide open. "That was the one thing I swore. And I…" The dam split. "I failed her, I failed her, I failed her…" The mantra poured out, frantic, unstoppable, each repetition a knife twisting deeper.

Memory stabbed through him: Evelyn barefoot in his Liverpool shirt, laughing in their kitchen, her voice calling him Jamie like he was hers alone. Alive. His. Real.

Now being erased from the earth.

His chest caved. A sound ripped out of him, not a command, not speech, but a strangled sob that tore the air apart. His shoulders shook violently, wrecked breaths heaving through him.

450

Mack grabbed the back of his neck, forcing their foreheads close. Not commander to soldier. Brother to brother.

That broke the room. Selena turned away, silent tears cutting her face. AJ dropped his head into his hands, shaking as lines of Evelyn's existence collapsed on his screens. Frost stared at the floor, face like stone. Bullet blinked furiously, swallowing down a sob. Irish finally saw james for what he was, desperate, exhausted and full of grief. He crouched at James's side, hand firm on his arm, whispering, "You didn't fail her, Jamie. You're still here. So is she. You haven't lost her yet."

But James couldn't look at him. Couldn't hear him. His whole body trembled under Mack's grip, broken sobs spilling from the man who was never supposed to break.

The farmhouse held the silence of a tomb.

Because Evelyn Blackthorn wasn't just missing.

She was being erased.

And soon, the only proof she had ever existed would be the grief in their chests.

Chapter 52

Day 61 – The Desecration of Evelyn Blackthorn

The safe house breathed like a tomb.

Everyone else was down, dragged under by exhaustion, but Selena sat in the comms room with her back rigid and her tea stone-cold. She had been staring at maps and static until her eyes blurred when the screen stuttered.

One blink. One glitch.

Then a file appeared.

The Desecration of Evelyn Blackthorn.

Her stomach lurched so violently she nearly retched. She closed the door, slid the bolt, and sat down like a woman lowering herself into an electric chair.

She clicked.

Static screamed across the screen, then text burnt through in jagged letters:

"You made her too hot to handle. Her death is on Obsidian's hands."

The image cut in.

Evelyn stood naked, skin a map of bruises and open cuts, bones jutting sharp under battered flesh. Her back was to the camera, hair matted with blood. She stood at the lip of a shallow grave. Black, wet earth glistened as if already feeding on her shadow.

A masked man shoved her between the shoulders. She stumbled, toes sinking into soil, but caught herself. Her voice rasped through cracked lips, raw but defiant:

"Fuck you. Go to hell."

The camera shifted. They wanted every angle.

Another shove sent her to her knees. She spat blood, red spraying across the lens. Laughter, low and cruel, from behind the mask.

One of them crouched beside her, his gloved hand fisting in her hair, jerking her head up to the camera. Her face was swollen, lips split, and one eye sealed with blood, but her gaze still burnt.

The man spoke directly to the lens, his voice muffled but gleeful.

"Paladin. You watching? This is what loyalty buys you. This is your wedding gift."

He slammed her face into the dirt, then hauled her up again by her hair until her spine arched and her jaw hung crooked.

"Say bye to your soldier," he sneered, pressing the muzzle under her chin.

She coughed, blood bubbling, then forced out one last, ragged whisper:

"Jamie, baby."

The shot erupted.

Her skull split open, red mist spraying into the pit. Her body folded like butchered meat, rolling deeper into the grave. One of them kicked her ribs with a wet crunch and barked a laugh.

The camera zoomed in, holding on her face, slackened, ruined, unrecognisable but still hers. The light caught her eyes. And this time… they were empty.

That was the moment Selena broke. Not the shot. Not the grave swallowing her. But the fire in those eyes going dark.

Her hands shook so badly she almost dropped the mouse. Tears came hot and silent, tracking her cheeks as she rocked forward, fighting the scream clawing at her throat.

The video didn't end.

The masked man leaned into the frame, filling it. His mask was blank, a black void where a face should be. His voice was cold, deliberate.

"You can keep hunting. You can keep bleeding. But Revenant is ours. She was never yours to save."

Then the screen cut to black.

Selena sat frozen in the blue glow, wet-faced, trembling. She didn't wake anyone. Didn't move.

Because she knew once the others saw this, there would be no turning back.

Only war.

Safe house – 02:06 AM

The hallway was unnaturally still, the kind of silence that pressed against your ears. Selena's bare feet slapped the cold stone, each step sharp with panic. Her breath came shallow, refusing to leave her chest.

She didn't knock.

She didn't slow down.

She shoved Mack's door open so hard it cracked against the wall.

"Mack... Get up! Please, get up!"

He was already moving, instincts snapping him awake. The sight of her, hair tangled and face pale, shaking head to toe, ripped the sleep straight out of him.

"Selena...?"

Her knees buckled before she reached him. He caught her, crouching low, both hands framing her face. His voice dropped, gentle, urgent.

"Hey. Look at me. What is it? What happened?"

Her lips trembled, words almost lost.

"Please... come with me. Tell me this isn't real."

She was on her feet before the sentence was done. Mack followed barefoot, heart hammering, dread crawling deep in his gut.

On the way, he shouldered Frost's door open. He was quickly at the bed, hand clamping over Frost's mouth before a sound escaped. Frost's eyes flew open, his hand instinctively darting for the gun under his pillow, until he saw Mack's face.

"Quiet," Mack whispered. "Sel's in a bad way. She needs you. Now."

That was enough. Frost rose, half-dressed, no questions.

The ops room glowed with the cold blue light of monitors. Selena sat rigid at the desk, tears carving hot streaks down her face, shoulders shaking. Frost crossed the room, pulling her into his chest, her sobs muffled against his skin.

Mack's eyes landed on the screen. His gut turned.

File: The Desecration of Evelyn Blackthorn.

The words alone winded him. His throat closed.

"No."

Frost's jaw tightened. He reached out, hand trembling only once before he hit play.

Static. Then text.

"You made her too hot to handle. Her death is on Obsidian's hands."

The image cut in. Evelyn. Naked, bruised, carved in blue and purple. Standing at the lip of a shallow grave. Her body was bone and defiance, her eyes still burning.

The shove. The spit. The punch that cracked bone. Her knees in the dirt. The hand in her hair, forcing her face to the lens.

"Say bye to your soldier."

Her voice was shredded, but hers.

"Jamie, baby."

The gun went off.

Her skull snapped back, red spray painting the earth. Her body folded into the grave, limbs loose, ribs caving under the kick.

The camera zoomed in on her face, slack and ruined. The fire in her eyes was gone.

Mack dropped into a chair like his legs had given out, one hand clamped over his mouth. His chest heaved, air scraping raw in his throat.

"That can't be her. That can't…"

Selena's whisper split the air, broken and final.

"It is."

Frost held her tighter, eyes locked on the black screen that followed, jaw pressed to her hair.

Mack bent forward, elbows to his knees, head in his hands. His voice cracked open.

"She fought so fucking hard…"

The silence after was suffocating.

Then Frost, voice low, grim as death itself:

"We have to tell James."

Safehouse Dorm – 03:11 AM

The dorm was dark, the kind of dark that pressed on the chest. The soldiers slept hard, their breathing steady, the brittle rhythm of bodies stolen by exhaustion.

Mack stood in the doorway, his shadow long across the floorboards. He didn't move. Didn't speak. Once he did, there would be no pulling it back.

James lay on his side, with one arm under the pillow and the blanket twisted low at his waist. In sleep, his face was softer, with no clenched jaw and no hollowed eyes. The only peace Mack had seen in weeks.

He crouched close, his voice a whisper gentler than anyone had heard from him in years.

"James... brother... I'm so sorry. You need to wake up."

James stirred, blinking blearily, voice rough. "Is it Ev? Did you find her?"

Mack's mouth opened. Nothing came. His jaw worked once, twice, then failed.

James's gaze sharpened, catching the silence. Catching Mack's face. Recognition hit like a bullet. He knew that look; he had seen it once before, in the desert, when men didn't come back. The finality in Mack's eyes said everything.

His body went rigid.

"No. Mack... don't. Don't look at me like that. Please." His voice cracked hard, like agony was trying to crawl out of his body through his mouth.

From the top bunk, Irish dropped down, feet thudding on the floor. He looked between them, his own face sinking with the truth before Mack gave a single, heavy nod.

"Fuck no Mack..." Irish's head rested onto the side of his bunk and then he found the only small ember of strength he had and locked his arm under James "Come on lad. We have got you."

Down the hall, each door opened as the rest of the team emerged from their rooms, drawn by the shift in the air.

James pushed upright, his movements slow and mechanical, like a man walking into his own execution. He didn't ask again. Didn't speak at all.

The corridor stretched ahead, longer than it had ever been. Each step dragged in silence. The shadows moved with them, their number growing: Irish, Bullet, AJ, and Rose. A quiet procession following James into whatever waited in the glow of the ops room.

Safehouse – 03:17 AM

The corridor bled them into the ops room one by one, their shadows dragging heavy across the warped boards. Selena stood stiff at the console, her face pale, eyes raw. She didn't look at James. She couldn't. She just stepped back.

On the monitor, the title was burnt in jagged font:

File: The Desecration of Evelyn Blackthorn

James's chest locked. He moved like a man already falling. His finger clicked the mouse.

The static broke.

A voice rasped through, warped by distortion, low and cruel:

"Paladin. You watching? This is what loyalty buys you. This is your wedding gift."

The screen cleared. Evelyn stood naked in the harsh light, her body a ruin. Bruises spread like continents across her skin. Cuts striped her thighs and her arms. Cigarette burns cratered her back and shoulders. Her collarbone jutted like broken glass, ribs sharp under wasted flesh. She was so thin she looked carved down, but still, impossibly, she stood.

Her head turned slightly, half her face swollen, one eye sealed shut, and her lips split and bleeding. And still, her gaze burnt through the lens.

459

"Jamie…" Her voice cracked, hoarse, but unmistakable. "Jamie, baby."

James's knees almost buckled. His hands shot to the edge of the table, white-knuckled. His throat convulsed around her name, but no sound came out.

Then the shove, rough and merciless, that sent her stumbling forward to the edge of a shallow grave dug into wet earth. She caught herself and spat blood back at her captor.

"Fuck you."

The answer came with a fist to the jaw. The crack of bone echoed through the speakers, spraying crimson across the dirt. Evelyn collapsed, her knees smashing into the grave floor. She tried to rise. Her arms shook.

A gloved hand knotted into her hair, yanking her up so hard her body arched. The balaclava man leaned to the lens.

"Say bye to the camera."

The muzzle flash filled the frame.

The shot blew through her skull in a spray of red and grey. She fell into the pit like a doll, limbs boneless, hair soaking in the mud. A boot shoved her deeper. The camera zoomed in on her slack, ruined face, blood pooling from eyes that had finally gone dark.

The video cut to black.

The room erupted.

AJ doubled forward, retching hard onto the floor, bile splattering over cables and concrete. Rose dropped to her knees

460

beside him, one arm around his shoulders as he heaved, her own face blotched and streaming with tears.

Bullet staggered back into the wall, with both hands over his mouth. His eyes went wide, then screwed shut, his forehead thunking against the plaster once, twice, like he couldn't believe what he'd seen.

Irish slammed a fist into the doorframe, the crack of bone on wood jolting the room. His face was carved raw, eyes bloodshot and wet.

Selena folded in on herself against the desk, silent, sobbing into her hands with Frost beside her, arms locked around her.

And James.

James didn't move. His breath came ragged, tearing. His eyes stayed fixed on the blank screen like if he blinked, she'd vanish for good. His mouth opened, but only one word made it past the wreckage of his chest.

"Ev…"

He looked down at the chain in his fist, the ring digging deep into his palm until blood welled between his fingers. The room shrank around him, the air choking, the silence heavier than gunfire. And every one of them, through their horror, grief, and sickness, they all saw it.

Something in James broke.

His voice frayed into a whisper. "It might be fake."

Mack's arms were folded tight across his chest, but his tears cut clear tracks down his face. "They didn't just kill her," he said hoarsely. "They staged it. They made it theatre."

461

Selena snapped, wild with grief. "AJ! Habibi... tell me it's fake!" She was on her knees now, sobbing, pleading with her body leaning against the desk to keep her up straight.

AJ moved from Roses's arms, pale, shaking, wiping the vomit from his mouth. He dropped into the chair, with his hands trembling over the keys, tearing through data, timestamps, and metadata. His fingers blurred. Then stilled.

He didn't look up. Just whispered: "Oh no..." His hands shook harder. "...it's real."

He slammed the laptop shut, it fell off the table and clattered across the floor filling the room with a sickening conformation. AJ gasped hard, like the air was being siphoned out his lungs and finally he collapsed forward into Roses's arms.

The silence after was worse than the footage.

James just stood there in a daze, his hands trembling, his chest heaving. His bloodied fists clenched so tight that his veins rose like cords. The pressure in the room thickened until everyone could feel it in their lungs.

Then he detonated.

Both his fists crashed onto the desk; the crack sounded like brutal gunfire. Coffee mugs were thrown and shattered against the comms screens. A discarded laptop was smashed face down, glass shattering across the wood.

"EVERYONE OUT."

His voice was jagged agony laced in steel and torment.

No one moved, they were all anchored in absolute horror, watching their friend and commander losing the last part of his humanity that he had tried desperately to hold on to.

"I SAID OUT!" He roared, heaving the desk sideways into the wall with a crash that rattled the windows.

Irish stepped forward. "James…Jamie…"

"Don't… Don't you dare call me that… EVER!" James's voice sounded ragged and feral. His eyes were wild and dangerous. "You didn't feel her die in your bones."

Bullet desperately tried to reach for him. James shoved him back, hard enough to warn. "OUT!"

Rose dragged AJ towards the door, the young man could bearly stand like heartbreak itself had taken his legs. Selena lingered, her eyes were red, until she saw the fracture in him, something feral, beyond reason, and she went. Mack was the last to hold his ground.

"Brother…"

"Go." James's voice cracked wide open. A plea wrapped in rage. "Before I burn this place down."

The door clicked shut, as a procession of broken souls found their places to morn. Some together, some on their own. For those moments time stopped, and agony filled the gap where the seconds and minutes belonged. Even the emotionally guarded amongst the team were shrouded in darkness and disbelief.

For a moment, James stood in silence.

Then he threw the chair into the rotting wooden wall, causing timber to splinter and buckle under the strain of it. He kicked the desk until it skidded across the floor, he welcomed the pain that shoot up his feet as the desk came apart. Then his boot came down on the laptop hard again and again until it was twisted metal, like that was the answer of erasing what he had just seen.

"Fuck… fuck… fuck!" His voice broke into a raw sound, not words, just pure misery torn straight out of his fractured soul.

He smashed his fists into the wall until his skin split, he felt the break as blood streaking down his arms. Papers rained down as he ripped the bookshelf loose and sent it crashing across the room.

Finally, the rage bled out. He sagged forward onto what was left of the desk, blood dripped adorning the wood in small red crescents.

"Ev…" he whispered, once, twice, like a prayer, like a plea.

Then he dropped to his knees. Shoulders hunched. Head bowed. Broken beyond repair.

Chapter 53

The room was wreckage. And so was he.

A stillness had overtaken, there was no sound except for James's breathing, ragged, jagged pulls that sounded like tearing cloth. He knelt amid wreckage, with his blood dripping from split knuckles onto shards of glass. He could see his reflection of what he had become in splinters of the broken laptop screen. He was not James anymore and he will never be Jamie Baby ever again.

The door creaked open, just slightly. Mack stepped cautiously in, his boots crunching on the fallen debris. He took in the overturned desk, the mangled laptop, and the holes in the wall.

"You done?" His voice was low, even but not judgmental.

James didn't move. He couldn't even if he tried.

"If not," Mack added, "I'll give you more time."

That pulled James's head up. His eyes were red-rimmed and hollow. He looked like a Revenant himself, distorted in grief. Sweat streaked his face. For a second he looked at Mack like he was a stranger.

Mack crouched low. He waited. His calm was a counterweight to James's storm.

But James suddenly lurched up, pacing like a caged animal. His boots thudded against the floor, breaths tearing out of him.

"Did you see her body, Mack?!" His voice cracked. "Did you see what they did to her?!"

Mack rose slowly. His own voice was hoarse. "Yeah. I saw it."

"She was broken!" James roared, slamming his fist into the wall again, with no care for his broken hand. The plaster split under the impact. He didn't flinch. "I promised to keep her safe…and they…" His voice shredded.

"She still fought. Still spat in their faces. And they stripped her and kicked her into a grave like she was nothing!" His chest heaved, with tears spilling. "But she's not nothing. She's mine…" His voice collapsed into a rasp. "She was mine…"

The last word broke him. His knees buckled. He hit the floor hard, with fists pressed white into the boards.

"My girl. The only reason I breathed. And I failed her."

The silence after was stifling.

Mack lowered himself beside him, their shoulders brushing. He didn't try to talk him out of it, there was no point. He just stayed. As a steady wall as James's grief tore him apart.

After a long stretch of broken chaotic breaths, James lifted his head. His voice was shredded, raw. "I need to find her body."

"You won't," Mack said gently. "No landmarks, no tells. Could be anywhere."

"I need to feel her, Mack. I need…"

Mack's grip tightened on his shoulder, steady as bedrock. "Selena's already booking flights back to Virginia. Let's get you home."

James closed his eyes. For the first time, he let someone guide him. Mack hauled him up, bearing all his weight.

466

When they stepped into the hall, almost like a guard of honor, for their fallen brother as well as sister. A part of James had just died and they all knew it. Eventually the team looked up.

They didn't see Paladin.

They saw James.

And he was broken.

No one spoke. They filed out into the night in silence, the cold air biting their faces. Mack stayed tight at his side, the others falling in behind like shadows. Even a single word felt like it might shatter him completely.

The drive to the airstrip was short, but in James's head it stretched like miles of empty road. He sat in the back, elbows braced on his knees, staring at the floor. The video looped behind his eyes, every kick, every bruise, the defiance in her eyes before the gunshot.

By the time they reached the tarmac, the jet's lights cut through the dark. Engines hummed, the sound was far too calm for the storm inside him. The wind stung his face, but he climbed the ramp like a man walking to his own execution.

The cabin was dim, the steady drone of engines filling the silence. James dropped into a seat at the back, facing the window. Mack slid in beside him without asking, solid as stone. Across the aisle, Rose curled into herself, her fingers tight around her pendant, her eyes never leaving James.

Bullet hunched two rows ahead, muttering into his hands, shaking his head like he could rattle the images free. Selena typed furiously at her laptop about transports and contingencies, pausing only to shut her eyes when her control slipped. Frost watched her like a hawk and eventually, wrapped her in his hoody when sleep finally took her. He was in his own grief, he put his headphones in and listened to the songs that him and Ev used to play together on the guitar and bass. The thought hit him. *We will never play together again.* Then he let his tears silently come.

AJ hid at the far end, hood up, earbuds in. But the rise and fall of his shoulders betrayed him: he wasn't listening to anything. He was just drowning. He remembered the moments that she had acted like mum when his mother was gone. He remembered the nights when she would let him rest his head on her lap and she would tell him that everything will be ok. He lost the last member of his family, and the grief was crippling.

Irish prowled the aisle, restless hands twitching. He could mend bone, stitch skin, and restart a heart, but there was no fixing this. The helplessness gnawed at him raw. Now was not his time to break, he would save that for when the world didn't need him.

James said nothing. Didn't eat. Didn't drink. He just stared out at the black sky, hands locked so tight the tendons stood white against his skin. His jaw moved sometimes, silent words, maybe prayers, maybe curses.

When the wheels touched down in Virginia, no one moved. The seatbelt sign clicked off, but the cabin stayed frozen, waiting.

James stood eventually, slow and stiff. He stepped down the ramp into the heavy night air.

The others followed, carrying the weight of Evelyn's absence between them like a coffin they couldn't set down.

Chapter 54

The Devil and the Commander

The observation room was dim, lit only by the sterile glow bleeding from the glass wall. Beyond it, Evelyn lay strapped to an inclined restraint table, her wrists and ankles locked in black composite cuffs. Her skin shimmered faintly with the blue pulse of nanites flaring and fighting inside her, each surge rattling the monitors tethered to her body. The foetal heartbeat thumped steadily over the intercom—thump, thump, thump—a merciless metronome.

Kashir sat at the desk before the glass, calm as a king on his throne. His fingers were steepled beneath his chin, eyes fixed on her trembling body as if she were a painting meant only for him.

The wall screen flickered alive. A U.S. Army commander appeared, posture iron-straight, voice clipped, eyes cold.

"Our informant confirms Reaves and the Obsidian team are returning to Virginia. They've taken the bait. They believe the subject is dead. You are clear to proceed with Project Eve."

Kashir leaned back, his smile slow and serpentine. "Good. Reaves was… amusing. His desperation is almost poetic. But they were close. Far too close."

His head tilted slightly, predatory. He didn't look at the commander; his gaze remained fixed on Evelyn thrashing faintly against the cuffs.

"How is our asset?" the commander asked.

Kashir's eyes gleamed. "Alive. Stronger. Every nerve has become an instrument. Pain has made her obedient; she resists, yet her body obeys. She will fight for me as though it were her own will."

The commander's face was carved from stone. "And the child?"

Kashir's tone shifted, hushed and reverent. His gaze dipped toward the steady spike of the foetal monitor.

"Growing. Fed by her agony. Every surge of cortisol, every spasm of fear, carving the foetus into something… exquisite. It will not be born crying. It will be born commanding."

The commander's jaw flexed once. "And the extractions?"

Kashir's smile bared his teeth, the reflection of Evelyn's restraints gleaming in his eyes.

"Three embryos. Harvested clean. Stable. Each carrying her perfected strain. Not soldiers, Commander. Heirs. Legions I will raise in my image."

The commander nodded once. "Keep me informed."

Kashir leaned forward until his face filled the feed, his voice lowering to a whisper, velvet and venom.

"Oh, I will. And when I am finished with her…" His grin widened, too sharp, too human to be sane. "…she will be unrecognisable. To you. To Reaves. Even to herself."

The feed snapped to black. In the reflection of the dead glass, Kashir's smile lingered. On the other side of the observation window, Evelyn's body convulsed in a flare of blue light, nanites fighting against the chains while her muffled groan fogged the air.

Kashir didn't look away. He just watched, patient, the devil at the end of a bargain already signed.

Facility IX – Sublevel Isolation Ward

The lab stank of bleach, iron, and rot masked beneath chemicals. Fluorescent lights buzzed overhead, casting a sickly pallor across the steel and tile. Evelyn lay strapped to the restraint table, her body tilted upright like a specimen pinned for dissection. The black composite cuffs at her wrists and ankles were built for something more dangerous than a human being. Her skin was clammy, her lips cracked. Every shallow breath rasped like it cost more than she had left to give.

The sound filled the room.

Thump… thump… thump.

The foetal monitor was steady and merciless.

Kashir leaned in, his bare hands gliding over the restraints with a mockery of tenderness. "Strong little heart," he murmured. "It feeds on you, Evelyn. You're writing rage into its marrow with every scream you try to swallow."

He flicked a switch. The monitor split into feeds: the ultrasound in stark monochrome, the foetus shifting, and beside it, her neural response. A jagged red line spiked up.

Evelyn's back arched against the table as current ripped through her system. A strangled groan burst past her lips, her eyes snapping open, wide and bloodshot.

The strobe of her brain activity fed straight into the second display, mapping in violent bursts.

471

Kashir adjusted the dial higher, fascinated. "Yes… yes. You see? Cortisol, adrenaline, neural overdrive, it's all stimulus. Every surge you suffer, the child adapts. You are building me something the world has never seen."

But then it happened.

Her skin lit up.

At first it was faint, a shimmer under her veins, like constellations blooming beneath her flesh. But then it pulsed, violent and raw, flaring out of sync with the foetal heartbeat. The nanotechnology that was already interwoven in her DNA ignited and fought back, crashing against the foreign programming and tearing at her biology.

Her body seized in the restraints, every muscle trembling as two systems warred inside her. The monitor spiked, screens juddering between her vitals and a storm of unreadable data.

Kashir's smile faltered. He leaned closer, watching the glow bleed through her skin in chaotic bursts. Not obedience. Not integration. Rebellion.

"Ah…" he whispered, half awe, half irritation. "Your strain resists."

She bared her teeth, a ragged hiss escaping her throat; her voice shredded but still hers. "Not… yours…"

The cuffs screeched as she pulled, her wrists bleeding against the composite. Sparks of blue light jumped from her skin to the restraints, little arcs of static crackling like something alive.

Kashir's eyes burned. "Oh, Evelyn… this is exquisite. Your child grows stronger from both, the agony I force into you, and the war you wage inside yourself. Nature and nurture, rewriting each other in real time. You think you're defying me, but you're only perfecting my creation."

The glow flared bright enough to throw shadows across the wall. Her veins blazed like rivers of fire, pulsing violently against the monitor's rhythm. The foetal heartbeat hammered thump-thump-thump in perfect rhythm, and Evelyn's nanites fired back like starbursts under her skin.

Her head snapped forward, hair matted across her face and her eyes blazing through the bruises. "You won't... break me."

Kashir only smiled again, wolfish, cruel. "No. I won't break you. I'll make you eternal."

He dimmed the lights until the blue flicker in her body looked almost celestial, like she was glowing from within. To him, she was no longer a prisoner. She was a prototype.

The hum of the machines swallowed her gasping breaths. The monitor kept on beeping, relentless. And Evelyn stayed strapped in chains, fighting a war inside her own body, her nanites clawing against Kashir's design, each flare of light a reminder that she wasn't finished yet.

Chapter 55

The machines hummed in their endless rhythm, cold and merciless, after Kashir's footsteps faded into the hall. Evelyn lay pinned to the table, her eyes fixed on the ceiling where the fluorescent buzz seemed to be eating the silence alive. The thump-thump, thump-thump of the foetal monitor wrapped around her like the last thread tying her to hope.

Her lips parted, the words scraping out so faint they barely stirred the air.

"Stay in there, little one. Hold strong, no matter what. You're mine, always mine. I don't know if Jamie is your father... But if he knew, he'd love you like you were his. You'd love him too. He's beautiful. Strong. Brave enough to rip the world apart for us. He is coming, I know he is."

Her breath wavered; tears burnt hot as they slipped into her hairline. Still, she forced the promise out.

"Daddy will find us. That's what he does. So stay with me. Stay strong. No matter what they do, I'll die a thousand times if it means I get to hold you in my arms. I swear it. I'll keep you safe. We're in this together... you and me."

For a moment, silence answered.

Then... light.

It bled from her stomach in a faint, shimmering ripple, blue-silver like moonlight bending through deep water. The glow pulsed with the beat of the monitor, thump, thump, thump, and spread outward, licking along her ribs, curling down her hips. The torn cuts in her skin began to knit at the edges, the raw flesh

474

softening, bruises blanching from black to yellow in slow, deliberate waves.

Evelyn's eyes widened, her breath catching sharply in her chest. She stared down at the faint constellation of light spidering under her skin with nanites stirring, not at Kashir's command but at her child's.

Her lips trembled into the ghost of a smile, weak but fierce.

"Thank you, little one…"

The heartbeat monitor kept pulsing steadily, as if the child had answered back.

Observation Chamber

Kashir stilled.

Through the glass, Evelyn slept, curled around her stomach. The shimmer rolled beneath her skin in rhythm with the foetal monitor—thump, thump, thump—each pulse glowing faintly blue like moonlight bleeding through veins. Her cuts knit shut. Bruises drained to yellow. The healing wasn't hers.

The foetus had reached out.

The child had healed her.

Kashir's smile faltered. This wasn't his design. He had calibrated for pain-fed obedience, for aggression sculpted in the womb. What he saw now was autonomous, untamed. A force acting of its own accord.

He leaned hard on the console, isolating the moment, frame by frame. The shimmer wasn't a trick of light. It had a signature, nanite resonance, but was wrong. Not the mother's strain. The foetus's.

And worse, it was grafting.

He watched the scans bloom across the screen, his pulse quickening as the data sharpened. Evelyn's neural map stuttered. Whole pathways blinked out, then relit with new branching, like vines overtaking a wall. Her blood markers flickered between her profile and a second signature. Not separate. Not parallel. Merging.

Her body convulsed once on the table, subtle but enough to make the leather restraints creak. On the scan, a cascade of lines lit like wildfire: foetal nanites bleeding into maternal tissue, rewriting her cell by cell. Not infection. Integration.

Kashir's lips peeled back from his teeth. "Impossible…"

But there it was. A patch of her ribcage had healed into ridges of denser, almost metallic cartilage. The cut on her temple had closed, but the scar tissue glowed faintly under the scan, threaded with nanite filaments that hadn't existed before. Her biology was being overwritten from within.

He pressed the intercom, his voice stripped of mockery, hard as bone.

"Lab One. I want a full re-scan—neural, hormonal, cellular. Mother and foetus. Triple redundancy."

A tech hesitated. "Sir… Is there a change?"

"Yes," Kashir hissed. "Something… unplanned."

He cut the line and locked the chamber to Level Black. No one entered now but him.

Through the glass, Evelyn's chest rose steadily, her hand twitching against the restraint as if trying to shield her stomach

476

even in sleep. The monitors showed her vitals stabilising, but on the cellular feed, her DNA was no longer hers alone. It was splicing. A hybrid helix, knitting strands of her code with the foetus's.

Not mother and child.

Symbiosis.

Kashir stood frozen, watching the readouts. His mind raced between horror and exhilaration. He wasn't just looking at a weapon. He was looking at an evolutionary event.

Finally, his smile returned, sharp, feral, and reverent.

"Oh, little one," he murmured to the glass. "You're rewriting her already. And when you're finished… neither of you will belong to her anymore."

Observation Room One – Forced Evolution

The theatre stank of antiseptic and ozone, undercut with the acrid tang of scorched flesh. Evelyn hung against the restraints, her body trembling in the cold light. The foetal monitor pulsed steadily behind her—thump, thump, thump, the only sound keeping rhythm with her shallow breaths.

Kashir adjusted the dials with no hesitation.

The restraints crackled. A surge of current slammed through her body, arching her spine so violently that the leather cuffs strained against the bolts. Her scream broke, raw, echoing in the chamber.

On the monitors, her vitals spiked into the red. The foetus remained steady, serene.

"Too calm," Kashir muttered, turning the dial again.

Heat bled into the cuffs, blistering her wrists and ankles. The stink of cooked skin thickened the air. Evelyn sagged, then convulsed as her body betrayed her with a guttural sob.

The shimmer came. At first faint, then blinding. Iridescent veins lit across her stomach, blue-white, spidering up her ribcage, through her arms, and down her legs. The burns shrank. The cuts sealed. Tissue crawled back together under the glow.

But something else happened too.

Her pulse slammed higher, then flatlined for a breath. Neural activity surged in jagged, unnatural spikes. The foetal readings mirrored it; for the first time they were not calm but fighting.

Kashir's lips peeled back. "Ah... there you are."

He pushed the dial to its limit. Evelyn convulsed, eyes rolling back, a strangled noise tearing from her throat. Her muscles locked so tight that the restraints creaked like bone under pressure.

The shimmer roared. This time it wasn't gentle; it was violent. Blue light tore through her veins in violent pulses, her skin bulging, writhing as if something beneath was pushing to the surface. Her stomach rippled, with her muscles spasming as nanites ripped through damaged tissue faster than it could break.

On the monitors, her heart raced erratically, skipping beats and stuttering back. The foetus's response was brutal: surges of adrenaline, waves of regenerative spikes, each one crashing harder, faster, like the child was fighting a war from inside her womb.

Evelyn's back arched until it looked like her spine might snap. The scream that ripped out of her throat was barely human, choked by blood pooling in her mouth.

Kashir watched, transfixed. His voice was a feverish whisper.

"Yes. Break her. Break her and let me see how far you'll go to put her back together."

Her wrists split open against the restraints, her skin flaying, bone glimpsed beneath, only for the light to flood in, knitting it shut in seconds. Her ribs visibly shifted under her skin, cracking from the current, then snapping back into place as the nanites repaired them mid-break.

It was no longer healing. It was warfare.

Mother breaking. Child rebuilding. Over and over.

Her body was the battlefield.

Kashir leaned in toward the glass, grinning like a zealot before an altar.

"You're not just surviving, little one," he whispered. "You're rewriting her. You're mine. Both of you."

He killed the current at last. Evelyn sagged against the straps, drenched in sweat, her chest heaving, eyes glassy with pain and exhaustion. Her lips moved weakly, forming words not for him but for the life inside her.

"I'm still here… Stay with me…"

The foetal monitor answered: steady, defiant, unbroken.

And Kashir, watching with fever-bright eyes, knew he had unlocked something new. Not a subject. Not an asset.

A weapon that fought back.

Chapter 56

James didn't even remember turning the key in the lock when he reached the house. But the moment the door swung open, the air hit him like a punch.

It still smelt like her.

His boots scuffed over the floorboards as he stepped inside. And there they were, her boots. Kicked off by the door, lying on their sides exactly where she'd left them. He stood over them for a long time, his throat tightening until he had to look away.

In the living room, her Liverpool Football Club blanket was draped over the couch, folded in that lazy, half-hearted way she always left it after curling up to watch a match. The sight of it made his chest ache so sharply he had to steady himself against the wall.

On the back of the kitchen chair hung the battered grey hoodie she always stole from him, creased, smelling faintly of her perfume and smoke. Her dog tags lay on the counter beside it, the chain coiled loosely, as if she'd only just taken them off. He remembered her doing it on their wedding day, smiling as she tossed them aside like she was finally free of them.

His feet felt heavy as he made his way to the bedroom.

The door creaked softly when he pushed it open. For a moment, he just stood there, staring. The bed was unmade, the sheets tangled exactly as they'd been the morning she left. Her side was empty now, but the dent in her pillow was still there, a hollow in the feathers that once drove him mad when they stuck out and scratched his face. Now, it felt like the most precious thing in the world.

On the nightstand sat the coffee cup she'd abandoned before leaving that morning, the faint brown ring at the bottom long dried. It was still where she'd put it down, like she'd meant to come back for it. Like she'd meant to come back for him.

The silence pressed in on him from every side.

He sat on the edge of the bed, his elbows on his knees, staring at nothing. Every corner of the room whispered her name. Every object, every crease in the sheets, and every faint trace of her perfume was a reminder of how violently she'd been torn away from him.

And for the first time since he'd seen Mack's face in that barracks, James let himself fall apart.

James lowered himself slowly, as though moving too fast might break something in the air around him. His hand brushed the dent in her pillow, his fingers curling into the fabric like he was afraid it might vanish if he let go. He pulled it toward him and lay down on his side, facing her empty space.

The scent hit him instantly.

It was her: that faint mix of her shampoo, the perfume she wore when she wasn't on a job, and the ghost of cigarettes from nights spent on the porch together. It poured through him in a way that was both comfort and torture.

He pressed his face into the pillow, breathing deeply until it hurt. If he closed his eyes hard enough, he could almost believe she was right there beside him, his legs tangled with his, her hair spilling across his chest. He could almost feel her shifting against him, making those quiet little hums she made when she was just on the edge of sleep.

But there was no warmth. No weight. Just the hollow space she'd left behind.

His fingers tightened around the pillow until his knuckles ached. He pulled it into his chest, holding it like it was the last piece of her he'd ever have, like letting go would mean losing her all over again. The ache in his chest sharpened until he thought it might break him apart.

His breath hitched. Once. Twice. And then the sound broke out of him—a raw, guttural thing he didn't recognise as his own voice. It tore through the stillness, bouncing off the walls, a sound born of love and fury and loss all tangled into something that had no place in this world.

He buried his face deeper, whispering her name against the fabric. Over and over. Like a prayer. Like a plea.

The pillow still smelt of her.

And that, somehow, hurt more than if it hadn't.

Irish sat on the edge of the couch, shoulders hunched, his elbows resting on his knees. The room was dim, the only light coming from the small lamp in the corner, casting everything in a muted amber haze. Rose was beside him, one hand curled around his, the other stroking through his hair with that quiet, steady rhythm she'd used on him in every dark moment since they'd met.

After a long silence, he finally shifted, leaning sideways until his head rested in her lap. She didn't say anything—just continued combing her fingers gently through his hair, smoothing it back like she could untangle the ache knotted deep in his chest.

He stared off toward the far wall, jaw tight. His voice, when it came, was low and rough.

"I can't shake it, Rose."

Her hand stilled for a moment before she coaxed it back into motion, her thumb brushing over his temple. "Can't shake what?"

He swallowed hard, his throat working. "That feeling. The one you get in the field... when you just know." His voice cracked slightly. "That medic's gut. The one that's never wrong."

Rose's breath caught, but she didn't interrupt.

"I think..." He closed his eyes, the words seeming to cost him more than he could afford. "I think James didn't just lose Ev." His chest rose and fell with a shudder. "I've got a horrible feeling he lost his child too."

Rose's fingers froze completely this time, her hand resting lightly against his head. She stared down at him, the weight of his words sinking in like cold water. There were no platitudes, no easy reassurances, because she knew. And she knew that gut feeling he was talking about. The one that had saved more lives than she could count.

She bent forward, pressing her lips to his hair. "Oh, Conall. You can never ever tell our James. He doesn't need to know. It will kill him."

His hands curled into fists on his chest, eyes still closed, like if he didn't look at her, the words might somehow be less real. "I hope to God I'm wrong," he whispered.

But neither of them believed it.

The door to James and Evelyn's home hadn't opened in forty-eight hours.

James hadn't answered a single call, not the dozens that had hit his personal phone, not the ones that came through his military line, not even the encrypted comms the team used. He had shut the world out completely.

Word had already leaked through the close-knit military community. The official line was the same old cold lie, "killed in a training accident." Everyone knew it was bollocks. That phrase was only ever used to wrap a death in something neat and non-threatening, something the public could swallow. But this wasn't neat. This wasn't clean. And people in the community had long memories. Over the years, he and Evelyn had worked with soldiers across every branch, every country, every corner of the battlefield. Word like this... it travelled fast.

He had taken her Liverpool Football Club blanket two days ago, wrapped it around himself, and hadn't been able to let it go since. It smelled faintly of her shampoo, her skin, the way she always smelled when she came in from the cold, wind, warmth, and something he couldn't name. He hadn't eaten. Hadn't showered. Hadn't even cleaned his teeth. His body was running on fumes, but his grief didn't need fuel. It burned on its own.

His knees had gone stiff from the way he'd been sitting, on the floor, back against the side of the bed. He couldn't bring himself to lie in it. He didn't want her scent disturbed, didn't want the smell of her pillow to be buried under the weight of his own grief. The dent her head had left in the feather pillow was still there, the same pillow he used to hate because the feathers poked out and scratched him. Now, it was a relic.

Time had stopped meaning anything. It was just one long, heavy stretch of silence.

The quiet broke with the faint creak of the door. No knock, no voice, just the sound of it easing open. There was only one person who could walk into his space unannounced and not risk being shot.

Irish.

Mack had given him the key.

Irish stepped inside the bedroom and shut the door quietly behind him. He didn't speak. He just stood there for a moment, looking at the man who had once led them all, who had held them together through hell. Now James looked like he'd been hollowed out, caved in around an ache so deep it seemed impossible to breathe through.

Irish crossed the room and sat down beside him, shoulder to shoulder. The silence between them was heavy, but familiar, the two men who didn't need to fill the air to understand what the other was feeling.

After a long moment, Irish's voice broke through, low and rough.

"You know what she said to me once? Back when you first pulled us together as a team?" James didn't look at him.

Irish's mouth twitched into a faint smile, his eyes somewhere far away.

"She said, 'He's got the emotional range of a tactical rock, but I swear that man blushes when I call him commander in a Scouse accent.'"

James's throat shifted, a muscle twitching at the corner of his jaw.

Irish kept going, his voice softer now, but still heavy with ache.

"She told me once that if you ever kissed her, the world might explode—'so maybe it's for the best he doesn't,' she said, 'I'm not sure I could defuse that.'" He gave a quiet chuckle, but it was thin, watery. "She said you made her knees go stupid. 'Stupid, Irish! Who the fuck invented knees? Sack 'em.'"

James's fingers clenched tighter around the edge of the blanket.

Irish's eyes softened. "She told me about the time you made her tea with the wrong milk, and she drank it anyway. Pretended it was perfect just so you wouldn't feel bad." He nudged James's arm lightly. "That's love, brother. Stupid, aching, ridiculous, real love."

For a while, James said nothing. When he finally spoke, his voice was barely there.

"She's not gone."

Irish nodded slowly.

"The version of her in that video…" James swallowed hard. "…that wasn't Ev. That was a woman who fought harder than anyone should ever have to. I need to remember her before that. Not broken. Not bloodied. Not thrown in a grave. I need to remember the beautiful nutter who called everyone lad, who ate peanut butter and salt in yogurt for breakfast. The woman who danced in the kitchen and played Fuck Her Gently on Frost's guitar that night at Mack's… and swore it was the best love song ever written."

James's voice cracked. "I held her, Irish. She was warm. Alive. Fuck… she was laughing at me the next morning because I couldn't find my socks."

Irish's eyes shone. "She called you Jamie-baby," he whispered.

James covered his face with both hands, and the sound that broke out of him wasn't just a sob, it was a full collapse, the dam finally giving way.

Irish didn't try to stop it. He just reached across, pulled him into a one-armed embrace, and held him there through his desperate demise into the abyss. And by god Irish felt it. This was the two men who loved the same fierce, fire-hearted woman. One as a husband, one as a brother.

"We'll find Kashir," Irish said quietly into his ear. "And then we end the cunt."

James stood suddenly.

No sound, no warning, just movement, slow and deliberate, like something mechanical grinding back to life. Irish didn't move. He just watched, his eyes fixed on the man in front of him, reading every shift of muscle and breath.

James's face was stripped bare of grief now. No softness, no tremor, no tears. Just something cold, sharp, and dangerous. War.

"I need to get her body," he said, voice flat.

Irish blinked. "James, we've talked about this..."

"Fuck what we've talked about." His tone could cut steel. "I need to trace where they buried her."

It didn't sound like he was talking about Evelyn anymore; it sounded like he was talking about an objective. Another op. His jaw was locked tight, eyes fixed on something far beyond the room.

"There's footage," he continued. "Timelines. Shadows. Angles. I want the metadata stripped and run through location triangulation."

He already had his phone in hand, moving like a man who had just chosen a target. Within seconds he was barking orders into the receiver.

"Selena. Get AJ. I want everything pulled from that file...light angles, cloud patterns, soil composition. If they dumped her, I'll find her."

Irish stood slowly, alarm creeping into his expression.

"Mate, think about what you're asking. You'll make them watch it again...AJ's not coping, and Selena..."

"I'm thinking clearly," James cut in, voice like stone. "For the first time in two days, I'm thinking exactly like they need me." His eyes narrowed. "They think they buried her. I'll dig up the fucking world to bring her home."

Hours Later – Obsidian HQ

Selena, AJ, and Irish stood around the war table. James didn't sit, instead he hovered at the edge, with his hands clamped onto the metal lip of the table, a stare burning into the big screen like he could force it to give up its secrets.

"You said it was wasteland," James growled. "We could cross-reference topography, wind patterns…"

"We did," Selena said quietly. "Every angle. Every cloud shadow, light temperature, insect noise. We broke that footage down to the fucking atoms."

AJ shook his head, defeated. "It's like they built a fake sky."

"Digital wasteland," Irish muttered. "Could be anywhere. It's like someone airbrushed the planet."

James's knuckles whitened. "The metadata?"

"Scrubbed to hell," AJ replied, voice hoarse. "No GPS. No server ID. No real audio outside of what they wanted us to hear. It wasn't leaked, it was sent. That grave could be in the Sahara or a bunker in Greenland."

The silence was heavy enough to crush the air.

"They don't want us to find her," James said finally, voice low.

"No," Selena agreed. "They want you to remember her like that. James grief doesn't make you braver. It makes you dangerous if you let it drive you. So we remember her right. We honour her correctly. But not like this, this will kill you."

James's body went rigid. Then he stepped back and slammed a fist into the wall hard enough to crack plaster.

"Fuck. Fuck!"

Irish grabbed his hand before he could swing again. "Stop! She'd hate this…"

"So that's it?" James's voice was a blade. "She's gone? All I get is that video? That grave? That—execution?"

Selena's silence was answer enough.

James's fists came down on the table, once, then again, until a coffee mug shattered, porcelain skittering over the war map.

AJ caught his fists. "Stop Baba… Stop hitting things… this is not you… she would be so angry if she saw you hurting yourself like this… please!"

"What the fuck do I bury?" He roared. "I'm drowning in missed calls from people we served with. I'm her husband. I'm the head of Obsidian. And I can't even bring my wife's body home. What the fuck does that make me?"

No one spoke.

"What do I put in the ground? A uniform? A fucking picture? She was mine! She deserves more than an empty hole in the dirt!" His voice cracked. "What am I supposed to do? Bury an empty casket?"

The silence fractured when Mack stepped closer, his voice low but steady. "James… you know the rules. No one can know how she died. No footage. No names. Not when it's this black."

James looked at him like a man staring down the edge of a cliff.

"You're right," Mack said. "We need to bury her. Even if it's just to give her people somewhere to stand and say goodbye. She deserves that." He hesitated, and the next words seemed to hurt coming out. "But we're not going to find what's left of her. They made sure of that."

James didn't blink. He just turned, walked out, and shut the door so quietly it was worse than if he'd screamed.

James didn't argue when Mack spoke the last words.

He didn't slam the door. He didn't shout. He just turned and walked out of the War Room, the quiet of it somehow heavier than any scream.

Down the corridor. Past the barracks. Past the hangar where the hum of Obsidian's heartbeat didn't touch him.

Outside, the winter air bit his skin but didn't slow him. He went straight to the motor pool, took the keys to the Jeep without a word, and drove.

Virginia blurred past in cold, empty miles. He didn't stop for fuel, food, or the dozens of calls still lighting his phone. Every ring was ignored, every notification buried under the roar of the tyres.

By the time he pulled up to their house, the sun was gone. The street was quiet. The kind of quiet that presses against your ribs until it hurts.

He unlocked the front door. Their space, built for two soldiers who somehow managed to create a home out of war zones and vinyl.

It swung open with a soft click.

The silence hit harder than the footage ever could.

Everything was exactly how she'd left it.

A single boot kicked off by the mat, as if she were mid-story and had paused to grab a snack. Her jacket was draped over the back of the armchair, where she always tossed it after a mission. The book she was reading—some half-witchy, half-horror pulp thing—was spine-up on the armrest, open at the chapter she'd last mocked aloud.

And there it was on the coffee table. Her Liverpool shirt. His shirt, really, but she'd claimed it years ago. Worn. Soft. Drenched in memories of late-night tea and her head on his chest, humming after the chaos had passed.

He picked it up, pressed it to his face, and sat.

Then he saw it.

Her Fleetwood Mac vinyl. *Rumours.* Still on the player. She'd been playing *Dreams* the morning of the wedding. Said it was a "soft chaos omen" and laughed.

The needle hadn't been returned to its place.

His hand hovered, then trembled as he lifted the album jacket and tucked it under his arm.

And in the corner, her bass guitar. Matte black. Strings slightly loose. He knelt before it like it was sacred. Like it might still hold her fingerprints.

He gathered all three things slowly:

Her Liverpool Football Club shirt.

The record.

The bass.

"If there's an afterlife," he whispered, voice raw, "these are the things you'll miss."

He didn't sleep there. Couldn't.

He left the apartment with her spirit folded into his arms and locked the door like sealing a tomb.

The base was humming with quiet motion when James returned with his arms full and heart hollow.

He didn't speak. He didn't need to. Everyone knew where he'd been.

The War Room was half-lit, the hum of equipment low and constant. Frost looked up first from the corner and froze when his eyes caught on the bass guitar in James's grip. Not slung over his shoulder like weightless kit, but cradled like it might break. Like he might.

Selenas's hand tightened around her mug of tea. AJ went perfectly still, seeing the precious relics that they all knew so well. Mack's spine straightened. Irish's eyes dropped to the floor. Because he knew what James would pick. He'd always known, its exactly what he would have choose, James knew her gypsy soul as well as he did.

James walked past them all and set the things down on the conference table with careful precision, as if arranging relics for a shrine:

Her Liverpool top, creased at the collar, number faded but proud.

Her *Rumours* vinyl sleeve was worn soft at the edges from countless rainy-night plays.

Her bass guitar, black, heavy, silent.

No one moved.

James stepped back, looking at them as if they could answer him.

"I'm sorry for how I've been acting," he murmured, his voice low and rough. "These were her. Not a uniform. Not a file. Not a weapon. These."

He touched the shirt. "She was 'Red' because of this. Not because of blood, but because of Liverpool. Because she swore their anthem had more soul than the army ever did."

His hand shifted to the record. "Stevie Nicks was her fairy godmother. She'd dance around in her socks, screaming, every lyric to Go your own way, like it was prophecy."

Then his fingers curled around the neck of the bass, and his shoulders caved a little. "She and Frost would jam for hours. Frost on guitar, her on this. I'd pretend it annoyed me, but it didn't. I loved it. I'd lie on the floor and let it thrum through me. It was the only time the noise in my head ever shut the fuck up."

Frost swallowed hard. "She… she was a rhythm section."

James gave a small nod, running both hands down his face. "I don't want to do this. I don't want to bury songs, or shirts, or memories. I want her back."

Irish stepped forward and laid a steady hand on his shoulder. Mack followed. Selena's voice came soft but certain. "She's in all of this, James. These aren't just objects. They're anchors. Until we know the truth."

He stood there for a long moment, breathing in the quiet, before finally reaching out to turn the vinyl sleeve so Stevie's face looked into the room.

"Let's bury what we have," he said. "And never stop hunting for what we lost."

Chapter 57

The night before the funeral, James stayed at Mack's house. He couldn't face their home. The silence, the walls and her absence.

He didn't hear the knock. Or maybe he did, but days without sleep had blurred the line between sound and memory. The door creaked open anyway, spilling in a thin strip of hall light.

"Mate… it's time." Mack's voice was careful, like he was coaxing a wounded animal.

James didn't move.

The blackout blinds kept the room thick with stale air, sweat, and grief. Mack crossed the room and sat on the edge of the bed. He didn't push. He just waited.

Eventually, James rolled onto his back. His eyes were red, lashes crusted with sleep that hadn't healed him. His beard was patchy and uneven. His jaw twitched from nights of grinding teeth.

"I can't," James rasped, his voice breaking. "I can't get up."

Mack only nodded. "That's alright. I've got you."

He left, then returned with a bowl of warm water, a towel, clippers, and a razor. Setting them down, he pulled the pillow from beneath James's head.

"Lift your chin, brother. Ev would skin me alive if she saw you like this."

A sound caught in James's throat, half laugh, half sob.

Mack shaved him slowly and gently, wiping each stroke like he was handling something sacred. He trimmed his hair next with no fuss, just neat, steady hands. The quiet rhythm filled the room in place of words.

By the end, James's head dipped forward, not from comfort, but from the sheer weight of everything pressing down.

He whispered through cracked lips. "How the fuck do I bury her, Mack?"

Mack's hand rested firm on his shoulder.

"We'll bury what she loved, her music, her fire. The rest, we carry."

He helped James stand. His legs shook, and Mack kept a hand at his back.

"She'd never want a flag over her," he murmured.

"Then we won't," Mack said. "Just the three things. They're her."

James stepped forward, picked up the Liverpool blanket, and pressed it to his face, breathing her in.

Mack turned away. Not because he couldn't bear to watch, but because grief didn't need an audience.

It needed space.

James gripped the bannister like it was the last solid thing in the world. Mack stayed close, a steady shadow, never rushing, never touching, just there.

Step by step, James descended. His Obsidian blacks hung heavy on him, medals catching muted light. His face was freshly shaven, but his eyes were hollow. In his breast pocket, tucked sharp against his heart, was a red Liverpool scarf, the one Evelyn had shoved at him two seasons ago, making him swear to wear it "when we next crush United."

The team was waiting in the hall. Silent. Sharp. Each dressed in their black obsidian uniforms, each with a scarlet scarf folded into their collar. Mourning. Proud.

Irish stepped forward first, something folded in his hands.

"I know you've still got yours," he said, voice roughened by grief. "But I've got hers. From the last match we went to. They won, and she left it in the pub, the daft cow."

James's chest cracked open at that, something warm and excruciating bleeding through the cold.

Irish unfolded the scarf with revanace. It still smelt faintly of beer, her perfume, and the shampoo she'd stolen from James's side of the bathroom. Without another word, he looped it around his neck.

James's hands trembled. His voice scraped out raw. "I can't let go."

Ruby stepped forward. She didn't ask. She just wrapped her arms around him, easing the blanket from his grip with a tenderness only she could.

"It's alright," she whispered. "You're not letting her go. You're letting us carry her now."

The sound that tore out of him was sharp and broken, a sob edged with survival, not meant for hearing. His knees buckled, and Mack caught him. Ruby didn't release her hold.

Outside, the black cars waited.

Inside, James stood ringed by the only people who would never let him fall.

The frost still clung to the tarmac when the six of them stood at the edge of the airstrip, waiting for the casket, they had to make it look devastatingly real.

That was the order. But James hated it. Hated that this funeral was a lie, that the box they would bury was light, hollow, and wrong.

A couple of months ago, he'd worn a suit he despised just to marry her. Now he stood in his obsidian black dress, medals pinned across his chest like they might hold him together. A red Liverpool scarf, hers, was tucked into his collar. Defiant. Sacred. She'd once hurled popcorn at him for cheering too late during a match. He would've given anything to hear her yell at him again.

Mack stood at his side. Irish next. Then Frost, AJ, and Bullet. Shoulder to shoulder, every man wearing the same scarlet scarf. Not issued. Not sanctioned. Just hers. Together, they would carry her.

The casket was light, and that made it worse. Inside lay only three things that belonged to her soul. That was all they had left of Evelyn Blackthorn.

They carried her through the silence. Military brass and old friends stood in small clusters, faces solemn but distant. Most knew only the official headline: Captain Evelyn Blackthorn. Killed in training. No further comment. Only Obsidian and her fellow solders knew the truth, that she had been stolen from them, and that this was theatre.

James's fingers twitched on the handle. His body moved, but it didn't feel like his own. Irish's gaze stayed locked ahead. AJ's face was hollow, Bullet's jaw trembled. Mack's lips moved in a prayer he hadn't said since Belfast, and Frost stayed silent, eyes fixed forward. They moved as they always had, in formation. But none of them had ever been trained for this.

The casket lowered into the ground under a dry, stubborn sky. The bugler played, crisp and slow. James stood at the front, staring down, whispering through clenched teeth, "She didn't even like flags."

Irish swallowed. "That's why we gave her a scarf."

Brass read her file from the podium—her name, her age, her tours, her decorations—delivered like a weather report. No fire. No fight. No, Evelyn.

James stepped forward, paper trembling in his hand. This time it had to be written, not like there wedding. There were no words that could just flow, not for this, not ever. The words on the page blurred, useless. "She was…" His voice cracked. He tried again. "She was the kind of woman who would burn every rule to protect someone she loved…" His throat closed. His body shook violently.

Mack's hand landed on his shoulder, steady. He took the paper gently from James and read for him.

"She was the soul of this team. Not because she was perfect, but because she wasn't. She was messy. Loud. Brilliant. She made us better just by being hers. And I don't think she ever believed she was worthy of love. That's why we never stopped showing her she was. Every damn day."

501

James's knees buckled. Ruby caught him, her arms locked tight around his waist, holding him up as the gun salute began.

Crack—he flinched. In his head, it wasn't the ceremony—it was the video.

Crack—her body jerking sideways in grainy footage.

Crack—the final shot. The image of the bullets on their wedding day.

Irish's voice rose, trembling, carrying the hymn that had carried them all since childhood:

"When you walk through a storm, hold your head up high…"

The melody wrapped the grave like a shroud. AJ wept openly. Frost turned his back as Selena held him, keeping him up straight. Bullet pressed his scarf over his mouth, muffling the sound of his sobs.

The folded flag was pressed into James's arms. The red scarf beneath his collar choked him. Ruby held him harder as something inside him gave way completely.

The world blurred, with sound falling away until all that was left was her laugh, her heartbeat, and her voice, in his head. *"you're a muppet Jamie baby, but I love you lad."*

Chapter 58

Her Dive Bar, Her Rules

The place smelt of stale beer, wet concrete, cigarette ghosts, and the low hum of a jukebox older than most of the regulars.

Exactly the way she liked it.

The dive had never seen good days—hell, it barely held itself together—but Evelyn had loved it for that very reason. "Polished places don't hold real stories," she'd once said. "This place? This place remembers everything."

Tonight, it remembered her.

The bar was packed wall-to-wall. Soldiers, mercenaries, SEALs, spooks, civilians, and people who had no business breathing the same air, except for one fact: every single one had been marked by Evelyn Blackthorn.

The noise was chaos. Laughter, swearing, crying, the scrape of stools, the slam of glass. It was grief at full volume, burning itself out in cheap whisky and louder songs.

Someone had shoved all the tables against the walls. The bar itself was drowning in pint glasses and rum shots. Above the till, taped in messy handwriting:

"Tonight, we drink to Red."

The jukebox had been rigged to cycle only Britpop, 90s anthems, and the rock anthems she'd blast in the van until someone threatened to throw the stereo out. Every chorus came out too loud, too out of tune, and absolutely perfect.

People carried their own relics of her. An old service mate marched in with a sun-bleached pillowcase with a bra stitched onto it: CAMP TITS! scrawled in thick black marker, a deployment joke that had somehow gone legendary. The room howled and cheered in unison when it went up on the wall.

Then another friend unrolled a faded Manchester United beach towel. The word 'UNITED' had been slashed out with paint and replaced, in messy block letters in her unmistakable hand: 'ARE TOSSERS'.

Both items went up beside her photo, her hair wild, beer bottle in her hand, a cigarette dangling from her lips and her middle finger flipping someone, probably Irish. The whole place shook with laughter, the kind that cracked through tears, the kind she would've demanded.

Her red Liverpool scarf, the one James had worn at the funeral, was now tied around the mic-stand like a war banner.

AJ and Bullet had claimed the "dance floor", if you could call the sticky space by the jukebox that. They slammed into each other to *Common People* by Pulp, Bullet's pint sloshing everywhere, while poor AJ, who was stone sober, just shouted the chorus like an idiot anyway.

Mack leaned against the wall, eyes glassy, listening as a corporal retold the time Evelyn had reprogrammed the base vending machine to cough up cider instead of Coke. He swallowed a laugh that tasted like grief and promised himself— quiet, fierce—that every firepit night from now on there would be a bottle opened for her, a small ritual to keep her seat warm and her voice in the dark.

Irish worked the bar like a man performing a ritual to stay upright—measure, pour, slide the glass across the scuffed wood, repeat. His hands moved with grim, professional precision, but the edges of each motion trembled; every shot was another stitch holding him together. Rose moved down the line handing out shots, her face the colour of old paper, her mouth clenched so tight no sound escaped.

To everyone else it looked like grief, with her soft eyes, but Rose's silence was a different beast: guilt folded small and constant behind her ribs. She watched the team like someone counting casualties: the way Mack swallowed a laugh that wasn't a laugh, how Selena's fingers brushed a cigarette and didn't light it, how Frost stared past the room as if the next thing he'd see would be her. Hardened men and women broke in their own private ways, and Rose felt each crack knowing she'd caused it.

Selena spent most of the night with her arms threaded through Frost's. He'd fought harder than he ever let anyone see; she'd held him while the armour slipped. But he broke for her the way she broke for him — two broken things pressed together, sanding one another smooth in the dark. Since Evelyns death they had slept like that, night after night, hands and breath learning the map of the other's fear. They didn't drink. They didn't dance. They just kept each other awake enough to survive the nightmares.

Throughout the night the stories avalanched.

Someone shouted about the squad of Marines she'd convinced to salute the camp goat every morning, complete with parade rest and a kazoo rendition of the national anthem. The bar roared. Another chimed in about her glitter bombs: how half the

505

Middle East still sparkled from the inside of kit bags she'd sabotaged.

Near the pool table, a group of Brits, some in uniform, some long retired, stood with Obsidian, drinks in hand, shaking their heads through their grins.

"Oi, d'you remember Iraq?" one asked. "When she tried to light a fag off that burning building?"

The whole group groaned, laughing already.

"Proper Scouse back then…" someone muttered.

But the question hung. "D'you remember what she said?"

As if rehearsed, the entire group bellowed in unison:

"Ya messin'…… I nearly took me lashes off then!"

The place erupted. Beer sloshed. Someone wheezed from laughing too hard. And James, who had been a carved statue of grief all night, let out the smallest, reluctant smile.

It wasn't much. But it was real.

The laughter rolled on. AJ told the story of her looking a NATO general dead in the eye and declaring his "war face" looked more like constipation. James's mouth twitched. Then Bullet launched into his reenactment of Evelyn drunk on a pool table, broom in hand, belting *Wonderwall* until she toppled flat on her arse mid-chorus. And James, finally, let out a sound. A quiet, broken laugh.

For a few minutes, it was like she was still there. Cigarette dangling, eyebrows arched, daring the world to keep up.

But past midnight, James finally stood. Slow. Careful. The room stilled, as if it had been waiting for him. The jukebox hushed. Conversations thinned to silence.

He looked at the wall and the scarf, the pillowcase, the towel, and her messy handwriting frozen in time, and it hit him like a fist to the ribs.

His voice was low, but it carried.

"I don't know how to do this." His throat worked, swallowing down the splinter. "I don't want to do this."

"I should be telling stories right now. About her being a legend. About her stubborn, impossible attitude. About her awful attitude and her even worse driving. About how she could make you want to punch her and thank her in the same breath."

He paused, glass trembling in his hand. His voice dipped lower, rougher.

"But all I can think about is how quiet the house is. How cold the bed is. How wrong it feels that the world hasn't stopped to acknowledge she's gone."

He downed the drink in one go, slammed the glass onto the counter, and leaned forward like the weight of it might break him.

"She was the best of us. Not because she was perfect… God knows she wasn't… but because she fought like hell. For every broken part of herself. For every broken part of us. And she won. Every damn time."

His eyes glistened as he looked out across the room.

"And fuck the brass. I'm not calling her Captain Blackthorn tonight. Her name was Evelyn. Red to those who loved her. She played bass like a goddess. Danced like no one was watching. And if you were watching… she made you feel like you didn't deserve to be in the room. She loved harder than anyone I've ever known. That was my wife."

His voice softened, splintering at the edges.

"She hated being called a hero. So don't. Just call her ours."

AJ was the first to raise his glass, his voice breaking but loud enough to carry. "To ours."

A forest of red scarves and raised glasses followed.

"To Evelyn."

The jukebox clicked over, the opening chords of *Live Forever* spilling into the room. The entire bar sang like she could hear them from the other side. And maybe, just maybe, she could.

James stayed until the music swelled, until the noise blurred into one relentless chorus. Then he slipped toward the door, pulling his jacket tighter against the cold.

Halfway through the crowd, his head lifted, scanning the room.

Looking for her. For the flash of blonde hair, the crooked smirk, and her boots propped on the nearest chair. For her to grin at him while he said, *'Time to go, Red.'*

But there was no one there. Just the echo of her voice in his head.

He stepped out into the night alone.

To be continued…

About the Author

N. M. Cotton was raised in Merseyside and holds a Bachelor of Science in Evolutionary Anthropology. Her fascination with genetics, human evolution, and resilience informs her fiction, where science and storytelling merge in raw, character-driven narratives.

A neurodiverse writer with a strong awareness of mental health, she brings authenticity and empathy to her work—particularly in exploring the hidden struggles of men and the resilience that emerges from them. Her debut series, Warborn, blends academic depth with a love of found-family bonds, loyalty under fire, and the fierce, fragile ways people survive love and loss. Grounded in Liverpool's grit and humour, her stories are visceral yet tender, cinematic yet intimate. When she isn't writing, she's lost in music, tracing her Celtic roots, or enjoying family life—usually with a book in one hand and strong coffee in the other